To Catch the Summer Wind

Crossway books by Doris Elaine Fell

Seasons of Intrigue Series

Always in September
Before Winter Comes
April Is Forever
The Twelfth Rose of Spring
To Catch the Summer Wind

SEASONS OF INTRIGUE

BOOK FIVE

To Catch the Summer Wind

Doris Elaine Fell

CROSSWAY BOOKS • WHEATON, ILLINOIS

A DIVISION OF GOOD NEWS PUBLISHERS

To Catch the Summer Wind

Copyright © 1996 by Doris Elaine Fell

Published by Crossway Books
         a division of Good News Publishers
         1300 Crescent Street
         Wheaton, Illinois 60187

Cover illustration: Chuck Gillies

Cover design: Dennis Hill

First printing 1996

Printed in the United States of America

Library of Congress Cataloging-in-Publication Data
Fell, Doris Elaine.
    To catch the summer wind / Doris Elaine Fell.
        p.   cm.—(Seasons of intrigue: bk. 5)
    I. Title. II. Series: Fell, Doris Elaine. Seasons of intrigue; bk. 5.
PS3556.E4716T6 1996   813'.54—dc20   96-26675
ISBN 0-89107-914-9

04		03		02		01		00		99		98		97		96
15	14	13	12	11	10	9	8	7	6	5	4	3	2	1

*Why should we
be in such
desperate haste to succeed,
and in such
desperate enterprises?
If a man does not keep pace
with his companions,
perhaps it is because
he hears
a different drummer.
Let him step to
the music which he hears,
however measured
or far away.*

—Henry David Thoreau

To Howard and Elsie
my brother and his wife

. . . .

When I count my blessings and my friends,
you shine brightly among them.

Prologue: London

May, 1986. Olivia Renway waited alone in the Chelsea dining room, her slender, well-manicured hands clasped tightly in front of her. She was a striking, genteel woman of sixty-two with russet hair and intense blue eyes framed by velvet black lashes. She sat with her back straight in the brocade chair, feeling out of place in this restaurant that catered to a lunch crowd of corporate executives and rakish artists. Even the masculine paintings on the paneled walls were of fox hunts and men riding to hounds. Somber waiters in crimson cummerbunds moved soundlessly across the plush red carpet, balancing trays of steaming broccoli and roast lamb trimmed with parsley and mint jelly.

She sent her platter back, untouched, leaving only a rose-bud lying in the center of the linen cloth where her grand-son had tossed it; its pink petals were taut except for the one Ian had torn free. Olivia wanted to grab her Burberry and briefcase and flee out into the rain-drenched city and never come to London again; but Ian would come back to the table looking for her, trusting her to be there. He was too young to abandon even though leaving him might save his life.

The man from Prague who had followed them this morning sat across the room, still wearing his damp raincoat and defiantly tapping the ashes of a thin cigar into his cup as he met her gaze. She placed him at twenty-six to thirty, a not unattractive man with a narrow face and hair so blond that it looked snow-white. At once Olivia glanced down at the wedding band with the five-carat diamond sparkling on her finger. Above the ring the sapphire bracelet—a fragile memory of the war years—pinched the skin of her narrow wrist. These were Olivia's two worlds—the life with Uriah Kendall and her hidden past.

Her knuckles blanched as she reached out to rearrange the crumbs around the fallen petal. Why had she insisted on going to London without Uriah? His finely chiseled face and handsome smile stayed locked in her memory. Thoughts of him sent tiny ripples along her spine, arousing her need for him. She longed to fly home to Maryland, to those tender, wide-open arms, but it would be better for all of them if she could outrun the man from Prague and slip away into oblivion. Then Uriah and Ian would never bear the humiliation of her past. Escape? But what would become of her promise to meet Uriah at their Cotswold cottage in June?

As she fingered the lone rose petal, soft and fragrant as her own skin, Olivia saw her thirteen-year-old grandson bounding back from the loo. Somehow she had to get him safely to Heathrow and on a plane back to Maryland as quickly as possible.

"I was worried about you, Ian," she said.

He flopped into the chair scowling, a rangy lad with one trousered leg swinging impatiently. Olivia loved him fiercely and felt fury at the new threats that might distance her from her grandson. He was her jeans and T-shirt boy, looking miserable in a suit and tie. And yet the two of them were so much alike—both tall and fair with piercing blue eyes—Ian with sandy red hair, her own beginning to gray at the temples, his unruly with one wavy lock slipping over his forehead and almost hiding his scowl. He had Uriah's cheeks and jawbone and strength of character, but that stubborn streak and his narrow nose and sensitive mouth were so like her own.

His lips twisted as he tugged at the tie. "Are we going to sit here all day, Grams, just because it's raining?" he asked.

"Just until the waiter brings the check."

She fumbled for her credit card. Thoughts of last night's phone caller with his distinct Czechoslovakian accent wiped the beginnings of a smile from her face. In those years before Uriah, she had faced trouble head-on with a Beretta tucked safely at the bottom of her bag or a Bren automatic hidden in the boot of her car. But she would never risk carrying a gun in Ian's presence.

"What took you so long?" she asked.

"I went to the bathroom."

"Twenty minutes ago."

He met her concern with silence and then said, "There was a man in the loo asking about you."

"That stranger across the room?"

His glance was obvious, his nose screwed up in boredom. "That's him. I think he followed us this morning."

"He seemed to be everywhere we went," she admitted.

"Are you afraid, Grams?"

Yes, I'm frightened, she thought. *Frightened for both of us.* But she smiled and said, "Not when you're with me."

"I told him you were my grandmother, but he said you were Olivia Renway, the suspense novelist."

"Not Olivia *Kendall?*"

"Don't think he knew that."

"I'm always running into people who think they know me."

"Dad hates that. Says you never had time to be his mother."

"Aubrey exaggerates," she said.

But Aubrey was right. Mothering had been difficult at best. Even now in his mid-thirties, Aubrey still sulked in her presence.

"Ian, your father was a demanding child," she said.

"But Dad said you spent all your time writing books—that you never had time for him."

"Aubrey exaggerates," Olivia said again. "I gave him everything money could buy—the best clothes, the best private schools, the opportunity to travel." *But what was all of that when she had failed so miserably at being his friend, his mother?*

"He thinks you should go by your married name."

"I do. That's who I am. Olivia Kendall. But Uriah wants me to keep my professional life separate."

Ian shrugged. "I like you both ways."

Aubrey's resentments had passed on to Ian's older brother, but Ian had wormed his way into Olivia's heart from the day he was born. She didn't want anything to weaken the bond between them. Motherless from birth, Ian had needed her in a way that Aubrey and Grover never had.

"Ian," she whispered, "I'm sorry I disappointed your father."

"Doesn't matter. Gramps is proud of you."

"He's proud of you, too. He wants you to go to Sandhurst."

"Can't. I'm not a Brit."

She smiled again. He was more English and more loyal to his grandfather's country than he realized. "Uriah will think of a way."

"No. I want to be a cyclist, not a Grenadier Guard."

"Couldn't you be both?"

"No." Clear, definite.

At thirteen he was already racing and doing well in the junior classics. Ian was committed to a career in cycling when he grew up so he could be an American hero like Greg LeMond—even if he had to defy family traditions to make his own mark in life. "Maybe you'll win the Tour de France for me someday, Ian."

He cocked his head, giving her the Kendall appraisal. "Will you be there?"

Her throat tightened. "Just try and stop me."

"You won't get too old?"

"No. I'll always be young." *And I'll always love you, always pray for you, no matter what happens.*

Unexpectedly he said, "Gramps will like your new dress."

She touched the jeweled neckline of the stylish dinner dress with its Italian label. "Uriah won't like the price."

"He'll like you in it. Wear it when we meet him next week."

"Ian, he won't be coming. I'm sending you home."

He stared in disbelief. "Grams, what did I do wrong?"

"Nothing. You've been an angel, but I'm going back to Czechoslovakia."

"I'll go with you."

"It's a business trip this time. Next summer maybe or even in the fall, we'll go to all the places we planned to go." She knew even as she made the suggestion that there would be no trip—next summer, in the fall, ever. "I'm sorry, Ian."

"But we always do something special in June."

"I know. I promised you a summer filled with rainbows, four weeks together in Italy and the Greek islands and then to Paris to watch Greg LeMond ride in the Tour de France. Honey, I want that as much as you do, but we'll go some other time."

"Don't send me home. I won't get in your way."

Her despair matched the gloom and disappointment on his face, a look of betrayal so intense that she stood and slipped into her Burberry as a bolt of lightning flashed behind the church spires. She had to calm herself. She would have the chauffeur drop her off at Westminster Abbey so she could slip inside for a moment of solitude. Then she would walk the rest of the way to Downing Street for her appointment with the prime minister.

As the waiter picked up her credit card, the man from Prague was paying his bill, too. "Ian, I have an appointment on Downing Street. After that we'll drive out to Heathrow."

"Aren't we going back to Stratford first?"

"No, I want you to catch a flight out of Heathrow this afternoon. I'm certain I can get you on board."

He shuffled to his feet, his lip quivering. "Don't send me away, Grams. Dad will think I made you mad."

She touched his cheek with her gloved fingers. "I'll call Uriah and explain everything. He'll let Aubrey know. Maybe you and Uriah could go on down to Disney World."

"That's kids' stuff."

"Then go camping in the Blue Ridge Mountains."

"Gramps always forgets the matches."

"Then have him take you to one of the junior classics."

"No! I don't want to watch a race. I want to ride in it, and I can't do that again until I get my new bicycle."

She had promised him a racing cycle for Christmas—yellow like the one Greg LeMond rode. From the corner of her eye, she saw the white Towncar emerge through the downpour and brake to a stop in front of the restaurant; its windshield wipers were swishing rhythmically, working overtime. Across the River Thames, another crooked streak of lightning flashed above the Albert Bridge. "Ian, dear, we have to leave now."

She put her hands on his shoulders for what she knew would be the last time and leaned down and kissed the top of his head. "I love you, Ian. You must always remember that."

Tears balanced on her lashes as she flicked the bracelet from her wrist and tucked it into his pocket. Before he could protest, she touched his lips. "Take care of it for me, Ian."

"Until you get back from Czechoslovakia?"

"Until I ask you for it."

Across the vast room, the man with the cigar stood and began wending his way toward the revolving doors. "Hurry, Ian," she said. "We must not keep Charles waiting."

"I don't like Charles."

"Honey, I know he's not our regular driver, but Michaels is sick. Charles is just filling in for the day."

"I still don't like him."

Outside the Fox Hunt Restaurant, she hesitated, protected by the canopied arch above her. As Ian shivered beside her, Olivia heard the man from Prague coming through the revolving door. She gripped Ian's hand and ran toward the waiting limousine.

The chauffeur tipped his cap as they slid across the back seat. "Westminster Abbey, Charles," she said. "While I'm there, take Ian to the cycle shop. He's interested in a yellow racer." A lump rose in her throat. "I promised him one for Christmas."

"Very good, Miss Renway."

As he eased the car from the curb, the London traffic darted in every direction, merging and doubling back on itself. Charles studied Olivia in the rearview mirror, his shrewd hawk-eyes fixed on her face. "When should Ian and I be back?" he asked.

"By two. I'll be at Downing Street. Meet me there."

⚉⚉⚉

Olivia stood inside the hallway as the door to number 10 Downing Street closed behind her. Beyond the narrow entryway, two houses had been joined together with a stairway that rose to the prime minister's small but well-kept flat at the top of the building. She knew from her last visit that the prime minister's personal touches were everywhere: a porcelain collection on display and art treasures like the Turner painting that hung in the White Drawing Room. British history cried out from the very walls of this building with striking portraits of Nelson and Wellington and a lifelike painting of Churchill in the Cabinet Room that had made Olivia feel as though she were facing the man himself.

Near Olivia a magnificent sculpture fit perfectly into the alcove. Above it hung a picture of Londoners asleep in the underground during the Blitz. Olivia had lived through a blitz of her own, a frightening escape from Czechoslovakia, a poignant memory that came crashing back as the painting stirred the remembrance of air raid sirens and Luftwaffe planes roaring overhead.

She turned at the sound of the secretary's light footsteps in the hallway. "Miss Renway, I'm Cynthia. We're sorry to keep you waiting. The prime minister had an unexpected phone call."

Someone protesting my visit. Butterflies kicked at Olivia's stomach as she followed Cynthia up the stairs to the private flat in the rafters. Cynthia left her at the study door where one of the most powerful women in the world sat at the desk poring over briefs that affected scores of nations, an empty coffee cup pushed off to one side. As the woman tugged at a pearl earring, the desk light cast a golden sheen on her reddish brown hair.

"Should I come back another time?" Olivia asked softly.

The prime minister stood, her face serious, her hands outstretched in welcome. "It's been a long time, Olivia."

"Two years," Olivia said. On previous occasions, Olivia had been an invited guest, the first time with Uriah, grandson of Lord and Lady Kendall. On her second visit, she had sat with the prime minister for an hour, reminiscing about Oxford. But two years ago, a brunch at the Chequers estate had ended in a bitter debate over Uriah's removal from British Intelligence.

"Please sit down, Olivia."

As she eased into a chair across from the prime minister, she glanced around. The study had been repapered since her last visit. The ugly sage-green wallpaper was gone, and a cream stripe brightened the room. Their eyes met again. "You've had a busy year. The G7 Summit in Tokyo earlier this month, wasn't it?"

The prime minister flicked a thread from her gray tweed suit. "Yes, along with a quick visit to South Korea, and I'm just back from that trip to Israel. It will be Camp David in November."

"I almost called you when you came to Washington a year ago."

"Why didn't you? We're old friends, Olivia."

"My friendship may have cost you that bombing in Brighton. I've been afraid that something I wrote risked your safety—"

"Since when have you teamed up with the Irish Republic?" There was a tongue-in-cheek pause. "Brighton was an IRA bombing."

Olivia snatched another glance at the striped wallpaper. "Czech terrorists may be the next real threat."

"To Brighton or Chelsea?"

"To you," Olivia said.

"And you've come here to warn me?" The prime minister pushed the empty cup farther away. As the seconds passed, a mixture of independence and wisdom, of amusement and annoyance, of concern and kindness showed in those alert eyes. "We're on good terms with Czechoslovakia. I have no briefs to the contrary, no word on any Czech subversives in the country. But, Olivia, I'll pass your concerns on to Dudley Perkins over at MI5."

"Perkins won't believe you. If it weren't for your intervention, he would keep the Kendalls banned from this country forever. Now he's convinced Uriah works for the CIA."

"Does he?"

"That would amuse Uriah. You know that he's retired."

"Isn't Langley just across the Potomac?"

Olivia shook her head. "Not from our place."

"Have you had tea, Olivia? We don't keep a live-in, but the deep freeze is well stocked. Or I can stir up a poached egg on Bovril toast if you prefer."

"I've eaten. I didn't want to take up much of your time."

The smile went back to quick and friendly. "That's right. You have a book signing this afternoon."

"That was canceled. Actually I have an appointment with my publisher. That's why I'm in London." She snapped her briefcase open and handed an autographed copy of her novel across the desk. "This is the one on industrial sabotage and chemical weapons snaking their way out of Europe into Asia." She tapped the unfinished manuscript in her case. "This will be a sequel to it."

"Uriah must be bursting with pride."

"Yes, but he's against my writing on a steel plant that produces chemical weapons for mass destruction. But I knew I had hit upon the truth when the phone threats started a week ago."

The prime minister's hand went involuntarily across the folder in front of her as Olivia slid a single sheet across the desk. "Are you familiar with these companies?" Olivia asked.

With a quick appraisal, the PM said, "Nishokura Steel? No, but this steel plant in Munich, Germany—I recognize that one."

"And the old Van Rindin architectural firm?"

"I don't believe I've heard of that one either."

"Also in Germany—also a family-run business with a branch facility not far from Prague." Olivia's voice turned bitter. "They're both thriving and prosperous since the late 1930s, but someone should have put them out of business a long time ago."

The warmth between them chilled. "A personal grudge, Olivia?"

Olivia's throat spasmed. "I'm convinced the Russelmanns and Van Rindins helped design the concentration camps of World War II. If it hadn't been for them, my father would still be alive."

"The war has been over for more than forty years, Olivia."

"No, it's very fresh for me. But what a marvelous excuse. They made the bomb, but they didn't drop it. They designed the ovens, but they didn't stoke them."

The prime minister's quiet reserve seemed to shout across the desk that separated them, saying, *You've gone quite mad, Olivia.*

Olivia continued, "Otto Russelmann founded a steel company in the Ruhr Valley in the early thirties. He prospered throughout the war designing weapons of death—and died of a stroke before they could drag him into the Nuremberg trials. The whole family was acquitted of war crimes. Only God knows why. It was so unfair."

"You speak as though you knew them personally."

I did. But I can't tell you that, not without risk to Uriah. Accountability. She was demanding accountability of others when she had never rendered her own. She touched the blanched line around her wrist where the sapphire bracelet had been and felt the racing drumbeat of her own heart.

"I know enough about them to know they were evil, and it passed down through the generations." *Oh, Uriah—dear family of mine—what unhappiness my life has cost you.*

"Olivia!" The clear enunciation of her name drew her back. "Perhaps collaboration was the only way the Russelmanns and the Van Rindins could survive in Nazi Germany."

"They could have fled from Germany—left it all." *As I fled from Prague.*

Across the shiny desk their eyes met again, the prime

minister's steady and unblinking. The corner of Olivia's mouth twitched. She said, "I don't know about the factories in Munich and the Ruhr Valley—but after the war Otto Russelmann's family enlarged the steel plant in Czechoslovakia."

"State-controlled, wasn't it?"

"No longer, not since the Communists left. But for some reason the Russelmanns fared well even during the Communist rule. I know. I just came back from Prague. Jarvoc actually—the village where I was born."

"You promised Uriah you would never go there again."

"My brother Dorian's wife died. I went home for the funeral. While I was there, I hit upon this idea for a book sequel when I recognized someone I had known in the war."

"Did that person recognize you?"

"I didn't think so at the time. But last night there was another threatening phone call—all in Czech. And this morning someone followed me. I'm frightened for my grandson Ian. He's with me today." Olivia paused. "I'm certain that I saw that same man at the factory where my brother Dorian works."

"At the Russelmann Steel factory in Jarvoc?"

"I'm certain of it. The Russelmanns have contracts with Nishokura in Japan and with the office of Jon Gainsborough."

"The steel magnate here in England?" the PM asked.

"Yes. I can't let history repeat itself. If it's the last thing I do, I have to buy my brother's way out of the Czech Republic." She rubbed her blanched wrist. "I have something that the Russelmanns want. That's why I'm going back to Prague. I'll barter with them for Dorian's freedom—before I expose them."

Olivia studied the cream stripes on the wall again as she tried to stop her fears from leapfrogging within her mind. Her facial muscles drew tight. "I have an old account to settle. Uriah knows nothing of my plans, but I'm telling you, dear friend, in case something goes wrong."

"I'm afraid for you, Olivia."

"Don't be. I don't expect you to understand, but it goes

back a long ways—to the assassination of Reinhard Heydrich."

"The head of the German protectorate in Czechoslovakia?"

"Yes. The Germans retaliated by destroying Lidice—and most of my family. It's still a bitter pill for Dorian and me to swallow. . . . When I saw that man in Jarvoc, it all came back."

"If you're in danger, Olivia, I'll call Scotland Yard."

"Please don't. My brother and childhood nanny are the ones in danger. I brought her back with me, but Dorian refused to come. At least my old nanny is safe from the younger generation of Russelmanns and Van Rindins." *Safe from Altman Russelmann.*

The prime minister's smile turned sympathetic. "You were always imaginative—even back at Somerville—and totally absorbed by novels of intrigue, especially Dorothy Sayers's, as I recall. But don't hold the younger generations guilty for the past. Trust me, Olivia. I keep abreast of the threats worldwide."

Disappointment flushed Olivia's cheeks. "What if the Russelmanns are still stockpiling toxic nerve gases?"

"British Intelligence will keep me informed. If there's a problem in Jarvoc, they'll contact Czech Intelligence for me."

"No. For the first time since I married Uriah, I may be able to prove that the things Dudley Perkins said about me were lies."

"Dudley was just an ambitious junior officer back then. Trying to do what he thought was right."

"He ruined Uriah's career. Robbed him of his honor, his knighthood."

The coffee cup was repositioned. "Leaving M15 was Uriah's choice. It was that or not marry you—a difficult decision at best. But if it helps, I never believed the rumors."

"Then why didn't you come to our wedding? Never mind. Some of those rumors were true, but I never spied against Britain. I want my husband's good name cleared. I want Uriah's title restored." Olivia snapped her briefcase shut. "If anything happens to me, the research in here will be proof enough."

They both stood, like strangers now. "We must keep in touch, Olivia. The next time Uriah is with you, why don't you have Sunday brunch with us out at Chequers again?"

In spite of Olivia's last visit there, the invitation struck a pleasant chord. She loved the prime minister's Elizabethan country manor with its highly polished furniture and antique treasures—a weekend refuge from the pressures and formality of London. Mostly Olivia remembered holding hands with Uriah as they enjoyed the tangy smell of a winter log burning in the fireplace.

"Oh, we'd love to come," she said.

As the phone rang, Olivia added, "I'll see myself out."

"You could leave by the back way through the gate."

"No. I have a ride waiting. Besides, if someone saw me come in, they'll be waiting for me to leave the same way."

"Not your Czechoslovakian terrorists?" the PM asked kindly.

"Perhaps."

🏵🏵🏵

The nervous tapping of Olivia's heels against the rain-washed sidewalk mirrored her thumping heart. She felt anger at her chauffeur for parking the Towncar at the end of the block. As she hurried toward it, a gangly young man with a large black umbrella elbowed her to the curb. She stepped aside to let him pass, but as he came abreast he said, "Miss Renway, may I have your autograph?"

Her grip on the briefcase tightened. "You've mistaken me for someone else," she said.

His amicable grin faded, leaving a puzzled expression on his face as though once confronting her, he was suddenly speechless. And then he shook his head. "No," he stammered, holding up the book. "See, this is your picture here on the back cover. I'd know you anywhere. I've read all your books."

In the picture, her hands rested on the chair back, the

sapphire bracelet in full view. She pushed around him and hurried on toward Whitehall. He turned and fell into step with her, holding his umbrella over her head. "Please. Just sign it for me. I've waited out here in the rain for an hour."

Reluctantly, she set down her briefcase and took the book.

"Name's Nedrick Russelmann," he volunteered.

As she repeated his name, the dryness in her mouth came back. Could it be—but, no, there couldn't be any connection.

Russelmann ran the back of his hand across his lower lip, those black-browed, dark eyes tugging at Olivia's past. She had to reach the safety of the Towncar. She opened the book jacket, scrawled her signature, and shoved the novel back into his hand. "Nedrick, I must go," she said, but her voice trembled.

He stepped back. "Here, Miss Renway, take my umbrella."

Olivia took it and picked up her briefcase. As she stepped off the curb, she saw him raise the book and wave it in the air.

She heard the gunning of an engine and tilted the umbrella back just in time to see the gray Renault bearing down on her. The impact of the vehicle sent her hurtling into the air and slammed her into the gutter—the back of her head striking the curb. The tires squealed as the car turned on a dime and fled back toward Whitehall.

For a moment, she felt nothing; then all of her nerve endings awakened in a thrust of pain so severe that she gasped. In her blurred vision, she saw Russelmann kick the twisted umbrella aside and grab her leather case. *My book draft and my notes on Prague!*

As pain ravaged her body, she cried out, "Why, Nedrick?"

Nedrick turned back, his face chalky white, his eyes desperate. He tossed the case toward her and fled along Downing to Whitehall as the passersby gathered around her broken body.

The stagnant smell of a cigar overwhelmed her as the man from Prague leaned over her. His raincoat lay open, his rich brown tie almost touching her cheek. His powerful fingers dug deep into her limp wrist. "Where is it?" he demanded. "Where is it?"

My bracelet. He wants my sapphire bracelet. "It's gone."

He stood, snatched the briefcase, and merged into the gathering crowd. Next week, next month he would stalk someone else. In the distance, she heard the plaintive wail of a siren and knew that it would not arrive in time.

"Help is coming," a uniformed bobby said as he knelt beside her and put his hand gently on her shoulder.

"My briefcase?" she cried.

He took a quick survey. "We'll find it. Tell me your name."

She gazed around dazedly. Where was Charles and the Towncar? Surely her chauffeur would come to her rescue. Wait . . . there was Charles. He was walking away. She struggled to lift her head and uttered the single word, "Charles."

Olivia caught a glimpse of him stepping into the limousine. She heard the door slam and the motor rev. She stared after him. As the car sped away, Ian's terrified face pressed against the back window, his hands pounding against the glass.

"I love you, Ian," she whispered.

Rain pelted her face, but a glimmer of sunlight broke through the darkened clouds, touching the sky with pastel ribbons of a rainbow. Beneath her breastbone something exploded. Her breathing was cut off. Spurts of blood filled her mouth and trickled down her chin. As the constable patted her hand, the excruciating pain eased. Olivia felt herself floating, drifting away. The solitude of her moments in Westminster Abbey flashed back. She mouthed the prayer again. The constable's face blurred. For a moment she thought she saw her beloved Uriah, and then her tunnel vision glimpsed a dazzling white light. Her fingers relaxed. She felt no fear, only peace. A peace like the calm that had swept over her in the Abbey.

❦❦❦

As the bobbies cordoned off the area, the emergency phone at the prime minister's residence rang with a third warning. The brittle Czechoslovakian voice on the other end said coldly, "A bomb is set to go off at number 10 Downing in the next fifteen minutes. . . . "

Moments later the gates on the property swung open, and a limousine sped down the driveway, the prime minister and her personal secretary shielded on the backseat.

Chapter 1

June 1, 1986. A low mist hung over the city as Uriah Kendall's Rolls Royce followed the stark white hearse bearing Olivia's body. The small procession wound its way slowly along the River Thames as his beloved Olivia took leave of London for the last time.

Uriah sat in the backseat with his grandsons huddled silently beside him. He could offer the boys no comfort; he had none to give. As Ian kicked at the upholstery, streaking it with brown shoe polish, Grover glared up at Uriah, wide-eyed, visibly annoyed, as though his grandmother had deliberately betrayed him by dying.

Uriah felt numb, his dark blue eyes almost as lifeless as Olivia's. He was distinguished looking, a well-groomed man meticulously attired with not a strand of his thick sandy hair out of place. Uriah's despair deepened as he thought about Olivia's five-carat diamond lying in his pocket, securely wrapped in a white linen handkerchief. Not stolen, but safe. He fixed his gaze on the gloves and walking stick on his lap and asked himself for the hundredth time, *Why, Olivia? Why? Why have you left me?*

Another lump rose in his throat as he listened to the thump, thump, thump of Ian's shoe. It was impossible for Uriah to swallow. Impossible to think clearly. There were so many words left unsaid, so many dreams unfinished. Behind the closed doors at Scotland Yard the constable had given Uriah a detailed report of the accident. Everything had blurred for Uriah when he read the medical report: Olivia's body bruised, battered, crushed by a hit-and-run driver. Olivia dead on a rain-swept London street with a man's umbrella by her broken body.

Dudley Perkins of MI5 had been there, coldly stating that Olivia's death had not been accidental. Perkins was right. Olivia would never step blindly from the curb without looking both ways.

"Can you explain the man's umbrella, Uriah?" Perkins had asked. "We must know the name of the man who accompanied her."

Without answering, Uriah had signed a release for Olivia's possessions, her beautiful things stuffed into a white plastic bag. He listened mechanically as the constable read off each item. The expensive dress stained with her blood. Red shoes with a broken heel. Her watch cracked. Her rings undamaged. *And the ugly black umbrella.* Uriah had taken the rings and refused the rest. He kept silent about Olivia's missing sapphire bracelet and leather attaché case, the one he had given her.

The funeral procession moved steadily over the motorway, following the river that Olivia had loved back toward its source. Uriah insisted that the procession take the hour's drive to Oxford to the academic world where Olivia had graduated from Somerville College—and where she had found her measure of peace in the college chapel at Christ's Church, not far from the narrow footpaths that edged the winding Cherwell.

In the deadly silence of his own heart, he pictured Olivia as he had first seen her standing in the rain on the Cotswold bridge, turning in slow motion to face him—cautious, watchful even then. At first all he had seen was a young woman in a charcoal gray trench coat leaning desolately against the railing, her slender feet pressed into beige pumps, her russet hair damp against her cheek. Startled by his sudden appearance, she had stood her guard, wary, ready to take flight, her delicate features like a mirage, her enormous blue eyes swallowed up in sadness.

Days later she told him that she had come to England as

a Czech refugee, stealing over the back streets of war-torn
London, creeping around elusively like the fog that crept
over the Thames. But once she became his wife, Uriah lav-
ished on her the good things of London: art galleries and
concerts and wild spending sprees on Oxford and Regent
Streets.

In the front seat of the car, Aubrey gripped the steering
wheel. "Dad, we should have taken Mom home to
Maryland," he said grudgingly. "Why are we leaving her in
England?"

"We've been over that already, Aubrey. I want to bury
your mother in Kendallshire—in the village where we met."

"Away from the prying eyes of her fans—away from her
family?"

"That's enough, Aubrey."

Ian stirred and leaned against Uriah. "There are only five
cars following us, Grandpa. I thought Grandma had a lot of
friends."

Uriah reached out and drew the boy closer, and then his
eyes riveted once again on the white hearse. *Six cars and a
hearse. We make a strange lot of summer mourners,* he
thought. *Family and a few close friends and Dudley Perkins.*

Perkins was riding in the fourth car, there on behalf of
the prime minister. Edwin Wallis, a young constable from
Scotland Yard, rode with him. Wallis was an alert thirty-
year-old with horn-rimmed glasses and little interest in the
funeral itself. *He doesn't know about the missing briefcase or
bracelet,* Uriah thought. *How could he? I haven't reported the
loss.*

Miles beyond Oxford, they left the steep hills and gullies
and passed through the thick woodland into the village of
Kendallshire where old friends lined the main road. The
hearse led the way on through the gated cemetery to the
knobby knoll where Uriah would bury Olivia beside his
parents. During the graveside service, the vicar tried to offer
Uriah comfort, but his words fell on deaf ears. Uriah stared
into the dirt crevice as they lowered Olivia's casket into it
and vowed that he would allow nothing to tarnish her
memory. A sudden breeze blew gently over the flowers on

the grave, scenting the air with the sweet fragrance of the lilacs and roses that she had loved; it was as though she had opened her slender hand and blown him one final kiss.

Afterwards Aubrey broke their silence. "Dad, the boys and I are driving back to London. Will you go with us?"

"And leave Olivia?"

Aubrey licked his lip, the tip of his tongue touching his thick mustache. Aubrey's eyes were wide and brooding, blue and intense like Olivia's, but his skin was coarse and ruddy from too much sun and too much drinking. Uriah stared off at the gentle valley with a Cotswold river running through it. The rustic bridge where he had first seen Olivia spanned the rippling water. "Your mother and I were happy here, Aubrey," he said.

"I know, Dad. I grew up here—remember? But there's nothing more you can do for Mother."

You're wrong. I can stay with her a little longer. "Son, there's room at the cottage. Come, spend some time with me."

The Kendalls' charming two-story cottage with its brick chimneys and steep thatched roof had once belonged to his great-grandparents. A dry stone wall surrounded the garden—Olivia's garden filled with the smell of wild thyme and marjoram and alive with colorful roses and lilacs. "Stay," Uriah urged.

"We can't, Dad. Ian saw what happened to Mother. Please fly back to the States with us."

"I'll stay at the cottage for a few weeks." His heart ached as he tried to lift his head to face his son. "I wish the Gregorys had come."

"Miriam's doctor wouldn't release her from the hospital. 'Pneumonia,' she said. I promised I'd call the minute I got home."

"Does Drew know yet?" Uriah asked.

"We still haven't reached him. Miriam's lawyer tried. I tried."

Uriah sighed. "I wish the prime minister had come."

"She sent flowers."

"They were friends. Did she have to send Dudley in her place?"

"She had to stick with the business in London. There was a bomb threat at the residence shortly after—" Aubrey cleared his throat. "Shortly after Mother was killed."

"But it proved a hoax."

"The bomb in the financial district wasn't. A Czech terrorist group took credit, *not the IRA.*" His mustache twitched. "Perkins says there's a connection between Mom's death and the terrorists."

Behind them Dudley Perkins's car door slammed shut. "We have to go, Dad. Perkins offered us a lift back to London, but the constable from Scotland Yard is staying on if you do."

"Edwin Wallis? Absolutely not."

"It's a precaution. Wallis knows about Mom's missing china closet and round table. He will be around if you need him."

"Your idea, Aubrey? Are you trying to find some link between the robbery at the cottage and your mother's— your mother's accident?"

"Yes. I've called the agency in London. Charles, the chauffeur, doesn't exist. They never heard of him. Edwin Wallis stays."

"Aubrey, we need to get something jolly well straightened out before you go. I make my own decisions. I'm not an invalid, son. Just—just a widower. I won't have Constable Wallis hanging around here and snooping through your mother's private papers."

"Do we have something to hide, Dad?"

Uriah swayed. For a moment it looked as though Aubrey would put one of his broad, sun-freckled hands on Uriah's shoulder. Uriah would have welcomed the grip. When it didn't happen, he glanced past Aubrey and saw Perkins drumming his fingers on the car window.

"You'd better go, son."

As he walked Aubrey to the car, Ian flung himself at his grandfather. Uriah lifted Ian's quivering chin. "Ian, no one is blaming you for what happened."

"Gramps, I couldn't go to her. Charles wouldn't let me."

Charles, the chauffeur. "I know, Ian." Uriah leaned down and embraced the boy. "We'll talk when I get home."

Aubrey glowered. "You're not to mention the accident to Ian again. He's to erase it from his memory. That's what I plan to do."

۞۞۞

The next morning tears stung Uriah's eyes as he left the bedroom he had shared with Olivia. He went into the empty sitting room. The walls were faded where the antique china closet and end table had once stood, but Olivia's desk sat by the window as neat as she had left it. Why would a thief steal her favorite treasures from her childhood home in Czechoslovakia? No, a thief would not be so selective. But if Olivia sent those treasures away herself, she never intended to come back to him.

He moved mechanically across the room to the desk. As he rummaged through the drawers, his housekeeper came into the room. "I've made you a cup of tea, Mr. Kendall, and some of those scones you love. You just sit yourself down."

He obeyed because he was too tired to argue after working late into the night, poring over boxes of Olivia's private papers. As she arranged the tray, he asked, "Maddie, did my wife tell you why she was going into London?"

The wizened eyes glanced toward the spot where the china closet had stood. "No, Mr. Kendall. But a few days before—before the accident—your wife and grandson took a place over near Stratford to be near an old family friend from Prague."

Beatrice Thorpe? Alive? Startled, he asked, "Whereabouts?"

"Mrs. Kendall said it was best if I didn't know. Told me not to worry about the cottage for a few days. I was just to leave it unattended. Of course, I couldn't do that." She swiped at a speck of dust with her gnarled fingers. "Your wife seemed different after her trip to Prague for the family funeral."

"I begged her not to go."

"That's what she said, but she was better when the boy

arrived. They were a special pair, those two. And the last thing she told me was to have the cottage spotless for your arrival and fresh flowers in the bedroom. I know she was pleased that you were coming."

"Then why did she call and tell me not to come?"

Maddie picked up his empty cup. "When your wife went away, she took boxes of her manuscripts with her. I've been thinking maybe that's what you've been looking for." She cleared her throat before saying, "I carried a box of family pictures out to the car for her. She said that friend of hers wanted to see them."

The pictures from Prague. Beatrice?

"There were other papers, Maddie. Private records. Her birth certificate. Some insurance papers. I can't find them—"

"She must have taken them with her. It's a good thing. That Mr. Wallis from Scotland Yard was asking about them yesterday—before you came back from the cemetery."

"What?"

"It's all right, Mr. Kendall. I sent him scudding off. Told him he ought to be ashamed coming here with his questions on a day like that. Especially with you grieving so."

"He'll be back, Maddie."

Uriah waited until Maddie went into the kitchen before he began another frantic search. He flung open the doors in the cadenza and checked the hall closet. No more boxes. Even the backup files on Olivia's computer had been wiped clean. These, like Olivia, were gone. She had left little behind to tarnish her name or reveal the truth about her last few days in London. Comforted with that thought, he left the house and made the lonely trek to Olivia's grave. He could lock the memory of the accident on Downing Street away even as it was already locked in Ian's mind.

Four weeks later Uriah left the Rolls Royce at the gate of the cemetery and went once more to the knobby knoll where Olivia lay. He shed no tears as he knelt and placed an orchid there. "My darling, I have to leave you now. I have burned the few papers that I found. I can do no more for you."

When he returned to the gravel road, a young man in jeans and a threadbare sweater was running his hand over the bonnet of the Rolls Royce, envy in his dark eyes. A well-worn backpack lay on the ground beside him. As Uriah approached, he reared back on his worn sneakers and jerked his thumb toward the car. "Yours, mister?"

"Mine," Uriah told him. "My London car."

"What I'd give to have a Rolls!" Using his sweater, he wiped a smudge from the chrome and then with unexpected bluntness said, "I'm sorry about your wife, Mr. Kendall."

"You know about Olivia?"

"Everybody in the village does."

"But you're not from here."

"No, I was born in Czechoslovakia. I've been bumming across Europe ever since I dropped out of school. But I always carry a couple of Miss Renway's books in my pack here."

He grinned, an amicable grin, as he bent down and flipped his canvas pack open. He held the book out and said, "See, your wife signed this one for me the other day in London."

A burst of rage shook Uriah. What right did this stranger have to boast of seeing Olivia alive? Alive in London. The image of Olivia on the rusty bridge here in the village—Olivia vibrant and beautiful—taunted him. He no longer wept at the thought of her dying. Tears had exhausted him. But inside he cried out. To be the last to see her alive—that was Uriah's right, Uriah's privilege, taken from him violently on Downing Street.

When he saw Olivia's signature in the front of the book, Uriah felt as though he would retch and empty his gut while the boy watched. He pushed the book away and walked around to the driver's side of the car.

The boy's watchful gaze followed him. "Don't be angry with me, mister," he said. "I'm like you. I lost my family, too."

Something about the sensitive mouth and the piercing dark eyes reminded Uriah of Olivia. She had looked that way when he first met her—an aloof young woman with velvet-lashed eyes, someone who needed a friend. This young man, eighteen or nineteen at best, was a loner like Olivia, a boy in need of a friend. Someone who read Olivia's books.

Impulsively, Uriah opened his wallet and took out a twenty-pound note. "I'm leaving now, but get yourself something to eat."

"You don't have to do that, Mr. Kendall."

"I want to."

The long fingers wrapped around the money. "I'd like to drive a car like this someday." As Uriah slid into the driver's seat, the boy asked, "Could you use a chauffeur, mister?"

Uriah laughed as the engine hummed. He hadn't laughed since Olivia's death, and the release was overwhelming. "I don't make my home in England anymore. You'd have to move to Maryland."

"That'd be okay. Anything to drive a car like this."

Uriah tapped his forefinger on the steering wheel. His mind had never cleared since the funeral, and now it seemed even more befuddled. If he drove away—left this stranger in the dust—he was leaving something of Olivia behind. This stranger had seen Olivia alive. Alive like Uriah wished she could be. He reached across and opened the passenger's door. "I'm driving back to London today. Right now. Would you like to ride along with me?"

"That would beat walking."

Dumping his backpack onto the backseat, he slid into the car beside Uriah and bounced on the leather cushion. "Like I told you, if you're looking for a chauffeur, I'm good with engines. Oh, by the way, Mr. Kendall, my name's Ned. Nedrick Russelmann."

Chapter 2

New York City, spring, 1996. It was Chase Evans's kind of day—a marvelous spring morning with the heat of seasonal changes nipping at the calendar, threatening the city with the early onset of a broiling Manhattan summer. Chase strolled lazily over the Columbia campus, her light-weight beige sweater tossed jauntily over one shoulder, a load of textbooks balanced in her suntanned arms. The pressure was off, her oral comprehensives behind her, and the plans for a summer abroad rapidly coming together.

As she drew abreast of the students sprawled on their backs on the south lawn, she realized that one of the classes had spilled out from the stuffy building into the freshness of an outdoor lecture. Instead of awakening the bespectacled student near her, the blistering sun was lulling him toward slumber. He lay with his head pillowed on a pair of dirty Nikes, a blade of grass dangling limply from his mouth. She allowed her gaze to wander back to the speaker. He wasn't the usual bearded professor with horn-rimmed glasses riding the tip of his nose, but a striking marine captain in full-dress blues. From head to toe he was spotless, his military cap tucked in the crook of his arm and his voice deep and sad as he vividly described his bitter years in the jungles of Laos.

She nudged the student, the sharpness of her polished toenail digging into his arm. Squinting up at her—his alert eyes magnified by thick lenses—he brushed her sandaled foot away. The blade of grass in his mouth raced from corner to corner as he grumbled, "What's your problem? You've got the whole lawn. Sit down."

She slid down and dropped her books on the ground between them. "What's a marine doing on campus?" she asked.

The blade of grass got a fresh gnaw. "He's just talking about the old conflict in Southeast Asia."

"The Vietnam War? The political club won't like that."

"*You* in particular?"

"He's probably off the wall."

Ignoring scowls for silence, he rolled to his side and braced himself on his elbow. "You got something against the military?"

"I believe in peaceful settlements."

"Wars don't work that way." With a flick of his finger, he opened one of her books. "Chase Evans, eh? I'm Kelly Carlson. You named for the old Chase Manhattan Bank or something?"

"No, for a close family friend."

"Some friend. Our marine hero up there has a tag, too. His old man is a retired admiral."

"Is that what got him on campus?"

"That or having an ex-father-in-law in the Senate."

"So he's political? Has he said anything worthwhile yet?"

"A bit on the blunders in Washington. That should please you. Bet you'd like to see a woman in the White House. Right?"

"Why not? If she qualifies." Chase was convinced that a woman would be there one day, a conviction that had sprouted at Vassar and intensified at Columbia. "I keep up an ongoing correspondence with senators and congressmen," she admitted.

"Demanding equality for women?"

"Lately I've been defending the rights of the elderly in nursing homes and fighting for more funding for AIDS patients."

"Like I said, you'd like that top office."

"Not really, but I want my vote to count when the time comes."

The blade of grass was back in Kelly's mouth, slurring his words. "Maybe that's why our marine hero went back to Vietnam three times—to make his vote count."

As a glowering student sought a quieter spot on the lawn, Kelly turned back to Chase. "I feel sorry for the captain. Some turncoat left him for dead in the Laotian jungles twenty years ago."

"Then he's the marine in the news lately?"

"Yeah. Caught in a government cover-up. Even took the rap for being a traitor. But he's an American hero now. That's politics for you. That's why I'm in chemistry. Science makes sense."

Chase swept her hair from the nape of her neck and felt the air cool her skin. "Why the uniform? Is he running for Congress?"

"It didn't help Ollie North any. I don't think this Luke Breckenridge will fare any better even if he is an admiral's son."

"Kelly, he's got good looks going for him."

"If you like older men with somber, unsmiling faces."

Yes, she could easily like this one. The marine captain had handsome, well-chiseled features. His sandy hair fringed with gray at the temples added to his good looks. And the deep scar that cut along his neck intrigued her.

Breckenridge's voice stayed well modulated as he said, "We could have won that war."

"Why didn't you, Captain?" Chase challenged from the rear.

Captain Breckenridge's piercing dark eyes fixed steadily on her. "I've asked myself that for twenty years."

"Then why did you go back there? Vietnam was a lost cause."

"Patriotism, ma'am," he said. "That's what motivated me."

With a chuckle, Kelly shouted, "Patriotism gets you killed."

Chase saw mocking indifference on the faces of the students around her, the response that she often gave her father when he spoke of Vietnam. She was willing to put odds on it—if these grad students had joined any war, it would likely have been on the side of the protest marchers. She wanted to unmuddy the waters and take back her own sarcastic comments, but it was too late.

She turned to Kelly. "The captain has walked into a den of lions. Like I did when I took my comprehensives."

"Breckenridge's choice. He was supposed to lecture us on the restored diplomatic relations with Vietnam. Instead he's defending America's right to be there twenty or thirty years ago." Kelly shrugged. "Forget the captain, Chase. What'cha doing this evening?"

She did another quick appraisal. Not bad looking, but his Nike laces were frayed and dirty, his T-shirt smudged. Her father would never approve. "I'm on my way home to Long Island," she said.

"With a stopover at the Halverson House?"

"How did you know about that?"

"I know Jeff Carlson."

"Oh, no. You're Jeff's brother!" she exclaimed.

"Yeah. I'm the brother *without* AIDS."

"You should see Jeff more. He talks about you all the time."

Kelly stretched on his back again. "Nothing to talk about. He got himself into that. I didn't."

"He needs you, Kelly."

"Why? Doc says he'll be dead in a few weeks." Kelly spewed the blade of grass from his mouth. It stuck to his T-shirt. "Jeff never was very smart."

He chewed hard on his lower lip and drew blood. Embarrassed, he looked away and then faced her again. "You can't save him. You can't make him well. Why waste your time?"

"I'm just trying to make a difference."

"Yeah, nurse said Jeff would have been gone weeks ago if you hadn't befriended him, but I don't think you did him a favor." His words startled her.

"Your brother is afraid to die."

"Aren't we all? How can you hack it? You're just wasting your time trying to right the wrongs in that place."

"I just read to Jeff and the others or play music for them."

"High classical stuff, Jeff tells me." He plucked another blade of grass and chewed it thoughtfully. "I think you sat in on one of my poly sci classes last semester, didn't you?"

She did a double take. "Yes, I had to drop out a week later for a business trip to Geneva with my father."

"You should have stayed with us. Then you'd understand what the man up front is trying to say."

"Do you?"

"I'm not interested in Vietnam or in any American company hog-jumping on business opportunities in Hanoi. We should account for the MIAs first." Kelly rolled to his side again and picked up the book with Dorothy L. Sayers's name in neon green. *The Mind of the Maker?* What are you, Chase? Some kind of a religious zealot?"

She laughed, an easy ripple that turned more eyes their way. "I'm doing my doctorate on Miss Sayers and Olivia Renway—women novelists who tried to make a difference."

"To dying people like you do? You are an idealist."

"That's what my father says."

Kelly ran his fingers over Sayers's book again. "Don't you have any interests in life besides working on a Ph.D.?"

"Tennis. Sailing. Concerts. Dinner shows."

"Then have dinner with me tonight."

The idea repulsed her. "I have to get back to Long Island. I promised your brother that I'd drop by to see him this evening."

"Chase, don't you date?"

She glanced at Captain Breckenridge. "Older men preferably."

That wasn't true, but she'd never see Kelly again unless she ran into him at Jeff's bedside. She dated all the time, young men in their middle-to-late twenties who often bored her. She took Sayers's book from his hand. "And I study a lot, too."

"So you can't squeeze in time for a hamburger tonight?"

"Not really."

Captain Breckenridge had finished his speech and cut the crowd off on their seventh question. He took his visored cap and squared it on his well-shaped head. "Thank you for your time," he said.

He was booed from the rear as an unenthusiastic applause echoed in the crowd. Chase put her own hands lightly together and then, pitying the handsome captain, began to applaud loudly. Over the heads of the other students their eyes met momentarily.

Kelly swung to a sitting position, pushed himself to his feet, and brushed the grass from his patched jeans. He held out his hand and jerked Chase to her feet. "Well, I guess you'll be off then to right my brother's wrongs?"

What Chase wanted to do was apologize to Luke Breckenridge. She said, "Kelly, you could help Jeff if you visited him more."

"Sorry. Count me out. I get all choked up when I see him." He hoisted his book pack and Nikes to his shoulder. "I don't even plan to go to Jeff's funeral."

He started to walk off barefooted and then turned back to face her. "That's not true. I just don't know what to say to him."

"Jeff said you were close as kids."

"Real close." His eyes shadowed. "If he died in a war—died for some cause like that marine talked about—maybe I'd understand."

❀❀❀

As Luke Breckenridge watched the crowd break up, he knew he didn't want to lecture about Vietnam and Laos ever again. He wanted to pack his uniform and ribbons away in mothballs and never put them on again. He needed to get on with his life. More than anything, he wanted to fly back to Europe—back to Sauni in Busingen, to the only woman he had ever loved.

Today's attempt to stretch the minds of these students and give them a glimpse of the hard choices made twenty years ago had failed, but strangely enough, he felt like saluting their backs as they sauntered away. His moment of jubilation was snatched from him as he saw a young woman push her way through the crowd toward him. He recognized her—the charming heckler who had applauded him. There was a fashionable simplicity to her outfit. She wore a short skirt and an orange tank top with a thin black belt pulled snugly against her narrow waist—and, Luke noted, she wore them well.

But don't come, he thought. *Not if you want to argue about the lost cause of Vietnam.*

The crowd was gone. It was just the two of them now. She stood there eyeing him from her five-foot-five vantage point, her long bare arms a copper tan. The sun gave a golden luster to her light chestnut hair. It fell in a stylish blunt cut, chin-level. He disliked hair hanging in a woman's eyes, but this girl's bangs had been swept back in a single wave above her left brow. He cocked his head, studying her as she studied him, feasting his eyes on a face that had surely been touched by an artist's brush. She was stunning in a wholesome way. Her wide brown eyes were open and direct, the long lashes curled up, the brows thinly arched like Sauni's.

"Did you miss my narrow Bartholomew nose, Captain?"

That was something Sauni might say, off-the-wall, direct, challenging. "I didn't know it belonged to the Bartholomews."

"Something I inherited on my mother's side. Satisfied?"

"Very much so."

With a quick comeback she said, "You're not bad yourself. Or maybe it's the uniform you're wearing."

He chuckled with a total sense of freedom.

"It wasn't that funny."

"No, but you are delightful."

"You didn't think so during the lecture." Without apology she said, "I'm Chase Evans. Bet you're glad that speech is over."

"The heckling was worse than going into battle."

She gave him a do-or-dare smile. "But you drew up the wrong battle lines, Captain. The students around here only remember the Bosnian war and the one in the Persian Gulf. So forget *your* war. You'll never convince my fellow Columbians that the American position was justified. I'm not sure you've convinced yourself."

He saw something of Sauni in those eyes, heard the challenge that Sauni had thrown at him so many years ago. "I believed in it back then. And you?"

The suntanned shoulders shrugged. "It's my father's opinion that America is rarely wrong. He was a marine there, too." Luke forced himself to concentrate on her words as she went on. "Captain, I'm afraid some of the Columbians of the Vietnam era are remembered for their protest marches, not their patriotism. It's passed down to my generation. Let's forget it and go have coffee."

"I am thirsty," he admitted.

She thrust her books into his arms and with a light, happy-go-lucky step walked through the campus with him. They ended up in a small cafe where Luke ordered orange freezes instead of coffee.

As they sat there, Chase said, "It would have gone better for you, Captain, if you hadn't worn that uniform."

"Are you all anti-military?"

She considered that. "No. I just thought you were using the uniform to impress us. Are you running for Congress?"

He choked on his drink. "I'm not interested in politics."

"You must have been twenty years ago."

"That was different, Chase."

She twisted her straw. "No. That war was all politics."

"At the time I thought it was all patriotism."

"You and my dad both. But you have Lyndon Johnson to thank for your tours of duty in Vietnam." Without missing a breath, she said, "Captain, has it been rough since you've been back home?"

Lightly, he said, "The last two months have been a nightmare. I felt like a nameless case number in hospital pajamas."

"Walter Reed Medical Center?"

"Germany first."

That's where military doctors had thumped and

pounded his body and taken pictures until he felt X-rated. Shrinks with placid smiles did their best to squeeze Luke's twenty years of exile into capsule form. High-ranking brass with gold braid on their shoulders interrogated him for hours, their mental calculators running at quad-speed. Things looked hopeless right on up to the day when the *Washington Post* headlines started the Associated Press wires sizzling. "Marine Hero Exonerated—Full Pardon Expected." Within days public opinion at home rallied to his defense, forcing his immediate transfer to Walter Reed in Washington.

"You don't talk much, do you, Captain?"

"Not about myself," he said.

"Were you this quiet when you first hit the States? Or did you at least show a little emotion?"

"I cried," he said honestly. "I came back to America on a medical evac." With a passport in his own name and with an honor guard standing at attention when his plane arrived. Langley intended for it to be a quiet reentry, but the public acclaimed him as a hero. "And then I was admitted to Walter Reed and had to face more debriefing and thumping and pounding and X-rays. And those endless couch-potato interviews."

"The shrinks, eh? Did it help?"

"In a way. But my mom says I'll get the most help on my knees."

"Praying?"

He laughed. "It's not a foreign language."

They sipped their orange freezes slowly and were lingering on a refill when her smile turned impish. "Why don't you dump that uniform and do something you really want to do?"

"Chase, I'm not sure what that something else is. I was trained as a military advisor."

"Haven't you heard about the military cutbacks?"

"Senator Summers, my ex-father-in-law, keeps me posted."

"That old filibusterer? How do you stand him?"

"He's changed. He's been supportive since I came home."

"So what does the ex-son-in-law of Senator Summers want to do with his life besides talk about Southeast Asia?"

"I honestly don't know. But no more speeches after today."

"Smart move. But you could make a mint writing that book on your lost years. At least that's what the news commentators say."

"I'm not lost anymore—so I didn't sign the book contract."

Whatever I do, he thought, *I don't want to do it without Sauni.* He pushed his frosty glass away. "Now tell me about you, Chase."

"There's not much to tell." She grinned. "I've spent *my last twenty years* living in New York. For the last six of them I've been a professional student. Dad calls it bumming around in the ivy halls. He wants me to get a permanent nine-to-five job. Pronto."

"So why don't you go to work, Chase?"

"I will next June when I finish my doctorate. I want to teach at the university level, Captain. If I can convince my father."

Luke couldn't see her confined to a stuffy classroom with a chalkboard behind her, but he said, "Then go for it."

"Over my father's dead body?"

He grinned. "I wouldn't get that drastic."

She held his attention talking casually about the Bartholomews, neither apologizing nor bragging about her family wealth. She spoke warmly of her friends in the nursing home. And then she grew heated as she told Luke that someone had to find a cure for AIDS.

"Let's try abstinence and higher moral standards," he suggested.

"What about babies born with the disease?" she countered. "Or innocent hospital patients who get it through blood transfusions. No, Captain, I'm concerned about people dying with an illness, not in lecturing them on cause and effect."

Luke took her rebuke quietly. He found her intelligent and sensitive, yet political; knowledgeable about her study program, but too idealistic. And he found her attractive, very attractive. He said, "You've sparked my interest in literature again. I'm going to read up on Sayers and Renway—and on AIDS."

She tugged at a tiny teardrop earring. "Then we can discuss them the next time we meet. Will you be in New York City long?"

"I'm leaving for Ocean City this afternoon."

She sighed. "How sad. I love New York City."

"Somehow that doesn't surprise me."

"I was seven before I realized that not everyone lived in a lovely old brownstone house and had a father working in the financial world." She took a final swallow through her straw. "I'm going to London this summer. I'll miss all of this."

"Then why go?" he teased.

"It's part of my research project on Olivia Renway. She left an unfinished manuscript behind—a lost manuscript. So I'm off to merry ole England to dig in the news files."

"Don't take on something you can't finish," he warned.

"I won't. I'm stubborn that way."

"I'll be in Europe myself. Look me up. I'll introduce you to my friends." He named them and added, "The Gregorys live in London." He wrote down Sauni's Busingen number. "Phone me when you get to Europe."

Chase's brilliant eyes sparkled. "You won't mind?"

"Of course not." *Funny kid,* he thought, but as she flushed with anticipation, the warning flags unfurled again. *Sauni won't like this.* Still he said, "I'd love to see you again, Chase."

۝۝۝

Kendall residence, Maryland. For Uriah Kendall thoughts of Olivia's death were always the same. Senseless. Unfair. Too soon. So long ago. That moment ten years ago still lay half-submerged in his memory, all but forgotten for weeks at a stretch. Then some wisp of wind stirred the leaves outside their bedroom window. Or sounds of the London symphony playing *Fantasia* called Olivia back to him—her face so vivid in his mind that he reached out to touch her soft cheek.

The letter on the mantel had brought Olivia back this time, intensifying the thoughts of her that always flooded his mind toward the end of May. He was staring over at the letter when he heard Nedrick Russelmann coming into the study, a quick bounce to his steps, that friendly flash of a grin on his lean face.

At twenty-eight Ned was a gangly man with wistful dark eyes and a persistent troubled frown that wedged between his thick black brows. The frown and the wistfulness disappeared when he smiled. "Sorry, I'm late. I lost track of time."

"I thought you were out tinkering in my workshop or polishing that car again. Kept hoping you'd come in for a game of chess."

Ned averted his gaze. "I took the car for a spin."

To Washington again? Uriah wondered. Often without a word Nedrick left the house to cruise up and down the streets of Washington where the embassies were located. Calmly Uriah asked, "Did you drive on Linnean Avenue today?"

"On Reservoir Road this time. Saw a German diplomat arrive."

The car was Ned's territory—where he went, Ned's business. But Nedrick's intense interest in foreign embassies worried Uriah. They'd been together—the car, Uriah, and Ned—ever since Olivia's death. Ever since Ned ran his hand over the other Rolls Royce in England and asked, "Could you use a chauffeur, mister?"

Ned had dropped into Uriah's life at a time when life itself had come to a standstill. Now Uriah thought of him more as a son than a chauffeur, as part of the family—someone more loyal and dependable than Aubrey had ever been. "What about that game of chess, Ned? Or checkers?"

"Later."

Uriah's throat constricted as Ned went straight to the mantel and thumbed through the pile of mail. "Looking for something special?" Uriah asked.

"Yes, this letter from Chase Evans. She has no right bothering us about Olivia."

Us? Uriah thought. He often felt a strange closeness to Ned, a tie that he could not define, as though Ned were his son and not Aubrey. In unexplained ways, Ned reminded him of Olivia—solitary, sensitive, and fiercely independent. Ned had devoured Uriah's friendship as though he had been starved for it all his life. They brought out the best in each other, Ned refusing to allow Uriah to slip into permanent mourning. He'd miss Ned if he ever moved away.

Nedrick shook the long white envelope. "Have you done anything about getting rid of this Chase Evans yet?" he asked.

"My lawyer has called her twice now. Three times maybe."

"Is she blackmailing you, Mr. Kendall?"

"Blackmailing me? For what? No, money isn't the problem. Miss Evans is one of the New York Bartholomews." Weariness gripped him again. "What she really wants is to read Olivia's last manuscript."

Nedrick spun around, his dark eyes solemn. He ran his hand through the thick dark hair that whipped back from his high forehead. "Her unfinished novel? I thought it was lost."

"More likely stolen. Olivia had her attaché case with her when she left the prime minister's residence moments before her death."

"That was ten years ago. How can you be so certain?"

"She always carried it. It's the one I gave her."

Ned tapped the letter in his hand. "May I?" he asked.

Uriah stirred in his leather chair as though he were sitting on tenterhooks. He had no doubt that Ned had already seen the letter, but he said, "Of course, read it. Miss Evans seems to know everything about my family. The war. London. Olivia's days at Oxford. She even knows Ian is in Gascony preparing for the Tour de France." *But I pray she hasn't found some link to Prague that would tarnish Olivia's memory.*

Ned's scowl deepened. He slapped the letter. "She can't be serious. She plans to see Ian in France. Can't you stop her?"

"From writing her dissertation on the works of Olivia Renway? No. In a way it's flattering. But I won't let her disturb Ian and bring his grandmother's death back to him."

Ned forced a good-humored smile. "Ian can hold his own as long as he keeps his mind on winning that yellow jersey."

"Lately my grandson doesn't have the mind-set of a winner."

Ned grabbed the telephone as it rang. "Kendall residence," he said. "Oh, it's you, Gregory. Yes, Uriah's here. Just a sec."

Uriah bellowed into the phone, "Drew, where are you?"

"In Paris on my honeymoon."

"Then why are you calling me?" Without waiting for Drew's answer, he said, "I'm sorry I couldn't make the wedding."

"We understood. This time of year is rough for you."

"Yes, it's hard without Olivia. But Ian was there."

"We're worried about your grandson, Uriah. There are rumors that he's dropping out of the race. That he doesn't have the stomach for it since the death of his friend Alekos."

"Ian can't drop out. It won't matter if he doesn't win."

"It does to Ian. Why don't you fly over and be with him? Bring Nedrick with you. Or are those two still at odds?"

"They have their problems."

Uriah glanced at the letter back on the mantel. "Drew, there's a young student doing her doctorate dissertation on Olivia."

"Good choice."

Uriah reserved his opinion. "I'd like you to stop her, Drew. Her name's Chase Evans. She's bound to ask Ian where he was when Olivia was killed."

"But I'm on my honeymoon, man. Well—maybe Miriam and I can detour by way of the hills of Gascony for a visit with Ian."

"I'd be grateful. So would Ian."

"Gotta go, Uriah. Miriam is coming."

Uriah cradled the receiver and turned to Ned. "Could you

spare a month or two for a trip to Europe? I'd like to see Ian."

"Ian and I don't get on, Mr. Kendall."

"You could try for my sake."

Ned braced against the mantel, his hands in his pockets, his eyes dark with despair. "It's not just Ian, is it? You want to find your wife's missing attaché case before Miss Evans does."

"I've never wanted to find it," Uriah said. "The contents of that case may have cost Olivia her life."

"Why should I be interested then?"

Uriah closed his eyes trying to shut out the expression on Nedrick's face—trying to ward off the prickling doubt that rose again. Sometimes Uriah pondered on their chance meeting in the Cotswold cemetery. He wondered again now and heard himself saying, "I'd think you'd be very interested in the contents of that case."

❧❧❧

Uriah knows. Ned wanted to cry out and defend himself. *I was there, but I left your wife's leather case behind when I fled.*

Nedrick dropped into Olivia's old chair and stretched his legs toward an unlit fireplace. Beside him Kendall looked suddenly old. "What did Gregory have to say, Uriah?" Ned asked.

"He said Ian blames himself for the death of his friend in Sulzbach. That's worrisome. When Olivia died, he withdrew for a time, lost in his own grief. We can't let that happen again."

A new threat, Ned acknowledged silently. Shock might force Ian's memory of Downing Street to surface, but it seemed unlikely that he could place Ned at the scene. The Towncar had been parked half a block away. Yet any risk was too great to take.

"What about it, Ned? Will you go to Europe with me?"

Ned dragged his heels across the rug. "I have other plans."

"I know, but I need your help." Uriah pressed his fingertips together, his smile faint. "I'm homesick for England, but I can't face going alone. Ned, will you put your own plans on hold and go with me?"

Nedrick greeted the question with silence. If he went to England, he risked losing everything. Ned glanced around the study. He'd come to love this old, well-furnished place. Ten years of good living. He owed Uriah something. "Okay, I'll go with you, and if Miss Evans gets to be a problem, I'll take care of it for you," he promised. *The Russelmanns always took care of problems.*

Chapter 3

Miriam came back into the room looking lovely in her sheer white dressing gown, her creamy skin glowing as she stepped gracefully toward Drew. Her hazel-brown eyes were radiant, her smile full and expectant. He took her in his arms and caressed her, his chin resting against her lightly scented hair. "*Liebling,*" he said, "I never dreamed I could be so happy again."

They began to dance without music, Drew humming the song so familiar to both of them. "Yes," she whispered, "I will be your partner for the rest of our lives."

He whirled her around the room, and they fell breathless on the edge of the bed, sitting there facing each other. Laughing, smiling. "You're such a gorgeous woman," he said.

She cupped his cheeks with her slender hands. "I love the way you stretch the truth." A frown touched her brow. "Drew, you were on the phone. It wasn't Langley, was it?"

"No."

"Don't tell me Troy Carwell knows we're here in Paris."

"Carwell won't bother us."

As CIA station-chief, Carwell tended to isolate himself within the embassy walls, a man committed to doing a job well. Drew knew that Troy's wife might be out climbing the steps to the Eiffel Tower, but Carwell would hold to his twelve-hour days on the Avenue Gabriel.

Miriam lured Drew back. "How can you be so sure?"

"He'd have to call every hotel in Paris to find us."

Drew had promised that there would be no evasive answers this time around. They'd go into marriage with the Agency on the back burner. He'd be up front with her as much as he dared without revealing Company secrets. Why was he finding it so hard to break old patterns? He gave himself a mental thrashing and said, "I was talking to Uriah Kendall."

"You called Uriah on our honeymoon?"

"That's what he asked. I told him Ian needs him."

She tightened the sash on her gown. "Did he believe you?"

"He will. Ian's his whole life."

"Drew, he has Aubrey and Grover."

Useless assets, Drew thought. "Yes, a grumpy, disagreeable son and a greedy grandson. Bet they make Uriah's life miserable."

"You do go on about them. I always got on with them both."

"You're diplomatic, *Liebling*."

"I did it for Olivia. She never forgave herself for not faring well with Aubrey. She gave him everything."

Everything except herself. She struggled there. Drew smiled. "Olivia and I both had trouble giving ourselves."

"You're doing better," Miriam said softly.

"Miriam, when we leave Paris, let's hit the hills of Gascony and check on Ian."

"Uriah's idea?"

"I agreed to it. Uriah is worried about a young grad student who's researching Olivia's life and writings."

Miriam's dazzling eyes widened. "He should be pleased."

"Hardly. He doesn't want the girl anywhere near Ian. And he definitely doesn't want her digging into Olivia's past."

"Is that why Uriah ignored me after Olivia died? It wasn't until I opened the art gallery in Beverly Hills that we were in touch again. Even then he sent Aubrey to pick out the pictures."

"And you don't sell the cheapest paintings."

Those well-set brows arced above her brilliant eyes.

"Drew, if it doesn't sell for a million, I feel like I've been cheated."

He ran his finger gently across her lips. Miriam—gifted and beautiful. Would he ever have her completely to himself, or would a part of Miriam always be committed to the art world?

"Uriah wants us to meet the student," he said.

"Just for a friendly chat? Or in full battle armor?"

"Whatever it takes to keep Chase Evans from stirring up haunting memories for the Kendalls. Uriah doesn't want her to bother Ian. And he definitely doesn't want Miss Evans to know that marriage to Olivia cost him his career with British Intelligence."

"I always thought it quite romantic that Uriah gave up so much for the woman he loved."

"He didn't give up the British throne—just his career."

Her lips parted and then closed again. Drew was grateful that she didn't remind him of what his own job had cost them. "The Kendalls had a good marriage, Miriam."

"I used to envy them." She stroked his arm. "I wish Olivia knew that we were back together again. She wanted that for us."

"Not half as much as I wanted you back again," Drew said. "Back then we troubled the Kendalls. And now they worry me. I know that Uriah is hiding something about Olivia's past, something so important to him that he was willing to sacrifice our friendship."

Her joy slipped to a half smile. "Let Uriah work it out."

Drew's grin stretched the somber lines around his gray-blue eyes. "Bad idea, eh? Especially with us still on our honeymoon."

"I'm glad you remembered."

"I did. I even made reservations for us on the Riviera."

"Oh, Drew, a day or two in the sun, and I'll look like a lobster. Why don't we go to Prague instead? I promised one of my clients that I'd look into some paintings there."

Business. Miriam's business. Miriam's career. Drew sprang to his feet, leaving her alone on the bed. He paced across the room to the window with its magnificent view of the Seine.

Drew could sketch a map of Europe with his eyes closed, even the changing boundaries that had come with the fall of communism. He'd hit so many of the main cities in the Cold War, often in the dead of night. But the logistics were impossible even with open borders. Prague and the Riviera were miles apart.

He turned to argue. He was not willing to let her job come between them, but from across the room she met his gaze, her eyes shining. He couldn't marshal any enthusiasm for Prague, but he said, "If that's what you want, I'll cancel our reservations on the Riviera."

"It was just an idea, Drew."

"I'll have you on the Charles Bridge before you know it. But I thought the Riviera would please *you*." His smile swept away. It was happening all over again—this tiptoeing over eggshells. "Miriam, I thought we were going to be up front with each other."

She brushed her hair back from her forehead. "I'm sorry. I want you to be happy, and yet I really want to go to Prague. For Olivia in a way. I've been thinking of her a lot lately."

Miriam and Olivia had been special friends, their age difference insignificant, their love of the art world a strong bond. He hadn't been there for Miriam when her best friend died.

"*Liebling*, you can't bring Olivia back."

"She's never been far away, Drew. I can't tell you how often I've thought of her and our special times together."

"Promise me you won't do anything foolish in Prague."

"Like looking up her brother Dorian?"

"Let's just stay at the Adria a couple of days."

Prague would make their schedule tight; it might even prevent them from sidetracking to Germany for a surprise visit with Robyn. He'd planned a special surprise for Miriam and his daughter. The Von Tonner Art Museum was opening soon, and he planned to be there when Pierre and Robyn cut the ribbon.

"*Liebling*, I have to be back in London by the first of July and back at the embassy bright and early the next morning. That was the agreement with Troy Carwell."

"Is that what you really want—to go back to the embassy?"

No, he thought. *I want to spend a lifetime with you, whatever lifetime I have left. But I know you so well. You need space to move in—an art gallery to run.* "Langley is counting on me staying on at the embassy for a while. I told them I would."

The old code of silence rose between them. He could not tell her that there were problems at the embassy—that Langley wanted an insider checking it out. The trail of betrayals that Porter Deven and Aldrich Ames had left behind was still turning up rough edges with the threat of other betrayals in the ranks. This new threat of more traitors would keep him at his post in London.

"I don't want to think about getting back to England. Right after that, Drew, I have to fly home."

"London is home now, Miriam," he reminded her.

Her cheeks flushed. "Yes, and I'm anxious to get our new apartment in Chelsea looking just right for you."

"For *us*. And to rescue me from my old dark, dismal flat."

"It is dreary."

"Except for the painting you gave me."

She laughed. "Don't forget the hearth rug."

"I won't be happy seeing you off to Los Angeles."

"But, Drew, we agreed that I'd take frequent trips back to Beverly Hills until the gallery is running smoothly without me."

He held out his hands. She went to him, and their fingers entwined. "I'm sorry I can't fly to Los Angeles with you."

She leaned against his broad chest. "It's all right."

It wasn't all right. He knew she was terrified of flying alone. America was being plagued by terrorism now. He had never told her that a college friend—a former CIA officer—had died in the Oklahoma City bombing. The less she knew, the less she worried. But the worry shoe was on his own foot. Miriam's gallery on Rodeo Drive was an easy target for terrorists. He didn't want to lose Miriam, not when he had just found her again.

"It'll work out, Miriam," he said, trying to pour confidence into his words. "We'll make it work this time."

"We already have. I love you, Drew Gregory."

She reached up on tiptoe, and he leaned down to encircle her in his arms. "Drew, I always liked our reunions—even in the old days. I'll expect roses on my desk when I get to California."

"Yes. Eleven red ones," he promised.

❦❦❦

Jarvoc, several miles west of Prague. Hanz Russelmann spaded the soil by the back porch, turned it over for the third time, and then stood up as tall as his hunched shoulders would permit. A proud man by birth and family tradition, his once-handsome profile remained strong, the bony German features distinct, well-chiseled. As his sun-weathered hands rested on the shovel, sweat streaked down his bristly cheeks and dropped on his gray work shirt. As far as he could see, the land was his own. The Russelmann farm spread out over the rolling hills and dipped down through the valley to a narrow winding branch of the Vltava River, and yet he was miserably unhappy. Despondent.

"*Guten Morgen,* Uncle Hanz," Mila called.

He looked up. His niece was leaning out an upstairs window, her face filled with more sunshine than the sky itself.

He waved as she exclaimed, "I love this time of year!"

Indeed, the bleakness of winter had ended, and the countryside had turned chartreuse green with the spring rains adding both life and color to the land. The distant slopes were blotched with yellow buttercups, and the wilting red geraniums in the window boxes had perked up.

"Oh, Uncle Hanz, just think—in a few weeks the hills will be an emerald green."

He envied her. Mila Van Rindin saw everything in golden hues and brilliant greens. His own sense of color had dimmed to grays. Sadly he said, "And then all too soon, winter will strike again."

"You worry too much about winter," she told him.

And why wouldn't he? In six months he would move reluctantly into another decade, ten years past his threescore-years-and-ten. Mila was twenty-six, but the winters of

Russelmann's life were running out. He shifted on his lame leg. The shattering war wound had made him an inch shorter and left him even now with throbbing pain at night. The ugly scar ran from his hip to his ankle, a constant reminder that he had once worn the uniform of a Luftwaffe pilot—that he had once dropped bombs over London, killing men who may well have walked the halls of Cambridge and studied with him before he was called home to serve on the losing side of the war. *Friends at university. Enemies at war.*

"Come down and help me. Tilling the soil is a lonesome job."

"I don't like gardening," she said.

"Then we'll pick berries."

"Some other time. . . . You miss her, don't you, Uncle Hanz?"

"Blanca?" The truth was, he rarely thought of her. He had been widowed for almost as many years as he had been married to her. She had been blinded by a stroke, wheelchair-bound, but Blanca had been a good companion. Yet he had never loved his wife. Even in marriage, his memories often strayed back to an air raid shelter in London and the girl he had left behind. His hasty departure from London in the dead of night during one of the worst air raids of the war robbed him of the chance to say a proper goodbye to his beloved British spy. Hanz had never forgotten Olivia Renway and never forgiven her. She had cost him half a million dollars in Kashmir sapphires.

"Uncle Hanz, do you think Nedrick remembers how beautiful it is in Jarvoc in the springtime?"

If it were not for the shovel, Hanz's legs would have buckled. His grandson was coming home. Yesterday's cable from Nedrick lay crumpled in his back pocket. Nedrick had disappeared from their lives ten years ago, his interest in the Russelmann factories in the Ruhr Valley, Poland, and Jarvoc nonexistent. Mila would never leave the farm, not when she was hoping that Nedrick would come back to her again. They had planned to run off together—second cousins, friends and dreamers—but Nedrick had gone without her.

Hanz felt her pain. His hope for the Russelmann family had always lain in Nedrick—Altman's only son. But Altman would not welcome Nedrick's return. Gruffly Hanz said, "Don't shed tears for my beloved grandson. It's best if he never comes back to us."

Mila disappeared behind the curtain, leaving him alone again, still leaning on his shovel. He felt beaten by time. His sons Altman and Josef considered him too old to make company decisions at the mill, but his mind was good, set in concrete against all war and all destruction. Only his body—that once sturdy six-foot-two frame—failed to keep pace with the demands of the Russelmann steel plant.

Hanz had only to turn to the south—as he did now—to see the gray ghostlike buildings. Funnels of black smoke rose from the chimneys of the far plant, curling up innocently toward the cerulean blue sky. It was eerie—like the rings of smoke and stench that had risen from the ovens and darkened the Czech skyline. Fifty years had slipped from him, but not the memory of the ovens. His factory? No, his son's now, but on paper Hanz was still the head of the family inheritance that had reaped devastation in the thirties and forties. He could never remove the stain of the evil that his father and grandfather had permitted. He could not even stop what was happening now.

As time grew closer for Hanz to render up an account of his own life, his flawed past haunted him. In recent months, Hanz had sought to find the peace of his Lutheran boyhood. Always when it seemed within reach, peace eluded him. The curling black smoke, the stench of the ovens, the blast of bombs took it away. He was certain there could be no peace for Hanz Russelmann, but he must stop Nedrick from coming back to Jarvoc. For Ned's own safety.

As Mila came out the door with a tray in her hands, Hanz propped the shovel against the wall of the house. "Here, let me take that for you, Mila."

She hesitated, her glance dropping to his lame leg. "It's heavy. I'm taking it to my father and the others."

Hanz shaded his dark eyes with one hand and stared out

toward the barn where the others were meeting. Then he reached out. "I was going out there anyway."

She pulled back, uncertain. "Then let me get another cup."

He waited, the wonderful aroma of hot coffee filling his nostrils. Mila came back at once and put another mug on the tray. She patted his hand. "Will you be all right, Uncle Hanz?"

Like Nedrick, Mila was filled with wanderlust and misgivings about the future. She had the Van Rindins' harsh German features, and the sun on her skin had robbed her of real beauty, yet she had an inner sensitivity, an unspoiled honesty. Impulsively he kissed her cheek, and then Hanz limped off toward the barn, the agony of the walk tearing at his limb.

His youth was playing itself out in the lives of his sons. Altman—the bastard son of the only woman Hanz had ever loved—and Josef the son of Blanca. He saw in them some of the old Nazi love of power—so gripping that they would do anything as long as they became rich in the process. For too long he had turned a blind eye to his sons' nefarious transactions with third world countries that wanted nuclear power. His sons were pleasant-appearing men, but they were trapped in the unforgivable scurvy of deficient minds—men capable of the atrocities of past generations of Russelmanns.

Hanz's hip felt on fire, his leg dragging at his commands. Still he walked proudly. *I am walking into hell itself*, he thought. *But I will beat my sons at their own game.*

Somehow. Some way.

🛢🛢🛢

Altman Russelmann stood in the open barn door, his back to the others. He toed out his cigarette, grinding the butt angrily into the ground, and turned to face Jiri Benak and Gustav Van Rindin, Mila's father. Gustav's two sons were there, too—Pavel who looked browbeaten and Franz with the brooding, dark face.

"My father is coming," Altman told them.

"Good," Gustav said. "Do you want me to tell him that he is no longer in charge?"

"No, Gustav. I can handle my father."

Gustav smirked. "You haven't done a good job of it lately."

Altman tossed a pack of cards on the table. "Shuffle those, Franz, and, Charlie," he told Pavel, "go and help my father before he stumbles with that bum leg of his."

"Isn't that the scar of the old Fatherland?"

"Don't let Hanz hear you say that, Charlie."

Pavel glowered through his tinted silver-rimmed glasses. "Don't call me Charlie. My name is Pavel. I hate your constant reminders that I botched that job in London."

Gustav's fat jowls bobbed as he looked at his son. "That was a long time ago, Pavel. Ten years. You just weren't cut out to be a chauffeur. We know that now."

Pavel's bitterness festered as he fingered his thick mustache with angry strokes. "Altman, you never told us you planned to kill Olivia Renway."

"How many times have I told you—that wasn't the original plan? Franz got out of control. We just wanted the Russelmann sapphires back." He thumbed their attention to the blond man at the end of the table. "But Jiri blundered that one."

Jiri tapped his cigar against the chair arm. "Renway wasn't wearing the bracelet that day. At least I grabbed her briefcase."

"What good did it do us?" Gustav asked. "It's rotting in Altman's safe with none of the rest of us privy to its contents. And for what? Renway wasn't as well-informed as we thought."

Wrong, Altman knew. *But we won't go into that.* A copy of his own birth certificate had been in the briefcase, proving that he was the son of Olivia Renway. And the manuscript pages and notes were full of veiled references to the Russelmann factory with their Japanese and Iranian interests clearly marked out. But how had she known? Hanz? Had his father confided in her?

Altman tried to speak, but for a moment hostility controlled his tongue. He could never be reasonable where Olivia Renway was concerned. Even her death had not alleviated his constant suspicions. She remained in his mind, not as his mother, but as a threat to his financial empire. His mandates had destroyed her—his own hands left pure white as Franz and the others obeyed his orders. But Altman had not destroyed what his mother knew about the Russelmann family.

His voice wavered. "We couldn't risk what she knew."

"You set us all up, Altman," Pavel said. "Renway's young grandson saw the accident. He saw what happened to her."

"Forget it, Charlie. It happened a long time ago."

"Do you think the years erased it for that boy?" He nodded toward the open door. "Go carry your own father's tray, Altman."

Jiri's narrow face grimaced. "It's Nedrick who should be angry, not you, Charlie. He didn't know who she was. I just said, 'Talk to her, Ned. If she's Olivia Renway, get her autograph.'"

"I have no doubt that my son knew that she was his grandmother. Nedrick and my father were always close. Always sharing things," Altman said. "I should never have trusted Nedrick—never have allowed him to be there when Renway died."

Franz rubbed his temples. "He got even taking refuge in Uriah Kendall's home. But, Altman, doesn't it bother you? Renway was your mother!"

In the split-second silence that followed, Altman's rage burned hotly against Olivia again. "She deserted me because I was the son of a German pilot."

Gustav overlapped the chair as he sat down. "We may be cousins, but let me remind you—thanks to your mother, you are half Jewish. If you had been in Germany during the war, you would have been tossed into a concentration camp."

"I am not Jewish," Altman shouted.

"Deny it then, but Olivia Renway was part Jewish. Never mind, Altman, being British was bad enough."

Altman forced himself to ignore Gustav as Hanz entered the barn and limped across the room. As Hanz spanned the distance between them, coffee sloshed over the edge of the tray.

Hanz's eyes looked dark and sad as though life had cheated him of its best treasures. Perhaps death would come sooner than Altman expected. With any luck they would not have to wait long for his demise. But in truth, he was reluctant to lose his father. The old man's approval still meant something to him.

Hanz glanced around at the others. "Well, what is it this time? Has another Japanese contract gone awry?"

"The opposite," Gustav said. "Foreign sales are up—especially with our Nishokura account. No thanks to your vote."

Altman raised a hand, silencing the threat of another verbal duel between the two men. "Father," he said, "Gustav and I have been discussing your resignation."

"Your takeover plans, you mean? Wait a few years and I'll be dead. You won't need my resignation then."

"Father, it's time to sign over your responsibilities to me. You've earned the right to just putter in your garden."

"Apparently your brother is not in agreement. Where is he?"

"Josef is at the plant overseeing new orders."

"Orders for steel or orders for warheads?"

Altman stiffened. "That's preposterous."

"That's what I thought." Hanz didn't know, but he said, "I know about the stockpile of weapons now. And about the sarin."

"We don't manufacture nerve gas. We're a steel industry."

"That's what my father and grandfather said of the family business in the thirties. But they lied. I know they lied."

Gustav pounded the table. "Hanz, we had nothing to do with those Tokyo disasters—nor the one in Korea."

"And you haven't tried to break the embargo on Iraq?"

Gustav lumbered from his chair, his fat cheeks scarlet.

"Sit down, Gustav." Altman's voice steadied as he turned back to Hanz. "We have legitimate contracts, Father, worldwide. Check the records if you want. But we've never sold any nerve gas or any of its components to the Orient."

"But perhaps one of the countries you do business with did."

Altman watched his father's gaze go slowly around the table to the faces of the men he had come to despise. Hanz was right. They were all clever, power-hungry men, himself included. Jiri had been given too much power, Pavel too little. But his father's contempt seemed to bypass Gustav and the others and settle once more on Altman. He braced himself for more ridicule.

"Don't get involved in sabotage, Altman."

"That's strange coming from you, Father."

Gustav butted in again. "You've gone mad, Hanz. One way or the other, we plan to take over the plant."

"No, you may need me at the helm a little longer."

Hanz took Nedrick's cable from his pocket and slid it across the rough tabletop within inches of Altman's long fingers. "Go on, son. Read it."

Altman snatched it up and read it. "It's from Nedrick. My son is coming here to Jarvoc." He held the cable in his fist and shook it at the others. "Some nonsense about a young woman who wants to research Olivia Renway's life and find her missing manuscript. But she won't find it. It's safe."

Hanz rested his head in his hands as though he could no longer sit upright in the chair and face his illegitimate son. Behind them a clucking hen scratched her claws against the straw. "Do you think Olivia was so unwise as to have only one copy of that manuscript?" he asked.

Gustav's scowl deepened. "She was clever enough to marry a former British agent, but Pavel and Jiri found none of her manuscripts at the Kendall cottage in the Cotswolds. Altman, I'm against your son coming to Jarvoc again. He'd just be trouble."

Altman flicked his fingers, willing the numbness to ease. "No, my son comes. If Ned has betrayed us, we'll deal with that later. If necessary, we'll destroy him."

Hanz lifted his face, his voice strained as he said, "Altman, don't you understand? Nedrick is concerned about us. Why else would he contact us after all these years?"

"He contacted *you*, Father. The cable is addressed to you."

"No, Nedrick is reaching out to all of us. That should be warning enough that this girl—this Chase Evans—cannot be trusted. Perhaps Evans is a plant—or worse a CIA agent herself."

"Then we'll silence her, Father. But all of this is of no consequence to you. Your beloved Olivia is dead."

"Son, to me she was dead long before she died."

But for Altman, his mother would never be dead. She haunted his memories. He was part of her. He had tried to destroy her—but she was there. Her marriage to Uriah Kendall had locked her into intelligence work. Now with terrorism spreading throughout the world—and the family coffers growing as a result—he would not risk Chase Evans uncovering the facts that Olivia had gathered.

Slowly Hanz pushed himself up, balancing on his lame leg. "Was there anything else, Altman? Did you want me for anything else?"

"We want your resignation, Father."

The older man shook his head. "I'm staying on at least until I talk with Nedrick. If there is anything that I can still do for this family, it is to keep that boy away from the rest of you."

"Father, he is not a boy. He'd be twenty-eight by now."

"I'd forgotten. He's still eighteen when I think of him."

"No, he's a grown man now." Altman suddenly brightened. He thumped the cable in triumph. "There's a slim hope. He's a Russelmann, Father, and he's coming home. Coming back where he belongs. He can be most useful to us."

Hanz's craggy face, lined with years, paled. "Altman," he said, "I've regretted the day I went to Cornwall and found you. I would have been better off if I had never known you existed."

"We would have both been better off, Father."

Chapter 4

Early Wednesday morning Chase Evans left her home on Long Island and stopped off at the Willowglen Nursing Center before catching the train into New York City. The Willowglen was a three-winged single-story building buffed white by the annual paint job. For the ninety-nine residents inside, the fresh coat of paint and the smell of a newly mown lawn did little to lift their spirits. Two days ago old man Wellington had died in his sleep, and, surprisingly, his bed was still empty. The ninety-nine simply waited as Joe Wellington had waited for the toes-up departure that would eventually come to each one.

As Chase walked down the wide corridor, a lump rose in her throat. Just a week ago she had sat beside Joe Wellington in the chapel service, strangely moved by the hymns that had lulled Joe to sleep. For hours afterwards she had chewed on the words of the squat, round-faced young preacher with fuzzy blond hair. With a booming voice for one so stunted, he had described the wide and narrow paths on which he seemed certain the residents of Willowglen tottered. His face had turned purple as they dozed off, and Chase, out of kindness, had given him her attention, even nodding in agreement as he spoke of heaven and hell. Heaven had been whispered softly around the Evans's household—a question mark behind it—when her grandmother Callie died; but hell seemed always channeled to the ravages of war and the battlefields of Vietnam, which her father described as "hell itself."

Lately Chase found herself caught up with growing uncertainty. What could she offer to her friends here at Willowglen or to the AIDS patients at Halverson Wayside House? She could hold their hands while they died, but she could not promise them an eternal tomorrow; she didn't even know whether anything existed beyond this life. She never held Callie Bartholomew's hand, not until the last day. Callie, Chase's maternal grandmother—although she never dared call her that—had spent the last few weeks of her life at the Willowglen, refusing visits from her oldest and dearest friends.

At seventy-three, while still a glamorous woman, Callie left the oncologist's office, canceled her world cruise, and put her much-loved brownstone home in New York City on the market. Without a word to her family, she had moved to Long Island and admitted herself into a private room at the Willowglen. Even as the tentacles of death encircled Callie, she had tried to convince herself that when you died, you died. Nothingness. Chase hated thinking about it. What if Callie had been wrong? If so, all the Bartholomew millions didn't gain her entry into what lay beyond.

On her last visit in that antiseptic room, Callie had held out her thin hand, and Chase ran across the room to take it. "Dear Chase, I've been a foolish woman," she had said, her glazed eyes full of fear. "Hold my hand, child. I'm so afraid."

"It'll be all right," Chase had promised.

"No, it's too late to prepare for tomorrow. Too late—"

Then having turned her back on family care and spiritual comfort, Callie had done her toes-up in the middle of the night when the private duty nurse had stepped briefly from the room.

Willowglen did nothing but remind Chase of Callie and those spur-of-the-moment flights to Paris and Milan to buy a fashionable outfit for the latest New York ball. Chase had inherited much of Callie's vivaciousness and her unrelenting devotion to causes, even if it meant stepping on the toes of the wealthy. Callie was stinking rich herself, the

Bartholomew name as well known as Rockefeller or Kennedy.

What Chase had liked the most about Callie was her marvelous sense of humor. At the dedication of the Bartholomew Library in memory of her late husband, Callie had tripped on the way to the podium. Strong arms had lifted her up and set her back on her feet. With a flick of her jeweled wrist she had said, "My beloved husband would have been embarrassed, but he's not here—at least I don't think he is—so let's get on with cutting the ribbon, and you students can get on with your lives."

But it hadn't been an accident. Hours later pain seared through Callie's leg, setting off the alarm that would end in a diagnosis of bone cancer. After Callie's death—or perhaps because of it—Chase had gone back to Willowglen to fill the lonely hours of others.

She turned into the west wing and found her friends in the back dining room, lined up in rows on both sides of the table—mouths sagging, lips parted for a spoonful of lumpy mush. Marie spotted her first. One by one the youthful faces of yesterday turned her way. Chase tried to imagine how they must have looked before the wrinkles appeared, before they had grown inevitably old and were confined in wheelchairs. Peg must have been tall and stately, not hunched and toothless as she was now. Maude squinted through half-blinded eyes that were once a brilliant blue. They were all there—all but Joe Wellington. Alice with the angelic smile, Daphine with the arthritic fingers, and dear Marie. How could Chase tell them that she planned to be gone for the summer? How could they tell her that they, too, might be gone before she got back?

She managed a quick "hi" for Alice, a hug for Daphine, a whispered "I love you" for the new little lady with the vacant stare. Then she pulled up a chair beside Marie and met those faded blue eyes with a smile. Marie's yellow-white hair had been pulled back from her face into a single ponytail that hung to her waist. Her face seemed thinner this morning, her grip on Chase's hand feeble. "I missed you, Marie, but I'm only here for a few minutes. I'm on my way to the university," she said as she offered her some juice. "But I'll come back."

At least once more before I leave for London.

Twenty minutes later she was on her feet, squeezing the blue-veined hand. She pressed Marie's head against her, and then, with a quick wave to all of them, she left the Willowglen in tears.

She indulged in a self-pity party as the train rattled into New York City. A subway ride later she was on the Columbia campus making her way to Doc Hampton's windowless cubicle with a slit of light showing beneath the door. Chase stopped and knocked. She rapped again seconds later. Hampton, she was certain, would be glaring down at some student's final exam, a red marker in his hand, his mood aggravated by the disturbance outside his door.

She risked a third brusque rap and heard his gravelly response, "Come in. I have all the time in the world."

Chase thrust the door open. "Good morning," she said. "I'm sorry I'm late. I stopped off at the Willowglen again."

He thumped the papers on the desk. "I wasn't going anywhere."

Nigel Hampton was not her image of a British don strolling leisurely across the lawns and walkways of Oxford in a black flowing robe—hair windblown, conversation philosophical, his honors too numerous to mention. The truth was, he had little hair to be wind-tossed; thin strands of washed-out brown stretched across his balding head, secured in place by something with a pleasant, albeit unfamiliar, scent. Chase had no doubt that he could easily match the intellect of C. S. Lewis and handle hours in the pub dissecting literary topics and wars and politics. Sometimes in the classroom, Hampton scared her half to death, but she liked the man and admired his brilliance and wit.

"You wanted to see me? About my prelims?"

"If you could have stuttered on paper, you would have."

Her heart sank. "Doc Hampton, I didn't—"

"You did well. Four major exams, and you did well."

He seemed both surprised and pleased. She heaved a

sigh, but he still didn't smile. "It's not my comprehensives?" she asked.

His voice seemed as grave as his expression. "I should never have persuaded the committee to hear your orals early. You could have used another week or two to prepare."

"But you're leaving for England."

"Someone in the department could have filled in for me."

"Yes, one of Prof. Marsten's old cronies."

"A prospect that's shaky at best," he admitted.

Chase's long legs locked at the knees. "Prof, didn't I make it?"

He seemed determined to extract something from the old-fashioned inkwell on his cluttered desk. Chase fixed her own gaze on the crook in his wide nose and then on the cleft in his chin.

His narrow face drew down to his long, sagging jowls. "I warned you to be confident when you took your orals. You looked terrified," he said.

"What did you expect with the six of you throwing all those curves my way? It was like a lion's den."

He chuckled. "And Prof. Marsten put up quite a roar."

"Professor Hampton, what about my orals?" she persisted.

"They went well. You're a good student, Chase, but sit down. Let's salvage your research project."

She lowered into the chair. "I thought you approved it."

"I did provisionally, but Marsten put thumbs down on any comparative study of Olivia Renway and Dorothy L. Sayers. She says you're putting too much emphasis on Renway's missing novel."

"They both had unfinished works. Sayers left an unfinished biography of a nineteenth-century novelist. Someone else finished that. But Renway! No one knows where her last manuscript is."

"Do you?" he asked.

"No, but it's important to my research project. I know it sounds brazen, but I'd like to find it and finish it for her."

He gave her a hard, brittle laugh. "That's unlikely, Chase."

Involuntarily, Chase's imagination went wild. Had Olivia Renway been carrying that thirtieth novel in her briefcase as she walked down the rain-soaked street, an umbrella clutched in her other hand? In her mind's eye, Chase could see the London rain splashing against Renway's ankles and could hear the horrible screech of brakes and the final cry of pain as Renway's battered body was crushed by the speeding car.

She tried to calm the frustration in her voice, saying, "Prof, two weeks ago I wrote a letter to Olivia Renway's widower to ask his help. I heard from Mr. Kendall's lawyer instead."

"Not good," Hampton said.

"Mr. Kendall refused any interviews, but the attorney did say that Kendall is going to London for the summer. Probably to his Cotswold cottage." She crossed one slender leg over the other, her sandal balanced on her big toe. "I haven't figured out how yet, but I'd really like to look him up when I get there."

Hampton shuffled through the mess on his desk, finally finding his thick spectacles in the clutter. He scowled as he put them on, making deep horizontal lines across his forehead and three vertical lines between his brows. "Pry too much and you'll need a lawyer of your own."

She shrugged indifferently. "I'm a Bartholomew, sir. I don't let lawyers scare me off."

He stared absently at the old-fashioned inkwell again. "Chase, are you certain you don't want to consider a project on Thoreau instead?"

Hampton seemed to be backing away from her. Without his support, Marsten would tear her project apart. "Is the committee going to reject my proposal after all the work I've put in?"

"With a bit of a rewrite, I'm certain we can get it passed."

"But you're flying back to England." She could never muddle through without him. "I wish they'd extend your sabbatical another year."

"My wife doesn't. But don't worry, Chase. I've convinced Marsten that we'd have your revised proposal back on her desk in a fortnight. That's the best I can do for you. So there's nothing stopping your trip to Europe."

"My summer abroad is dependent on my dad's funding."

The three vertical lines on his forehead became one. "Isn't it time you paid your own way? You're twenty-three now, aren't you?"

"Twenty-four. In another nine months I'll cash in on my inheritance that's been tied up in the courts for months."

Hampton's mouth twisted as he asked, "What would happen to you if your father's financial world collapsed?"

"You don't know my father. Everything he touches turns to gold—at least, into stocks and bonds and mutual funds."

Seymour Evans's calculated risks had taken him the whole nine yards—a CEO in the aircraft industry, a mansion on Long Island, a Blue Water sailing yacht for his weekend pleasure, banking reserves in Switzerland, and a foreign account in London. Chase felt a sudden urge to defend her father, to trace his long journey from barefoot boy to wealthy Long Islander.

"I won't apologize for my father's success. He's worked hard for it. Dad grew up in poverty and joined the service to put clothes on his back and three meals a day in his stomach."

"Is that why he married into the Bartholomew family?"

"He didn't marry the family—just my mother. Dad came out of the marines twenty-nine years ago before the Vietnam War had gone full scale and persuaded my mom to marry him."

Hampton's chair squeaked as he turned. "Posthaste—before her parents found out, according to Marsten."

"Marsten wasn't there. But she's right. The Bartholomews were outraged," she admitted. "But my dad earned every dime he has himself. And I'm not letting a doctorate slip between my fingers just because I'm Seymour Evans's daughter."

Her outburst seemed to please Hampton. "Good," he said. "And after your doctorate, what then, Chase?"

"I'll teach at the university level like you do. You keep

telling me there's nothing more promising than to touch a student's life and mold his mind."

Hampton's smile turned generous. "So you have been listening to me! Can I tell Marsten that you'll be getting back to her in a fortnight with a revised proposal?"

"Yes, but when I tell my dad I'll be in Europe, he'll have fits worrying about me driving on the wrong side of the street."

"I'm prepared to make you an offer that he can't resist." She met Hampton's twinkling gaze across the desk as he said, "You can stay with my wife and me at Oxford, safely out of the traffic jams in London. I'll be your mentor. Marsten approves of that."

"Oxford? Why would you do that for me?"

He looked away. "I considered voting with Marsten to stop your project. I wanted to stop you," he said darkly. "Marsten wanted me to persuade you to do your dissertation on the Inklings—Tolkien and C. S. Lewis with Sayers thrown in—"

"And omit Olivia Renway?"

"Yes, but whatever your reasons, you have to choose your own study." His eyes were back on her, his expression full of concern. "I won't try to stop you," he promised. "I can only pray that nothing happens to you while you're abroad."

Pray? She had never thought of him as a man who prayed. "You're not making sense, Dr. Hampton."

"Renway's tragic death was a topic of conversation at Oxford. She was one of our own, a Somerville graduate, you know. Whatever skeletons lie in her closet are best left there."

"You sound like you dislike her."

Again he hesitated. "You'll learn soon enough that Lord and Lady Kendall disapproved of Renway marrying their son."

"Why?"

"There were questions about her background that threatened to ruin their son's career. In the end it did."

"Prof, I'm interested in Renway's writings and in Dorothy Sayers's influence on her life and career."

"You're a stubborn one, but then if you took my advice and studied Thoreau, you wouldn't be coming to Oxford this summer. No, the committee won't stand in your way if I support you," he said, giving way to a faint smile. "But, Chase, you're going to have to decide how to handle Sayers's belief in a deity."

"Do you mean God?" she asked, surprised. "Marsten is tough enough."

"Sayers wrote more than mysteries. Among other things, she was a persuasive theologian." He slapped the desk. "Enough. What about Oxford? You'll find us a bit more traditional."

"You're not a totally hip campus?" she teased, glad that his mood had lightened.

"We didn't exactly rush out and get wired, so don't expect a new million-dollar computer lab at your disposal."

"Will I have access to the libraries?"

"I'll arrange it."

"Will your wife mind my coming?"

"She's fond of my students. She'll be particularly fond of you, once we tell her about your friends at Willowglen."

He ran his fingers through his thinning hair, his green eyes turning merry. "You and my wife will get on quite well," he said. "She drives about an hour each day to an elderly residence. The Eagle's Nest, they call it. Half of them can't walk, let alone fly, but my wife spends all of her time there where no one has any recollection of Chaucer or C. S. Lewis."

The literary ignorance at the Eagle's Nest seemed an affront to him. Chase said, "It sounds as if you don't like them because they don't remember."

"My wife accuses me of that." He was suddenly back to extracting thoughts from the inkwell. "Yes, you'll find my wife's place of business most interesting."

"Is it like Willowglen?"

"The residents are. Some of them are a pathetic lot." He thumped the marker against his hand, streaking his palm with red. "You'll want to get to know one of them. I think she's batting ninety-five. A jolly, independent old thing with nothing to do but knit multicolored lap robes. A dowager as old as the London Bridge."

"Don't make fun of her, Professor Hampton."

His bristly chin got a pensive rub. "You'll know what I mean when you see her. She sits in her private room in fancy clothes and a high felt hat as though she's stepping out any minute."

"Is her memory good?"

"At ninety-five? Better than mine will be. She's happy dwelling in the past. She may not know anything about Chaucer or C. S. Lewis, but she definitely remembers Prague."

"I don't understand, Prof."

"You will when you meet her. She knew Olivia Renway."

Chapter 5

Long Island, New York. At seven on the button, Chase came out of a fuzzy nap at the sound of her father's footsteps in the hallway. She had come into his private study after supper and taken over his sofa. She closed her eyes again, measuring his steps as he crossed the marbled hallway. Silence. He'd be by the stairs now, setting his attaché case down and hooking his hat—that he never wore but always carried in the car—on the shiny brass knob at the foot of the cream rail. Precisely, keeping the folds perfect, he'd lay his suit coat neatly over the railing. She heard his warm, muffled words to the dachshund puppy that had somehow won favor with him and taken up residence inside the family mansion. Puddles and all.

He called up the stairwell. "Nola, it's me. I'm home."

He'd forgotten, as he always did, that Nola was never home ahead of him on Wednesdays. Her Wednesdays were crammed full with committee meetings—she chaired four of them—or with playing bridge, which she hated losing.

That confident thud of Seymour's steps came closer as he entered the study and brushed past the sofa without pausing. His leather chair squeaked as he sat down and slapped his case on the desk. Chase thought of her father as heart-attack prone, a man in a pressure cooker, but his blood pressure only shot sky high when he talked about her inability to settle on a permanent career.

She was not afraid of her father, but she could not please

him—not unless she quit being a professional student and landed a top position in some corporate office in New York City as her brother Tad had done. It frustrated Chase that her father always came out on Tad's side. The only other way to long-lasting approval would be to marry a wealthy New York attorney as her sister Adele had done.

Chase's father was a marvelously successful man himself: self-made, well-disciplined, professionally groomed. He was as predictable as the seasons. His day started at 5:00 in the morning when he slipped out of his king-sized bed, showered, dressed, and took breakfast alone: one egg, two pieces of rye toast—one with jam, one with butter—and two cups of black coffee, sugarless as he was. Promptly at 5:45, he would leave the house, toss one of the two morning papers into the car with his hat, and drive off to work in his Lincoln Towncar, arriving well ahead of his employees. Except for phone calls and one luncheon date a week with Nola, Seymour stayed out of touch with the family until seven in the evening.

In spite of his demanding schedule, Nola had adapted to dinner at eight and a companionable evening sitting together in the family room, Nippy the dachshund nestled on one lap or the other. At eleven straight up, Seymour flipped on the evening news. At midnight Chase's parents went up the wide steps arm in arm. They'd talk—and sometimes laugh—for another fifteen minutes, and then silence until Seymour's loud snoring echoed through the walls.

Saturday was reserved for his wife's social calendar, Sunday for an eighteen-hole round of golf with three of his friends. On lucky Sundays he would invite Chase to go along to fill in for a missing partner. She played well, somehow pleasing him.

For another minute or two, Chase heard him rattle papers on his desk, and then across the room from behind his large mahogany desk, he said, "I assume you want to talk to me, Chase?"

She swung to a sitting position. "Do you have time, Dad?"

Curtly he snapped, "I always have time for my family."

She didn't argue. At unexpected moments, he did set

aside his work, however briefly, to talk with them. Into his rigid schedule, he sometimes reserved a slot for family matters—his wife's guest list, Tad's latest speeding ticket, Adele's marital disharmony, or Chase's endless aspirations. She realized that this was one of those golden moments as he asked, "Well, what is it?"

"I'm going to Oxford this summer on a study program."

Only one brow lifted. "How do you propose to pay for that?"

"I was hoping you'd help me."

A twinkle glinted in his eyes. "You mean, pay your way. Your last study program in Europe was a total fizzle."

"That doesn't count, Dad. I was seventeen then, off to a year of finishing school in Switzerland."

"It about finished us. You almost flunked out."

Chase took the old fight with her dad good-naturedly. "Dad, I was majoring in social activities. And I did learn French."

"And I paid through the nose—a heavy endowment to the school to keep you there and an outlandish fee for two tutors, *not one,* to thump something into that featherbrain of yours."

She smiled. "My I.Q. is much higher than that."

"When you choose to capitalize on it as you did at Vassar."

He didn't mention Nathan, but she felt a flush in her cheeks. Nathan, that gorgeous thirty-five-year-old Swiss tutor, had spent more time flirting with her than teaching her calculus. When her father caught on, Nathan had been dismissed. Once Chase came home and entered Vassar—a miracle in itself—she did a complete turnaround, taking honors, and pleasing herself as well as her parents. She was hooked. Learning was addictive.

She walked across the room and sat down in the chair facing her father's desk. He was meticulous in his wrinkle-free blue shirt with a navy silk tie knotted in place. He looked every inch the CEO of his own company, the commander-in-chief of his own household. Chase could never decide whether he was handsome or not with his silver-foxed hair and Grecian skin; his eyes were so dark brown that they appeared black as she looked at him.

"Dad, I'll have my doctorate in another year."

"Do you have to go to England to get it?"

"I'm studying up on two novelists who lived there."

He straightened a pile of work sheets, already in perfect order, and placed them in his attaché case. Then he drew the household ledger toward him—each dime, each purchase neatly penned in the appropriate column. Accounting records were essential to Seymour—as though at any moment the poverty of his youth would catch him unawares. He seemed always braced for his own financial crash. The crash of '29—she'd heard it a thousand times— had left his family unemployed and his mother in long bread lines.

He opened the ledger. "How much will it cost? Ten thousand?"

Hopefully she said, "Fifteen, maybe. And then I'll need an expense account and my air fare."

The figure Chase named was small—her father dealt in million-dollar contracts. He folded his hands on top of the ledger. "I suppose you've discussed this with your mother?"

"Once or twice."

Chase saw the first hint of defeat in her father's face. "It doesn't worry your mother—your constant chasing after the wind, your endless schooling. But it worries me that a daughter of mine still doesn't know what she wants to do with her life."

She didn't want to hear a repeat of her father's rise from emptying wastebaskets to a top position in the corporate world. The thought of her teaching at the university level would blow him straight out of his leather chair. He wasn't into tenure and long-haired students, musty libraries and research papers. Teaching, she knew, wouldn't offer the advancements that he coveted for her.

"Chase," he demanded, "these British authors—are they accomplishing something worthwhile with their writings?"

"They did before they died."

"Two dead novelists? What started you on this wild idea?"

"I've been wondering what happened to Olivia Renway's missing manuscript."

"And who is Olivia Renway?"

Chase's mother answered from the doorway. "If you read books for mere pleasure, you'd know. She was a British-born novelist. Quite well known. And, dear, very rich! That should impress you."

No, Czechoslovakian, Chase thought.

Nola crossed the room to the cushioned chair near Seymour's desk. Her soft brown hair was cut short; the blue-gray eyes wide, the skin folds above them puffy. She looked tired, but then she slept poorly, catching most of her sleep after Seymour stopped snoring. She had a built-in time clock that made her spring from the bed by 7:30 and be on the go, full speed ahead within the hour. Nola loved the out of doors—swimming and sailing, golfing and gardening. Long hours in the sun had taken their toll on her skin, leaving it coarse and blotched with wrinkles long ahead of time. But what Chase loved about her mother was her happy smile and the straight, open gaze that met hers now.

Nola sat down and crossed her legs, one open-toed slipper tapping the air. She folded her large-knuckled hands, one on top of the other, her chin resting on them. "I gather that you and Chase have been discussing London," she said.

"So this is another of *your* schemes, Nola?"

"Why not?" his wife asked. "I want you to fund Chase's summer. If you don't, Seymour, I will."

Her threat was real. She had become financially independent again with the Bartholomew inheritance. Seymour leaned back in his chair, his interest finally aroused. "How will a summer abroad prepare Chase for the business world?"

"If you mean investments, it won't. Your Dow Jones averages don't interest her. Nor me, really."

"They should. My wise investments keep us in luxury."

"Don't take all the credit, my dear. My parents taught me about wise investments long before you came along."

"Nola," he said patiently, "writing a dissertation that sends her chasing off to England is a waste of time. She could just as well pick a political theme like America's involvement in the war in Southeast Asia. She could even include that marine hero who lectured at Columbia the other day."

"Luke Breckenridge?" Chase asked, clearly remembering that handsome face. "Dad, he wasn't anything spectacular. Oh, he's a handsome hunk, but he's no football or basketball star or pop singer. Strip away that marine uniform and what do you have?"

"May I remind you, Chase, I was a marine."

"You remind us often enough," Nola said.

"And Vietnam was my war. It would make a good topic for your dissertation."

Chase shrugged. "And you didn't even start that conflict. It doesn't matter, Dad. I don't want to research Breckenridge's life. He's been out of circulation for twenty years." The memory of Luke's sad smile filled her mind. "Dad, he was kind of shy and out of place in twentieth-century USA!"

"Twenty years of captivity does that," Seymour said. "Never mind, Chase, with your mother on your side, you win. Forget the marine hero."

"I may see him again. He told me he's going back to Europe."

"What's wrong with the good old USA? When I came back from Vietnam, America was good enough for me."

"He hates the crowds and the news media, so he's going to help set up some art museum in Germany. And," she said with an air of mystery, "he expects me to call him when I get to Europe."

Seymour unbuttoned one shirt sleeve with jerking motions and folded it above his wrist. "I don't want you contacting him over there."

Nola laughed. "So now you don't trust the marines. Then why don't you laser off that *semper fidelis* tattoo of yours?"

Her mother had scored. Seymour almost always wore long-sleeved shirts, even in the sizzling summer, anything to hide his tattooed biceps in public. He still boasted about his days with the marines, but he withdrew when his wife or daughters pressed him for tales of his wild and woolly days as an off-duty marine.

"Chase, phone the captain and let your father talk to him."

Seymour gave the idea a quick thumbs down. There was no appeasing him. "Dad, Prof. Hampton invited me to stay in his home in Oxford. He's offered to be my mentor for the summer."

Seymour stared at her, more disgruntled than ever. "I trust that's all. Attend Oxford? What will that cost me?"

In that flash Chase decided that if she ever married, it would be on the run. She wouldn't dare wait for her father's approval. "It's a private arrangement. Prof. Hampton promised me access to the libraries there. It's a chance of a lifetime, Dad."

"So is getting a permanent job."

Nippy chose that moment to enter the room and piddle on the plush ash-blue carpet. For a second no one moved, and then Seymour pointed angrily at the dachshund. "Get that dog out of my study. I have work to do. We'll talk about Oxford later."

Without even glancing at Nola, Chase went to the door and mopped the damp rug with her sweatshirt. She scooped Nippy up into her arms as she left the room. His squat body and drooping ears draped over her arm as she hurried down the long, spacious hall and skidded to her listening post. The intercom system went throughout the house. She flicked on the button into the study—a trick that Tad had taught her when they were children.

Her mother's voice came through clearly. "Seymour, don't say that again. Our daughter is not lazy. She chalks up twenty hours a week volunteering. And that on top of her studies."

"All at my expense."

"It costs less than Tad's speeding tickets, and it doesn't hurt your reputation. I constantly hear about Seymour Evans's lovely daughter—the good she does for the abused elderly in nursing homes, her hours with children on the pediatric ward."

"It's her time at the Halverson Wayside House that both-ers me. Risking her health with those AIDS patients."

"Sometimes, Seymour, I think you are totally witless. She will not contact the virus by reading to them."

"She's a stubborn one, that girl."

"She is, unfortunately, a chip off the old Evans block."

"Hardly," he groused. "You won't find me in any AIDS march. I wish Chase would keep her political convictions to herself."

"You never did."

"Nola, I can't support this Oxford whim of hers."

"She'd have her own money if you hadn't talked my mother into adding that codicil to her will—just before she died. It was unfair to delay Chase's inheritance—to want her treated differently from Tad and Adele."

"I simply suggested that none of the children should inherit until they were twenty-five. Your mother agreed."

"Callie loved Chase. You took advantage of mother's ill health. You used her to try and force Chase to stop going to university and find a permanent job. But I'm proud of Chase. She's the only one of our children who will have a Ph.D.!"

"She's the only one without gainful employment. I don't want her to be thirty and jobless. I can't foot her bills forever."

"Funny," Nola said sadly. "You never stand in Tad's way."

"He's always made the right choices."

"Your choices for him. It has left him a social disaster." Pain crept into her voice. "In case you've forgotten, Chase never went off on drugs like Tad did. She's a good girl, Seymour."

"She's a woman."

Chase kept her hand cupped around the puppy's mouth and heard her father drumming his pen on the desk. "Tad's okay now. I'm proud of him."

"Are you proud of his divorce, too? Seymour, she can't be like Tad, and surely you wouldn't want another Adele. Give it nine months; then Chase will have her own money. Thanks to my mother. But help her now, please."

The pen clapped more loudly. "A doctorate won't change her."

"Oh, Seymour, if only Chase could please you."

He coughed. "You said that about me once to your mother."

"Callie came around in the end. 'My self-made son-in-law,' she called you. She just wanted the best for you."

"I want the best for Chase. I want her to marry well."

"That may not mean marrying into money, Seymour. We had nothing when we started out."

Chase expected her father to explode. Instead, he said huskily, "I hated it when your parents cut you off. It took me so many years to provide for you the way they did."

"It didn't matter. We had each other."

"Your mother never forgave me for not taking you on a proper honeymoon. She told me that a day or two before she died."

Nola's laugh turned merry. "That did eat at Callie's pride. Dear mother! She never admitted to her friends that we went off for six days to a broken-down summer cabin."

Seymour's voice lightened. "And we came back flat broke without even the foggiest notion of how we would survive or where we'd live. When your father called me in for that Bartholomew lecture, I could have thrashed him for suggesting an annulment."

"I almost fainted when you told him that it was too late for that. But I did think he would offer you a job."

"You know I refused it. I told him I'd make it on my own."

"Yes, you earned your own way from the day I married you. Chase is so much like you. She'll be all right, Seymour."

Chase predicted what would happen next and heard her Dad's husky voice saying, "Nola, I love you."

"That's why I've stayed with you all these years, Seymour." With a breezy laugh Nola said, "Wouldn't you like a summer alone? Just the two of us again?"

Chase pictured Nola slipping behind the desk and leaning her sun-browned cheek against Seymour's. "I'm sorry. I am guilty of spoiling our children."

"You win again," he said quietly. "Chase can have her

way. Pack her up. I'll open another account for her in London."

"Can we send a new laptop computer with her?"

"What about that state-of-the-art system in her bedroom?"

"She can't carry that on board the plane."

"Anything, Nola. I'll have my secretary tend to it. At least I won't have to be embarrassed with Chase waving banners on some street corner in Long Island for three whole months. She can take her causes to the streets of London."

Chase was about to switch off the intercom when he added, "But, Nola, I'm uneasy about her trip abroad. All alone."

"You always worry about Chase, darling."

"It's different this time. It's not just the money. I keep thinking back to that Oklahoma City bombing and the disasters in the Tokyo subways. I couldn't bear it if anything happened to Chase." His voice faltered. "I'm quite fond of her, you know."

"Then why don't you tell her that?"

"I don't know how." He sighed heavily. "It's easier to write out a check."

Chapter 6

Ocean City, New Jersey. Luke Breckenridge stood at the attic window in the bedroom he had once shared with his brother Landon and stared across Asbury Avenue. The media trucks were gone. Not a single out-of-town visitor gawked up at the shingled two-story house with its front porch spotless from his mother's scrubbing. He swung open the shutters and sucked in the ocean air, wondering if he'd soon be free to walk the boardwalk of his hometown and not be recognized. He longed for anonymity, even for the isolation that he had known for all those years when people thought he was dead in the Laotian jungles. A dead traitor.

Betrayal in the jungles of Laos remained a vivid memory. His captivity had left his back and jaw scarred, his mind often in the torture mode. His stateside reentry process and the long weeks of tests and interrogation had added to the pressure. If Luke had appreciated any of the top brass who grilled him, it was the lanky shrink with the bushy eyebrows and half-mast eyelids that hid an amused twinkle. Sid Grozfelt had a slow drawl and a backwoods approach that didn't win ribbons from his fellow officers, but they won Luke's approval.

Even now Luke smiled at their last interview. As Grozfelt had come into the hospital room at Walter Reed, Luke had snarled, "Is the black crepe for a traitor still hanging on my door?"

"Didn't notice," Sid said as he sat down by the window.

"I'm fed up with these four walls that separate me from my family." *Sequestered even from Sauni.* "I might as well be dead."

"Nothing wrong with the view from this window, Captain."

"It would look better from the outside."

Sid turned, grinning. "That's what I told the committee after another phone call from your wife. She sent her love."

"You heard from Sauni? I haven't."

"The switchboard is still monitoring your incoming calls. The operator gave Mrs. Breckenridge a bit of a run-around before transferring her call to my office." He chuckled. "I wouldn't want to cross wires with your wife often, Captain."

In his slow drawl, he quoted Sauni, "'All this political maneuvering—they've been holding Luke's family in mourning for twenty years now, and they still won't let him go. Do I have to fly to Washington and talk to the president himself?'"

Grozfelt leaned back in the chair, a silly grin on his face. "Captain, your wife thinks I'm your chaplain. I do make a rather good confessional sometimes."

Before Luke could react, two officers from Langley barged straight into Luke's private room. Chad Kaminsky shut the door and leaned against it as Harv Neilson, the better groomed of the two, stormed toward the bed where Luke was sitting.

"CIA big boys," Luke hissed.

Grozfelt unraveled from his chair and placed himself firmly in Neilson's path. "Sir, may I help you?"

"We're here to see Breckenridge about his escape from Laos," Neilson said. "And his time at the mercenary camps in Europe."

Sid took a small notebook from his shirt pocket and flipped to a blank page. "No need. We've already discussed those issues. Besides, when Captain Breckenridge leaves here, he goes with a clean bill of health from Walter Reed. *A free man.*"

"But we're from Langley."

"So Breckenridge tells me."

"It's all right, Grozfelt. Sooner or later they'll track me down." *Or have me killed*, Luke thought. "Let's hear them out."

Neilson was a bookish man with law degrees and a brusque manner that turned nasty as he said, "We'd like to speak with Breckenridge alone."

Sid's voice remained calm. "I'm his doctor. I stay."

As Neilson glared down at him, Luke asked, "Are you here to discuss my CIA mission in Laos?"

"No, but if you were held in Southeast Asia against your will—as you claim—how did you escape from there?"

Luke had answered that question a hundred times already in the hours of interrogation. Again he stuck consistently to his belief that his escape from Laos had been Russian-orchestrated.

"Russian?" Neilson mocked.

"If not Russia, then it was the work of the CIA."

"Next you'll tell me Porter Deven arranged your freedom."

"No," Luke said. "Porter Deven wanted me dead."

Though Neilson hounded him, Luke remained guarded about his time at the mercenary camp in the foothills of the Pyrenees.

Neilson's eyes hardened. "You were the brigadier commander there."

Luke's response remained polite, clipped. "Yes, sir."

"You were there for monetary gain?"

"No, sir."

"Where are the men you served with?"

"I don't know, sir."

Neilson no longer denied Luke's brief association with the CIA, but he didn't admit to it either. Luke could imagine the detailed triplicate reports that would follow the Neilson-Kaminsky visit. At the door as they left, Neilson's gaze slipped past Grozfelt and settled angrily on Luke. "Porter Deven was a good man. You ruined his career, Breckenridge."

"He was a traitor, Neilson—the traitor who betrayed me."

The muscles on Neilson's jaw throbbed. "You should have died in that mercenary camp, Breckenridge."

"Nice chaps," Grozfelt said as the door slammed behind them. "But, Breckenridge, you really got to them with that 'Yes, sir. No, sir. I don't know, sir.' Where are those men now?"

"In Africa perhaps or bloody-well wounded or dead, many of them lying in unmarked graves in Bosnia or Chechnya."

"And you think you owe those men something?"

My silence mostly and only sketchy recollections for the record. Aloud he said, "There have always been foreign legions, Sid, filled with misfits and renegades willing to fight another man's war for a price. That wild riffraff of mercenaries trusted me. No matter what price I have to pay, Sid, I won't expose them." But he would, as he did often now in the deep quiet of his soul, pray for their safety.

"Well, Breckenridge," Grozfelt had said on discharging him the following morning, "I've talked the brass into setting you free. You've got a good mind, Captain. Forget Porter Deven's betrayal. Don't let the bitterness of lost years destroy you."

With an unmilitary stance, Grozfelt extended his freckled hand and gave Luke a phone number. "If you ever want to talk things out again, call me. We can't give you back the years you lost, Captain, but make the time that's left count."

Luke didn't even wait for his parents to drive down to Walter Reed to pick him up. He rented a car and sped home to Ocean City, a resort town already bracing for the summer crowds, home to the best set of parents a man could have. As he settled into the familiar environment, his thoughts often strayed far from the Jersey shore to Sauni in Busingen, Germany. Sauni Summers was the only woman he had ever loved, the gal he had married, the young wife who had left him when he went back to Vietnam for a third tour of duty. Since coming back home, he had racked up enormous phone bills with his transatlantic calls just to hear her say, "I still love you, Luke."

His solitary musings were interrupted by the sound of

the front doorbell ringing. He dreaded the thought of another reporter with a new angle on the Luther Breckenridge story.

"Luther. Luther." The soft, mellow voice of Amy Breckenridge echoed up the narrow stairs. "Luke, dear."

He went to the top of the stairs and smiled down at his mother, a genteel woman, her kindly eyes full of love for him. "Dinner won't be until seven. But you have company."

"I was afraid of that." Luke ducked his head to avoid the low-pitched ceiling and made his way down the steps. He kissed Amy on the cheek. "Who is it, Mom?"

"Said he was a friend of yours. A stranger to me."

Luke found his guest engrossed in the rogue's gallery that went the length of the hallway. "You have to see this to believe it," Sid Grozfelt said staring up at the generations of Breckenridges in uniform. "I take it that this one is the admiral."

Luke nodded toward the sitting room. "That's him in person."

Luke's dad dozed in his maroon leather chair, his stocking feet on the hassock, his unused pipe on the table beside him. He looked old and beaten sitting there, aged in the long years of Luke's absence. He was no longer the proud, rigid man that Luke had known as a boy.

"Let's not disturb him," Grozfelt said. "Why don't we take a drive, Luke? Or a stroll on that boardwalk of yours?"

"What's wrong, doctor? Or do you always make house calls?"

"I haven't heard from you since you left Walter Reed. Thought I'd drop by and check on you myself."

"A three-hour drive?"

Luke's mother watched them from the kitchen door. "I'll be back in a couple of hours, Mom," Luke promised. He waved and followed Sid to the porch. "Where to?" he asked.

"Your brother's grave. Your high school. And the boardwalk."

Luke didn't question Grozfelt. His therapeutic approach didn't fit the textbook. "Let's hit the boardwalk first," Luke said. "It's just a few blocks walk from here."

"How's your recovery program, Luke?" Sid asked as they strolled along.

"I'm better. This is the first day without the news media. But I don't feel like a hero. I don't even want to be one. Maybe I should have stayed back at the mercenary camp."

"That kind of retreat would be like going back to the leeks and garlic in Egypt."

Luke sighed. "Mom tells me that life will get back to normal. But when, Sid? I've spent half of my life in exile."

"Vietnam wasn't your fault, Luke."

"But the mercenary camp in Spain was my choice."

"Understandable. You had no place to go. No legal papers to identify you. Porter Deven robbed you of a lot of years. But don't forget you have a full pardon now."

"Are there any other decisions in Washington I should know about?" Luke asked.

"Besides balancing the budget and giving tax advantages to the wealthy? Some good news for you. Public opinion swayed Spain to drop the charges against you."

Luke grabbed Grozfelt's arm. "I've been expecting the worst, but this means I'm really free to go back to Europe."

"I'd say so. But there's still some concern in the House about your training of mercenary soldiers. It'll take time."

Grozfelt sauntered over to a hamburger stand, ordered, and went heavy on the mustard and relish. He spoke with his mouth full. "Luke, what about those book contracts—in seven figures, right?"

"Is that why you're here? Do you have a problem with that?"

Sid almost choked laughing. "No, just my curiosity."

"I turned them down. I don't want to repeat the Laotian story ever again. I don't even want to remember it."

Sid stopped in the middle of the boardwalk. "Is your wife behind your decision to drop the book contracts?" he asked.

"Not really. But a university student thought I was crazy."

Chase Evans—that was her name. A pretty, young woman with chestnut hair and tiny earrings at her well-shaped ears. He ran down the fragmented recollections: lipstick that matched her polished nails; a stylish, low-cut tank top; and a voice light and quick like a summer breeze. "We had a chat after I blew a lecture at Columbia University. She spent the next hour trying to convince me that my speech hadn't been all that bad. Nice girl, Sid. You'd rate her high on your scale."

Sid wiped the mustard from his mouth. "What's important is whether she means something to you or not."

"Just friends. She's to call me when she gets to Europe."

Grozfelt let that one ride as they ambled over to the railing and stood there watching the four-foot waves wash away the top layer of the beach. In the deafening roar of the water, as the waves crashed beneath the boardwalk, Luke tried to recapture the carefree days of his boyhood. But his thoughts kept somersaulting back to sea, trying to beat the raging Atlantic to the other side of the world where Sauni lived.

"Any more trouble with nightmares, Luke?"

Luke gave Grozfelt a twisted grin. "Coming home was just what the doctor ordered. I feel as safe as a little kid again."

"No flashbacks? No anger?"

"Will they ever go away, Sid? Sometimes I think I still hate Porter Deven. He ruined my whole life."

"He can only destroy what you let him destroy. Tell me, Luke, is your former wife still in the picture?"

Luke wiped his palms on his jeans. Miserable flashbacks of Southeast Asia and Spain—those faces from the past— kept Sauni at a distance. "I can't ask her to share the torment of my personal battles."

"Do the battles have faces?" Sid asked.

Luke couldn't voice them: the bamboo cage in the Laotian jungle, the roving Pathet Lao troops that hunted him down, the mercenary camps in Europe where he trained men to kill, and his unrelenting rage at Porter Deven—the CIA officer who had betrayed him. "Sid," Luke confided at last, "I can think of Vietnam and Laos now and dwell more on Neng Pao's friendship than on the betrayal. Without my friend Neng, I would never have made it. Maybe it will be that way with Porter Deven in time."

"A day at a time, Luke. Use some of those mental gymnastics that helped you survive in Southeast Asia. You'll come through, especially with that young woman in Busingen rooting for you."

Luke turned. "You've been in touch with Sauni again?"

Grozfelt's eyelids opened wider, his amusement more apparent. "Several times. She still thinks I'm the chaplain. Imagine—a nice, little Jewish boy like me! Mrs. Breckenridge is quite a woman! When will you two get back together?"

"I don't feel good enough for her."

"There you go again, putting yourself down. Look at the bright side. She never remarried. She went to great lengths to clear your name. You're still young, Breckenridge— vibrant and virile. Getting back with your wife is quite feasible."

Grozfelt didn't wait for an answer, but said, "I won't ask about your financial state, but Congress and the military are still dragging their heels. They did make one decision— seems like nothing will be done about the life insurance policy. They voted against asking your parents to pay it back."

"I have some back pay coming to me from the marines. That will tide me over for now."

"Twenty years' worth?"

"That hasn't been decided. But at least I'm covered for the captivity time in Laos."

It was 7:15 before they got back to the house. "Come in and have dinner with us," Luke suggested.

"No, I need to get back to Washington."

"And turn in your reports on me?"

"No reports. We'll just chalk this up as a visit with an old friend." Sid's handclasp was firm as he said, "Keep in touch, Captain. Call me collect if you have to, even from Europe."

Luke waited until Grozfelt drove away, and then he went back inside the house. He paused at the sitting room, a lump rising in his throat as he saw his father still sleeping in the chair. Luke longed to walk across the room and put his arm around the admiral's shoulders. He smiled instead and left him undisturbed.

When he reached the kitchen, he grabbed an apple and leaned against the sink watching his mother. She searched Luke's face. "You've decided, haven't you, son?"

He met her honest gaze. "Yes. I'm going back to Europe."

"You're not happy here?"

"Sauni's over there."

"Your dad and I will miss you. Dreadfully. We like having you up there in your old room or spending your evenings with us."

"Europe may not be permanent. It depends on Sauni."

"There's something even more important for you to consider."

He touched her wrinkled cheek. "I know. Your prayers haven't been wasted. Nor Sauni's. I'm sorting all of that out, too. But I'm still having trouble believing in God's Son when He took yours."

Tears filled her eyes. "Don't, Luke. Landon was so ill. I prayed that God would set him free."

Luke couldn't buy that. "Did you pray that way about me?"

"No." She turned on the faucet and filled the teakettle. "Even when we buried what we thought was your body, I didn't want it to be true. Not when you weren't at peace."

"Landon was at peace," Luke said. "I want that, too."

"It's all right, Luke. Even if you don't believe completely yet, at least believe the miracles. Your honorable discharge. The miracle of your survival. Surely God had a purpose in this."

"You talked about miracles when Landon and I were boys."

"I'd forgotten."

"I didn't. I thought of it often these last twenty years."

Her hands looked dishwater red, her steps slow as she took her kettle to the stove. Inside, Luke knew, she was a tower of strength. She'd always been there—for all of them.

She turned on the burner and looked back at him. "Luke, do we have much longer with you?"

"Several days. I'm scheduled to speak at the graduation at Ocean City High before I can leave."

"And you're to be introduced at the Tabernacle."

The Tabernacle was as familiar to him as the boardwalk and Shriver's salt water taffy. The old building had been replaced with modern architecture with a cross on top; it was as much a part of his mom's roots as the house they lived in. Her pride was wrapped up in his speaking to the town where she could hold her head up—now that he was no longer called a traitor. He winked. "I'll spend those fifteen minutes bragging about my parents."

She picked up his apple core and threw it in the garbage bag. "Did you go over to Landon's grave again today?"

"Yes. Grozfelt went with me. He's my shrink, Mom. He was assigned to help me sort out the last twenty years."

"But the cemetery is a private matter, Luke."

"I told Grozfelt that I could always talk things out with my brother. He knows I still miss Landon. Like you do, Mom."

Her lip trembled as she lifted the lid on the vegetables. "Luke, work it out with Sauni. If you get back together, we'll come to see you." She sighed. "Have you told your father yet?"

"No. He'll worry about not being here when I get back."

"Your father is good for a number of years. We both are. Having you alive and back in our lives was all we ever wanted." She brushed strands of her silvery hair away from her face. "I'll fret about you being alone over there. What will you do while Sauni teaches all day?"

"Drew Gregory's daughter offered me a job at the Von Tonner Art Museum for a few weeks." He grinned, confident now. "I promised her four days a week making picture frames. That leaves my weekends free to drive up to Busingen."

"Luke, you won't get involved with Drew Gregory, will you?"

"I thought you liked him."

"I do. Very much. But, Luke dear, he's still with the CIA. Dad and I don't want anything to happen to you."

"Mom, I'll be careful, but I can't forget that Drew saved

my life—at least he gave it back to me. I was CIA once. Remember? Briefly in that one big mission in Laos."

She swayed and had to lean against him. Wiping her hands on her apron, she said, "Oh, Luke, we're going to miss you. You won't leave until after that visit to the White House?"

"No, Dad's counting on it. I think he'll get more kick out of shaking the president's hand than I will. I think this full pardon was forced on the president."

"It won't hurt his political position either."

"While I'm in Washington, maybe he can get me an invitation to Annapolis before I leave." Luke tried not to sound bitter. "I'm not exactly their favorite son in spite of my full pardon."

"But, Luke dear, you're my favorite son."

🥀🥀🥀

Chase waited by the phone, hoping that Luke Breckenridge, the tall, handsome marine hero, would call her. She kept picturing the distinguishing gray strands that edged his thick sandy hair and those dark eyes, one moment sad, the next hypnotic in their intensity. The uniform with all its ribbons had set him apart, making him appealing, easy to think about.

They would meet again! Even if she lost all of her luggage on the flight, Chase had no intention of losing Breckenridge's address. Luke reminded her of the strengths that she most admired in her father, someone who would surely go places. Luke was far more exciting than her usual dates—and there were plenty of them: Tom who saw dating Seymour Evans's daughter as an open invitation for a day on board the family yacht, Randy who hated it when she won at golf, and Calvin the bookworm who was dry as dust even on a dinner date.

Captain Luther Breckenridge had not been boring.

She closed her suitcases and locked them. As she reached the stairs, her father glanced up at her. "Well," he said, frowning at her oversized bags, "I see you packed lightly this time."

He met her halfway up the steps and took her luggage. "You won't change your mind, Chase?"

"About the trip? No, Dad."

"I hate to see you go. It's an unsettled world out there."

As they reached the porch, she touched her father's cheek in a rare show of affection. "Once I get my Ph.D., I'll go to work. You'll see. If all else fails, I'll get a job sweeping floors."

"You don't have any experience with a broom, Chase."

He was right. "You don't mind driving me to Kennedy?"

"I insist on it. But hurry. Nola is in the car waiting."

Ten minutes later he pulled to a stop in front of the Willowglen Nursing Center. "Chase, Mother and I thought you'd like to say goodbye to your friends one more time."

"And I'm going in with you," Nola announced.

"It won't bother you, Mother?"

"Of course, it will. I haven't been back to this wretched place since your grandmother died."

Seymour drummed his fingers on the steering wheel. "Don't be long. I want to get to Kennedy International on time."

Nola took Chase's arm. "Your father has a business appointment at two. We don't want him to miss that."

As they passed the room where Callie had died, Nola said, "I hate this place."

"Mom, coming here to live was Callie's choice, not yours."

Marie's arms were already outstretched when they reached her, the thin face lighting with joy at the sight of Chase. "I'm going away for the summer, Marie, but I'll come to see you as soon as I get back."

The old woman's frail grasp tightened.

"Honest, Marie. I'll be back." *But you won't be here. You're thinner than last week. You're failing rapidly.*

Unexpectedly, Nola crouched down beside Marie's wheelchair. "I'll come to see you while Chase is gone," she offered.

The watery eyes fixed on Nola. "Really, Marie. I'll come and bring you flowers and read Chase's letters to you."

What letters? Chase wondered. *I usually telephone.*

They left Marie and walked to the car in silence, their sad mood weighing them down all the way to Kennedy. Tears still pricked Chase's eyes as they stood at the departure gate.

"Write," Nola told her.

"Just call us collect," Seymour advised. "That way we'll know you aren't lost on the back of beyond."

"I'll do both, Dad. How's that?"

"I still don't like you traveling alone."

"You're old-fashioned."

"I'm cautious. I don't even like Tad going off alone."

"Tad seldom does."

"Chase, your ticket is *round* trip," Nola reminded her.

"I'll keep that in mind. And thanks for Paris, Dad."

"I don't approve of you going there first, not alone, not after that series of bombings there last year."

"But the last time I saw Paris—"

Her father's face went gray as the boarding gate opened. "No jokes, Chase. This is it. I want you back here in September to finish your studies. Please be careful. Stay out of the way of bombs and strangers and don't leave your luggage unattended."

His fears came at her like leeches. She had an uneasy feeling that unless she looked both ways all the way to England, she was in for trouble. She scolded herself and said, "Stop worrying, Dad. Nothing's going to happen to me."

Gruffly, her father pulled her to him, hugged her, and said what she had never heard him say before. "I love you, Chase."

Chapter 7

Paris lay far behind the Gregorys as they rode over the winding hills of Gascony and crested the steepest elevation. Below them was another quaint village nestled in the verdant valley. Drew let up on the gas and coasted toward the village, avoiding the children at play and the sheep lazily crossing the dusty road that ran through the center of town. He crept past the white-steepled church and headed toward the stone hotel with three chimneys poking up from its slate roof. A cobblestone path led to the door where colorful flower boxes hung in each window.

"Oh, Drew. Let's stay there!" Miriam exclaimed.

He smiled—he'd been doing a lot of that in the last few days—and said amiably, "Why not? We're at least within earshot of Ian Kendall. I'm sure of it."

"Does he know we're coming?"

"I thought we'd surprise him."

"He might surprise us and be gone."

He answered her arched brows with a shrug of his broad shoulders. "No, Jon Gainsborough gave me Ian's schedule. He's the British industrialist who sponsors Ian's cycling team."

"You don't sound as though you like him."

"Jon's all right, but he and Dudley Perkins are thick."

She patted his arm. "Reason enough to be careful."

They parked in the rear and entered through the patio dining room where the tables were set with sparkling pink goblets and freshly picked flowers. Stepping cautiously over the mopped tiles, they found the hostess dozing in a rocker, the mop bucket still at her side. She came to with a jerk and fired such a quick round of French at them that even Drew had to listen intently.

Within minutes she escorted them up a narrow stairway to the only unoccupied room on the second floor, *a chambre sur la cour.* Outlandish green wallpaper ran in wide strips from ceiling to floor. A sink and a bidet stood beside the tub in the corner, as old-fashioned as the mahogany wardrobe with its chipped finish.

Before he could suggest traveling on, his bride who loved luxury ran her fingers over the porcelain pitcher and wash basin as though she had been ushered into the queen's palace.

"Take the room, Drew. I love it."

He wanted nothing more than to please her. "We'll take it," he said, and feeling a bit romantic at the isolation, nodded appreciatively to their hostess. "Make that two nights."

Drew regretted it five minutes later when he flopped down on a bed as hard as a limestone slab. The pillow roll felt equally rigid and unyielding beneath his neck.

"Miriam, we'll never sleep on this four-poster."

She laughed and tossed her cashmere sweater to him. As he tucked it under his head, she said, "Darling, it's just for two nights. But forget the bed. Come here and look at this view."

Reluctantly, he struggled to his feet to stand with her by the open shutters. The air smelled sweet and fresh, as though they had just come through a rainstorm. A thick vine framed the window, and red geraniums poked their colorful heads up from the window box below. The far-flung slopes rose and fell in patterns of emerald and jade and loden greens. Trees and bushes, flowers, and more stone houses dotted the verdant hillsides.

"Miriam, let's look for Uriah's grandson while we still have daylight in our favor."

She leaned back against his chest. "I'd forgotten about Ian. I'll have to freshen up a bit first."

"And I need a bath after that long drive." He stepped away from the window and started to strip down.

"Where's the bathroom?" she asked.

"The water closet is at the end of the hall and the tub," he said, thumbing toward the corner of the room, "is there."

"But there's not even a shower curtain."

"Doesn't look that way. But," he said, running his finger under the tap and sinking lower into the tub, "the water's steaming. Care to join me?"

⚉⚉⚉

The Gregorys left their charming room an hour later and followed the scribbled map to a large chalet on the other side of town. They were directed to a private room in the back, an odoriferous enclosure that accommodated exercise equipment and five metal tables, all occupied. Riding gear and helmets lay piled against the wall, the outfits emblazoned with the red and blues of the Jon Gainsborough cycling team.

Ian was easy to spot with his lanky body and flaming reddish hair. He lay facedown on the middle table, a sheet draped over his buttocks and thighs, his upper torso gleaming with sweat, his bare feet toes down. A physical therapist stood by his side working his back muscles, taut after a long day's drive.

"Keep your eyes straight ahead," Drew teased as he led Miriam to Ian. He stooped down. "Kendall, it's Drew Gregory."

Ian looked like he would sprint from the table with a backward flip. "Don't get up, Ian," Drew warned. "Miriam is with me."

Ian stretched his arm back and blindly gripped her fingers. "How's this character treating you, Miriam?"

"Like royalty."

"Good. Then I won't get up and settle accounts for you."

She laughed softly. "No, Ian, I'm more than happy."

"Good," he said again, and there was a catch in his voice. "If you're here for the race, you're six weeks early."

"No," Drew assured him. "We're just doing the countryside, so we swung by to see you."

Ian's answer vibrated as the masseur dug deeper into his shoulder muscles. "A hundred kilometers out of your way? A deliberate detour? How'd you find me?"

"Gainsborough gave us your schedule. How are you doing?"

"Coach Skobla said my timing was better today. But yesterday—dismal at best. I'm still considering dropping out."

"The Kendalls never quit," Drew told him.

Ian nodded toward the other tables. "The team won't thank me if I lose. And Gainsborough would have coach's head if I did."

"Give it your best. It doesn't matter whether you win."

"It does to me, Drew."

"Just go for it. If you don't win the yellow jersey this time, try again next year. You're a young rider. You have time."

"A rider without friends. Orlando and Chris don't wait around for me anymore, not since Alekos died at Sulzbach." His shoulders arched. "They think Alekos would be alive if it hadn't been for me. I really messed up."

Drew slipped his arm around Miriam, his thoughts on sixteen missing years in his marriage. "We all make mistakes, Ian."

Kendall rolled to his side and swung himself upright, maintaining his modesty with the sheet over his lap. He waved the masseur off with the flip of his hand. "What happened to Alekos in Sulzbach really *was* my fault."

"No," Drew said, "Alekos made some careless choices."

"He just wanted to win the race—to beat me."

"Then go out there and race for him," Miriam said gently.

"I promised my grandmother that I'd win the Tour de France for *her*." Ian wiped his eyes with his sun-freckled hand, allowing Drew relief from those probing blue eyes so much like Olivia's. Ian's voice dropped to a husky low. "Sometimes I almost forget my grandmother, and then at other times she seems to be in the next room, influencing me like she always did."

"Ian, you were so close to her."

"Yeah, Miriam, but I was angry with her the day she died. She told me she was sending me back to Maryland." His jaw tightened. "Once she made up her mind, nothing stopped her. I almost hated her for breaking her promise to me. It didn't matter to her that I was counting on going to Italy and the Greek islands with her."

Long ago Drew had broken a promise to his own daughter. Now he tried to see Ian's hurt from the perspective of a child. But his friendship had been with Uriah and Olivia. He couldn't call up more than a time or two when he'd paid attention to the thin-lipped, scrawny Ian. Ian had been a nice-looking kid but withdrawn and sensitive. Drew had bought him a baseball mitt and tossed a ball or two his way. He'd bought him a chocolate ice cream cone that Ian had dripped over the red leather seat of Drew's new car. And he had pushed him on a swing at a Kendall picnic back when Ian was six or seven—because Miriam had told him to.

Now Drew faced a stranger sitting there on the metal table in front of him. The brief openness that Ian had shown in Sulzbach when Alekos had died was gone. There was a barrier between them again, a wall that said, *Come no further, Drew Gregory.*

The room had emptied slowly—Ian's teammates grabbing up their clothes from the floor and slipping out without even a glance at him. Drew knew he should leave the past buried in that Cotswold cemetery, but as he tossed a towel around Ian's shoulders, he asked, "Ian, what really happened on Downing Street ten years ago? I want to hear it from you."

Ian jerked his head toward Drew. "You want a rerun?"

"I want to help you."

The agony on Ian's face was fresh; his blue eyes darkened even more. "Drew, I saw the car hit my grandmother. I couldn't even reach her."

"Uriah told us it was an unwitnessed hit-and-run."

"Come on, Gregory. I was there."

"You were just a kid."

"A thirteen-year-old with two eyes. My grandfather rarely

talks about it. It's as though Downing Street never happened."

A mask of indifference settled on Ian's face, but his roupy voice gave him away. "You won't believe me, but Dudley Perkins still insists my grandmother was an enemy agent—that she was deliberately killed on Downing because of it."

Miriam braced herself on the metal table. "Not Olivia! Not my best friend," she whispered.

Ian gave her a cursory glance. "Your husband wants the gory details. Does your Agency want to ruin my grandmother's reputation, Drew?"

"If she was killed, it's time we found out the truth."

A hard sneer distorted Ian's fine facial features. "Perkins accused my grandmother of being involved in espionage back in the war. We could live with that. But Perkins would like to take my grandfather down with her. He insists that she was still an agent until the day she died."

Miriam linked her arm in Drew's and leaned against him. Drew felt numb. "Perkins wants to connect Uriah with acts of espionage? Tell me, Ian, what did you see that day on Downing?"

Ian rubbed his forehead. "Not much. Enough. I don't know."

"Try us. Did Olivia pass her attaché case to anyone?"

His puzzled frown deepened. "No. I don't think so. At first it was just my grandmother walking along the street—and then the stranger and the crowds and the siren—"

"Back up. What happened first?"

"We had lunch together. That's when she told me she was sending me home. I thought she was mad at me for taking so long in the loo, but she kept asking me about some man sitting across the dining room from us."

"What restaurant?"

"It was in Chelsea somewhere."

"It's important, Ian. Her death was well publicized. Some waiter might remember her."

"How? I can't remember what Charles the chauffeur looked like or the man in the dining room. I try, but they're always faceless." He pondered. "I think I could take you there. I'm sure it was a popular restaurant—the kind my grandmother liked—but this one had a horse motif and thick red carpets."

"The Fox Hunt?"

"Yeah, that may have been the name."

Drew grabbed a pen from his pocket and jotted it down. "Did anyone follow you to Downing Street?"

"I don't know. My grandmother went alone. She was visiting the prime minister."

Drew and Miriam exchanged glances. "You met her there?"

He frowned, forcing his thoughts back to something he didn't want to remember. Finally he said, "Charles and I were parked at the end of Downing, on Whitehall. We saw my grandmother coming toward us, but I was still mad at her—almost hoping that something would happen to her because she was sending me away."

He wiped perspiration from his face. "She was halfway to Whitehall when she put down her attaché case to autograph a book for a stranger. Imagine signing a book in the blinding rain."

Ian stared beyond Miriam and Drew as though part of the veiled mist on Downing Street was clearing for him. "The stranger gave her his umbrella, and then my grandmother stepped off the curb." He focused on Miriam. "Maybe I'm crazy—I'm not sure."

Drew tightened his hold on Miriam's arm and waited.

"I—I think that man waved the book in the air as if he were signaling someone. Yeah! That's when that Renault gunned its engine and moved in on my grandma, full speed." Ian's cold expression wavered. He swayed on the metal table. "And then the car hit her. If only I could have warned her—"

❁❁❁

Miriam considered it a plaintive cry, as if Ian had just heard the thud of the Renault slamming into Olivia. At twenty-three, in spite of the misery on his face, he was a handsome young man, good looking as Olivia had been. "Ian," she said softly, "it could have been accidental."

"It wasn't."

Coldly Drew asked, "You've known this all these years and said nothing?"

"When I was a kid, I used to think it was my fault. I was so angry with her. I wanted something to happen—"

"You've thought about it a lot since Alekos died. Right?"

"Until then, Drew, I didn't want to remember. But they were both cut down deliberately."

The fragrance of Miriam's French perfume barely offset the smell of Ian's sweaty body, but she broke free from Drew and put her cheek against Ian's bristly cheek. "Whatever Olivia's reason for sending you home that day, I know she loved you, Ian."

He pushed her away. "She was going to Prague without me."

"Why Prague?" Drew asked.

"Something to do with her unfinished novel. She wasn't supposed to go back there. She'd just come back from a family funeral. She promised Gramps that after the funeral, she'd never go there again."

Drew sighed. "Sometimes I think we never really knew her."

"We knew her and we loved her," Miriam said. "We just didn't know everything about her."

Miriam thought about Olivia, the guarded part that sometimes kept her distant. They had met at an arty luncheon in New York City, a dining room teeming with artists and museum curators and art buyers. Olivia was a beautiful woman, elegantly turned out, poised and graceful. Age had separated them, and yet immediately they had been caught up with their mutual love for Rembrandt paintings. Even now she still mourned Olivia. Missed her maturity and wisdom. Missed her friendship. She was not prepared to discover another side to her old friend. She didn't want to know the truth about Olivia.

She tilted her head, studying Ian. His troubled gaze and

features were so much like Olivia's. "You remind me of your grandmother," she said.

"Because I'm moody and pigheaded?"

"Because you're gentle and kind under that mask of yours. You have her depth and sensitivity, Ian, those special strengths that I so admired in her." She squeezed his hand. "It's a good thing I see Uriah in you, too. He's flying over in a few days."

"Just for the Tour de France?"

"He's coming just for *you*, Ian."

Drew hand-brushed his silver-streaked hair and laughed. "Maybe he's coming to protect you from Chase Evans."

"Huh? Chase Evans? A girl by that name checked into the hostel where we're staying." He grinned. "This one is kind of pretty. Comes from Long Island." His facial muscles had relaxed, allowing his wry grin to widen. "Orlando was tongue-tied around her, so I took her out for a soft drink."

"The famous Kendall rescue?" Drew asked.

"You might call it that. I suggested that she go back to England with me." He pointed to his cycling gear on the floor. "But she's out of my class. Quite a dresser."

"Sounds like the girl we're talking about. Did you tell her about yourself?"

"Guilty. We flirted a bit. Talked about the Tour de France."

"And about Uriah and Olivia?"

"I never even mentioned them. Too busy getting to know her." He considered. "I think she said she's here for the summer. Yeah, that's it—some kind of project that her father is funding. But what's my grandfather's interest in a young woman like that?"

"She wanted your grandfather's help. She's doing a comparative study on two novelists."

"Oh, that's right. She's going on to Oxford. Wants a Ph.D.—like I said, that's out of my line. I don't care what she writes about. Once she leaves here, I'll never see her again."

"You will. She's researching your grandmother's story."

"Why didn't she tell me?" Ian wet his lips. "Does she

know about Prague? Has she been in touch with Dudley Perkins?"

"You'll have to ask Miss Evans. But according to Uriah, she'd contact the queen if she thought it would help her. Now get showered and dressed, Ian, and we'll take you to dinner."

❦❦❦

Chase Evans was sitting on the steps when Ian got back to the hostel. She was pretty even in the evening shadows, her chin cupped in her slender hands as she looked up at him and smiled. She was wearing white slacks and a teal turtleneck sweat top, her hair falling softly around her face.

"Hello. I wondered if you were coming home."

"I've been out," he said guardedly.

"I thought we were going to have a Coke together."

"I wasn't thirsty this evening."

He remembered last night and his quick heartbeat as he had sat across from her. Resentment and disappointment filled him now.

"Ian, are you angry with me?"

He put one foot on the step and paused. "Yes. About New York and your Columbia University study program—"

"I meant to tell you."

"After you quizzed me about my grandmother?"

"I didn't plan it that way."

"Yeah, I'm sure of it." He took another step.

"Don't go."

"I need my sleep if I'm going to ride in the morning."

"Will I see you tomorrow?"

"We won't be coming back this way." *I'll make sure of it.*

"But you invited me to travel back to England with you."

"I changed my mind."

She actually looked hurt, as though he had let her down. "I'm still going to stay over and watch you ride off in the morning," she said.

He swung his sweater over his shoulder. "Don't bother."

"Ian, I'm sorry. Really. I would have told you, but it was too soon. Please, why not introduce me to your friends?"

"Orlando and Chris? You've already met them."

"No, I mean the couple you had dinner with this evening. Orlando said they were close friends of your grandfather's."

"Leave the Gregorys alone. I don't want you pumping them with your questions."

"But I can't blow my doctoral dissertation, not when I've gone this far." She shook her head. "I don't understand your family. Most people would be pleased to have their grandmother remembered. You act like there's something to hide."

The door had almost slammed shut when he heard her mumble, "Don't help me then. But I'll find out my own way."

Chapter 8

Nedrick Russelmann made his way across the Westminster Bridge and walked briskly along the River Thames, idly pausing now and then to watch a swirling whirlpool or to stare at the quiet waters pooled by the embankment. Three hours ago when he left Uriah Kendall alone at the Cotswold cottage, he had said, "Uriah, I have business in London."

Wise, cagey Uriah. His smile had turned marginal as he dropped the car keys into Nedrick's hand and said, "Do what you must then." *As though betrayal no longer mattered.*

In despair Ned had followed the river as it wound its way gently around the scenic country roads into the center of London. This River Thames coursed through Uriah's veins, this great city of London, this country—all of it part of Uriah's makeup, part of his strength. Nedrick tossed a stone into the water and watched its rippling effect spreading out, forming its own little whirlpool. One lie. One lie to Uriah had led to another, churning the little eddies into a violent maelstrom, a raging undercurrent in Ned's mind that was luring him back to Prague.

The resonant, deep chimes of Big Ben sounded out the hour, narrowing the time until Nedrick kept his appointment with Jiri Benak, the Russelmanns' errand boy. Ten years ago Nedrick had turned his back on the prosperous Russelmanns and had gone off as a determined eighteen-year-old to find his own way, to find the gentler side of himself, as his grandfather had called it.

"You'll never be a true Russelmann," Popshot had said, and there had been both sadness and pride in Hanz Russelmann's voice.

For Nedrick, his grandfather's words were the ultimate rejection. Even as a boy Nedrick had wondered why the Russelmann Steel factory prospered when other businesses failed during those long years under communism. The Russelmanns' success dated back to Otto and Karl Russelmann in World War I, but the struggling engineering company suddenly flourished in the Nazi regime, turning out steel for a nation at war. After his war injury, Hanz had been assigned to the facility in Prague. Now Nedrick's father Altman and his Uncle Gustav vied for leadership. Engineers and architects. Men poring over blueprints and architectural plans. And why? Did a steel factory require all of that?

As Nedrick reached the age of accountability, the twisted thinking of his father took a tighter grip on him. He saw a whole lifetime spread out in front of him that wouldn't cut beyond the Prague borders. He'd be saddled permanently with the generational commitment to the steel mill— Altman would see to that.

The plant nearest the forest always had dark smoke rising from its chimney, a twisted black funnel that Popshot hated. Nedrick came to hate it himself. Not knowing why, not even caring. Its curling mass had engulfed Ned emotionally, leaving him with the inner urge to cut the family ties before greed and power meshed him into a Russelmann statistic.

He tossed another stone into the Thames, pebble-size this time, and then turned from the river and made his way toward St. James Park. Of all the family, he most admired his grandfather Hanz Russelmann—Popshot, his own nickname for the man. He longed to see him again, but perhaps the old man had died. Perhaps there would never be another chance to go fishing together; Hanz had taught him to cast a line and to hike for long hours in the woods, sighting a rabbit or deer—not for the kill but for the pleasure.

Maybe it was already too late to plow through another winter snowstorm, his grandfather limping beside him.

Nedrick grew up believing that his grandfather had been a flying ace. Then the bitter truth came to the surface. Hanz had not been a Czech pilot defending Czechoslovakia, but a Luftwaffe pilot—a German, a Nazi, both still hated in the country in which Nedrick had grown up. He had gone to Hanz to question him about the veiled secrecy that surrounded the family business.

"Popshot always tells me the truth," he told his cousin.

Pavel laughed. "Uncle Hanz knows nothing of truth; your hero has lived a lie all these years, and you've swallowed it."

Weeks later Nedrick quit school, packed up, and, without even saying goodbye to Mila, left. Plain-faced Mila, his second cousin, his friend, the girl who trusted and loved him. Mila, the girl with shiny dark hair, dark eyes, and a sad, whimsical smile, had made his boyhood tolerable, romping the fields with him, casting a better fishing line than he could himself. In his own self-centered way, he had loved her. At sixteen he had promised her the world, at seventeen himself. At eighteen he had looked out the farm window and watched her happily planting flower seeds beside his grandfather. Nedrick left her to find her own way out of life on the Russelmann farm.

But he realized as he elbowed the crowd on the busy London street that his most nostalgic memory of Prague always went back to his grandfather in the garden—a man's man turning the soil, planting flowers and vegetables and finding pleasure in the color and crops that resulted. And he remembered Popshot's library. They'd often strolled the streets of Prague, browsing in bookstores to add to the collection. He was with Hanz that day in Prague when Hanz found one of Olivia Renway's novels.

Popshot had grasped that book and stared at the picture on the back cover, his eyes hardened to an iceberg blue. "Olivia," he cried. "Olivia. She's still alive."

Nedrick snatched up a second copy and ran his fingers over the color photo. She was a well-dressed, stylish woman, unsmiling and elegant—with eyes like his own—and a beautiful bracelet on her slender wrist. "Popshot, who is she?"

"She was part of my past."

After that Hanz scoured the bookstalls in Prague in search of all her books to display in his vast library. Those he couldn't find, he ordered. He read and reread them and for a time slipped from the self-assured head of the family into a brooding shell of a man, his sadness evident even when he spaded the flowers. Nedrick read Olivia's books, too, sometimes thinking that he had heard the stories before on fishing trips and on those hikes in the woods or on that vacation trip in Spain.

"Who is she really?" Ned had asked days before leaving Prague.

"Your grandmother—the gentler side of you, boy."

🌀🌀🌀

Nedrick left the crowded streets of the city and approached St. James Park along Birdcage Walk. Through the magnificent oak and beech trees he could see the Whitehall rooftops, and yet the roar of traffic had mellowed in the serenity of the gardens. Mothers sat in hired deck chairs near the water's edge watching their children toss bread crumbs to the ducks. Contentment surrounded Ned— pigeons, pelicans, and people, and the heady fragrance of summer flowers in bloom. Unlike the murky waters of the Thames, the pond seemed clear, bluish. He passed the beds of azaleas and tulips that edged the walks before he spotted Jiri Benak leaning against an ageless shade tree, his thick head of hair so blond that it gleamed snow-white in the sun.

Jiri was wearing his familiar beige trench coat, his hands thrust deep in his pockets, one no doubt wrapped carefully around the revolver he always carried. His sardonic grin twisted like a gnarled tree branch. "Nedrick, who is that man following you?"

Nedrick's gaze followed Jiri's to the English gentleman in the pinstriped suit. A black bowler hat rode low on his brow shadowing wide, inquisitive eyes in a gaunt face. His

starched white shirt was loose at the neck, the tie ridicu-
lously plain. He leaned on his umbrella like a walking stick
and took a sudden interest in the pelican at his feet.

"I don't know him," Nedrick said.

"It's all right. Pavel is nearby if we need him. We'll walk
along and see whether the man still finds us interesting."

Jiri set the pace, an easy, unconcerned gait that aggravated Nedrick even more. Jiri had been right. In their
silence, he heard the Englishman's long-stemmed umbrella
tapping against the sidewalk, dogging their steps. Jiri's
mood remained unperturbed; he bit into danger like one
biting into rich chocolate cake, savoring the moment, wanting more. Nedrick had no stamina for counting on his wits
to outmaneuver an enemy.

Or was Jiri—as he had always done—mocking the weak-
ness of Hanz Russelmann's grandson? Nedrick ran the tip
of his tongue across his upper lip and still it felt dry and
cracked. He had forgotten that the Russelmann clan
depended on force and weapons to achieve their purposes.
Those who stood in their way were removed. Why then had
they never found him in Maryland and destroyed him? Jiri
would delight in the assignment, seeing it as an opportunity to clear the path for his own promotion. Jiri despised
the favored sons—finding both Nedrick and Pavel obstacles
to his own success, but Jiri found no threat in Franz. Franz
was a weak, powerless man, a follower, a loser.

Nedrick had thrived on the luxury and comfort of the
Kendall home in Maryland, enjoying the amiable friendship with Uriah, and eager for those rare moments when
Uriah spoke openly about Olivia. Ned never risked identi-
fying himself—never made claims to the blood line that was
rightfully his own. But lately he had come to fear being discovered for who he was, threatened by an unknown honor
student determined to unravel Olivia's past. Kendall was a
reasonable man, but he would never tolerate Nedrick living
a lie.

Jiri nudged him back saying, "Do you remember your
Czech, Nedrick?"

"Some."

"Then we'll speak in Czech. Did Uriah Kendall question your coming to London this morning?"

"Why would he? He gives me free range," Nedrick said.

"And the girl? Has she contacted Kendall yet?"

"We haven't heard from her again, but she could be a problem."

"Don't tell me the old blood line is flowing again? Loyalty to the Russelmann clan never motivated you."

Not like it influenced you, Nedrick thought.

No, Nedrick's fear of being discovered, his own cowardice, had put wings to his feet. If Chase Evans unveiled Olivia's past, it would lead back to the Russelmann farm and straight to Hanz Russelmann—a past that included Nedrick, a threat that might disrupt the shrewd practices of the family business. It had never mattered before whether the business toppled, but the blood line had a new hold on him. He didn't want to see his family come to ruin, no matter how unscrupulous their dealings. Again he ran the tip of his tongue across his dry lip, searching his memory for the language of his boyhood. "Once a Russelmann, always a Russelmann," he said.

His words did not please Jiri. "Why did you come back—stirring up trouble about Renway's missing manuscript again? We know she wrote about some steel factory in Czechoslovakia—but we're not the only steel mill in the country."

"She meant the Russelmanns. I'm certain of it. Why else would she have mentioned the plant in the village where she was born?"

"She's dead, Nedrick. The book died with her."

"She died because of that book. And I'm convinced that you ordered that hit-and-run, Jiri."

"Hanz gives the orders. Always has."

Nedrick sucked in his breath and stopped in the middle of the crowd. The tapping of the Englishman's umbrella against the pavement ceased. "Popshot would not give that kind of order."

"Ask him yourself when you reach Jarvoc."

"Then my grandfather is still alive?"

"He's too obstinate to die. Besides he wants to see you—and Miss Evans. She's flying into London from Paris. Pavel will be going out to Heathrow any minute now to meet her plane."

"What was she doing in France?"

"Contacting Kendall's grandson. With a few phone calls, we traced Evans to the Bartholomew family and then to the Evans mansion on Long Island, but she outsmarted us by going to Paris first. What does she have, Nedrick, that worries you so?"

"A healthy curiosity."

"That's no problem."

"It will be, Jiri, if she stirs up the old memories that Ian Kendall has blocked out for ten years. And it's a problem if she finds the missing manuscript. Renway's death is still on file at Scotland Yard. Trace that stolen manuscript back to you, Jiri, and they have the one who murdered her."

A sneer disfigured his thin face. "Franz drove the car."

"But you planned it."

They had circled around and retraced their steps to the Birdcage Walk. "That manuscript is not a problem to us," Jiri said. "If it had been, your father would have destroyed it. But there may be missing pages, segments, notes on the steel mill. She would never have destroyed them. We must find them."

"What could she possibly have known?"

"Nothing. Everything. She must have passed them on to someone—Kendall, for instance."

"Impossible. Uriah Kendall destroyed anything that threatened his wife's reputation."

"Renway was in Prague days before her death. Talking about the tunnels."

"Perhaps she played in them as a child," Nedrick suggested.

"Or maybe she walked through them when the war ended—when the Russians liberated the people." Jiri's mocking tone was as cold as his expression. "According to her brother, she wanted to link the mill and the tunnels to the old internment camps of the forties. So she nosed around. Took notes. She may have photographed some important papers that could link us to chemical sales like those used in the subway disaster in Tokyo. Now after all these years of cooperating, Nishokura is threatening to stop doing business with us unless we triple their fees for doubling their risks."

Nerve gas? Nedrick's throat constricted as he thought of the black smoke at the waste plant that had evoked unsettling feelings in his grandfather and uneasy stirrings in himself as a boy. "But we only sell steel to Nishokura. Always have."

"We have other business interests at stake. Renway urged Dorian to stop working for us. Told him we were nothing but modern-day designers of death."

Nedrick fought off his boyhood apprehensions about his father's business. "Was there any truth in what she said?"

"She thought so. She told Dorian that she knew something might happen to her. She planned ahead."

"Meaning?" Nedrick asked.

"That she would have trusted someone with her research—someone who would finish her work for her."

"Her brother?"

"Someone outside of Prague."

"She was friends with the British prime minister."

"Someone less obvious, Nedrick. A friend left Prague with Renway ten years ago. We've never been able to locate her. They were in the resistance movement together." They were nearing the end of the path. "Whatever Chase Evans learns about Renway could be helpful to us. Let me know when Evans contacts you."

"Are the missing notes really that important? My grandmother is dead. You act like she could still destroy the Russelmanns."

Jiri held out his hand and offered Nedrick a cold-fish shake. "We can't take that chance, can we?"

🌀🌀🌀

Dudley Perkins watched the men shake hands and take their leave in separate directions, the blond going casually up the walkway past the azaleas toward the main boulevard. He had understood snatches of the conversation, enough to know that the man was foreign-born, straight from Prague, no doubt. *But*, thought Perkins, *you made no effort to hide that, and you were aware of my presence.*

He nodded to Lyle Spincrest standing nearby in his stark white tennis shorts. Lyle took Perkins's signal and started out on a jog behind the man in the trench coat.

With a toss of bread crumbs to the pelican, Perkins brushed his hands clean and left St. James Park, his pace casual as he lagged behind Uriah Kendall's chauffeur. Kendall's man seemed in no haste now, aimless and dejected, and then suddenly he ran for a double-decker bus, swung aboard, and managed to leave Dudley standing on the sidewalk, hands on his hips.

Twenty minutes later, Perkins walked into Scotland Yard. "Constable Wallis is expecting me," he said.

He was ushered into a compact room where Edwin Wallis sat buried under a mound of paperwork. At forty Wallis still wore his thick horn-rimmed glasses and his dark blue letterman sweater from his Oxford days—for rowing or cricket, if Perkins remembered correctly.

"Edwin," he said impatiently.

Wallis looked up. His cheeks were full, his nose long and narrow like a bobsled run. His sleepy gaze belied a sharp awareness. "Perkins," he said. "How can I help you?"

"I'd like you to open an old case for me."

Interest lit in the sleepy eyes. "Not without just cause or the queen's edict."

"It was a hit-and-run ten years ago. On Downing Street."

Wallis swiveled in his chair, the tip of his pen to his lips. "Not Olivia Renway?"

"I tried to convince you that it was more than an accident back then—that it was tied in with the bomb threat on the prime minister's residence. I still think so."

Dudley had struck the right button. Wallis reached out to a microfiche on his desk and began to flip the dials. "I went along with you to her funeral. Married to an American, wasn't she?"

"No, British. They made their home in America."

"Here it is. Never solved. Uriah Kendall's wife. Kendall was a friend of yours, wasn't he?"

"We worked together after the war."

"Oh, yes. He was washed out of MI5 because of you." Wallis's grin was wary. "Now I remember. I was new to the force. You dragged me off to the woman's funeral."

"For the protection of the Kendall family, Edwin. The prime minister's idea. The Kendalls were personal acquaintances of hers."

Wallis leaned back in his chair. "So you are still trying to connect the bombing in the financial district with Renway's death?"

"Edwin, the Czechs claimed credit. And Renway was Czech."

The intelligence reports back at Dudley's office pointed toward a new problem—Czech-oriented and ill-defined threats from an unidentified splinter group. Bomb threats. Several in Paris. London could be next. Even the Cotswolds were threatened. Dudley had put little stock in it until Uriah Kendall phoned and said, "Perkins, I want you to check up on my chauffeur. I met him ten years ago, and this morning for the first time I'm not sure I really know him. . . . "

Uriah's Czechoslovakian chauffeur.

Wallis rolled his pen across the desk. "Perkins," he said, "it's unlikely that we'll ever find the driver of the car that killed Renway. There are unsolved hit-and-runs all the time."

"But what if this one was murder?"

Chapter 9

Chase arrived at the airport just in time for her short flight to Heathrow. She had dressed in what she considered to be a simple, eye-catching outfit—her Saks Fifth Avenue ecru blazer, the off-white lace shell, and a soft voile skirt—guaranteed to be wrinkle-proof. Yet she had followed her grandmother's axiom to be classy and stunning head to toe.

She hurried to the VIP line and was given prompt, courteous service, as she knew she would be. Even the passenger who had rushed up to the check-in counter beside her watched Chase with an unblinking gaze, not particularly flattering, but not unusual either. He was thirtyish, his eyes darkly brooding in an otherwise attractive face. Without taking his eyes from her, he shoved cash across the counter and insisted on upgrading his ticket to first class. "I would like a seat near this young lady," he said.

Displeased at his brashness, Chase hurried off to the boarding gate. She had grown accustomed to the amenities of traveling first class and liked boarding early and having ample room for her long legs. As she sank into the wide-cushioned seat, a smiling flight attendant dropped a hot white towel into her hands. It felt refreshing as she held it against her cheek and leaned back against the soft cushions of her window seat.

The economy passengers pushed and shoved their way along the narrow aisle as the attendant squeezed her way back to Chase. "I'm Angeline Melbourne," she said smiling. "There's time for a glass of wine before we take off." She held out the wine list.

Chase, who had never acquired a taste for alcoholic beverages, ordered a glass of iced tea instead. A gooey French torte came with it. She was a muncher at heart—chips and dips, mixed nuts, and low-salt pretzels—with too much boundless energy to let the fat stick to her ribs or to ever tip the scale at more than 118. She forked the French pastry politely, savoring each bite, but as she did so, her spiral notebook toppled to the floor. It was impossible to retrieve it with the tray on her lap. As she waited for the hostess, she glimpsed the last passenger boarding—the brash, young man from the ticket counter. His sly, sullen eyes sought hers as he handed his canvas satchel to the attendant and strode to the seat behind Chase.

By the time her teacup was empty, the seat belt sign was on, and the aircraft door had been secured, leaving the seat beside her unoccupied. She buckled her strap as the plane taxied down the runway—smothering her disappointment that her phone calls had failed to reach Luke Breckenridge. Even her contact with Ian Kendall had ended on the hills of Gascony when he pedaled off at the head of the pack without saying goodbye. Ian was, she decided, not a man of his word. After all, he had invited her to ride the English "Chunnel" with him.

Until yesterday Chase's goal had been literary, a search for intriguing facts about Olivia Renway for her dissertation. Ian changed all that. There was something about Olivia Renway that his family wanted to keep buried with her. But what? Renway's death had been accidental, so why had Ian warned her off? As preposterous as it sounded, she wondered if Ian had asked the man on the plane to follow her.

The seat belt light was off. She unsnapped her belt and with growing concern scanned the floor for her missing notepad. Nothing! She snapped open her attaché case and thumbed through the contents. One spiral notepad was definitely gone, but she grabbed a postcard and began to write as the plane leveled off.

Dear Mom and Dad,

We just left Paris behind. London next. It's goodbye to the Eiffel Tower and Notre Dame and hello Big Ben and Westminster Abbey. It seems unreal not having Callie traveling with me and fussing about the scant snack they're serving to us now. Hugs to Marie. And, if you don't mind, could you call Halverson House and see how Jeff Carlson is doing?

Bushels of love from your wind-chaser.

With two days in London, she would have time to check old newspapers and even to walk Downing Street. Then it would be off to Oxford and the Cotswolds to visit some of the places where Olivia Renway had spent her life.

The flight attendant was back, serving a second drink to the man behind Chase. Again Chase glanced down at the floor, wondering whether he had picked up her notepad. Impulsively she got up and followed Angeline to the galley. "Could I have a cup of coffee?" she asked.

She took a sip, hating the bitter taste.

"Is something wrong?" Melbourne asked.

"Yes. I've misplaced one of my notebooks." She held up her hands, designating the size. "It's small, but important to me."

"Let me help you look."

"No, don't. I was just wondering—what do you know about the gentleman sitting behind me?"

"I know he likes his Bloody Mary strong."

Chase allowed herself a casual glance around first class, her eyes settling on him. Dark hair. A faint stubble of beard. Denim shirt and brown leather jacket. Receding hairline. Ears flat against his head.

Melbourne leaned against the galley counter. "If he's

bothering you, the pilot could call ahead and have someone from British Airways escort you through customs to a taxi."

"Thanks, but I'll just catch a taxi direct to my hotel." She put the cup down. "Do you know the man's name?"

Angeline hesitated before glancing at her passenger list. "Franz Van Rindin." Her smile was ambiguous, her eyes watchful. "You'd better sit down, Miss Evans. We'll be landing soon."

As Chase went back to her seat, she deliberately met the man's gaze. He was poker-faced, unblinking, his expression empty, as though he had little hope of happiness along the way.

"Good flight," he said to her, and even his voice sounded wooden, unimpassioned.

۞۞۞

Franz Van Rindin took the last sip of his drink and allowed the flight attendant to whisk his glass away. As she moved on down the aisle, he dropped Chase Evans's notebook on the floor and toed it under the seat in front of him. Then he fastened his seat belt and put his hands over his kneecaps, his fingers blanching as he held on. His uncle Hanz Russelmann still treasured his medals from his days as a Luftwaffe pilot—still loved flying. Franz hated it, especially taking off and landing. As the airliner lowered beneath the clouds and the British Isles stretched out below them, he focused on the passenger in front of him. She seemed to be making a last-minute search for her missing notebook; bending down for a final quick check, she retrieved it.

It's all there, he thought. *I didn't touch your shorthand scribblings on Olivia Renway.*

Like Altman, Franz was convinced that the girl was CIA. They'd already checked. Evans was a Columbia University honor student with strong political opinions; the CIA had tapped an intelligent young woman to serve them.

His grip on his knees tightened as the earth came up to meet him. In spite of the order from the Russelmann farm,

Franz had never intended to kill Olivia Renway on Downing Street. His plan had been to frighten her—as he was frightened now—allowing Jiri Benak just enough time to snatch her briefcase and the Russelmann bracelet. But Renway's visit to the prime minister changed all of that. She had gone too far! As she stepped from the curb, Franz had gunned his idling engine and roared toward her, his foot to the floorboard. She had frozen at the sound of his car. Franz could still recall the stark horror etched in her lovely face and then the impact of her body against the hard metal of his vehicle.

For ten years nothing had come of Renway's threat to destroy the Russelmanns. Had she fooled them all? Or was Altman right? The CIA had chosen Evans to take up Olivia's crusade and bring them all to ruin. What was worse in Franz's mind was the fact that Evans had contacted Uriah Kendall, an ex-MI5 officer. That meant the British and Americans were in this together.

Evans looked harmless enough, but then the Americans liked a pretty face—as Franz did. Still he found it hard to believe that they would send their intelligence agents first class. As the plane banked over the English Channel, he caught another glimpse of her profile reflected in the window. *Young*, he thought again. *Chic, smartly styled.* Maybe that made for a good agent. Her appearance did not arouse suspicion. The only second glance you'd give this girl would be with romance in mind. She had an easy smile, a breezy, jaunty gait that was both feminine and confident, and clothes too form-fitting to hide a weapon.

The flight attendant stood in the aisle, pleasantly announcing their momentary arrival at Heathrow. She frowned at Franz and then sat down for the landing. He closed his eyes and fought nausea, his muscles taut as he braced for the runway. The plane hit hard, bounced, and then they were earthbound, the wheels braking and squealing across the tarmac.

Melbourne shot to her feet. Chase Evans sat quietly, her seat belt still buckled. It was his time to fool them both. He'd be the first one off the plane. With no luggage to worry about except his empty canvas satchel, he'd signal his brother and disappear into the waiting room. Let Pavel take up the watch.

☙☙☙

Chase's soft, sheer skirt swished as she moved through the passenger line, her bone t-strap pumps snug on her tired feet. Her grandmother would have looked on her with favor, pleased that she was following the Bartholomew cardinal rule to look first class when she traveled and wrinkle-free when she arrived. Callie Bartholomew had chosen her wardrobe from Paris and Milan and always accented it with expensive jewelry. Chase was more content with selections from Neiman Marcus and Saks Fifth Avenue. She often kept her accessories modest as she had done today—pierced earrings, her ruby ring, a single strand necklace. Right now Chase longed for comfort—her familiar Koret City Blues and a bright tank top—but these were at the bottom of the suitcase that would any minute be torn open for customs inspection.

Security had increased following an upsurge of IRA terrorism—leaving Chase and other foreigners in a long line. For all of his haste to disembark, Van Rindin was being delayed, arguing loudly in a Slavic accent, "The satchel is all I have. My luggage was stolen in Paris. Gone," he repeated, his wide palms extended.

"Sir," the agent countered, "why is your satchel empty?"

It was her turn now. Chase smiled at the dour customs agent. He fitted her father's image of a British official—tight-faced and aloof, a decent sort of man with serious eyes and actions more assertive than his words. It seemed as though the exposed newspaper headlines near his elbow had been deliberately placed there: "Bomb Threat Against Whitehall." Heathrow was on full alert.

She handed him her passport and snapped her pullman open. She'd learned another traveling tip from Callie. "Customs agents have big hands. Give them room to poke around. And allow yourself a chance to close your case again without sitting on it." Or losing ummentionables as Callie had done on a flight to Munich.

"Security seems heightened this morning," she said.

"Just precaution," he assured her.

Her attention was drawn back to Franz Van Rindin arguing heatedly a few feet from her. Was he making a deliberate scene? *Yes*, Chase decided. *He wants to be noticed.* He had turned his face toward the crowd, and she caught that flicker of recognition in his expression, that indiscernible nod toward her.

Was he signaling someone that things were not going well at the customs table? Or warning them that the young woman five passengers behind him was the one to follow? She searched the faces in the crowd for Van Rindin's contact without success. Fresh fury at Ian Kendall rose with the nigglings of doubt.

"Your destination?" the agent asked.

"Oxford."

"To study?"

"For the summer. I'll be staying with friends."

That was another family axiom, and she'd just blown it. Never offer information before it is needed. She considered using Nigel Hampton's name and decided she could just as well say Chaucer or Shelley and get the same response. The Londoner looking up at her right now didn't care where she stayed as long as she wasn't carrying stolen jewels or a lethal weapon.

From the corner of her eye, she saw Van Rindin resisting restraint as he was led into a small room. At once the agent relaxed. "Your destination in London, Miss Evans?" he asked, returning her passport.

"The Ritz for two days and then Oxford."

He shoved the lid down, ignoring the rest of her luggage, and flashed what proved to be a charming smile. He pushed her suitcases toward her. "Have a good stay. Next."

A burly porter loaded her luggage and led the way through the terminal, making a wide path for her with his luggage cart. As they reached the exit and stepped out on the sidewalk, two men cut across their path—a young man light on his feet and a serious-faced man with thick black hair and tinted glasses.

The younger man, with a boyish, lopsided grin, reached her first. "Miss Evans," he said, his accent clipped and British, "I'm Peter Quincy. I'm sorry I'm late."

The second intruder hesitated, spun abruptly, and disappeared back into the terminal. Alarmed, she brushed past Quincy and followed the porter to a waiting taxi.

"But, Miss Evans," Quincy protested, "I'm to drive you to Oxford. Mr. Hampton—"

She cut Quincy off with a shrug. Nigel Hampton knew she was staying in London a few days. *Take someone else with you,* she thought, *not me.* She turned her back to Quincy and faced the taxi driver. "The Ritz, please," she whispered. "And hurry."

He shoved the wad of gum to his other cheek. "Right on, miss," he said.

"Did he follow us?" she asked as they left the terminal.

"No, he's still standing there looking jilted. Lover's quarrel?" he asked.

"Just someone who wanted to take me for a ride."

She rode the rest of the way to the hotel in silence, taking in the familiar sights of London. The winding Thames. Westminster Abbey. Piccadilly Circus. But as they pulled up in front of the Ritz Hotel, Chase thought back to the strangers at Heathrow. The one had walked away abruptly; the other knew her name. Try as she could, she didn't recall which one had the mustache.

⊛⊛⊛

The Ritz doorman recognized her as he held out his gloved hand. As she stepped to the sidewalk and glanced up at him, he smiled. "Miss Evans, welcome back. Where is your grandmother?"

Chase choked as she said, "She died—months ago."

He let go of her hand apologetically. "I'm so sorry."

As she regained her composure, he averted his gaze and snapped his fingers for a bellman.

She would have settled on a quaint hotel on the other side of the Thames, but the Ritz was her father's choice. He fussed about spending money on her, but he always went high class. And this was—as her grandmother always said—blue blood at its best. Chase could picture her father confiding in a friend at a business luncheon, "My youngest daughter? She's staying at the Ritz in London, and then she'll go on for a summer at Oxford."

It wasn't that Seymour Evans was keeping up with the Joneses; he was simply striving to surpass the Bartholomews.

The inside of the Ritz was even more imposing—a restaurant with gilded chandeliers suspended from a painted ceiling, rooms that were marbled and French-styled, and the opulent Palm Court where she had had tea with Callie on their last trip to London. Chase was dressed for afternoon tea, thanks to Callie's traveling wisdom. As soon as she rested, she'd go down to the Palm Court for cucumber sandwiches and scones dripping with jams and cream.

Her room was spacious, well lit, pink, and feminine. She emptied her smaller case on the bed and hung up the items she would need over the next two days. Tomorrow would be full. She'd search out the newspaper morgues for clippings on Olivia Renway's death, and after that she'd walk to Downing Street.

With the suitcase stowed in the closet, she fluffed her pillows and stretched out on the queen-sized bed. She kicked off her pumps and wiggled her toes, staring out the hotel window on the city of London and thinking about the three lives that had brought her here: Olivia Renway, Dorothy Sayers, and her grandmother Callie Bartholomew. The Ritz was not a quiet reflective place, cornered as it was on a busy street. Outside she heard a double-decker bus roar by and the sound of a church bell chiming the hour. From her bed she could see the spire-topped cathedral in the Gothic architectural style that had fascinated her grandmother.

Callie had loved Paris and Milan, Florence and Vienna, but she had always been drawn back to the city of London. They both loved the afternoon teas at the Ritz, the tennis play-offs at Wimbledon, and the limitless spending sprees at Harrods. Mostly they loved browsing in art museums, never tiring of the Somerset House or the Turner Collection at the Tate Gallery. It struck Chase that she must see these alone now. She could never again bask in the beauty of the Cotswolds or the white cliffs of Dover with her grandmother. Never again would they stand on a rocky cliff at Land's End on Cornwall and thrill to the wild sea waters splashing their faces. She had shared so much with Callie, and yet some aspects of her grandmother remained a mystery. Callie rarely went into Westminster Abbey or St. Paul's, but when she did, she came out strangely moved, refusing to speak.

This was Callie's England, her London—the London that Olivia Renway would have recognized, a spectacular city spread out from the banks of the Thames. But it would have been unfamiliar to Dorothy Sayers; she had known the London that existed between the world wars. Sayers, a plain-faced vicar's daughter with pincher glasses and short, thin hair, had been a woman of independence and intellect, far ahead of her society. She threw off Victorian restraints— Callie would have applauded—and entered into the jazz and swing era just before the global depression of the thirties. In Sayers's life and her books she broke the rules, finding innovative ways to commit murder in her Peter Wimsey novels—and often wearing outrageous clothes or smoking cigars as she spurned her privileged background. Her career had spanned both wars, but she would not live to see much of postwar London and would not be alive for the Beatles or Margaret Thatcher's rise to power.

As Chase lay puzzling over the similarities between Renway and Sayers, she saw only differences. Renway had been glamorous, well-styled, politically oriented, but rarely outgoing; yet in the libraries of Oxford Renway had discovered comfort in the life and writings of the outspoken Sayers.

But why? Chase asked herself again. What linked the two? The London blitz? Their alma mater? The love of London? Their writings? There was no whimsical detective, no short, pampered Lord Peter Wimsey in Renway's books. Renway leaned toward the historical, her characters deadly serious and sometimes autobiographical. Chase's grandmother would have liked both women, but she would have liked Sayers best for her break with society, but definitely not for her religious convictions. Chase reached out to her bed table and picked up the book she had started on the flight from America, Sayers's *The Mind of the Maker.* The book was filled with Sayers's pursuit of the Trinity. Perhaps it was this part of Sayers's journey that had touched Olivia Renway's life.

Chapter 10

London. Vic Wilson finally persuaded Jon Gainsborough to lunch with him at the Fox Hunt, the restaurant where Olivia Renway had taken her last meal. When Vic arrived, he requested a table with a window view of London. The waiter led him to a straight-back brocade chair that faced the entry, seating him close to where Olivia had sat ten years ago.

Above Vic hung the massive painting *Riding to the Hounds,* the level of energy visible in the taut neck muscles of the horses and in the faces of the men who rode them. Vic thought of something Ian Kendall had told him. The boy remembered sitting beneath that painting, but why not? It was striking, vivid in color, full of action—something that would have caught the eye of Renway's curious thirteen-year-old grandson.

Kendall had confided something else to Vic. His grandmother had been afraid of someone sitting across the dining room from her. Involuntarily, Vic glanced around and was startled to see Dudley Perkins sitting nearby. So Gainsborough had alerted Perkins. Once again Drew had put his thumb on trouble. Vic would take it a step at a time. Outsmarting MI5 had been one of the fringe benefits of working at the American embassy.

He ordered a lemon and water, his stomach no longer tolerating alcoholic beverages. *Drew,* he decided, *would be proud of me, but for all the wrong reasons.* Vic's old lifestyle—

a charming date in every city with too many one-night stands—had brought him up short. Gone now even the small comfort that liquor had once given him. Vic hadn't admitted to anyone that he tired more easily. Add night sweats and little blackouts, and the picture looked glum. He hadn't risked telling his cousin Brianna about the new symptoms. She'd force him to go for another blood test, a test that might come up AIDS positive.

Wilson grabbed his lemon and water and cooled his parched throat with four great gulps. Over the brim of his glass, he saw Gainsborough standing between the potted palms, blocking the way of other guests. He was a short, squat man, his three hundred pounds squeezed into a Saville suit. The coat hung unbuttoned, his oversized trousers covering that portly belly.

Gainsborough took a quick survey of the room, turning first toward Dudley Perkins before he allowed his gaze to track the window row of tables. Vic gave him a quick salute, and Gainsborough barreled toward him, a business power-house, a steel magnate whose money did most of his talking. He came with a bold stride for such a big man, his hairpiece in front not quite matching the gray-streaked dark hair that fringed his head.

The waiter pulled the chair back, and Gainsborough lowered his hulking frame down with a thud. In a booming voice that carried to the tables around them, he asked, "Wilson, where's Drew Gregory?"

"Honeymooning. I'm filling in for him. Gregory sent word that you owe him one."

"The Sulzbach affair." He managed to soften his volume. "An unhappy recollection for all of us. I lost one of my cycling team there. Alekos Golemis—he was a good lad."

"That's why I'm here—to discuss your cycling team."

The sharp eyes narrowed. Jon hooked his umbrella over a palm branch and picked up the menu. "I didn't know Gregory was interested in cycling."

"He's interested in your plans for Ian Kendall. A drink first?" Vic asked.

"Business first. Ian's teammates don't want him to race."

"And you? Is that your way of punishing him, too?"

Gainsborough slid a glance toward Perkins who was non-chalantly munching his salad, a thick book in his free hand.

"Is it up to Perkins?" Vic asked.

"No, it's up to Kendall, but he's racing poorly."

"Ian has the weight of a dead friend on his cycle."

The fat jowls wobbled. He nodded toward Perkins. "I was just doing an old friend a favor. Coach Skobla opposed it. Never dreamed it would cost Alekos his life."

"Risky, wasn't it, breaking from their regular training?"

"It was that or Perkins would make certain Kendall didn't ride. I couldn't let that happen. Kendall is still our best chance for winning the Tour de France."

Vic felt contempt for the man drumming his fingers on the table. They were well-groomed hands with flashy rings squeezing the fat fingers. Gainsborough was buying his own margin of safety, bumping heads with Perkins, kow-towing to him. *It can mean only one thing,* Vic thought. *Perkins has a file on him.*

Where had Gainsborough gone wrong? In his business dealings? In his investments? Or was it something personal between the two men? He was nothing but a big, gutless man controlled by the staid Englishman across the room. MI5 was internal security, Perkins one of their top men. Had Gainsborough breached the security line just far enough for Dudley to find him useful?

"You have only a few weeks to decide, Gainsborough."

"Up until Sulzbach, Kendall had a real shot at winning."

"Your opinion or the coach's?"

"I depend on the men I hire. But Kendall's record is good. Montreal's Grand Prix. The Chambery Race. The Dupont Tour. He had good standings in all of them." Gainsborough's face sparkled. "You should have seen him take those cobbled climbs in the Het Volk. No question about it. The boy's good."

"You call the shots then? What about it, Gainsborough? Will Kendall ride in the Tour? He rode well in last year's race."

"Especially in the Pyrenees. He took those mountain curves at top speed, never braking once."

"Sounds crazy."

"It was. The coach was furious. But Kendall wanted to win, and he would have if that Italian hadn't crashed into him."

"I saw that crash on TV. Heartbreaking for Kendall."

Gainsborough rubbed his neck with his ringed hand. "It was disappointing for all of us. He'd taken three of the stages, but my boys are trained for team racing, not individual glory."

"And you think Kendall is racing for himself?"

"Kendall doesn't always go for structure. He wants space. That's Ian's weakest point, not always riding with the team in mind. If Orlando Gioceppi beats him at the Coors Classic, he's our next choice." Again his gaze shifted toward Perkins. "Ian has serious problems. It's as though the fight has gone out of him since Sulzbach."

"Kendall thinks you blame him for Alekos's death."

"Who else would I blame?"

"Yourself perhaps or Perkins. Why not square it away with Kendall? He needs to know you're not holding that accident against him."

"He's not the one with the threat of a lawsuit. Alekos's family is out to destroy the team now. Look, I'm hungry. Why don't we order?"

"Are you ready for that drink?"

"No, I want something solid." Gainsborough took time to study the menu and then reskimmed it before ordering a double portion of steak-and-kidney pie with roast potatoes, broccoli, and Yorkshire pudding. "And," he added, "I want creamy baked custard for dessert."

Vic kept his order simple. Eggs and toast and a pot of steeping tea. It was about all his stomach could handle.

They spent the next several minutes staring across the table at each other, starting a phrase or two and letting them go. When the food arrived, Vic said, "Gregory thinks Ian has lost his winning spirit."

"We'll know at the Coors Classic. He blows it there, and he's off the team. I can't support a loser."

"Perkins's idea or yours?"

He finished his first bite. "We were counting on Ian. The kid's a world pro. If I have to let him go, another team will snap him up. If I could only convince Perkins—"

"It's not up to Perkins. Your steel plant supports the team."

"True, but if Kendall goes, Coach Skobla will split with him. I'd lose everything."

What would you lose? Vic wondered. *Maybe you'd have Perkins off your back.* "Ludvik Skobla is new, isn't he?"

"Since the last Tour de France. One of my steel contacts in Prague recommended Skobla. He's been our best coach yet."

Vic wanted a name for the contact in Prague. He picked one from the hat and asked, "Not Cliff Harriman?"

Gainsborough's scowl made his fat face more homely. "No," he said. "The man's name is Altman Russelmann. The Russelmanns gave me my own start in the steel business. Altman knew Coach Skobla personally."

"Was he a good choice?"

"I think so. I trust Altman's recommendations. Skobla befriends the boys, but he trains them at high intensity. He's well organized and technical. Kendall needed that."

When the baked custard and coffee came, Vic nodded at the picture on the wall. "That fox hunt is one of Ian's favorite paintings."

"How would you know?"

"He came to this restaurant with his grandmother."

Food bulged in Gainsborough's cheek. He spoke with his mouth full. "Dead, isn't she?"

As you well know. "Afraid so, Gainsborough. She's the reason Kendall intends to win the Tour de France. He wants to wear the yellow jersey for her."

"We're a team, Wilson. If Kendall wears the yellow jersey, it's for the Gainsborough team. Not some dead woman."

Vic let that one ride. "When I talked with Gregory, he said that Ian raced well yesterday."

"One day is not enough. There are no miracles in cycling without good hard work. You can tell Gregory it all depends on the Coors Classic. If Ian wins that one, he will be our best choice for the Tour since Greg LeMond."

"Perkins won't try to stop Ian again?"

Gainsborough stuffed his mouth with the last spoonful of custard, his mood suddenly determined. "I won't let him."

"Drew has another request."

"I told you, there are no miracles in cycling."

"This one's under your control. He wants to ride in the team car next month."

"During the Tour de France? That's for the staff."

"It's a safety precaution. The men who killed Alekos were never picked up. They must know about the race."

Gainsborough's spoon clattered to the plate. He shoved the dish aside. "I'll check with Coach Skobla."

And who is he taking his orders from? Vic wondered.

Gainsborough held out his hand and tapped his wrist-watch. "I must be going. I'll pass your concerns onto the coach."

And to Perkins, I bet.

Even as Gainsborough stood, Perkins went on reading his book, making no effort to move. "I'm looking forward to the Coors Classic, Jon. It will be televised, won't it?"

"At least it will make the sports page." Gainsborough opened his wallet and pulled out several pound notes.

"No need," Vic said. "My treat. I'll walk you out."

They parted on the sidewalk, the big man taking off with full strides. Vic stood and watched him until that massive body was swallowed up in the pressing crowds. Then he craned his neck and glanced up at the shop sign, a brass carving of a horse and rider with a hound at their heels. Beneath the shingle were the bold red-and-white letters: The Fox Hunt.

Wilson had found his sly fox. *Two of them,* he thought as Dudley Perkins sauntered out of the restaurant. Vic turned in the opposite direction and headed for his car whistling.

Back at Brianna's empty apartment, he dropped into the

chair and spent the next hour making several business calls. Finally he dialed the Adria Hotel in Prague. When Drew picked up the phone on the third ring, Vic said, "I'm glad I caught you."

❁❁❁

Drew Gregory smiled into the phone. "Almost didn't. We're going out to dinner."

"What's on your schedule for tomorrow, Drew?"

Miriam sat at the desk, pen poised above the travel folders spread out in front of her. "Miriam's working on that. The Prague Gallery for one. She's into Renaissance paintings this week."

"Can you add the Russelmann Steel Mill to your schedule?"

"What?"

"Jon Gainsborough does business with them."

Drew turned his back to Miriam. "Didn't Gainsborough check out?"

"I have a few question marks. He didn't like lunching at The Fox Hunt, and he didn't want to talk about Olivia Renway. But he did let it slip that the Russelmanns gave him his start in the steel industry."

"A problem?"

"I picked up copies of the *Evening Standard* and the *International Herald Tribune* on my way back to Brianna's. I wanted to check the business pages. Then I made several calls this afternoon. One to an editor friend of mine, one to the Russelmann corporate office in Munich, a third to Jarvoc, Czechoslovakia." He chuckled. "I'll save the bill for you, otherwise Brianna will have my head when the charges come."

"Get to your point, Vic."

"The families of Gainsborough's friends were in business back in Nazi Germany. After the war, they eluded the Nuremberg trials."

Drew stared across the room at the pastel walls. Vic Wilson was one of those cocky guys born to crusade, born to push his convictions on others in a Newt Gingrich style. Tell Vic that they were going to clean up Congress and the Senate, and he would be on the bandwagon with his own ten-point contract for America.

"You still there, Gregory?"

Drew moved the mouthpiece closer. "Go ahead. I'm listening."

"The Russelmanns prospered all through the war. Branched out into Poland and Czechoslovakia during the war. Forced labor. Full profits."

"Thought everything was state-run in Czechoslovakia."

"Not since the Communists moved out."

Vic had always brushed off the Cold War and Communist rule. He even scoffed at the new leadership in Russia in a cocksure way that bugged his colleagues. He viewed the home front in the same way. He didn't care who was in the Oval Office. So why this sudden interest in a steel industry?

"Where's the factory, Vic?"

"In Jarvoc. That's west of Prague, not far from Kladno."

Jarvoc. The name clicked this time. Dorian Paschek's hometown. Olivia Renway's birthplace. Had Vic picked up on this, too? "I'll see what I can do, Vic. I'll check with Miriam first."

"So that's what happens when you get married?"

"It didn't the first time around."

Five minutes later, after an earful on Gainsborough and Perkins, Drew cradled the receiver and walked over to Miriam. As he gently massaged her narrow shoulders, she placed her cheek against his hand.

"I'm surprised at how many people know where we are on our honeymoon," she said. "I didn't even give our numbers to Robyn."

"I'm sorry. That call was my fault, *Liebling.* It was Vic."

"Not Uriah Kendall this time?"

"Vic was checking into some things for me."

"Something to do with Uriah?"

"Yes."

He studied her in the mirror and marveled again at her

natural beauty. She kissed the back of his hand. "Is Vic all right?" she asked.

"Sounds cheerful enough."

"Nothing about his illness?"

"Nothing new."

Softly she said, "You're going to miss him."

"He's not dead yet."

"Then why do you act like he is?"

Drew knew and hated knowing. Sooner or later he was going to lose his friend. He seethed at what was happening to Vic, but he couldn't alter it. And the truth was, he couldn't face it either.

He couldn't even find comfort in blaming it on Vic. Vic had made his own choices, always calling himself a free moral agent. That binding freedom had taken him on a wild journey from a girl in every port to no girls at all now. A year or two down the trail and Vic would test AIDS positive. The one thing Drew had promised himself was that nothing would spoil their friendship.

"You have been good friends, haven't you?"

"The best. We go at the job from different viewpoints, but we've always worked well together. He saved my life a couple of times. I'll always have that to remember."

"Drew, he is still alive. Don't treat him as though he is dying."

Gratefully he smiled at her in the mirror. "You won't mind having him in our home for dinners?"

"A little. The disease still frightens me."

"It frightens him, too."

She picked up her brush and ran it through her auburn hair, each stroke adding to the sheen. "I can't picture Vic afraid of anything."

"He's afraid of dying. He has no peace at all."

"But you do, Drew. Share yours."

"Right now he's not ready to listen."

"Someday he will. His illness—"

Miriam still couldn't bring herself to say the words HIV virus, as though verbalizing them would harm Vic more. Perhaps Drew was right. Vic would bear the reproach and rejection of his colleagues once the results of his blood tests reached the Agency.

Miriam cleared her throat. "His illness has polished some of his rough edges. It's like a new Vic at the helm."

"That's his cousin's doings. Brianna is like a rock. She'll stick with him all the way. But you're right. Being HIV positive has mellowed Vic." He tried to sound chipper as he added, "Thanks to Vic, I have good news for you, *Liebling*."

He stopped the brush mid-stroke, leaned down, and put his cheek against hers. "You'll be able to look up Dorian Paschek after all."

Chapter 11

Luke Breckenridge cracked his knuckles as the Swiss airliner banked over Zurich. For a moment it felt as if the jet hovered motionless against a sea of cumulus clouds, and then the gigantic bird shuddered as the wheels locked into place. Earth's patchwork fields came rapidly up to meet them. To Luke's left lay the wooded hills shadowed in deep purple and the mountaintops still crested in layers of snow. To his right stood the traffic control tower and in the distance the Zurichsee, blue and glistening.

On his last trip to Zurich, he had been in the custody of Drew Gregory, convinced that Drew would turn him over to the CIA, the victim of another man's treason. Luke had sat with Drew on the patio of the Schweizerhof Cafe in Schaffhausen contemplating a mad dash for freedom over the winding streets of the town. His thoughts had been far from ever seeing his precious Sauni again.

For twenty years she had thought him buried at Arlington. In a way he had been dead, dead inside. He had sat there unblinking, rigid in his flak jacket and khaki pants. Shiny black boots pressed against his callused feet; a one-inch stubble of beard covered his chin. And then—there at the cafe in Schaffhausen, Sauni came over the bridge that spanned the Rhine wearing a red dress and the heart-shaped locket that he had given her long ago. He would have known her anywhere—that lovely oval face, the sensitive mouth, that quick, light step of hers. From across the cafe patio, she met Luke's gaze, her dazzling blue-green eyes pained when she saw him. He knew she recognized him even though his strong features were marred by a jagged scar along his neck and by years of bitterness against the man and country that had betrayed him. In his rage, he would have destroyed Gregory for letting Sauni see him like that, but he could only voice his fury as she walked back over that bridge without him.

He hadn't counted on Drew's help. Gregory was gutsy, somber, determined, but he was a CIA officer. Luke didn't credit any of them with integrity. After all, one of them had betrayed him in the jungles of Laos. But Drew went doggedly after the truth. In the end he bought Luke's pardon at the cost of an old friendship with the CIA station-chief in Paris. Luke still found it hard to believe he was a free man, a man with his own passport, his name cleared of treason, the country hailing him as a hero. It seemed now that Gregory was the one who had come up short, condemned by his own Company, his friends blatantly against him. Gregory made no demands on Luke, expressed no regrets for helping him. Luke wondered whether he would have done the same for Gregory.

Sauni. Going on in life without Sauni held no meaning for Luke. His stomach knotted as the plane lined up with the runway. The pilot was committed to landing. Was Luke committed to facing Sauni once again? She had every reason to reject him. They were divorced, and he had allowed her to think he was dead for twenty years. Yet she stood with him through the roughest part of the journey back to freedom—had even threatened to storm the White House on his behalf. But when he was honored there on the lawn of the White House, she had not come to share his glory.

The wheels hit the touchdown zone, the belly of the plane shuddering as the tires burned the runway. The jet braked and came to a jarring stop at the terminal, its wing lights blinking. He let the others scramble to their feet and tug luggage from the rack as they fought for standing space in the aisle. Finally Luke stood, his lanky legs numb after the long flight.

One of the attendants made her way to him. "Sir, every-one is off the plane. Are you all right?"

He smiled down at her, his facial muscles tight. "I wasn't up to fighting the crowd."

"But you're all right? Someone is meeting you?"

"I hope so," he said.

He grabbed his briefcase and raincoat and followed her to the exit. She stepped aside, and he ducked as he left the cabin.

"Have a nice time in Zurich, sir."

I'd like that, he thought. "Thanks for a good flight."

He took off with long strides and caught up with the stragglers at the baggage roundabout. He had his luggage key and passport in his hand, but he was ushered rapidly through the customs line with only a cursory glance. Inside the noisy terminal, he envied the laughter and boisterous reunions.

As he searched for Sauni's familiar face, his neck scar pulsated, the sharp pain searing into his jaw and tracking its way to his temples. The violent onset of a headache startled him. He shouldered his raincoat and merged with the crowd, his disappointment so physical that he thought he would spill his guts as he had done in Laos when dysentery almost killed him.

She hadn't come. His sense of rejection was unbearable. He moved mechanically, inches taller than the passengers around him as they fought for space in the crowded corridor. The drone of voices sounded like the roar of a turbojet in his ears.

"Luke."

The voice sounded far away, distant like a memory.

"Luke. LUKE! *LUKE!*"

As he turned, people spread thin and walked around him. He saw Sauni hurrying toward him. He dropped his coat and briefcase. She was running now, her flimsy red dress restricting her speed. He held out his arms, his long-ing for her overwhelming.

She was there, looking up at him, breathless with an apol-ogy. "They told me the wrong gate," she said.

"I thought you weren't coming."

Her eyes smiled first. "Luke, you know me better than that."

He touched her cheek to make certain she was real, to make certain he was still alive himself.

"I was at the wrong gate for thirty minutes—and then I heard them announce your flight. I—"

He cupped her face and came down hard on those well-shaped lips, silencing her apology. For a moment she responded as warmly and passionately as he did. Then abruptly she pushed him away, her soft hands trembling against his broad chest.

"Luke, we'd better go." He heard panic and embarrassment in her voice. "I want to avoid the traffic."

"I'll drive," he offered.

"Oh, no. It's Annabelle's car."

Sauni kept up a nervous flow of chatter from the escalator to the parked car. She seemed relieved to get her hands on the steering wheel, to fix her eyes on the traffic. She glanced at him as they left the airport. "Luke, you look wonderful."

"My mother's cooking," he said casually.

"I'm afraid she spoiled you. You won't even like my meals."

"Mom said you've turned into an excellent cook."

A happy ripple of laughter swept through the car. "How would Amy know? We took most of our meals out when they visited me."

"She said you don't do burnt offerings anymore."

"Luke, how did you ever stand my first attempts at cooking?"

"I filled up at the mess hall before coming home."

She sobered with another glance his way, and then she was back to concentrating on the traffic. She drove defensively—the way he had taught her—and he was pleased.

"I called your mother this morning. Amy said your plane got off on time. She sent her love—said they miss you already."

"They were good about my coming. I had to see you, Sauni."

She cut him off, her voice gentle. "I told Amy I've taken a couple of days off from summer school to show you around."

"You didn't have to do that."

"I wanted to. You missed so much of Busingen the last time."

"We had that walk by the river."

"That's all we had, wasn't it, Luke?"

All we'll ever have, he thought. "Are you staying on at the school in Busingen?"

"I signed on for another term—after talking with the chaplain. He thought it was a good idea to go on with my life." To his silence she whispered, "I'm happy here."

"Teaching theology?"

"Oh, Luke."

He had always loved the way she laughed—from the day he met her on the steps of the Capitol. But this time he feared she was laughing at him.

"Luke, I teach literature—French and biblical both. My students come from all over Europe. Two even from the States."

She was still cutting him off, keeping her distance, choosing a life where there was no room for him. "Sauni, I'll stay at the hotel in Schaffhausen."

"Hotel? No, you're staying with my friends in Busingen. Right next door to me. We can wave from our bedroom windows."

It wasn't what he had in mind. Was she afraid of being near him? Or was there someone else? "I don't want to put anyone out."

"Luke, it's all arranged." Her laughter had slipped to impatience. "They're my friends. You'll like them."

His spine stiffened. These days he still didn't take to strangers and particularly to theologians. He didn't want her friends sharing the burden of his arrival. He wanted time alone with Sauni. "Will you be free to spend time with me, Sauni?"

"I told you—I took a few days off to show you around."

They covered several miles of beautiful countryside before she asked, "Did things go well for you at Walter Reed?"

"My debriefing and endless X-rays? I'm grateful it's over."

"Was it that rough?"

"The interviews with Langley were the worst."

"But Chaplain Grozfelt was nice to you, wasn't he?"

He started to say, "Sid is my shrink." But it might push her further away. "He's a good man—the easiest part of Walter Reed."

"He's the gentleman who—who told me to go on with my life."

Luke fought anger at Sid. "That's strange, Sauni. Sid is the one who told me to fly over and be with you."

❦❦❦

Sauni Breckenridge paced the living room for an hour after Luke left her, and then she crawled between the sheets and cried herself to sleep. She awakened in the middle of the night, her cheeks flushing in the darkness at the thought of Luke's kiss.

She had promised herself—no, she had promised Sid Grozfelt not to push their relationship. In a way, Grozfelt had snatched away the hope of any permanent reunion with Luke. He had warned her that Luke was on a long journey back, struggling to accept himself and society once again. Sauni had in those two long phone calls with Grozfelt confided her deep feeling for Luke, her longing to go back twenty years when they were the happiest, her willingness to marry Luke again.

Grozfelt's answer had been slow, like his Southern drawl. "There's no going back. It's one day at a time for both of you. Just remember Captain Breckenridge is walking a fragile line that cannot be hurried." Gently, he had added, "Luke is well physically, Mrs. Breckenridge, but coming back emotionally will take longer. The captain may never feel free to marry again."

"But you said he's well."

"His debriefing was not easy. There are some in Washington who would punish Captain Breckenridge for his time at the mercenary camps. An understandable concern, Mrs. Breckenridge."

"Luke had nowhere to go, Chaplain Grozfelt."

She heard him chuckle, but his words were sobering. "Right now he's finding it hard to forgive himself. . . . Celibacy could be one way of self-punishment."

No, Sauni knew Luke better than that. Deep inside Luke would always be a warm and caring man, expressive and romantic. Surely God hadn't brought Luke this far to walk a solitary journey. She wanted to call Luke and reassure him that she loved him no matter what. She propped herself up on one elbow and turned on the bedside light. The answering machine blinked, indicating two incoming calls. Had the phone rung twice while she was showering?

She pushed the message button and smiled at the sound of Luke's voice. "Sauni, I just wanted to say good night again."

But as she turned her attention to the second message, her happiness faded. "Luke," a cheerful young voice said, "it's Chase Evans. I've been trying to reach you for days. I'm in Europe. When can we get together? Please *call* me."

🜚🜚🜚

In Jarvoc the last whistle had blown. Except for a skeleton night crew, Russelmann Steel Mill had shut down. Hanz Russelmann stood by his office window in the air-conditioned facility and watched the lights dim on each floor. Outside, the parking lot emptied rapidly as the cars and bikes and trucks headed toward town and a round of drinks at the local pubs.

He longed for that kind of freedom, but those merry days of laughter and drinking belonged to his Cambridge years and the Oktoberfests in Munich—before the war and the twists and turns that had brought him to Prague—before these long, lonely years of living in isolation from the land of his birth. Fifty-five years ago seemed like forever.

Hanz had another twenty minutes before his office would begin to overheat. Still he waited in the dark, listening, trying to determine whether Altman and Gustav had left the building. He heard the elevator door shut and open. Shut and open. He used up ten of his twenty minutes, and then he moved quickly, for a man of such bulk and height, into the deserted corridor. His luck held. Using his passkey, he entered the well-furnished boardroom; the long oval table was covered with fingerprints from today's conference. Altman still allowed him to sit in on the daily meetings, but Hanz no longer voiced his opinions. Even when they discussed Nedrick and his usefulness to them, Hanz kept his tongue, listening. If there was anything good left in the Russelmann clan, it was Nedrick; it was up to Hanz to protect him.

By morning the boardroom would be spotless, the table highly polished, the plants freshly watered—and Altman, Gustav, and Josef ready to discuss Nedrick's fate. Time was running out for Hanz, too, but he had to beat his sons at their own game. He had to stay alive long enough to salvage his grandson even at the sacrifice of the factory. And by morning Hanz intended to know more about the contracts with Nishokura Steel in Tokyo.

From the boardroom he could work his way into Altman's spacious quarters. He closed the door cautiously, the click of the latch resounding like a drumbeat. He had been prepared to stand until his eyes adjusted to the darkness, but a wide streak of light came through the door that led into Altman's office.

The plush carpet allowed Hanz to move closer to a better vantage point. Eerie shafts of light from the desk lamp reflected against the massive painting of a Napoleon battle. The painting had been swung aside, and the safe on the wall lay open.

Altman sat at his desk deep in thought, the tip of a pen to his lips, a report of some kind in his hand. His suit coat had been discarded, the knot of his tie loosened, the cuffs of his lavender shirt rolled up. In profile Altman was an attractive man, fifty something now, not at all frightening as he was when people faced those cruel, unfeeling eyes.

Sitting there so pensively, he didn't look brutish, implacable, cold-blooded. With a fresh burst of remorse Hanz regretted the day he had found his son in Cornwall, England. Things might have turned out differently if he had never known the boy existed. Until that moment Altman had no past, no history, no known parentage, no one to claim him. The boy had been told that he was an orphan, the victim of the London bombings, his heritage lost in the rubble.

Five years after the war, Hanz had gone to England to finalize the arrangements with Jon Gainsborough for a satellite steel factory north of Oxford. Once the papers were signed, Hanz set out on a futile search to find Olivia Renway. He found no trace, no clues to Olivia's whereabouts—he heard only a persistent rumor that there had been a child.

Standing motionless in the boardroom in Jarvoc, he remembered back to Olivia vomiting morning after morning. He had comforted her, telling her not to be afraid of the air raids. He was there with her. She had said nothing, nothing about the baby. But if there had been a baby, she would have gone back to the Renways in Cornwall. Yes, that is where he would find Olivia's child. He remembered that day as if it were yesterday. . . .

❁❁❁

January 1950. Hanz took the train to Cornwall, retracing the familiar journey to the Renways' tiny fishing village. He had known Warren and Millicent Renway since Cambridge, their political thinking strongly aligned with his own. He had recruited them for the cause that was sweeping over Europe, convinced himself that the Nazi movement would restore Germany to power and lift her from the throes of a dying economy.

Hanz had considered it in his favor that Warren Renway

was a close friend of the Duke of Windsor, the man who had abdicated the British throne. Like the duke, Renway had many relatives born into German families and had been a frequent visitor in that country. Hanz soon learned that Renway and his wife had taken offense at the royal family's rejection of the duke once he married the American divorcee. Hanz nurtured Renway's resentments, playing mind games with him until Renway was convinced that England could best be served by siding with the cause that would unite the two countries and restore the duke to the English throne under German control. Warren's wife, Millicent, whose German roots went even deeper, agreed.

While war was still a rumor, Hanz had set the Renways up with a shortwave transmitter and put them in touch with German Intelligence. They wanted to avoid war at all costs, but if German pilots crashed in England, the Renways would help them escape by signaling German subs off the coast. Hanz, as it turned out, was one of the first Luftwaffe pilots to seek their help when his plane crashed during the early weeks of the Blitz. The decision from Berlin was for Hanz to remain in England to gather information that would bring the British Isles to her knees.

As his plane had limped toward the coast, the crash imminent, he had seen the futility of war and the bombs' destruction of the city of London. Hanz loved England. While he stood on the Cornish cliffs with the angry sea crashing against the boulders, he had resented the orders that would keep him there as a spy. It was then, in the darkest hour of his life, that he met Olivia face to face. He had known about her, the Renways' "adopted" daughter, but he had not met her until she came out to the cliff that day to call him home.

"Henri," she had said, "supper is ready."

Hanz turned, startled by the unexpected recognition. He had seen her once before in his life—the day the Germans moved into Prague. He had watched her flee with her father and take refuge inside the church, and he had let her go.

She was barely sixteen then, and now at seventeen her face was still waiflike, pale and thin, but her eyes were blue

and beautiful. She wore a leather jacket, stolen no doubt
from a downed pilot, men's trousers, and scuffed boots. The
top two buttons of her white shirt were open with a floral
print scarf knotted at her neck. The russet brown hair hung
in loose strands, blown back from her face by the strong sea
breeze. As he stared at her, her narrow chin jutted forward.

"You must be Olivia. I wondered if we'd ever meet."

"I've been in Czechoslovakia," she said.

Taking messages to the resistance fighters in Prague, he
guessed. He knew at that moment that she knew nothing of
the Renways' political leanings; and he knew that if she had,
she would have hated them. Olivia had simply sought
refuge in the home of family friends.

She came to supper that evening in a dress, her hair
brushed and tied back from her face with the same scarf she
had worn at her neck. Meeting her trusting, admiring gaze
over the supper table, he made the decision to use her. She
had already given a year of her life to the resistance movement in Prague. He would persuade her to help him.
Instead he fell in love with her.

Now he had come back to Cornwall, not to find Olivia,
but to find the child that she had borne him. The stone
church and the orphanage attached to it were set off from
the sturdy seafarers' homes that nestled securely in the
towering cliffs. A shingle with the weather-beaten words
"St. Michael's Children's Cove" squeaked in the wind. The
orphanage had been overcrowded with children during the
war, but now only fifty unwanted youngsters made their
home there.

Hanz followed the robed nun inside. An hour later
another somber-faced nun shook her head for the third
time. "I'm sorry, Mr. Russelmann. The birth records of the
children are sealed."

"Surely you can tell me whether there is a child here by
the name of Renway. He—she—would be around nine or
ten."

The Mother Superior folded her hands on the ledger in
front of her. "The children go by their first names. Perhaps
if you could be more specific about the child."

He went hopelessly to the window and stared out on the children at play. Taking the miniature binoculars from his pocket, he studied their faces. He was just about to give up when he saw the young boy standing by the stone fence. There was nothing about his solemn, morose face that reminded him of Olivia, but he saw himself in the boy.

"Sister," he said, "the boy over there—what's his name?"

She came to stand at Hanz's side, her long habit swishing at her ankles as she moved. "That's Altman," she said. "He's such a gloomy little boy. Rejected by the others."

Hanz sucked in his breath. *Altman was his middle name.* He could not take his eyes off the child. "Why do the others reject him?" he asked.

She folded her hands in front of her. "This late it shouldn't matter, but it still does. His father was a German— a soldier, I believe. And his mother partly Jewish."

He winced, remembering his own revulsion when Olivia admitted to her Jewish heritage. His throat tightened as he asked, "The boy's mother—is she dead?"

The nun glanced up at him. "Mr. Russelmann, I've told you, we don't discuss the children's records."

"It's important."

"To you perhaps. But not to the boy."

"Could I see the child and talk with him?"

"I see no harm in that, Mr. Russelmann."

As they walked to the playground together, he hounded her with questions. The boy's age? His likes and dislikes? His scholastic rating? The possibility of taking the boy out of England and raising him?

And then he faced his son, Olivia's son. Thick hair and eyes like his own with features that surely belonged to a Russelmann.

"It seems strange, Mr. Russelmann," the nun said as Altman chased after the soccerball. "You've asked many questions about the boy. But never once have you asked me who his father was."

Hanz felt as though he were back in the Luftwaffe uniform standing rigidly at attention, his commanding officer ripping the Iron Cross from his neck. He turned slowly, stiffly, and met her steady gaze. "Sister," he said with a catch in his throat, "I already know all about his father."

🏺🏺🏺

Hanz stood in the shadows of the boardroom, balancing painfully on his game leg, wondering what had become of that boy he had found in Cornwall, England. He tried to recall what his first impressions had been. They were vague. An angry child, raging like the seawaters on the Cornish coast. An unsmiling, sullen child chasing a soccerball. When Hanz told the boy he was taking him back to Germany with him, Altman shrugged and went on drawing lines with a black crayon. He showed no emotion at all when the nuns packed up his few belongings and he walked down the steps of the orphanage with Hanz to a new life. They had flown to Germany as strangers. They were still strangers.

Altman had grown from a child into a self-sufficient, power-hungry adult who still hated the mother who had rejected him. From where Hanz stood, he could see the muscles on his son's face contorting. The room had become suffocating with the air conditioner turned off, but Altman seemed unaware of the discomfort as he continued to browse through the thick report.

Unexpectedly Altman's fist came down hard on the desk, scattering the papers. As he shoved back his leather chair and struggled to his feet, one page drifted unnoticed to the floor. With the precision so characteristic of him, he put the report into the briefcase, placed it in the safe, and twirled the dial. Squaring the painting on the wall to his satisfaction, Altman snatched up his coat, switched off the lights, and left the room.

As Altman's footsteps faded, Hanz felt his way to the fallen sheet of paper and picked it up. He snapped the desk light back on and stared disbelievingly at the paper in his hand.

Olivia Renway's name ran across the top of the page, the title of her unfinished novel beside it.

Chapter 12

Prague. Early the next morning the Gregorys left their hotel room with its cheery yellow walls, took the stairs down to the Adria's marble-tiled reception room, and turned in the passkey. The electric doors slid open, and Drew and Miriam walked through them, out under the bright yellow awning onto Wenceslas Square. The hotel doorman, waiting politely by their rental car, opened the door of the Skoda with his gloved hand and wrapped his fingers around the tip that Drew gave him.

Drew maneuvered through the tangled web of one-way streets, then drove along the Vltava River not far from the Charles Bridge, honking impatiently at a horse-drawn wagon of manure and narrowly missing a nun on a motorcycle.

"Shades of New York," he complained.

"Have you forgotten, Drew? It's a heavy on-the-spot fine if they stop you for a traffic violation."

"It will probably be life if I topple that load of manure."

"Or, heaven forbid, hit that poor nun."

"Hmm." His thoughts turned back to the farm of his childhood in upstate New York, the Gregory Dairy Farm with its manure and shovels and hundreds of cattle. He could visualize the woods and the river where his brother Aaron had fished, but the face of his mom, the woman who had so molded him, blurred in his memory. He tried even harder to sketch the features of Wallace Gregory, the dad he had dearly admired.

Briefly the church of his boyhood laid claim to his memory. St. Bonaventure had been a small parish, later closed for lack of parishioners. He remembered the priest and his own days as an altar boy, but he could not remember any nun, and certainly not one on a motorcycle. The faith he had ignored and stomped on for years had become real to him once again in a simple transaction on a Sulzbach mountain slope. He'd made peace with God there, but what gripped him at this moment was the confident prospect that he would see his parents again. No one had told him that an eternal reunion was a fringe benefit, but the conviction had come on the same mountain.

Drew smiled as they left the crowded city of a hundred spires and drove west though rolling hills and gentle farmlands. The Czech Republic had few modern highways, but it abounded in scenic countryside. Wild flowers filled the hillsides. Melting snows had turned to small waterfalls. Splashes of yellow and green dotted the sprawling fields.

He bypassed Kladno, a thriving steel center, and drove northwest to Jarvoc. The town stood backed by a forest of spruce and firs, steep rolling hills rising toward the low-crested mountains. Railroad tracks ran along the edge of the forest where a long line of freight cars waited for loading. The river—more like a bubbling stream for trout—left the town as landlocked as the country, with no major outlet to the North Sea for shipping steel.

He could see the Russelmann factory as they drove along, black smoke curling from the farthest building. As he increased speed, Miriam said, "You passed Dorian Paschek's street, Drew."

"Did I? I thought the Pascheks owned a large farm."

"They did, but war and communism changed all that."

He shot a glance her way. "How would you know?"

"Olivia sent a card from Prague just before she was killed. She said the beautiful farmland had been turned into a factory town with crowded housing. . . . Please, let's see Dorian first."

He kept his foot heavy on the gas. "We'll still have time."

"No. You'll get to talking at the factory. Besides, in a town this small, Dorian will know all about the Russelmanns."

He gave in reluctantly as he turned the car back and bumped over the cobbled road to the Pascheks' faded yellow home. Its living quarters were still attached to the old barn. It sat beside a narrow row of newer, look-alike houses. There was a drabness, a sense of hopelessness to this part of town, as though a fresh coat of paint was out of reach. The housing still reflected the dull colors of communism. The narrow wood siding on Paschek's washboard of a place was worn and ridged, in dire need of a scrubbing. But the old barn had been turned into a shop. Ribbed glass plates and bowls were displayed in the window, another man's name on the shingle.

Drew parked at the end of the street. As they stepped from the car, he nodded to the sign. "Hon, Paschek doesn't live here."

"We have to make certain." She took his hand and tugged him along. Inside the shop, Miriam smiled at the woman behind the counter. "We're looking for our friend Dorian Paschek," she said.

The woman pointed along the side of the shop. "He keeps the cottage in the rear. Actually it's the old toolshed, but he fixed it up real nice and added a room or two." She fussed with the glass display. "No need to go back there. He's at work now."

Miriam never liked detours. "Where does he work?"

"Thought you knew him." Her sharp tone matched Miriam's.

Miriam mellowed. "We do—sort of. We knew his sister."

"His sister is dead. God rest her soul."

"I know, but we were friends. Very good friends."

The woman's interest turned to a dust speck on the counter. "Dorian won't be home for another six hours. He lives alone since his wife's death. We don't bother him. He likes it that way."

Drew picked up one of the glass bowls with its intricate design. "Where does Mr. Paschek work?" he asked casually.

"Same place everyone else does. There's my place. Four cafes. The pubs and the factory. But without the steel factory the town would have died long ago."

Drew put the bowl down. "We'll come back on our way out of town. We'd like to take a gift home to our daughter."

As Drew opened the door for Miriam, the woman repositioned a glass plate. "If you find Dorian, I wouldn't mention that sister of his to him. Not in front of anyone."

Miriam whirled around in the open doorway and put her foot against it. The door chime kept ringing. Above the clanging, the woman said, "Dorian never speaks of her anymore, not since she caused so much trouble."

"Trouble?" Drew asked. "She only came here for the funeral."

"And never when they really needed her. Dorian's wife was sick a long time. No," she said sadly, "Dorian's sister should have died back in the resistance movement. Then we could have put her name on the town monument—and forgotten her."

They walked back to the car in silence. As he slipped in beside Miriam, she said, "Why would Dorian feel that way? Olivia deposited money for him in Prague for years, ample enough to cover any medical expenses." She bit at her lips. "I should have told her we knew Olivia in America—that she was a good person."

"Somehow I don't think that woman would have believed you."

As they drew closer to the factory, the six-story air-conditioned building loomed up in front of them. The property was gated, the grounds well kept with trimmed hedges and a freshly cut lawn. Behind the modern complex lay acres of land with six or seven separate plants that surely contained the computer-controlled systems, the coke ovens and blast furnaces, the refineries and rolling mills that allowed the Russelmanns to produce tons of steel annually. The guard at the gate handed them a visitor's pass and waved them on.

Inside the main building the reception room was airy and spacious, the floors carpeted. A cushioned bench encircled the fountain in the middle of the hall, the sound of running water echoing through the empty room.

Drew strolled to the directory and scanned the long list of occupants. He knew enough German and French to know that many of the companies were foreign owned: investment and insurance companies, brokers and exporters, and one Japanese company—Nishokura Steel. Most of them were members of the European Community and had brought their businesses to Jarvoc, probably to avoid the monstrous rentals in the crowded city of Prague.

The Russelmanns' executive suites took up the entire second floor. "This explains it," Drew said, scanning the names again. "The Russelmanns may own this building, but they lease most of it to others." Grinning he said, "So let's go drop Vic's bombshell and tell them we know Jon Gainsborough."

"Is that what Vic wanted us to do?"

"It's the easiest way to look around."

"You won't forget Dorian?"

"Wouldn't think of it."

The Russelmann suite was more plush than the lobby. A tall, dignified gentleman in a gray suit stood by the receptionist's desk with *The Prague Post* in his arthritic hands. "I'm Hanz," he said, looking at Drew. "May I help you?"

"I'm Drew Gregory. We're looking for the Russelmanns."

"Which Mr. Russelmann?" the receptionist asked.

The older man cut her off, asking, "Were you interested in a shipment of steel, Mr. Gregory?"

"Not exactly. We're friends of Jon Gainsborough in London. He asked us to drop by."

Drew felt Miriam's jab to the ribs. Old habits were hard to break. He'd had years of small untruths and innocuous answers all in the line of duty, all intended to keep the code of silence demanded by the Agency. During those years, he was convinced that God and the Agency were incompatible. Now that he'd lined himself on the side of God, he still struggled with Company ethics.

Awkwardly he said, "Actually a friend told us to drop by. Said you and Gainsborough do business together."

The tired brown eyes blinked. The man's hair was gray and thin, his profile strong, his expression sad. "Gainsborough? He could be one of our long-standing accounts." The receptionist looked perplexed as Hanz slipped his I.D. badge into his pocket and said, "You'd have to check with Altman Russelmann. He handles the foreign contacts."

Drew glanced at the door marked President. "Could we see Mr. Russelmann?"

Hanz put a restraining hand on the receptionist's shoulder. "Altman is out in the welding plant. He'll be another two hours."

"Do you know Dorian Paschek?" Miriam asked, smiling up at Hanz. "Dorian's sister Olivia Renway and I were good friends."

For a moment Hanz froze. He remained stony-faced, but interest sparked in his eyes. "Dorian Paschek works for us."

Odd, Drew thought. *You don't recall an important foreign contract, and yet you immediately knew one of the employees.*

"Would it be possible to see Mr. Paschek?" Drew asked. "We're driving back to Prague shortly."

Without a word, Hanz limped toward them. Grabbing three hard hats from the hooks, he handed two of them to the Gregorys. "Dorian is in the field."

In spite of the limp he moved quickly, obviously not expecting them to accommodate their steps to his. He led them out the back entrance to a tram and shuttled them out past two more security gates directly onto the open fields. The guards saluted as he sped by them. The land seemed to stretch for miles, acres of property stockpiled with steel. A hydraulic pallet and a truck crane were parked in front of one plant, and wing pallets stood loaded with steel bars and tubes ready for shipment. Other trucks loaded with the wide-flange beams rumbled over the fields toward the freight cars.

"Wait here," he said and limped away.

As they waited for him to come back, Miriam pointed toward the building by the edge of the forest that looked like a military barracks with rings of black smoke rising from its chimneys. "Drew, what would they use that for?"

"Housing maybe, although it's a bit rundown for that."

He couldn't picture metallurgists and engineers finding the barracks satisfactory housing, especially with the railroad tracks running right past it. Drew turned back in time to see Hanz signal to a man in his middle years sitting high on the black seat of the forklift, his gloved hands gripping the wheel as he bounced along. The man braked and leaned over to listen to Hanz, then slid down from the yellow cab, and sauntered toward the Gregorys. He was a big man, solid but not tall. Fringes of straight gray hair hung beneath his hard hat.

He yanked his gloves and black-rimmed glasses off and slipped them into his pocket as he reached them. "I'm Dorian Paschek," he said.

He ignored the hand that Drew extended. "We're the Gregorys," Drew said. "Friends of your sister."

"Yes, she told me about you when she was here. What do you want?"

"Just to greet you," Miriam said. "We were fond of her."

It seemed as though his gray, lifeless eyes would brim with tears, but he looked away, toeing the dirt beneath his scuffed boot. Life had not been kind to Dorian Paschek. His work clothes were worn and patched, his mottled skin weather-beaten, his large hands rough and callused from working the forklift.

Hanz stood by the tram, his eyes unblinking as he watched them. "We won't keep you long, Paschek," Drew promised.

"Good. They'll dock my pay for every second." He looked from one to the other. "There's little lodging in Jarvoc." He was soft-spoken, his voice guarded. "And I've no room at my place."

"We're not staying," Miriam said. "We just wanted to meet you. I promised Olivia that I would visit her country one day."

"She came back once," he said. "For my wife's funeral.

Olivia should never have come. She was shocked to find the steel factory functioning again under the old leadership."

"You never told her?"

"Mrs. Gregory, we never wrote. When my wife died, I called Olivia. She was the only family I had left. I didn't expect her to come. But she insisted—"

"Is that when she discovered the Russelmanns back in business?"

"Yes, Gregory, and she didn't like what had happened to Jarvoc under Communist rule. To her it was like Lidice and the war all over again."

He shifted, turning his face from Hanz. "I've got to get back to work. But I'm telling you, Olivia was a fool coming back here." He ran the back of his big hand across his lips. "She came down to the factory with me—insisted on it. Her in all her finery. She took pictures and notes—it almost cost me my job."

Drew wanted to ask why Olivia had avoided coming home all those years. Or had she been told never to come back? What had clouded her past? Even Dorian seemed to reject her. Drew was convinced that it went back to the war years. Ian Kendall had hinted that part of Olivia's pain stemmed back to Lidice and the resistance movement—to Olivia's personal war against the Nazis. Somehow Jarvoc was part of the puzzle. On a gamble he asked, "Dorian, do you have your sister's notes on her last novel?"

Dorian's face hardened. "I refused to keep them."

"Do you know where they are?"

"I trust that they're in ashes like Olivia."

"Dorian, it's important to Olivia's family. Would you have any idea what your sister did with those notes?"

His gaze remained glum and dispirited. "We had a nanny when we were small, a governess actually."

"Beatrice Thorpe," Drew said.

Dorian seemed surprised. "She lived in Jarvoc, and when she could no longer care for herself, she moved in with my wife and me. But after my wife's death—"

Drew felt the man's pain. "Then you were glad when Olivia took Beatrice back to London."

He shrugged. "I knew Olivia would give her a good home. She'd be dead now, but she was the one person that my sister trusted."

As he turned to leave, Drew stopped him. "Why didn't you keep in touch with Olivia's family?"

"Her husband wrote right after Olivia's death." He tipped his hard hat forward. "Uriah wanted me to move to America."

"You should have taken him up on it."

He looked at Miriam. "I never answered him, Mrs. Gregory."

"Call me Miriam," she told him. "Olivia did."

"It was best for all of us to forget Olivia. You, too."

"*Never*, Dorian."

Drew slipped his arm around Miriam. "Paschek, we've taken up enough of your work time. I'm sorry. But look—is there anything that Uriah could do for you? Or my wife and I?"

"You can leave us alone," Dorian said.

He walked away, his grief evident in his slow gait back to the forklift. They watched him climb up into the leather seat and maneuver the truck backwards. He was scooping the prongs under a load of steel when Hanz pulled the tram up in front of them.

"I'll drive you to your car," he offered.

Drew nodded. *Good shot,* he thought. *A clever detour from any contact with Altman Russelmann.*

🏵🏵🏵

They were back in the Skoda, Drew with his hand on the key. He sat there, not turning on the engine. "The way Dorian acts, the economy here would be nothing without the Russelmann factory. The Russelmanns must control this town."

"At least they employ it."

"But, Miriam, Kladno is one of the major steel industries in the Czech Republic. Why competition like this so close by?"

"There are a lot of people in the surrounding areas, Drew. Competition is healthy. I'm not the only art gallery on Rodeo Drive, you know."

"It's a wild shot, *Liebling*, but if the Russelmanns control Jon Gainsborough, they may have a stake in the cycling team."

She looked horrified. "Ian!" was all she could say.

"When I talked with Vic, he said the Russelmanns set Gainsborough up in business. That means they backed him with plenty of pound notes and crowns."

He shifted his gaze. "That building in the rear—the one that looks like a Quonset hut—has been around a long time. The rest of the compound is modern, updated. But they left that one standing."

"The Russelmanns must like antiques."

"Maybe it's connected to underground tunnels. Maybe it's a reminder to the people of a bitter past."

"You're talking circles, Drew. And if we don't get out of here, the security guards will be ticketing us for loitering."

He ducked beneath the sun shield. "I'm more concerned about the gentleman up there on the second floor watching us."

She squinted through her dark glasses. "Who is he?"

"I'd say Altman Russelmann."

"But Hanz said he was out in the welding shop."

"I don't think the receptionist agreed."

"You're right! She was surprised when he said Russelmann was unavailable."

With a flick of Drew's wrist the engine hummed. "That's when Hanz took off his I.D. badge, Miriam."

"He didn't need a badge, Drew. He wasn't the custodian or some flunky. Everyone recognized him. And that suit was high-priced. Same for the shoes. I notice those things."

"My guess is he's part of executive row. Another Russelmann perhaps, so he'd be aware of the Gainsborough contracts."

🌀🌀🌀

The city of more than a hundred spires lay ahead, a city intricate in design. Modern and medieval. Landlocked, yet a crossroads of Europe. "Oh, Drew, Olivia loved this old city," Miriam said. "I understand why."

"Why?" he teased.

"Prague is everything—a modern city, a Bohemian countryside. Romanesque and Gothic architecture. Peaceful gardens." She laughed. "And those tangled one-way streets that you despise."

"Don't forget Prague's history."

"It wasn't all glorious," she said. "But I don't think I'll ever forget my time here. Because of Olivia. Because of *you*."

They could see some distinctive landmarks now. St. Vitus's Cathedral with the rose window between its twin spires. The Prague Castle high above the Left Bank of the Vltava River. The gold-crested National Theater. "I love this city," she said.

"Sounds like you're not ready to leave it, *Liebling*."

"I'd like one more day."

"Oh, sweetheart, I couldn't look at another museum. We've accomplished what we came for, did what Vic wanted us to do. Met Dorian Paschek. I'd rather leave."

"But, Drew, I came to enjoy Olivia's city."

"One more day," he agreed reluctantly.

"You won't make me check out of the Adria?"

"Why would I do that?"

She glanced at the sideview mirror. "Because that car in the distance has been following us ever since we left Jarvoc."

He patted her knee. "We'll be all right. We came into Prague as tourists. I plan for us to leave the same way."

"And if they keep following us?"

He winked. "We'll lose them by the third museum."

Drew fell into a moody silence as he turned the car over to the doorman at the Adria and took Miriam's hand. It was too late to take action this evening, without rousing her suspicions. But Drew was an early riser—always downing two or three cups of black coffee before sociability caught up with him. Tomorrow he'd let Miriam sleep in. It would give him time to contact Leos Cepek, an old friend with Czech Intelligence. He wanted to warn Leos that the Jarvoc steel mill bore watching. The call to Dudley Perkins in London would have to come later. He dreaded that one. Perkins wouldn't thank Drew for questioning the business integrity of Jon Gainsborough, the British steel magnate who was especially useful to Perkins.

As they reached their room, Miriam asked, "Drew, why do you think Dorian hates Olivia so?"

"He doesn't. He's troubled by bad memories. Somehow Olivia made it difficult for him. Maybe Hanz let it slip when he said they built the Russelmann factory on the ruins of Jarvoc."

Chapter 13

Chase groaned as the microfilm spun off its reel and fell on the table in a crumpled mess in front of her. Three hours ago she had hit a gold mine when a jaunty cameraman on the university campus tapped his camera bag and said, "I'm Andrew Forrestal. I'd like to take your picture."

Startled she had asked, "Whatever for?"

"For the evening news." He peeked under the brim of her hat. "Tell me you've done something newsworthy today, Miss—"

"Not a thing," she said. "I'm just here for the summer. And I'm Chase Evans. From Long Island, New York, before you ask."

"That's it, Miss Evans. The influx of tourists."

His voice and face seemed to smile at the same time. Somehow it pleased her. She had taken long enough to dress this morning, finally settling on the white-trimmed navy dress, a French design her grandmother had bought for her on their last visit to Europe. She had forgotten an umbrella, and at the last minute grabbed the wide-brimmed red hat that she had worn to the Royal Ascot races. It sat low on her forehead, putting the emphasis on her dark-lashed eyes. "I'm more of a student than a tourist," she said still laughing up at him. "But no pictures."

"A pity. You'd make such a splendid subject."

"Are you the roving campus photographer?"

He chuckled. "I'm ten years post-college, and even then I didn't graduate. But I'm good with this camera." He whipped it from its case and flashed another of his easygoing grins. "I just did a session with one of the retiring dons at Imperial College. Caught him at just the right angle. He won't even look bald."

"Is he part of the evening news?"

"Will be. Now, your turn."

He aimed the camera, and she pushed his hands away. "No pictures, Mr. Forrestal."

"Such a pity. But call me Andy." His voice rang with amusement as he fell into step with her. "Americans usually take their cameras to Piccadilly and Trafalgar Square. So what are you doing at London University with an attaché case in your hand?"

"Putting my International Student Card to good use. This is a marvelous campus."

"Another piece of British history like Westminster Abbey. Which piece of history are you looking for?"

"The death of Olivia Renway."

"An accident?"

"Yes."

"That's my usual beat. Accidents. Homicides. Murders. You know—the grisly scenes. Twisted metal. Grotesque bodies—"

"That's gross, Andy."

"I'm sorry. Forgive me. . . . Who was your friend? This Renway?"

"A novelist. She married a Britisher—and ended up dead on Downing Street ten years ago."

"Because of her marriage?"

"No! Her husband wasn't even in London the day she was killed. I'm researching her life. Yesterday I went bleary-eyed looking at microfilms and microfiche at the newspaper morgue."

She had browsed until her shoulders ached from standing in front of the Business Newsbank drawers searching out clippings. She flexed her angel wings as they walked along trying to ease the kinks that were still there. "And this morning I was back at the library looking at more film and records, but I haven't put my finger on what I want yet."

For a moment he actually looked sympathetic, his face serious. Then he gave her that sly grin of his. "At least you didn't have to thumb through a stack of yellowed newspapers. But try the Public Record Office. They might be able to help you."

She brightened. "I might try them in the morning."

"So what are you tracking down?"

"Olivia Renway's reason for being on Downing Street. If I could just get into the BBC files and find out what happened—"

"Sorry, the broadcasting center is closed to the public."

"And no amount of persuasion changed their minds."

They had reached the street corner, not far from her subway station. "I have to be going now, Andrew."

He slung his camera over his shoulder and pulled her back from the curb, his grip possessive. "Don't go. I can help you. I work for an independent television station. Our news files are as thorough as those stored at BBC. But my time comes costly."

She grabbed at his invitation. "How much?"

The sum had been high, but she was leaving for Oxford in the morning. *Too high,* she thought now as she stared down at the broken reel of microfilm. Andrew Forrestal would have to fix it.

She felt a surge of relief as he came back from the storage room, another film canister in his hand. Andrew's striped shirt was only half tucked in, the sleeves rolled up. His squint seemed perpetual, as though he were looking at her through his zoom lens.

As he reached her, he stared down at the twisted film. "What happened?"

"I ran the reel too hard. I'm sorry."

"No bother. I'll repair it. Did you find what you wanted?"

She tapped the frayed film. "It's the right time frame—the end of May ten years ago—but there's nothing on the accident."

"It had to be a major tragedy to make the evening news."

His indifference irritated her. "Perhaps it was only tragic to her family."

"Or some breaking news pushed it to the back page."

"Then why did I find clippings of her death over at the newspaper office?" Chase flipped her hair from the nape of her neck and bent her head back. The ceiling of the work room was drab, colorless, one strip of paint peeling away and hanging loose. Slowly her attention was drawn to the man who had arrived moments after she did. Periodically he glanced her way, an intense man with light hair and a petulant smile. He slouched forward, his trench coat thrown over the chair beside him. She pegged him as a grumpy TV news commentator pressed for time on an article for the evening broadcast.

Along the wall behind him stood four computers, the years marked at the top of each one. The last forty years of news highlights had been preserved in full text on floppy disks and CD-ROMs. With the press of a button the past came alive—four decades of breaking news stories that had pushed school plays and traffic accidents and obituaries to the back burner.

Chase spread her notes out in front of her and looked up at Forrestal again. He was checking his watch, his interest waning rapidly. "Andrew, if only this torn film were in one piece."

"I told you, I can fix it."

"Is there some other way to check the main headline for that day? I think it was something about a bombing—"

He picked up the twisted film. "Let me at that chair. Maybe I can hand-feed the film enough for us to find out."

She leaned over his bony shoulder. As he stretched the film back and forth, the bobbing pictures made Chase dizzy.

"What was that date again?" he asked.

"The twenty-seventh of May."

"Jolly good. The man over there is interested in the same date. There it is. Bomb scare at the prime minister's place. No wonder your friend's death went to the back page."

"The IRA?"

"Some Czech splinter group took credit."

She started to say, *Renway was Czechoslovakian*, but bit her tongue. "Can you run me a copy?"

"Impossible. You're the one who broke it."

"I told you I was sorry."

His attention went back to the bobbing microfilm. "Where did you say your friend was killed?"

"Downing Street—just off Whitehall on a rainy afternoon."

He grinned. "We have a lot of rain. Come back tomorrow. I could have this film spliced back together by then."

"Can't. I'm going on to Oxford in the morning."

He handed her his business card. "Be a love and leave your address. If I find anything else on this Renway, I'll let you know. I'll even drive up to Oxford and hand-deliver it."

As he pulled the torn film back and forth, she wrote the Hamptons' address on the back of his card and tucked it in his shirt pocket. "Here we go," he said. "An obituary on Renway."

She had leaned so close that her cheek was near his. "Andrew, would they have aired it over the telly?"

He picked up the canister and frowned. "American novelist . . . wife of Uriah Kendall, son of Lord and Lady Kendall . . . " He whistled. "Somebody had it ready for the evening news that night, but it was canceled."

"Why would they do that?"

His mood turned harsh. "I told you. Some late-breaking story bumped it, or someone ordered it off the air."

Someone important. She started to say, *Olivia Renway was a good friend of the prime minister.* But what difference did it make? The late-breaking news of a bomb threat had surely swept the report of Olivia's death from the evening news.

Forrestal stood and gathered up the frayed film and canisters. "Chase, why don't you let this business go?"

One of her father's cardinal rules popped into her mind. "You never stop in the middle of a project. If the answers don't come, you back up and start over."

From the look on Andrew Forrestal's face, it was time to

back off. "Andrew, I've taken far too much of your time already."

"That's not the problem," he said. "You knew all along, didn't you? That Renway's husband was with British Intelligence."

She avoided his eyes, not wanting him to know that he had just dropped a bombshell, but he saw her surprise and said, "You didn't know." Without his smile the worry lines cut deep into his face. "Chase, let me give you a bit of advice. In this country an intelligence officer is off-limits."

Chase stuffed her notes into her briefcase and swung the case off the table. She refused to take his warning. "But, Andrew, Olivia Renway and Dorothy Sayers are not off-limits."

⚘⚘⚘

Andrew watched her leave and then turned to face the other occupant in the room. The man was slipping into his trench coat, a perfidious sneer on his narrow face.

Unfriendly sort! Forrestal thought. *Never mind. He paid me a hefty fee for the privilege of being here.*

"Just leave the canisters on the table," Forrestal said, and then he sauntered into the storage room, his thoughts on the girl's Oxford address in his pocket.

He whistled as he spliced the split ends of the microfilm, and still whistling went to the aisle marked 1980-89. Tapping the canister against his open palm, he wondered why this sudden interest in an old hit-and-run? But the dead woman had been the wife of a former British agent. Could Chase be a security risk? He considered his options. The better part of wisdom suggested total silence. Stay out of it. Don't get involved. Don't let the staff know that bribery money burned in his hip pocket.

Or he could call Edwin Wallis over at Scotland Yard and suggest they meet at the local pub for an hour or two. He didn't always see eye to eye with Constable Wallis, but they had exchanged favors in the past. Why not now? If Wallis didn't remember the Renway incident, at least he'd have access to the records. He thumped the canister in his hand again. Even three sheets to the wind, Wallis would laugh in his face. Edwin Wallis had a unique way of cutting you down, making even your slightest suspicion seem like child's play. The first thing the constable would ask would be, "Did you get photos of her, Andy?"

Andy's whistle died, leaving the musty room unbearable. He shrugged and filed the microfilm in the empty slot.

Behind him he heard the squeaking of a shoe. He whirled around half expecting to see the girl again. He saw only the glint of the razor-sharp knife before it broke into his skin and thrust deep into his body. The scream was his own, the agony excruciating. He squinted, trying desperately to focus on the mocking face of his assailant. For a moment he clung to the bookshelf, his fingers chalk-white. As his grip weakened, he slumped to the floor.

The man in the beige trench coat knelt beside him, his fingers deftly searching Andy's pockets until he found the card with Chase Evans's address on it. His eyes were cold, unfeeling as he raised the knife once more and plunged it into Andy's abdomen. As the man fled, Forrestal gasped for air. His thoughts reeled. Blurred images like a strip of exposed film filled his vision. Indistinct silhouettes. Curled celluloid. *This is a homicide. . . . must take pictures for the evening news. . . . Constable Wallis will demand photographs.*

His hand lay limp on his chest, soaked in his own blood. He saw nothing now. Only grayness. Darkness. Utter void. He sensed the deathly silence of the room and felt the faint thump of his own heartbeat. He wanted the girl with the pretty hat to come back. He wanted her to hold his hand.

✿✿✿

Nedrick Russelmann made a quick decision as Chase Evans left the back entry of the television studio. Jiri Benak had not followed her out. It was up to Nedrick to set out after her.

She walked with a brisk, confident step, her narrow hips swaying slightly, that gleaming hair bouncing against her slender neck. Once she reached the embankment and passed the first elegant Victorian bridge, she slowed her pace, strolling leisurely along the tree-lined walkway. Moments later she paused on the footbridge. *Evans will make her contact here,* Ned thought.

But she gazed down at the River Thames like one beholding an old friend and enjoying the visit. Ned had not expected to find her so appealing. She seemed far more sophisticated and worldly wise than Mila, trapped as she was in the simple life in Jarvoc. He waited, but Evans seemed content to simply gaze down on the meandering blue-green river with its tiny whirlpools of polluted gray. Tugboats and tour cruisers drifted with the current; moored ships bobbed along the granite embankment. And then she moved on, those long legs stepping quickly.

Nedrick followed her, pausing briefly where she had stood. No package had been left behind. No chalk markings on the railing. He shrank back when he spotted a police launch patrolling the Thames and turned in time to see Evans bypass a call-box, too distant from it to chalk a message there.

As he reached the far end of the bridge, he kept her in sight, pacing his strides to hers—one moment pushing himself rapidly through the teeming crowd, the next feeling the press of the crowd against his leaden steps. Evans's leather briefcase banged rhythmically against her thigh, forcing Ned to think back to that never-forgotten moment when Olivia Renway had set her briefcase down to autograph a book for him.

He remembered the flicker in Renway's transparent expression when he had given her his name. Her fingers had frozen around the pen. She had recognized the name. He was certain of it. He had meant to hate her when he met her, to despise her for abandoning his father and grandfather. Instead he was stunned by her elegance, by the softness of her mouth and pensive gaze. Hanz Russelmann had loved this woman. Why then had he given the order to destroy her? To murder her! Popshot?

As the rain had come down harder that day, rolling off

Renway's designer clothes, Ned had thrust his black umbrella into her hands. He ached to say, *I'm Nedrick. I'm your grandson.* Instead, he said, "Here, Miss Renway, take my umbrella."

He had not been told that Franz would take the waving of her book as a cue to power-charge the car and hurl the gentler side of Ned's life into eternity. His umbrella had blocked her vision as the car barreled down on her. Ned still remembered the bloody designer clothes, the elegant face twisted in pain. He could still see her mouthing the words, "Why, Nedrick?"

Yes, she had known. Olivia Renway had known.

Later when he came to his senses—when the sheer exhaustion of running left him—he vomited in the gutter. In that moment he despised his grandfather. Renway's murder had taken away a part of Nedrick himself. Ned would never be able to tell Renway who he was, never be able to call her grandmother.

Thinking of it once more as he tracked the American, he wondered whether Jiri had intended for Franz to run *him* down, too, to leave him dead on Downing Street with Renway. Even now he feared that Jiri had no intention of letting him ever reach Jarvoc alive.

Ned had lost sight of Evans. He quickened his pace and finally saw her crossing the street and making her way toward the north side of Whitehall. *She's leading me back to Downing Street.*

Stone barriers blocked the entry into Downing. Chase had joined the queue of people standing behind the barriers, their cameras aimed toward the bobbies on duty at the famous doorway. Nedrick fought the rush of dryness in his mouth, fought the memory of Olivia Renway coming out that door, coming toward him.

"Distract Renway while I grab her briefcase," Jiri had told him. "And if she resists—"

But she hadn't resisted.

The gray Renault with his cousin Franz at the wheel had shattered his grandmother's body on impact. With squealing tires, Franz turned the Renault on a dime, making his own roundabout in the middle of Downing. He had careened wildly up and over the curb and bounced back into the street, the bonnet of the car rattling as he winged his way into the Whitehall traffic and disappeared.

Jiri plans the same fate for you, Ned thought as his eyes settled back on Chase Evans again. She spoke to no one. Touched no one. Passed nothing. If Jiri's prediction came true—if Chase Evans really worked for the CIA—someone would contact her. The attaché case would pass from Chase's hands to another agent's.

The man standing beside Nedrick held a crackling transistor to his ear. He slapped it and listened again. Turning to his companion in the Harris Tweed jacket, he said, "Some bloke just walked into a television studio viewing room and killed a cameraman."

"In broad daylight?"

He shook the crackling radio. "Just happened within the hour. Andrew Forrestal—"

"Forrestal? The one with all those award-winning shots?"

"Maybe one of them got him killed. Sad thing—they never catch up with those blokes."

The tweed coat was more confident. "They might this time. They keep hidden video cameras in those TV viewing rooms."

The sour taste in Nedrick's mouth stung like the bite of a bitter lemon. In front of him, Evans shifted her case to the other hand. For a second Ned thought she was passing it back to the man in the Harris Tweed, but without even noticing him, she set out once more on Whitehall, strolling toward Piccadilly.

If the cameras at the studio had caught Evans and Jiri Benak on film, Ned didn't plan to be found in their company. He struck out toward the Victoria Embankment and the nearest underground station. He'd ride a few stops, then transfer to the East London tube, and go from there to his parked car—Uriah's shiny Rolls Royce.

Nedrick felt sick thinking about the dead cameraman. The Russelmann blood pulsated through his veins, a mixture of disdain and loyalty. There would be no welcome for him in Jarvoc. No, he would take the tunnel under the English Channel and escape along the French coastline, crossing the Pyrenees into Spain where he would gladly settle in Madrid or in one of the fishing villages facing Morocco. His mouth tightened. He would change his name—to Nedrick Kendall perhaps. He knew the language. Someday he would send for Mila, and she would come to him.

But Uriah Kendall's friendship dug at his inmost fiber. He knew that before Madrid—before escaping to any fishing village—he must first head back to the Cotswolds and warn Uriah that Chase Evans was pursuing Olivia's story with deadly consequences.

Chapter 14

Chase left the Ritz too tuckered out to think about the fifty-mile drive to Oxford. As she hit the accelerator, the sun reflected on the Thames, promising a fair day to replace the two gloomy gray days she had spent in London. It was that way back home, too—the weather and the Hudson River always playing games with her.

The Hudson was her river; the Thames belonged to Olivia Renway, and yet for now it was hers as well. The River Thames was London. The city spread out on either side of its banks, no longer the great commercial port but still as much a part of the Londoner as the city's history and ceremony. Beneath one of the bridges, a fishing trawler churned the waters between the rusty piers, cutting its path through the blue-green foam, chugging along toward the next bend in the river.

Outside of London a gusty spring breeze whipped through the open car window; it brushed against her cheek, sweeping her back in time to the windy days of her childhood—to gentle summer days on the beach with the sea breeze blowing in off the ocean. Back to favorite snapshots. A smiling baby, sun-baked on a cloudless day. A happy-go-lucky child, her pretty clothes kite-whipped as she romped around the spacious home on the hilltop. A third grader, housebound by a winter northeasterner, sitting by a dollhouse that was bigger than any owned by her friends. A teenager frantically manning the sails on her father's yacht

when they were caught in an unexpected squall on Long
Island Sound. The Vassar student sometimes acting as mystical as the trade winds off the Atlantic. And the torn picture
of her father coming to find her during last year's bitterly
cold snowstorm that blew in across the Hudson. Chase
wasn't even a quarter of a century old, yet they had been
good years with her needs met by doting parents and her
desires lavishly fulfilled by her grandmother. Chase had
always been the recipient of Callie Bartholomew's favors
with many trips abroad.

The wind brushed her cheek again, taking a tear with it.
Something had happened to the snapshots of her teen
years. Without intending to do so, Chase had taken on some
of Callie's broad views of the world and her cynicism
toward an afterlife. And yet at this moment as Chase drove
along the River Thames—alone in England—the trips that
filled her fondest memories were the family outings with
her dad at the wheel as they followed the course of the
Hudson River. Life had been much richer before her dad
became so engrossed in the corporate world—before a good
public image had become the cardinal rule in the Evans
household.

Even now, in her empty car, she wanted to shout out,
"Daddy, where are we going?"

"Where do you want to go?" he'd ask in his deep bass
voice.

"To the Land of Oz." Surely it was just around the bend
in the Hudson River.

"Pick a place closer," he would say.

"Heaven," she had suggested once innocently.

"Don't know the way."

She admitted to herself that it was not just intellectual
pursuits that drove her these days. She was obsessed with
an unresolved personal search for peace. In the Evans mansion one tiptoed around discussions on finances and faith.
Finances were only discussed in the form of wise investments and faith and prayer only voiced at the grave. Even
her older sister had married in the family garden, and if a
prayer was expressed, Chase couldn't remember it.

Chase was forever stepping to a new drumbeat. In spite of having everything at her fingertips, she never felt satisfied. Something drew her to Renway and Sayers—she felt an emotional tie. Everything she read about Renway suggested restlessness and secrecy. Sayers was another woman out of step with her times, always dancing to her own music—another intellectual who broke with the mores of society as she left her mark on the literary world. Her writings spanned a wide variety of interests from the whimsical Lord Peter Wimsey to the subtle lessons on theology that would have placed Sayers behind a pulpit had she been a man in her own generation. Something had drawn Renway to an in-depth study of Sayers, something more than their degrees from Somerville.

As Chase redefined the purposes of her study program abroad, she smiled ruefully. Maybe she should call her dissertation "The Somerville Connection." Her father would like that one. Or "The Feminine Gender at Oxford." Or if she included Margaret Thatcher, she could call it "Somerville Women in the Political Arena." The political arena? Is that where Sayers and Renway belonged?

She stretched her arm out the car window and tried to cup the wind in her hand. That was as difficult as trying to link Renway and Sayers or please her father. With nostalgia she thought of those happy childhood days with her dad at the wheel calling back to her, "What are you doing, sweetie?"

"Catching the wind."

He had filled the car with his laughter. "Do that and you can do anything."

Nola, sitting close beside him, had said, "Seymour, if she wants to chase the wind, don't laugh at her."

Lately that seemed to be all she was doing—chasing the wind with her choices and rarely pleasing her father. He expected her to take top honors in grad school and to be on the competitive side of sailing and tennis, but her hours at the Halverson House and the Willowglen were an embarrassment to him. He adamantly opposed her friendship with Jeff Carlson, and he still took it as a personal affront that his affluent mother-in-law had chosen to die of cancer in a three-winged nursing home—trapped in diapers and a wheelchair in the very city where he was so well known.

Somehow Seymour Evans the airplane industrialist was not the father she remembered from her childhood, and now she faced displeasing him more. Once she had her degree and claimed her inheritance, she planned to speak out in Washington for people like Jeff Carlson and Marie at the Willowglen. She would have the Bartholomew wealth behind her and two names to flaunt. The Bartholomews of New York had been making inroads on Washington for generations, and the name Evans was not unknown. Her dad often packed a wallop at election time and was rewarded with continual government contracts. Chase didn't want government contracts. She just wanted the politicians in Washington to take up the cause of those who could no longer stand up for themselves. She wouldn't be chasing the wind then—she'd be battling a family blizzard.

Chase shifted gears and took the hill, wishing with unexpected nostalgia that Callie could be with her wending around the mighty Thames. It was from Callie that Chase had discovered the imperfect world that was left to the Bartholomews and the Evans clan to transform. Callie never doubted her own abilities to change the world. Chase had simply taken up her banner.

But the Halverson Wayside House had caused stirrings on Long Island that would have daunted even Callie. In spite of police raids and rock-throwing, loudspeakers and marches and legal maneuvering, the town's outcry against AIDS and those infected with it had been defeated. The Halverson House sat on a privately owned hill, surrounded not by gates but by well-trimmed hedges. When it came to a council debate, little could be done. The owner called the dying residents "guests in his home." The defeat in the city council infuriated Chase's father, which was reason enough for Chase to take up the rights of the residents there.

On her first visit to the Halverson House, she had arrived with only a vague plan of what she would do when someone opened the door. She was still knocking when a gaunt-faced young man peered around the partly cracked door, his dark eyes recessed and hollow. He appeared so weak that she expected him to fall forward and topple into her arms.

"Yes, ma'am?" he said in a voice without joy.

"I came to visit someone," she told him.

He opened the door farther and allowed her to step into the massive foyer. She realized then that he was barefoot, his skin as white as the painted walls behind him. "Are you a relative?"

"The truth is, I don't know anyone here. I just came—"

The hunched shoulders squared. "You from the city council?"

"No."

"You're not some reporter?"

"No, I came as a friend." She held up a book of Robert Service's poems. "Could I read to someone? Or just sit and visit?"

His eyes seemed even more sunken now, uncertain. "It's not very pleasant around here."

Down the hall she heard guitar music and a soft melancholy voice crooning a country song. "There's music," she said.

"We try to cheer each other up."

She glanced past him down the long hallway.

"Maybe you'd like to see Jeff. He ain't got no family. At least no one who comes regularly."

"And you?"

He looked at her now as he mumbled, "These guys are all the family I have now."

"Then perhaps I can visit you next time?"

"You'd come back here? We don't usually get much company."

"Where do I find Jeff?"

"He's at the end of the hall near the kitchen." He stepped back so she could pass him. "We made up a room for him on the first floor. He's too sick to climb the stairs."

"When I come back the next time, where will I find you?"

"Just ask for Mitch. I ain't planning on going nowhere."

"I'll see you later. I'll go read to Jeff now."

"You won't be afraid of him?"

She already felt creepy. "Of course not."

"He's really sick," Mitch called as she went down the hall.

At Jeff's door she panicked. Maybe she should have worn a space suit and a mask, and then she saw Jeff lying like a corpse against the sheets, struggling and gasping for each breath.

"Hi, Jeff," she said

He tried to focus on her. His eyes were an eggshell gray, his body emaciated, his long, thin fingers ghostly white. A silver earring hung from the lobe of his ear. He tried to move his lips, but they were too dry and cracked to speak.

"I'm Chase Evans," she said softly. "I came to visit you."

Before he could protest, she had crossed the room and pulled a wicker chair to his bedside. "I'm just going to sit here for a little while. If you need something—"

He lifted a limp hand and pointed to his lips.

"You're thirsty?"

He nodded.

She turned to the door and was relieved to see a nurse entering the room with a glass of ice chips. She smiled reassuringly. "Mitch told me you had a guest, Jeff. How nice. I'll leave you two alone."

The last thing Chase had wanted was to be left alone with this dying twenty-year-old. She forced herself to stay. He coughed fitfully as she rolled up his bed, but he urged her with those lifeless hands to roll him higher. Before she realized it, she was leaning against his bed reading Robert Service poems to him and spooning ice chips between those cracked lips. An hour later when she left him, he pled, "Come back again."

"I will."

She did, but not before she spent hours in the library poring over *The New England Journal of Medicine* and all the current information she could find. She wanted nothing more than a cure that would salvage Mitch and Jeff. She wasn't even afraid that second time when she knocked on the door. She had a smile ready for Mitch, but a nurse in uniform opened the door.

"Oh," she said happily. "Miss Evans, isn't it? Jeff kept hoping you'd come back."

"Where's Mitch?"

The smile of welcome clouded. "He's gone."

"He went home?"

"He's dead."

When Chase reached Jeff's room, he was holding his own glass of ice chips. Seeing her face, he said, "I didn't think Mitch would go first. He wanted to get well and go home to his family."

"What about you, Jeff? Don't you have a family?"

"My brother Kelly, but he doesn't come by here anymore."

Now Jeff was an ocean away, on the other side of the world, dead perhaps. He had cried when she left him. "Send me a picture of the Thames," he had said, "to remember you by."

As she gripped the steering wheel, she gazed off to her right where the River Thames surged with a sudden burst of energy, going from what had been a quiet stream to a rushing river. The whole fifty miles she had allowed herself to think about her childhood, her father, Halverson House— anything but Downing Street. The conclusions she had reached yesterday were too horrid to contemplate, but as she reached the Hamptons' house in Oxford, she faced them again.

Olivia Renway's last five novels had moved away from the familiar World War II settings to the threat of terrorism and chemical warfare in Asia. Chase tried to put the broken pieces together—Renway's friendship with the prime minister and the bomb threat against number 10 Downing as Olivia lay dying. Had the driver in a rented Renault been part of the Czechoslovakian terrorist group? Had news on the terrorists pushed the report of Olivia's death to the back pages of the newspaper? Chase could no longer think of Renway's death as a simple hit-and-run. *Someone had wanted Olivia Renway dead. But why?*

Jiri Benak and Pavel Van Rindin left the Ritz in London a few minutes ahead of Chase Evans. When they reached the car, Pavel peered at Jiri through his tinted silver-rimmed glasses. "I thought you were sending Franz to the Cotswolds with me."

"I sent him back to Prague. I couldn't risk him staying on, not after Heathrow security detained him for twenty-four hours."

Pavel ran a finger through his mustache. "I don't like going to Kendallshire alone," he said. "Not with all the rumors about a bombing in the Cotswolds."

"What rumors?"

"Turn on the telly. Or your car radio."

"Why would anyone broadcast our arrival? We're not the IRA with a fifteen- or sixty-minute warning before a bomb goes off."

"The news media refers to us as a Czech splinter group."

"They've narrowed it down to that? They're winging it."

"Are they, Jiri? Or is Altman wiping his hands of us both?"

Pavel's resentments against Jiri and the Russelmann family went deep. At twenty-nine he had been browbeaten and badgered too long, robbed of any leadership in the Jarvoc steel plant. He was a moody man like his brother Franz, not much for talking, but far more intelligent, quick with his mind. A real computer genius. But lately he had been given to bouts of depression with frequent glances back over his shoulder and long solitary walks in the woods behind the farm. And now this—total paranoia.

Pavel, Jiri decided, *was expendable, as Renway had been.*

"Come on, Charlie. I can join you in a day or two—"

"Cut the Charlie blather. You know my name. Use it. But I'm telling you the truth. They're publicizing bomb threats against the Cotswolds."

"They?" Jiri scoffed.

Pavel seemed near the breaking point. Jiri put a firm hand on the man's shoulder. "Nedrick is the only one who would leak information like that."

Or maybe Hanz was switching loyalties to protect the Kendalls. Or had Franz resented being shipped back to Prague?

"Just take it easy, Pavel. All you have to worry about right now is to find us a place to stay in Kendallshire. Then observe Uriah Kendall. We can wire a firebomb when I get there."

"We?" Pavel's laugh rang shrilly. "You don't plan to test the chemical compounds this time?"

Jiri toed the compact computer at Pavel's feet. "You concentrate on the remote control I will need to set off the bomb by the click of the computer keys. We'll be out of Kendallshire before they even know we've been there."

"I want no part of political terrorism, Jiri. No part of killing more innocent people."

Jiri laughed raucously. "What do you call the family business but political participation? The steel plant is nothing but a front for exporting weapons and nerve gas components to the highest bidders."

"Our company stays clean. Nishokura handles the sales to terrorists abroad."

"That is international involvement. If we were investigated, they could trace our sales through Nishokura back twenty years. That takes in a lot of terrorist activity."

"You're behind this. You and those fancy architectural drawings of yours, Jiri. Designing weapons of destruction. Uncle Altman still thinks you're the wonder boy architect. You have them all fooled."

Jiri had grown up reading blueprints and studying design in the family architectural shop in Germany. He took pride in knowing that his grandfather had been one of the architects of the Nazi extermination camps. "Don't mock it, Charlie. The skills I learned in the family shop have paid great dividends. Yes, they have served me well in Jarvoc."

"And in the end you'll take over the compound. That will be our thanks for taking you in. I've watched you, Jiri, slipping in and out of the old waste plant. I know what we store there."

There was a noticeable shrug of Pavel's shoulders. "As long as that building is left standing, the people of Jarvoc will hate us. Maybe someday my family will wake up and get rid of you before you destroy all of us."

"Not likely, Charlie." *They might want to put you to rest,* he thought, *but I'm too important to them.*

Twelve years ago when the Russelmanns ordered the vast reconstruction of the steel compound, Jiri had been invited to design it. Altman had insisted that one building by the railroad tracks not be torn down. He wanted it left standing as a gruesome reminder to the people of Jarvoc that the Russelmanns were in control of the town. And while Jiri was drawing up the blueprints for the new plant, he discovered the layout of the old labor camp.

He had been amazed. Extermination camps had existed in Poland and Germany. But in Jarvoc? Now Jiri knew the tunnels and storerooms better than Altman did—and he knew how to use every chemical stockpiled there. Jiri was a patient man. One day he would own the company and dispose of those who stood in his way.

He slipped into the driver's seat of his car. "Pavel, your orders are to go to Kendallshire. Mine—to follow the girl."

As Pavel sauntered away, defiance in his every step, Jiri wondered if he would ever reach the Cotswolds. Or would Pavel run back to Jarvoc, back to the farm?

By the time Chase came out of the Ritz Hotel and started on her trip to Oxford, Jiri's stomach burned like fire. He tensed at the sight of her, and more acid poured into his stomach. She came gracefully in her sling-back pumps, the quick bounce to her step giving no hint of caution. He found her alluring in her tailored blazer and sheer skirt. She eased into the car rental, smiled up at the doorman, and with a quick wave drove off.

Jiri followed the American at some distance, surprised at her reckless abandon as she reached the motorway. She held the car steady, but she drove like a Londoner. Twice she risked passing on the hill, and Jiri was certain she would hit head-on when she crested the top.

As he followed her through the peaceful English countryside, he drove with one hand; the other hung limply on his bony knee. At times he could picture himself taking up residence in one of the thatched cottages with sheep grazing on the hillsides—far away from the smoke-rimmed sky at Jarvoc. Considering it now, he attributed his fondness for the English countryside to the lay of the land, its intricate design and structure; its fabric and color appealed to him. Someday, when he owned the Russelmann Steel Mill, perhaps he would take a summer cottage in the Cotswolds. The cottage would be fresh and airy, the roof thatched, the grounds private. He would hire a gardener and plant a high hedge that would isolate him from his neighbors.

As they reached a bleak stretch of land, his thoughts strayed back to the dark gray storage plant at Jarvoc. It had taken him months to discover the secrets of the old plant and even longer to locate the blueprints. They were stowed in the corner in the back room as though the architect, the designer of death, had stepped from the room and would be back to complete the detailed drawings. Jiri had brushed the lacy strand of cobwebs away, unrolled the yellow sheets, and stared down at the structural drawings for an extermination camp. His grandfather's scrawled initials were still visible in the corner.

At first Jiri had felt repulsed, then later proud. It had taken a brilliant mind to contrive such an elaborate plan in the closing months of a war. It was all there. The deposits of coal. The water supply. The railroad track. Barracks designed to house hundreds of prisoners. A ventilation system had been built into the walls. Stairs—crumbled now—led directly from the train into the building. He found cracked tins that had once contained the pellets of hydrogen cyanide. Other containers—with part of the labels still on them—had once held gas crystals. And then he discovered the underground tunnel with shelves of modern containers filled with toxic components. Jiri had not one doubt that Altman Russelmann had plans to sell these to the highest bidder. Or did the plans belong to Hanz Russelmann?

The doors in the plant were airtight, the peepholes once used by the S.S. guards still there. Some of the pipes had rusted over the years, but Jiri had replaced the ducts leading into the sealed shower rooms and the old underground morgue. He planned it carefully. It would be a simple matter to remove his competition. Altman Russelmann and

Gustav Van Rindin made frequent inspections of all the buildings. When the time was ripe, Jiri would fill the ducts with gas crystals, seal Altman and Gustav in the shower room, and gas them to death in the old crematorium.

Bored, he switched on the car radio and twirled the dial. Rock music bombarded him. He liked classical—a Wagner overture or the Hungarian Rhapsody #9, music that for all of its triumphant notes had a peaceful quality to it. He rode with the windows open, chewing on his thin cigar, his brooding suddenly startled by the news commentator. "We interrupt this program . . . Yesterday's tragic slaying of Andrew Forrestal, one of London's noted photographers . . . dead at thirty-four . . . murdered in his own studio . . . Scotland Yard released the following composites."

Accurate descriptions of Chase Evans and himself followed. He had forgotten the hidden video cameras. Pulling off the motorway at the first exit, he drove to a wooded area and parked. He folded his trench coat with precision and placed it in the boot of his car along with his Gucci tie. He substituted the sweater emblazoned with "OXFORD UNIVERSITY," bought for just such an occasion.

Taking Forrestal's business card from his pocket, he memorized the girl's Oxford address and then set it ablaze with his lighter. With the ashes still warm, he knelt and replaced the license plates on the rental car with ones from his suitcase. Back in the car, he inspected himself in the mirror. The cigar had to go. He tossed it on the gravel.

Within minutes he was back on the motorway keeping his speed within the limits. If a police officer stopped him, he would tell him that he had spent the last week at Gainsborough's steel mill. Jon Gainsborough would vouch for him. Jon was cooperative that way. After all, he wanted to continue to do business with the Russelmanns.

In the distance Jiri saw a car cresting a steep hill on the wrong side of the street. Impossible. But, no, he had caught up with the crazy American.

Chapter 15

Chase parked on a side road kitty-cornered from the Hamptons' narrow street. The Hamptons' centuries-old home was brownstone in color, with a gabled roof and dormer windows, one of four units converted from what was surely a monastic building. It was brightened by flower tubs along the front filled with tulips and pink and white geraniums. She felt both disappointment and intrigue. Having no breathing space or lawn between your lodging and the neighbors' reminded her of the crowded tenements in Manhattan; yet the whole setting here was pastoral and peaceful.

In New York it would be blaring car horns, shifting gears, and angry drivers cursing. Here the squeal of bicycles and perambulators and a car or two broke the stillness. Here it was spired cathedrals in the distance; at home skyscrapers jutted into the skyline. In New York—in the city that she loved even more than Paris—the air was often polluted with smoke and bus fumes. Here on a wide patch of meadow, the air was fresh and clean.

Chase realized that the man in the gray Renault had driven by twice already. She caught a glimpse of light hair, dark sunshades, a university sweater. Perhaps she had claimed his parking space, but an unsettling thought pushed its way into her peaceful musings. The man was following her. She moved quickly and emptied the boot of her car before he could circle the block once more. She trolleyed her pullman and balanced her carry-on with her other hand. The gray Renault whisked by her again as she reached the curb on the Hamptons' side of the street.

Close up, the house seemed smaller. Where would they find room for her? She formed an unwanted picture in her mind of a worn sofa in the tiny living room and her suitcases stacked in the corner. There was no porch, no protection from rain.

The door swung open before she could knock. "Here," said a cheerful voice, "let me give you a hand with your things."

Chase recognized the boyish, lopsided grin. "Oh, no."

"Oh, yes. Peter Quincy. Remember?"

"You were at Heathrow."

"To meet you. I was supposed to show you around London."

"But you didn't say."

"You didn't give me a chance."

He gave her a mocking bow as she stepped from the stone-flagged walkway into the house. Peter was striking and robust, small of build, five-nine if he toed it. His dark tweed jacket was well cut, his shoes well shined. His lips twisted in a funny little way as though he were holding back a chuckle. Peter's hair was an oxblood brown, and those intelligent eyes must surely belong to one of Oxford's best and brightest.

"I'm embarrassed," she said.

"Don't be. Now let me take your luggage."

She glanced behind him. "Aren't the Hamptons in?"

"Dr. Hampton is with a guest. I volunteered to wait over and show you to your room."

And have a good laugh at my expense, I'll bet. "And Mrs. Hampton?"

"She's always late getting in from the Eagle's Nest."

"And you, Peter? Are you on a scholarship?"

"Yes. I plan to live at number 10 Downing Street someday, so I'm staying on—thanks to Dr. Hampton—for postgraduate studies."

"What did you do—take first honors in science?"

He smiled, not denying it, and picked up her luggage for the second time. "Let me run these up to your room. It's the first door on the left."

"Peter."

He paused halfway up, banging the cases against the rail.

"I'm sorry about the airport. I didn't know who you were."

"And you weren't taking any chances?"

"Not when my cabby told me someone was following us."

His eyes twinkled. "You'll have time here at Oxford to make it up to me. I'm your tutor for the summer."

"My tutor!" she exclaimed. Embarrassed again, she lowered her voice and said, "But Doc Hampton promised to help me."

"He'll meet with you weekly, but I'll arrange for your library privileges and any lecture classes you want to attend."

As he disappeared at the top of the stairs, she sighed. *If only you were Luke Breckenridge.*

❂❂❂

Nigel Hampton swept into his private study with his long black gown snapping at his ankles and was pleasantly surprised to see Constable Wallis standing with his back to the window.

"Edwin!"

Edwin Wallis had been a student at the college fifteen years ago, a studious young man who took his degree at his father's old school. But at the end of the first year, he had come to Hampton saying, "My goal is Scotland Yard, not the House of Commons."

"Your father will be disappointed," Nigel had told him.

"My father followed his own career."

Wallis had to be forty now, looking older with that receding hairline and those ugly thick-rimmed glasses. He came forward at once and shook Nigel's hand in a familiar bull-like grip.

"This is a surprise," Nigel said. "But a pleasant one."

"I'm here on business."

"I gathered as much." He pointed to a chair, and they took seats facing each other.

"How did your run go in America?" Edwin asked.

"It was a good school year."

"But Mrs. Hampton didn't go with you?"

My wife is not the business at hand, he thought. She had wanted no part of his sabbatical in New York. Her world revolved around the Eagle's Nest. They had parted for the school term with an ocean between them, an unhappy arrangement for Nigel, a satisfactory one for his wife.

As Wallis clasped his broad hands behind him, Nigel said, "My wife could not get away for a whole year."

"Not even for Christmas?"

So he knew that Margot had remained in England, refusing to ruin her holiday traditions with a trip to America. "We agreed it would be best. Christmas is a lonely time at the Eagle's Nest. Without Margot, there would be no tree or presents."

He didn't add that Margot would never go anywhere as long as Beatrice Thorpe was alive. "Edwin, I hear good things about you. Your recent promotions. Your success at the Yard."

"Fortunately you don't hear about my unsolved cases."

"Sometimes," Nigel said, smiling. "So what brings you here?"

"One of your students. An American, I believe."

He's going to ask me about Chase Evans. As he crossed and uncrossed his legs, they felt like lead. "Edwin, you know the boys get a bit rowdy during Eights Week."

"I wasn't referring to the boat race."

"But our boys were 'Head of the River' again this year."

"So Peter Quincy told me when I arrived."

"He was in the winning boat. A strong rower. Fiercely competitive, as you were, Edwin."

Edwin removed his glasses and placed a stem in his mouth. Now Nigel could see the dark circles under his eyes, the weariness in his face. "You're looking tired, Edwin."

"We've been up most of the night working on a case—"

"Long term?"

"No, a homicide in London yesterday." He took a black-and-white from an envelope and handed it to Hampton. "Is this the American student who is staying with you?"

"Chase Evans. She's a grad student from Columbia."

"In New York. We already know that. Comes from quite an influential family. Why this student, Nigel? There's no place for a woman in your all-male college."

"She was in my department at Columbia. I agreed to be her mentor this summer. That picture of her—where did it come from?"

"It was taken on a video camera at the television studio. I had them blow it up for me."

"Come on, Edwin. No jokes between us."

"There's been a homicide at the television studio. We need to ask Miss Evans a few questions."

"That's disgusting, Wallis. Evans is a fine young woman."

"Is she here?"

He considered denying it, but for the last several minutes he had heard voices in the sitting room. "Let me introduce her to you, Edwin. Perhaps you can get this mess straightened out."

As they entered the room, Peter stood up, and Chase glanced their way. "I'm here," she said cheerily, tumbling out of her chair. "Drove all the way on the wrong side of the road and didn't even get a dent in my fender."

Nigel's facial muscles felt too tight to smile.

"I didn't come at the wrong time, did I, Prof?"

Still unsmiling, he said, "This is Constable Wallis from Scotland Yard. He wants to ask you a few questions."

"Oh, dear. Is something wrong?" She smiled up at Edwin and extended her hand. Edwin wrapped his burly one around it.

Quietly, patiently he said, "You were at the television studio with Andrew Forrestal yesterday, weren't you?"

"Yes, for a couple of hours."

"Had you known him long?"

Nigel marveled at her unflushed cheeks. With utter calm

she said, "We just met yesterday and—well, he offered to help me."

"How?" Edwin asked without letting her hand go.

"He had some microfilm that he thought would be of particular interest to me. He's not in trouble, is he?"

"For helping you?"

"Well, I did pay him." She wrenched her hand from his grip. "I was driving here today and, well—I wanted to find out everything I could about a novelist named Olivia Renway while I was still in London."

Wallis's bushy brows arched above his thick-rimmed glasses. Watching him, Hampton's concern grew. "Chase is doing her doctoral dissertation on Renway," he explained.

Edwin's intimidating gaze never left her face. "Were you alone at the studio with Mr. Forrestal?" he asked.

"No. There was one other employee there—a rather surly looking man. We didn't speak."

"This man?" he asked, extending a black-and-white.

The picture was blurry. "Yes, I think that's him."

"He wasn't an employee—that's been confirmed."

"Who then, sir?"

"Chase," Hampton said, "why don't you sit down?"

She shrugged off his offer. "I don't need to sit down. What's going on, Constable?"

"Mr. Forrestal is dead," he said.

Hampton saw the involuntary shudder of her shoulders as Peter lunged toward Chase. Her face had turned ghost-like, the luster in her eyes wiped clean.

"It's all right, Peter," she said. "I'm okay."

It took her only seconds to meet Constable Wallis's accusing gaze. "What happened? Andrew was fine when I left him."

"He was murdered," Edwin said calmly.

Peter kept his steadying hand on her elbow. She stared at the photograph again. Only the tremor in her voice gave her away as she said, "You mean—"

"We don't know, Miss Evans. Perhaps if you would accompany me back to London, we could get this straightened—"

Nigel flashed a warning glance at Peter. If Edwin had anything definite on Chase, he would have sent his underlings. No, he had come himself, counting on his old friendship with his professor. Hampton had no intention of letting this happen. It was more than protecting Chase Evans. Nigel couldn't risk upsetting his wife. He said, "On what charge, Edwin?"

"I'll be responsible for her."

Nigel held his ground. "No, Edwin, she's my responsibility. A guest in my home. She's safer here than in London."

Edwin dropped the photograph back in the envelope. "Can you tell us anything more about this man, Miss Evans?"

"You have his picture. What else can I tell you?"

"The sound of his voice. His height—"

She hedged. "I didn't pay that much attention. He was sitting the whole time with his back to us. We didn't speak."

Chase's fears seemed well controlled now. She seemed to sense Peter's support and Nigel's concern. She turned back to the constable. "The man had light hair—like a Scandinavian. And he was well dressed, but you could see that in the picture, Constable." She looked up at Nigel, her confidence wavering. "He'd have no way of knowing my name or whereabouts."

She knows something, Hampton thought, *but she's not going to tell Edwin. She doesn't trust him.*

Hampton remembered Edwin's granite expression back in his student days. He was more intense now, his quiet voice more overbearing than if he had shouted. His eyes hardened as he looked down at Chase and asked, "Did Mr. Forrestal know you were coming to Oxford?"

She shot an apologetic glance toward Hampton. "I'm afraid I gave him this address. Andrew promised to get in touch with me if he learned anything more about Olivia Renway."

Not a muscle twitched in Edwin's face. "Nigel, we'll want to keep in touch with Miss Evans. If we have any more questions—"

"She will be here with us." *Thank God, she will be safe with us.* "Chase, why don't you go and freshen up for dinner. My wife will be home soon."

They watched her go in silence. As she reached the top of the stairs, Nigel faced his former student again. "Was it necessary to tell her what happened?"

"That's my job. She may well have been the last one to see Forrestal alive. She was there, Hampton, as much a suspect as the man she describes. Surely you understand that." He tucked the envelope under his arm. "There was no address on Forrestal's body. Nothing in his pockets or his wallet."

"Evans wouldn't lie to you."

"I don't suppose she would, if she's innocent. But it appears that our chief suspect has Miss Evans's name and address."

Nigel heard his wife's car arriving. "I'd rather not alarm Margot," he said.

"Of course."

"Thank you for coming, Edwin."

"I wish it could have been under more pleasant circumstances. But we'll keep in touch. If Miss Evans remembers anything, you will call—"

"You know that I will."

He walked Edwin to the door and kissed his wife on the cheek as she stepped from her car. It was too late to ask Edwin about Olivia Renway, but Hampton had seen Edwin's eyes brighten at her name. Margot was right. Nigel had been unwise in bringing the girl here.

🪷🪷🪷

As the Hamptons saw Constable Wallis off, Chase crept back down the stairs again. Peter Quincy smiled up at her and caught her hand as she reached the last steps.

"You've been crying," he said.

"Yes—a little. Is the constable gone?" she asked.

"Just. Are you all right?"

"I feel awful about Andrew Forrestal."

"Try not to think about him."

"But—he's dead, Peter."

"I'm sorry—sorry you're involved."

"Peter, I'm not involved. At least I don't think I am."

He released her hand. "I was watching you. You know something about the man at the television studio."

"He may have followed me to Oxford."

Peter urged her to sit down. "Why didn't you tell the constable?"

"I didn't like him, and I didn't want to alarm Doc Hampton."

He patted her wrist. "It's all right, Chase. I'll keep your secret. You'll be safe here. I'll see to it. In a day or so you will forget all about Forrestal. And you'll think that Hampton knows half the academia in Oxford." Peter's voice filled with admiration. "He counts several of the proctors and the vice-chancellor as best friends. He lectures with some, drinks beer in the pubs with others."

"He sounds like C. S. Lewis."

"He has a brilliant mind."

"And you're his prodigy?"

He frowned. "So was Constable Wallis fifteen years ago."

"So that's how the constable tracked me down."

"He would have found you anyway." His smile seemed infinitely patient. "Chase, I'll be by in the morning. Can you bicycle?"

"Yes, but I've rented a car."

"There's enough of a traffic jam in town with all the bicycles and perambulators. Mrs. Hampton will lend you her cycle."

"Are you supposed to go everywhere with me?"

There was no embarrassment as she met his gaze. "You'll find having a tutor isn't such a bad thing. Like I said, I'll arrange your library time and show you how to use our facilities."

"I don't need a tutor."

"That's the way we do it here, Chase. We have to get on this summer. I want that and Dr. Hampton definitely does."

Out on the walkway she heard the Hamptons' voices, low and heated. Then their words were muted by the tolling of a cathedral chime. "What's that?" Chase asked.

Peter glanced at his watch. "The bell at Christ's Church. It tolls 101 strokes a night."

"Have you ever counted them?"

"No, but let's do that some evening."

"Won't you have gate hours?"

"A few of the undergraduates still do, but that's a thing of the past for me."

Peter Quincy didn't match up to Luke Breckenridge, but he did know Oxford. "Then why don't we? I think that's the church Olivia Renway mentioned in her novels. She spent a great amount of time there."

"I'll take you there for evensong."

"Oh, but I should go with the Hamptons."

His mouth puckered again with the hint of a smile. "You'll know soon enough. The Hamptons rarely go to chapel anymore—only when Nigel's position obligates him—and even then his wife rarely goes with him."

He picked up his books, silent for a moment. "The college where Dr. Hampton teaches is all-male. It will be a bit unusual having a girl on hand."

"Me?"

The front door had cracked an inch or two, too wide to shut out the Hamptons' angry voices.

"I want the truth, Nigel. What was Constable Wallis doing here?"

"Edwin was one of my students."

"We're talking about now. How can a visit from Scotland Yard be a friendly one?"

"It wasn't. He came to see Chase Evans."

"Is she in trouble?"

"I hope not," he said. "But she knew Andrew Forrestal."

They heard Margot Hampton's quick gasp before she said, "The London photographer? He's dead, isn't he?"

"Murdered."

"Oh, Nigel, you should never have brought her here."

"I know," he said sadly. "I just thought it was for the best. I did it for you, Margot."

For a moment Chase was too stunned to move. Peter

shifted his books and touched her arm. "I'm sorry you heard that."

"No wonder you're not very happy being my tutor. I'm the unwanted guest."

"Things will work out, Chase. Hampton will see to it."

"He invited me—"

"But I'm not sure his wife did. They don't always agree on everything."

۞۞۞

Constable Wallis sat on the backseat of the unmarked police car drumming his fingers on his knock-knees as his driver merged with the motorway traffic. The attractive American, upright and quick with her answers, had irritated him. Even more he resented his old professor's defense of the girl. If it had not been for Hampton, Wallis would have insisted on the girl accompanying him back to Scotland Yard for questioning—not on the Andrew Forrestal murder but on her relationship with Hampton and her curious search into the life of Olivia Renway.

Edwin tried to put his drumming fingers on the missing elements. Nothing came together. In that brief encounter, he had seen that Chase Evans was clearly right-handed. It had been a left-handed thrust of the knife that had claimed Forrestal's life. Evans was tall and athletic, but she would not have been strong enough for the violence at the television studio.

What had brought them together—the American student, the London photographer, and Wallis's old professor? Renway linked them. Forrestal died because he had befriended the American. Edwin felt certain of it. Edwin struggled against his respect for Hampton, knowing that nothing would stop him from finding answers even if it led back to a scandal at Oxford.

He picked up the cellular phone. He rarely shared information with MI5—was rarely invited to do so—but with jerking motions he dialed Dudley Perkins's emergency line.

Chapter 16

Dudley Perkins sat alone in his drab office, his gangly hands folded on the plain, uncluttered desk. He pressed his spine against the hard-back chair and stared down at the emergency phone as though it were a coiled snake. Edwin Wallis's call had annoyed him. The death of the television cameraman was Scotland Yard's responsibility and not within Dudley's jurisdiction. He didn't even care about the possible link between Andrew Forrestal and Uriah Kendall. Dudley already knew that Kendall had reached his cottage in the Cotswolds. If the American student made contact with Uriah, Dudley would be the first to know it.

He had enough on his mind with the intelligence report on his desk marked top secret. Czech terrorists had threatened to set off a bomb in the Cotswolds—not in London. If the threat had been against the coal mines to the north or the steel factories outside of Oxford, he would have understood, but an idyllic village in the Cotswolds seemed preposterous.

He couldn't push it aside as some mental incompetent's prank. It had been too specific: west of Oxford, south of Cheltenham, north of Chipping Sodbury. A devilish plan with someone mocking from the sidelines. Dudley had pored over the map, his focus mostly on Gloucestershire with tourists at every turn. MI5 couldn't detain everyone for questioning nor even send out warnings with so many Cotswold villages to alert.

Dudley had run his knuckled finger over Kendallshire until the map was almost worn thin. He believed the isolated village of Kendallshire was the real target and found himself wishing that the terrorist's bomb would blow the graveyard apart, scattering Olivia Renway's ashes over the countryside. Or better yet, he wished the Czech splinter group would obliterate Uriah Kendall and his cottage. He flexed his long fingers over the report, hating himself for his lingering bitterness.

The chair squeaked as he turned and placed the folder in the file cabinet. Slamming the drawer shut, he secured the lock and swore silently. He would have destroyed Uriah Kendall many times, but he had failed. Failed miserably. Involuntarily he reached for his wallet. From behind the credit cards he pulled out the faded snapshot of Olivia Renway and laid it on the desk in front of him. A candid shot—he had caught her unawares. She had turned and blinked those velvet lashes, surprise in her eyes.

Dudley touched the tattered edges. "You were so beguiling."

From the pages of his past he remembered his first visit to Uriah's village. Yes, it was Uriah's village, founded by the Kendalls. A Kendall had always been Lord of the Manor, a position handed down from generation to generation. Dudley had never known such power, not until he fought his way to the top at MI5.

Long before the death of his son Joel in the Falklands— long before Molly had come into his life—Dudley had taken Olivia to Kendallshire with him. Beautiful, bewitching temptress. When they arrived, she insisted on going to a cottage on her own—leaving him infuriated, jealous of her every move, blinded to her past.

An hour later he went looking for her—ready to apologize, prepared to ask her to reconsider sharing his room. He found her on the stone bridge that spanned the river. She stood there talking to Uriah Kendall, her russet hair blowing across her cheek. Sheep grazed contentedly on the meadows behind them. With the hillsides ablaze with spring flowers, his colleague—his fellow officer at MI5—stole his girl. Moments later they walked away, not even noticing Dudley's presence.

After that Dudley dug into her past and with infinite patience built a case against her, convincing his superiors that Kendall bore watching. The resulting scandal cost Uriah his career with MI5. But it was true. Everything Dudley uncovered was true. Olivia Renway had been a spy.

Four months later—the day after Uriah became engaged to Olivia—Dudley did the next best thing. He married Molly—the rich, unglamorous daughter of Lord Gilmore, who threatened to disinherit his daughter if she went through with the wedding.

The door to Dudley's office opened quietly.

He looked up, drawn back to the present as his wife entered the colorless room. Molly was dressed to the nines, her homely face turning almost pretty as she smiled at him. She brought the sweet scent of her perfume with her as she crossed the room and stood behind him. He felt her warm lips on his thinning hair as she slipped her arms around his neck, her gloved hands resting on his chest. It was too late. Olivia Renway's ragged snapshot stared up at them. He glanced over his shoulder and saw the pain in Molly's deep blue eyes.

"You should have called before you came," he said.

"I did. You wouldn't take my calls."

"I've been busy."

"Too busy to come home? You haven't been there for three nights. It's lonely without you."

"We've been working long hours, Molly."

Her arms still rested around his neck as she leaned forward and studied the picture. "Olivia Renway, isn't it?"

"Yes. Uriah Kendall's wife."

"She's lovely," Molly said. "Did you love her, Dudley?"

"I thought I did."

"Why don't you let her go?"

"I thought I had."

Her cheek brushed against his, the fragrance of her perfume sensuous, overpowering. "You haven't shaved," she said.

"I had a business call from Scotland Yard. Give me a few moments to clean up, and then we can have lunch together."

"There isn't time. I'm going away, Dudley."

He took her hand and pulled her around to face him. "That's good. You need a holiday."

"It's more than that. . . . I'm leaving you." She leaned against the edge of his desk, her long-lashed eyes still on the snapshot. "I think you knew it was coming."

No, he hadn't even guessed. Molly was always there for him—defending him, supporting him, loving him. She was his rock, his mainstay. All through those bitter months after their son's death, no matter how grave the situation, Molly stood by him.

"Don't leave me, Molly. You've always been there for me. I would never have made it through Joel's death without you."

"We needed each other then," she said.

Dudley went cold inside. "I need you now."

"Do you? You've changed, Dudley, ever since Sulzbach—ever since that Russian agent's death."

"Marta Zubkov was nothing to me. You know that."

She ran her fingers over Renway's picture. "But Olivia was."

"That was a long time ago."

"I don't think she is ever very far from your thoughts. I've watched it destroy you. First it was Uriah Kendall's career. And then his grandson. Ian is only a young man. To threaten him with his grandmother's reputation—"

"Olivia Renway betrayed this country."

"Or did she betray you? Sometimes, my darling, I think you would have destroyed Joel, too, if he had lived long enough."

She straightened, tall and elegant, the silver of her hair and the blue of her eyes picking up the colors in her dress.

"Where will you go?" he asked.

"Paris for a while. Then to the Von Tonner Art Museum.

Friends at the Tate Gallery made certain I was invited. We both were," she said sadly.

It's always been both of us. How can she leave—go her separate way? He wanted Molly to urge him to go, but it would be a month or two before he could get away. "You'll have a good time."

"Yes, it'll be grand," she said, her voice melancholy. "They're opening the ballroom again, but it won't be the same without Ingrid von Tonner there."

"She was charming."

"And devious. Do you think I am devious, Dudley?"

Listen to us, he thought. *Empty, inane words, as though talking could hold us together.*

"But there's a nice young couple—the Courtlands. They're the ones opening the museum."

Drew Gregory's daughter and son-in-law. Then the Gregorys would be there. Suddenly it was important that Molly look more sensational than Drew's wife. "Buy yourself something to wear."

"I did. Yesterday. It's a Valentino evening dress." Her eyes brightened describing it. "Shoestring shoulder straps and a lovely ruffle on the bottom."

The Valentino label meant nine thousand pounds or more of Lord Gilmore's money. "You'll look lovely in it," he said. "Molly, will you come back to me after that?"

She reached out and touched his cheek. "I've made plans to stay with friends on a Greek island. I need time away from you."

"The last three days weren't enough?"

"You'll be all right, once you let go of Olivia Renway."

His pride was at stake, his bitter memories digging at him. He wanted to yank open the file drawer and shove the Renway folder into her hands. *Olivia was dropped back into my lap,* he wanted to say. *There's a terrorist connection, and Uriah and Ian Kendall are involved.* But he didn't really believe that. He knew only that the terrorist connection pointed toward an American student and traced back in time to Olivia Renway. Even now as he watched Molly, he was certain he could stop her from going if he could just tell her the truth. Instead he licked his thin, dry lips. "Molly, does Lord Gilmore know you're leaving me?"

"My father knows I'm going to Paris. That's all."

Dudley was not a demonstrative man, so the words did not come easily, but he said, "Molly, I love you."

She stole one more glance at the picture on his desk. "I'm glad," she said softly.

❦❦❦

On Friday morning in Jarvoc, Hanz Russelmann picked his way along the rusty railroad track at the back of the property. His blue chino shirt lay open at the neck, the sleeves rolled up to the elbows. His work trousers came loose at the top of his boots as he trudged along. He seldom came this way, but since Nedrick's cable old memories had flooded back. He wasn't even aware that the black-and-white collie had joined him until he circled the old gun-metal building that Altman had refused to tear down.

"Patek, where did you come from?" he asked.

The dog nuzzled his fingers, but as they drew abreast of the door, a low growl rumbled in her throat. The fur on the back of her neck stiffened.

"It's all right, Patek. We won't go inside. Not this time."

Next week when Altman and the others were in Prague meeting with the representatives from Nishokura Steel, Hanz would come back and force his way inside. He had not been there for years, but he remembered the general layout of the building with its thick walls and gas sensors hanging on the paneling. Vast storage space lay hidden under the structure with its labyrinthine tunnels running beneath the railroad tracks and cutting deep into the forest. It was important now to know exactly what Altman was storing there. Hanz had seen the silver thermos containers and the fifty-five-gallon drums that had been destined for the storage sheds.

For years he had been aware that Altman and Gustav had been stockpiling weapons, no doubt selling them. Hanz was not a fool. He knew that the "satchel" and "earmuff" charges and blasting caps that Jiri Benak designed had no place in the steel business. But he had protested strongly when Jiri came back from the merc camp in the Pyrenees foothills with new suggestions. "We can increase the company profits by slicing steel beams to accommodate blasting caps," he had said. "Or we can produce bomb castings for weapons. We can sell them both to third world countries."

Altman's eyes had glazed over. "No, we won't sell direct to third world countries. We'll keep on dealing with Nishokura Steel. Let them handle any circuitous route for our products."

The look that Hanz saw in his son's eyes—in Olivia's son—had been inhuman. He had seen that same look during the war in the eyes of Himmler and Heydrich as they planned the annihilation of another race. Like Heydrich and Himmler, hatred had consumed Altman. No amount of money pleased him. He wanted power. Sometimes Hanz blamed himself. He had given Altman everything. No, not quite everything. He had robbed his son of a mother. There was nothing of Olivia in Altman, not even in his facial features, but Hanz had seen Olivia's gentleness in Nedrick.

He tried to shut out the memory of Altman saying, "Jiri, I have other ideas, too, that will make the Russelmann profits soar." Altman had presented unbelievable methods of destruction in a calm, cool, meticulous way, and then looking at Hanz he had said, "You and my brother Josef must help us, Father."

For Hanz it was as though the diabolical thinking of the thirties and forties had come back to haunt his final days on earth. The possibility of his sons and nephew hiding chemical weapons at the Russelmann plant sickened him. Now with Nedrick coming home to Jarvoc, he feared for the boy's life.

With the blistering sun directly overhead, he walked slowly down the dirt trail back toward the farmhouse, the collie at his side, the daily news tucked under his arm. He tipped Altman's visored field cap to the neighbor and moved on before he could be persuaded to stay for a cup of coffee or a glass of Becherovka.

These days long walks tired him, putting added pressure on his game leg. As he limped along, dragging his 180 pounds, he felt as though heavy steel plates had been slung across his back, the weight of them cutting painfully into his thoughts.

Reaching the front porch, he dropped down on the top step and whipped open the paper. The stray collie panted in front of him, her woeful eyes on Hanz.

"Let me rest a bit, Patek, and then I'll get you some water."

Hanz skipped the bold headlines and thumbed on to the stock and business reports. Running his eyes down the export columns, he was grateful that foreign sales on steel and iron ore were high again. The Czech Republic continued to gain recognition abroad with the Russelmann profits listed among them.

In the far column a small headline caught his attention. A subway disaster had been averted in Tokyo with a renewed crackdown on the purchase of chemical weapons from other countries. For anyone caught, punishment would be swift. Hanz tried to imagine how nerve gas components could be shipped abroad in steel bar packaging or how his sons Altman and Josef might be involved. Sixty-foot steel rails and forty-foot beams or cylinders would be shipped unpackaged, but specialty parts—the smaller welded bars and flanged steel tubes—could be crated or shipped in barrels, allowing room to hide chemical components.

My sons have gone mad, he thought. *No, not Josef.* Josef was a simple man, hardworking and industrious like his Slovakian mother. Josef had Blanca's fine features and dark hair and some of her shyness and wisdom. Surely Josef had not been taken in by Altman's schemes. Josef had worked hard for his degrees in chemistry, but, sadly, he was still the son who had always lived in the shadow of his half-brother Altman. Hanz glanced toward the sky, wishing at the moment that he knew how to pray.

The only one who seemed to be listening was the collie at his side. "Josef is not a cruel man," he told the dog.

If Nedrick had been the son of Josef, Hanz would have understood it better. They were more alike, less greedy, less power-hungry. Of all the Russelmann-Van Rindin clan in residence at the farm, only Josef was welcomed in the local pubs. The people of Jarvoc would drink with him and to him as the Russelmann who stood up for the men in the plant.

Hanz's hand proved unsteady as he tore the Tokyo article from the paper and stuffed it in his pocket.

"Here," he said to the collie. "Give me a hand."

Patek drew closer and allowed Hanz to balance himself as he stood. The dog whimpered as she followed Hanz past the compost pile to the area where he burned the leaves and trash.

Pain seared through his sciatic nerve as he knelt on one knee. He touched his lighter to the damp twigs and leaves until they sparked. As Hanz fueled the fire with page after page of grimy newsprint, Mila Van Rindin came around the corner of the house. "Uncle Hanz, where have you been?"

"About," he said. "Good day for walking."

"Altman was looking for you."

"He's sure to find me."

She wiped soot from his face with the corner of her apron. "I see you found the collie."

"She's adopted me."

"Of course. It's Friday. You always find her on Fridays."

"Maybe it's the only day she breaks loose."

Mila picked up the hose and filled the bowl with water. "Here, Patek," she said.

"Treat her like that and she'll stay around."

"We'd both like that, wouldn't we?"

Of all the Van Rindins, Mila was the gentlest, genuine and caring. Hanz saw behind the harshness of her square, bony features, the protruding cheeks, the sun-weathered skin. Her eyes said it all—lit as they were now with compassion and kindness.

"Uncle Hanz, was there any word from Nedrick?"

"Not today."

"But he is coming home?"

He stumbled back to his feet, refusing the hand that she extended his way. "Yes, he'll fly into Ruzyne Airport soon."

Shyly she asked, "And then he'll come to Jarvoc. I have his old room ready. I want him to stay with us."

"It's been ten years, Mila. He may have changed."

"You don't know that."

"You're second cousins," he reminded her.

"I don't care. He promised we'd spend our lives together."

Hanz smothered his exasperation and ran his gnarled knuckles down her cheek. "Nedrick is in London with Jiri right now."

"Then I'll go to him. I fear for Ned when Jiri is with him."

"Let's wait and see what happens," Hanz said.

Her saucer eyes seemed troubled—for herself, for him. "You're unhappy, Uncle Hanz. You're worried about Nedrick, too."

"I'm just old and weary. I walked too far for an old man."

"You could retire. Father says—"

"That I'm useless?" He smiled. "What else does Gustav say?"

"That you hold the factory back from foreign sales."

"Do I?" As he shifted the weight to his good leg, he heard the crackle of the newsprint in his pocket. "We are high on the charts on foreign sales, Mila."

"But you're still unhappy."

He turned his back on Mila, not wanting her to know how despondent he felt. He shaded his eyes and looked off toward the factory. The glare of the sun fell across the rail-road tracks. It struck him now that certain days and certain points in history came back, each time with greater intensity. You could not erase the black days, anymore than you could relive the joyful ones. He had tried often to picture those months with Olivia in London. She was only seventeen when he had met her, seven years younger than himself. Her family was in Czechoslovakia. Alone and beautiful, she was in a foreign country, as he was, and he had loved her.

The joyful moments with Olivia had been overshadowed with betrayal, darkened by their last moments together in the Blitz. He had left her during an air raid, left her with a sapphire bracelet—a family heirloom he had called it. But if it had been found in her possession, it would have cost Olivia her life.

"Uncle Hanz," Mila asked, "did I say something wrong?"

He shook his head, still unable to speak.

Hanz had never seen Olivia again. Months later in May of 1942, he was in Prague, sitting on his bunk polishing his shoes, struggling with mixed emotions about the honor of flying Reinhard Heydrich into Berlin in the morning. He despised Heydrich, as he detested all loyal Nazis. But he particularly mistrusted the German-appointed head of the protectorate of Czechoslovakia, a man who led with bloody cruelty. Shortly before leaving for an evening concert with his wife, Heydrich—a towering six-footer, resplendent and arrogant in his S.S. uniform—had strolled into Hanz's room. He turned to the Luftwaffe pilot and said, "Russelmann, why don't you join us this evening for the concert?"

Hanz had remained at the castle where the Germans were quartered. The underground resistance network in Prague was extensive. So were the rumors about a possible assassination attempt on Heydrich. Hanz feared that Olivia's family might be involved. He had traced them to the Paschek farm where a wiry little woman with an English accent had insisted that Olivia had been parachuted back into Czechoslovakia. It could mean only one thing. Olivia was part of the assassination team. He must stop her.

The following morning when Heydrich's unescorted Mercedes slowed on a sharp bend of a hill, gunfire erupted. Heydrich took the fatal bullets. In the wake of his death, hundreds of Czechs were arrested and executed. As the hunt for the assassins continued, Hanz slipped out of Prague and went to Jarvoc to search once more for Olivia. The Paschek farm was empty. Fearful for their own lives, the neighbors told him that Olivia's father had remained in Prague with the resistance movement; the rest of the family had fled to

Lidice. The perky little woman with the English accent—
Beatrice, they had called her—had disappeared into the hills.
Five days after Heydrich's assassination, trains began the
journey from Prague to extermination factories.

Hanz shuddered as Mila touched his hand. He shook
himself free. In his mind's eye, he saw again the Prague
train pulling into the Jarvoc station. Heard the hobnailed
boots running. Heard the S.S. guards shouting, "Out. Out.
Achtung! Achtung!"

Olivia's father was part of the human cargo on that train.
Hanz remembered him stepping unassisted from the box-
car. With a sense of Czech pride, the man had placed his
shoes and spectacles in the boxes provided and then went
down those seven steps to his death.

"I didn't mean to add to your unhappiness," Mila said.

"You didn't, child. I was just thinking back—"

"A long ways back?"

"Yes. To when I first came to Prague."

She eased back into her favorite topic. "I'm glad you did,
Uncle Hanz. Otherwise I would never have known Nedrick.
Are you eager for him to come home?"

"Of course. I've missed him."

"And if he stays on and works at the plant, will that make
you happy again?"

He mustn't. "It would not be easy to work for his father."

"Nor for mine," she said sadly.

"Altman and Gustav will always be hard taskmasters,
Mila."

"Then I'll go away with Nedrick. You can come with us."

His tightened knuckle took another gentle run down her
pitted cheek. "Nedrick will do what is best for you."

"What's all this talk about Nedrick?" Altman asked as he
walked up behind them. "Surely you have better things to
discuss, Mila, than my son."

As she glanced up into Hanz's weathered face, some of
the brightness in her eyes clouded. "Do you want me to get
your hoe for you, Uncle Hanz?" she asked.

He brushed the dirt from his hands. "Not now, Mila. The
garden can wait. I think I'll have a word with Altman first."

"About what, Father?" Altman asked coldly.

Hanz pointed toward the gloomy structure by the railroad track. "About tearing down that old storage building over there."

Chapter 17

Chase unchained Margot Hampton's bike from the drain spout and stared beyond the cobbled pathway. It wasn't like Peter to be late. He kept to a strict time schedule. She wheeled the bike to the corner. Still no Peter. Beyond this quiet neighborhood lay the willow-lined Cherwell and the ancient university spires that stretched toward the cloudy sky.

In the ten days with the Hamptons, Chase had tried to put Andrew Forrestal's death from her mind, but since dawn this morning, his face had crept stealthily into her thoughts. He was dead. She accepted this, but it was frightening to think that she was one of the last persons to see him alive. If she had stayed at the station another twenty minutes, she may well have died with him.

As the days merged, she stopped looking over her shoulder for the man who had followed her to the Hamptons' house. Peter and the academic community kept her too busy to worry about strangers. She was becoming well acquainted with the city of Oxford. She could make her way through the medieval streets without getting lost now and distinguish between St. Michael's Saxon tower and the fifteenth-century bell tower of Magdalen College.

She had marked off certain landmarks for herself—the Bridge of Sighs would take her to the Hertford Quad; the Sheldonian Theatre was the place where Peter's honors degree had been conferred; and the Bodleian Library was the place to be at six because Peter didn't like to be kept waiting. She could make her way to High Street and Broad Street without Peter pedaling beside her. But mostly he refused to let her out of his sight until she was tucked away safely in one of the cubicles in the library.

As she gripped the handlebars, she looked around again for him and then remembered a book she-wanted to take with her. She wheeled the bike back to the house, ran inside, and took the stair steps on the run, her heart racing as she reached her nook of a room on the second floor. She found the book on the dresser and was about to lower her window in case of an afternoon shower when she heard the Hamptons on the back patio.

She leaned out the window to interrupt their breakfast with a cheery hello, but she muzzled the greeting when she heard Margot ask, "Nigel, have you heard from Edwin Wallis?"

"Almost daily. He's like a dog gnawing a bone—insisting that Chase was the last one to see Andrew Forrestal alive."

"Is Edwin accusing her?"

"He won't go that far, but sooner or later he expects her to remember something. Or someone."

"Has she said anything to you about it?"

"She tried. I stopped her. Edwin would be bound to drag it out of me." His voice lowered. "And I forbade Peter to discuss it with her."

"Oh, Nigel, would you rather have Edwin think her guilty?"

"I would rather not involve us in any way."

Chase had disliked Constable Wallis from the moment they met. Now she was angry. *I'm practically a suspect in a murder case,* she thought. *And now even the Hamptons distrust me.* She stepped back from the window and kept her tongue, silenced by the memory of the stranger with the snow-blond hair. *Sooner or later Chase will remember.* She had to tell someone that the man from the television studio had followed her from London. If she could get into town without Peter shadowing her, she would call Luke

Breckenridge and beg him to come take her away from Oxford.

She felt as limp as the curtain as she heard Nigel say, "Margot, try not to worry. Peter keeps close tabs on Chase. He's certain that no one has followed them. She'll be fine."

Margot's cup and saucer clattered. "What about *our* safety?"

Impatiently he snapped, "Nothing will happen to us."

"I'm alone on the motorway two hours every day. Since this Forrestal tragedy, I jump every time a driver cuts in too closely."

"Chase could go with you tomorrow. She wants to visit the Eagle's Nest."

"No, Nigel. What she wants is to quiz Beatrice Thorpe."

He ran his hand through his thinning hair. "Beatrice could help Chase in her research on Olivia. What harm could that be?"

"She's an old woman. You can't depend on what she says."

"Chase is good with people like that."

"I won't be at rest until she's gone."

"The old woman or Chase, Margot?"

"Both of them. You were foolish to bring Chase here."

"Don't you like her?"

"I've always liked your students."

"Is this one so different because she's a girl?"

"You've spent your whole academic life teaching men."

"Chase is a refreshing change," he said.

"You usually bring your students home for meals, not for a whole summer. Why did you ever tell that girl about Beatrice?"

"Chase would have found out. She's very thorough."

"Too thorough. Even Edwin knows she's researching Olivia's life. No wonder there's such renewed interest in her death."

The air in Chase's bedroom stood still as Margot's voice rose to a high pitch. "Wallis and Chase will drag us through the mud before this is over."

"And in the end you and the Kendalls will be free, my

dear. I've longed for that for ten years. I lost you when Olivia died."

Margot scraped back the wrought-iron chair and gathered up the dishes. "Isn't it all best forgotten?"

Not wanting the Hamptons to come into the house and discover her still there, Chase fled down the steps and back out the front door. Peter would be annoyed when he arrived and found her gone, but she grabbed the bike and pedaled off without waiting for him.

In town she was so anxious to find a BT phone box that she didn't see the small boy dart out in front of her. She slammed on her brakes, missed the child, and collided with another student, a dishwater brunette wearing tortoise-shell glasses. The girl glared at Chase as they tried to unlock their front wheels.

"I'm sorry," Chase told her. "Are you all right?"

She examined her skinned knee. "I think so. And you?"

"Okay." Chase pointed toward a nearby cafe. "Perhaps I could make it up to you with a cup of tea?"

Inside, with cups of steaming tea in front of them, the young woman said, "I'm Anna Walker. Somerville College."

"That's Margaret Thatcher's school."

"And a hundred others."

"I'm Chase Evans. Peter—that's my tutor—promised to take me to Somerville this afternoon."

Anna sipped her tea and studied Chase. "You're American?"

"Yes. New York. I'm just here for the summer."

"Why don't you ride over to Somerville Manor with me? That's one of our houses for upperclasswomen. Ten of us presently."

"I'd like that—but let me make a phone call first."

The answering machine at the Busingen number clicked in, and a sweet voice invited Chase to leave a message. She glanced at Anna over the mouthpiece. "No one is home."

"Leave a message."

Chase forced a cheerful smile as she hung up the phone and pocketed her father's credit card. "What I wanted was

Luke's number in Germany. Never mind. I'll see him next week anyway."

"Boyfriend?"

"Just a friend."

"Hmm."

The Somerville Manor, a narrow, three-story house on a cobbled street in the heart of Oxford, had been claimed by Somerville students for a number of years. The sitting room was filled with overstuffed sofas and several beanbag chairs that one of the American students had brought with her. Six bespectacled residents sprawled about the room poring over their books.

"Forget them," Anna said. "Let me introduce you to some of Somerville's better-known achievers."

Pictures of five women hung in the hallway. "None of them ever lived at the Manor," Anna admitted as they paused by the portrait of Suzanee Cumbertain. "They were all like Thoreau. They danced to their own music. I think that's what made them special. At least some of them."

Suzanee Cumbertain had gained recognition in science. Madelaine Louberry's short career was in the film industry—seven major French films before her death in Flight 103 over Lockerbie, Scotland. Olivia Renway held the middle spot and most of Chase's attention. Anna gave Chase an apologetic glance. "I don't like Renway hanging here. She wasn't British. In fact, she spent a good bit of her life in America."

"Two strikes and you're out?" Chase asked.

"It's not that. The residents here at the Manor know little about her personal life. She wrote a few books. That's all."

"I've read them all."

Anna shrugged and moved on to Dorothy Sayers's plain, bespectacled face. "Another writer," she said.

The close-up photograph of Margaret Thatcher completed the gallery of Somerville's best. Pride rang in Anna's voice. "I think of all our grads, Lady Thatcher has had the most influence."

Beside Thatcher hung an empty frame. "That's our constant challenge," Anna said, tucking a lock of hair behind her ear. "We hope someone from the Manor hangs in this frame someday."

"You perhaps?"

Anna grinned. "I came to Somerville because of Prime Minister Thatcher. I'm even majoring in chemistry." As she tossed her head, the long hair swept across her neck again. "She's always been my role model."

"One of mine, too," Chase said. "I've always admired her."

Chase left that magnificent portrait and moved back to look up into Renway's pensive face. She was struck by Olivia's beauty, but unlike Thatcher's bright, alert gaze, Renway seemed lost in her own thoughts. "That's a remarkable painting, Anna."

"Renway's husband donated it to the Manor when she died."

"I've been studying her life."

Anna shot Chase a cold glance. "Have you found the skeletons yet? She and Sayers both had a dark past. You won't find much on Renway. Her private life seemed just that. Extremely private."

"Perhaps that's why I find her so intriguing."

"Apparently the man across the street finds *you* quite intriguing," another girl said as she joined them. "He's been there ever since you came. A secret admirer?"

"Oh, that's probably Peter. My tutor." *My shadow.*

When she reached the open window, she stepped back in horror. The blond man across the street was much older than Peter. Andrew Forrestal and a beige trench coat tossed over a chair back flashed in her mind. The dryness in her mouth came at once.

"Are you all right?" Anna asked.

All right? Hardly. She was sure it was the man from the television station in London, the stranger who had been outside the Hamptons' house ten days ago—possibly Andrew Forrestal's murderer. "I don't want that man to see me leave here."

"Well, let's jolly well get rid of him," Anna offered. "Or we can call the police if you want."

Chase nodded. "Would you? I think—"

"While we do that, you cut out the back way to Holywell Street. Can you find your way to the library from there?"

"Yes, Anna. Yes, of course."

"We'll detain the gentleman and give you time to disappear. By then the police should be here."

But even through the thin curtains they could see that the stranger had already slipped away.

◔◔◔

The library was a massive room, its seventeenth-century architecture encasing a morgue-like stillness. The arched windows were high, the broad center aisle filled with oriental throw rugs, the vaulted ceiling like padded velvet. Mahogany bookcases crowded with musty volumes lined both sides of the room. The only sound besides her own breathing was being made by a student with dark hair and tinted glasses as he idly twirled one of the world globes. *Squeak. Squeak. Squeak.*

Chase sat in an isolated cubicle, trying to erase the annoying sound from her mind. She glanced down at her notes, a column marked "Renway" and one marked "Sayers." Both women were meticulous scholars and loners. Both had the advantages of private tutors and boarding schools. She ran her finger down the notations, comparing them as she had done day after day. Like herself, they had come from privileged backgrounds, rational thinkers with strong political views. Renway was a stylish woman, Sayers at times in her earlier years outrageously dressed.

She ticked off her list, searching for links between them: voracious readers, graduates of Somerville, gifted writers. Was she hunting for something that did not exist? The world globe twirled again. *Squeak. Squeak. Squeak.*

Chase tugged at the heavy volume chained to the library table, trying to bring it closer to her tired eyes. She scanned the article on Sayers's bohemian days when she incurred moral outrage at the birth of an illegitimate son. Whamo!

Chase ran her pencil under the words: "the birth of a son."
A child born out of wedlock.

Squeak. Squeak. Squeak. This time the sound came from
footsteps. Leather shoes. The globe spun by itself now. The
student had stepped from view, but he made no effort to
hide his approach as he walked over the hardwood floors.
From the next alcove of books, she heard his heavy
breathing.

"Who's there?" she cried out.

Behind her more footsteps. She whirled around ready to
defend herself by yanking the book from its chain. "Oh, Doc
Hampton—it's you!"

Hampton gently released her grip from the chain. "That's
how we protect our ancient volumes from slippery fingers,"
he said.

"Where's Peter?"

"At the house." He put his finger to his lips, grabbed her
books and notes, and led her out the back way. Outside he
took her elbow and hurried her along.

"Doc Hampton, we've forgotten your wife's bicycle."

"Peter will see to it in the morning."

"Is something wrong?"

"When the library is empty, don't stay in there alone."

"There was a student there. Didn't you notice him?"

"He ducked out of sight when I came in. Don't ever leave
the house without Peter again."

"Was Peter angry with me?"

"No, worried about you. Someone is looking for you,
Chase. He found Peter instead."

The man who murdered Andrew Forrestal. She sucked in
her breath. "Is Peter all right?"

"He'll feel better in the morning. We've talked to
Constable Wallis. He suggests that you leave Oxford for
now."

She dragged her feet and stared up at him. *Be honest with
me,* she thought. *Your wife wants me out of your lives.* But
where would she go? To the Cotswolds? Uriah Kendall had
surely reached there by now. "Tell him I'll go to the
Cotswolds," she said.

"Delay that visit until someone can go with you."

"Well, I won't delay attending the opening of the Von Tonner Art Museum in Germany next week."

"Is Peter going with you?"

"He wasn't invited. I'm going with Luke Breckenridge—at least I'm meeting Luke there." *And I won't have Luke see me with Peter,* she thought. *No way.* "It's by invitation only."

"Until then I'll send you to the Eagle's Nest with my wife."

"Will your wife mind?"

"Peter will mind."

He struck out toward the outskirts of town, his long robe snapping at his ankles. Hampton walked briskly, striding as though he had a man at his side. She took a deep breath and increased her speed.

As they strolled along, he said, "Chase, I took the liberty to mail your revised proposal back to Professor Marsten. We had to meet her deadline—or else."

"Oh, Doc Hampton, I left it on your desk. I forgot to mail it."

His words were as quick as his steps. "You and Peter have been busy. Besides, I added a long letter. I doubt that Marsten and her committee will give you any trouble." More seriously, he asked, "How's your project coming?"

"I'm filling my notebooks with bits and pieces. Sayers played a violin quite well, and Renway came from a country that's known for making violins. Little things like that."

"You don't sound very enthusiastic, Chase."

"I don't like thinking about them being cut down in the prime of their lives. Sayers with a thrombosis—"

"And Renway with a hit-and-run," he said hastily.

"No, Prof, I don't believe that anymore. I think someone killed her. She died and never finished her life's work."

"We all die with unfinished dreams, Chase."

"Not me. I don't intend to let this one go."

🌀🌀🌀

Relief swept across Margot's face as Chase and Nigel walked into the kitchen, but Peter looked miserable. He sat at the table, an ice pack in his hand. His right eye was swollen and bruised, the side of his face red, the cheek puffy. Crusted blood clung to his upper lip. Chase rushed across the room to him.

He winced as she touched his bruised face. "What happened?"

"Tell her," Margot said.

He peered at Chase with his good eye. "I came by for you this morning, but you had gone off without me. I set off alone, so angry with you that I didn't hear the rider come up behind me."

Margot lifted his hand and made him place the ice pack over his eye. "His bike collided with Peter's," she said. "Deliberately."

"Who would do a thing like that?"

"Chase, he didn't give his name and address. When I tried to stand up, he pounded my face."

She leaned closer. "Peter, I'm sorry."

He licked his swollen lip and tried to smile. "He wanted to know where you were. Said crazy things like—wanting to know what the CIA agent had given me."

"*You,*" Margot said indignantly, her voice back at high pitch. "The man who accosted Peter thinks you're with the CIA."

Nigel stood with his back to the sink, a cup of hot tea in his hands. "You should have told me, Chase. If I had known about your CIA connection, I would never have invited you here."

She sank into the chair beside Peter. "Where would he get a crazy idea like that? I don't even know anyone in the CIA."

The silence in the room was deadly. Peter repositioned the ice pack. Margot rubbed her hand on the side of her skirt. Nigel turned to the stove and poured himself another cup of tea.

His back was still turned to her when he asked coldly, "Is it true? Are you with the CIA and sworn to some code of silence?"

"Prof, you know I'm a student. Why would I work for American Intelligence?"

He faced her once more, his jaw set, his gaze unfriendly, suspicious. "They've been known to recruit students before."

She tried to picture him back at Columbia smiling, joking, challenging her. The lines under his eyes had deepened. His phone contacts with Edwin Wallis were turning him against her.

"Prof, I didn't kill Andrew Forrestal."

He sighed. "I want to believe you—I do believe you—but you were there at the television station with him."

"That doesn't make me a murderer. Andrew was just trying to help me."

"Were you old friends?"

"Not friends at all. I told you before—I met Andrew at the university that morning." She glanced cautiously at Peter. "Forrestal flirted with me and then asked to take my picture."

"A total stranger?" Peter asked, disappointed. "And you simply went off with him?"

"Chase." Nigel again. "The constable said that Forrestal had a hundred dollars in his pocket."

"It should have been more than that," she said. "I paid him to show me some old news reels on Olivia's accident."

Nigel's displeasure was apparent. "Did you give Forrestal anything else?"

She felt the way she did when her father cornered her and demanded answers. She resented the embarrassment as she admitted, "He promised to get in touch with me if he found any information on Olivia—that's when I gave him your name and address here."

Nigel drained his cup. "When I told Wallis about Peter's beating, he was not happy at all. He believes you know more about the man in the television studio than you've told us—"

"I tried to tell you about that day in the television studio, but you wouldn't hear me out." She rubbed her eyes. *Sooner or later she will remember.* "He was blond. Possibly your height, Dr. Hampton. Fortyish. Harsh looking. Carrying a trench coat."

Peter leaned forward, the painful effort obvious. "Chase, except for the coat, that describes my assailant."

"I told Peter a man followed me here from London. For several days I didn't see him." Fear. Blind fear. The kind that she could taste and feel up and down her spine. "And then today—I saw him again."

"The man at the library?"

"No. I never saw him before. There's something else. The man who was in the studio may have overheard Andrew Forrestal tell me that Mr. Kendall was British Intelligence."

From across the table, Margot asked, "Is Kendall working for American Intelligence now?"

"I don't know who he's working for," Chase said. "He's retired as far as I know."

Margot sat with her hands clasped. "Chase, Peter says you've been making long distance calls from town. You could have made your calls here."

Chase closed her eyes, trying to block out the nightmare. The hot flushing in her cheeks was more anger than embarrassment. She had wanted to keep her calls to Luke private. "I've been calling a gentleman friend," she said. "I tried to call him again today. I wanted him to come and take me away from Oxford. But it doesn't matter. It's all falling into place now. Dead as Olivia Renway is, she's involved in this somehow. Otherwise, there wouldn't have been such opposition to my writing about her."

She opened her eyes in time to see the Hamptons exchange glances again. "Margot," Nigel said, "Edwin is not available for a day or two. That makes us responsible for Chase's safety. I want you to take her to the Eagle's Nest in the morning."

"No, I forbid it. I'm more concerned about you, Nigel. You've worked hard for your career. We can't risk a scandal, not here at Oxford. It would ruin you."

"It's all right, Margot."

"No, it isn't."

"I've upset all of you," Chase said. "It all has to do with Olivia Renway, doesn't it? She really was killed. And it's best if we never know why. Is that how you feel, Mrs. Hampton?"

The resentment on Margot's face softened as Nigel walked over and took her hand. "Margot, Chase is leaving for Germany in a few days. Until then find her a place at the Eagle's Nest."

She tried to pull away, but he held on tightly. "For just a few days, Margot."

"Please don't ask me to do that. If I take Chase to the Eagle's Nest, Edwin will come looking for her. Won't he, Nigel?"

As he nodded, she yanked her hand free and turned on Chase. For a moment she just sat there, desolate, twisting the rings on her finger, and then sadly she said, "Tomorrow, my dear Miss Evans, you will have your way. You will meet Beatrice Thorpe."

Chapter 18

At seven the next morning Margot Hampton and Chase drove on the motorway in a companionable silence. Even so, Chase saw tiny ridges furrow her brow as she glanced in the rearview mirror. Without warning, Margot swung the wheel to the right. Horns blared as their car careened across two lanes and skidded inches behind a minivan. With another jerk of the wheel, Margot spun them on the curve of the off-ramp on three wheels.

"We lost him," she gasped as the car righted itself.

Chase caught her breath. "What was that all about?"

Margot's hands had blanched against the wheel. "I didn't wait to find out. He's been behind us for the last hour. I had to do something."

"You almost got us killed. He'll just go to the next turn-around and come back after us."

"But he won't know which country road to follow." Chase heard the tremor in Margot's voice as she warned, "Now we must forget that little encounter, or it will ruin our whole day."

Easy for you to say, Chase thought.

"Chase, you must not tell Nigel about my daring little maneuver."

"I promise. Not a word. I'll probably still be speechless."

Her touch of humor pleased Margot. "You're not a bad sort, Chase. We should have met on different terms. I think we would have been friends."

Leaving the rush of the motorway behind, Margot bumped over the last few kilometers to the tranquillity of the Eagle's Nest. As they left the car, a lazy breeze drifted across the sleepy valley, stirring the tops of the meadow's wild flowers.

They approached a low shingled building sheltered by tall shade trees and a tangle of thickets. The grounds had flowers planted everywhere and baskets of bougainvillea hung on the screened porch. White-painted benches faced the bird bath. As they hurried up the paved walkway, they heard the sweet, plaintive song of a goldfinch as it splashed in the shallow water.

Inside, several listless residents sat serenely in the lobby. Others still sharp of mind recognized Margot, waved, and returned her smile.

Putting her finger in a vase of flowers, she called to the nearest aide. "Charlene, freshen this up a bit and pick a fresh bouquet for the receptionist's desk."

Margot led Chase to the left wing. "Beatrice Thorpe has a private room," she said. "You'll be staying in the guest room next to hers. Beatrice doesn't take to strangers, but Nigel insists on your meeting her."

"And you don't agree?"

"She's an old woman. If you barge in there asking about Olivia Renway, she may throw you out. I don't want her upset."

"I'll do my best."

"To annoy her?"

"No, to be nice to her."

Margot smiled, her tired face pleasant for the moment. "She will try to talk you into having lunch in her room. She latches onto every excuse to stay in that old chair of hers. It's a fight every day to get her to the dining room."

As they walked the corridor, Margot ran her finger along the ledge. A few steps later she scooped up a swirl of lint from the floor. "I expect this place to be kept clean and neat for the residents. Except you will find Beatrice's room outrageous. All clutter. But clean."

"Most of the rooms we passed had two beds in them."

"I know. Beatrice has the only single room. I insisted on it. Otherwise, the staff would have quit long ago."

"But you're the administrator, Mrs. Hampton."

"Yes, and I'm determined to keep my staff happy. Beatrice wore down two roommates in the beginning, always afraid someone was going to take her possessions. I had three resignations on my desk in a week."

She stopped and tapped gently on the door before swinging it open. "Beatrice, good morning. It's Margot."

Beatrice Thorpe sat in a cushioned rocker by an open window, surrounded by antique collections. The knitting needles in her ringed hands clicked in constant motion. She was dressed in an old-fashioned royal blue blouse and a long beige skirt that matched the high derby hat on her head. She looked up, her Mediterranean eyes pale blue, innocent as a child's.

"Oh, Margot, did you bring Olivia with you today?"

"No, not today, Bea. But I brought another guest. Someone who likes Olivia."

Thorpe's hair was the same shiny color as her silver-rimmed glasses. Dangling earrings hung from the wide lobes of her pierced ears.

"Is she going out?" Chase whispered.

"No. She's always dressed to the nines. She was very fashionable in her day. And after those two years in the concentration camp, clothes meant even more to her."

Chase's mind raced. *Where? When? What concentration camp?* But she resisted asking. Instead she whispered, "She's lovely. She doesn't look ninety."

"She's not. She's ninety-five. You're on your own now until lunch."

The door closed behind Margot, leaving Chase alone with the old woman. She glanced around the cluttered room—a single bed with the side rails down, a china closet filled with treasures, a high round table with a lamp and candy dish on it. China plates and a magnificent Botticelli painting of the Madonna and the Child hung on the wall. On the crowded shelves beneath the Botticelli, books were piled on top of one another. Drawers and the open closet were jammed with boxes and papers.

"Stop gawking, young lady."

"I'm sorry."

Beatrice squinted. "What's your name?"

"Chase Evans. I'm from New York."

"New York. Then come," she said, kicking the threads of her unfinished afghan with her laced shoes. "I'm Bea. My friends call me Bea. Sit down beside me. I want to go to New York. Maybe I'll go after the war."

War? As Chase pulled up a straight-back chair, her own shoes caught in the lap robe. She reached out and touched the aged hand with the tips of her fingers and thought of Marie back at Willowglen, more fragile than Beatrice Thorpe, Marie's days little more than endless hours.

"Well, why are you here?" Beatrice asked. "You should be off helping Olivia. The boys need a safe route out of Prague."

Deep wrinkles cut from the corners of Beatrice's mouth to her double chin. Chase couldn't be sure whether those lines were twisting into a smile. The faded blue eyes stayed wide and direct, demanding an answer.

"W-What boys?" Chase stammered.

"The men of Anthropoid. We can't leave them in the church. The Gestapo will find them."

Chase touched the wrinkled hand again, at a loss for words. Beatrice pushed her fingers away and went on knitting. "You've got to get word to Olivia. I can't go. I'm a prisoner here."

Anxious to appease her, Chase said, "I'll try. Tell me how."

Beatrice bent over her knitting needles and whispered urgently, "They're hiding in the catacombs at the Karel Boromejsky Church."

"I don't know where that is."

Bewildered, Beatrice tapped Chase with a needle. "Think, child. It's in the center of Prague. Now be on your way."

Chase considered running, taking off before the eccentric old woman went completely off her rocker. The imploring look on Thorpe's face stopped her. Chase wanted to explain that they were in England—that "the boys" were undoubtedly dead now.

Thorpe's agitation turned quickly to tears. "Don't you understand? The soldiers are searching the city door by door. Margot and Olivia can't hold them off much longer. . . . We've got to rescue them. There's a price on their heads. . . . We've got to get those boys across the border."

As gently as she could, Chase said, "She's gone, Beatrice."

"Gone. Olivia's not coming back?"

"She died in a traffic accident a long time ago."

"Oh! I'd forgotten about that. Then I have nothing left."

"Bea, she left her books for you. I've read all of them."

"Not the last one. You didn't read the last one on Czechoslovakia. She was killed for that one." Beatrice had come back to the present as calmly as she had left it, her rambling thoughts back in focus. She pulled the multicolored lap robe up around her waist. "No one believes me," she said, "but Olivia was killed for that manuscript."

Chase's chest tightened. "I believe you. That's why I came to see you, Miss Thorpe, to find out how she died."

Beatrice cackled. "It's Mrs. Thorpe. No one ever questioned Olivia's traffic death before except me. *And you*. And the boy."

"What boy?"

"Ian Kendall."

Ian Kendall! "You know Olivia's grandson?"

Confusion wrapped around Thorpe again. "There's no grandson. Olivia left her baby boy at St. Michael's Cove in Cornwall before she went back to Prague."

The breeze from the windows blew the long lace curtains back against a row of war photographs on the wall. A gentle wind. A fragile mind. Chase watched a troubled expression flicker on Thorpe's face again. "Can you take a message to Olivia for me?"

"I can tell Margot."

"Yes, she'll help us. Tell her the boys from the Czech Brigade need help. They've been training in England near Warwick. They did us proud, didn't they."

Chase nodded. "I'm sure they did."

"You understand, don't you? The German head of the protectorate of Prague was ruthless to our people. He had to die."

"A Nazi?" Chase asked.

"Yes. So proud and arrogant even when he played the violin. Did you know he liked music?"

"I don't know anything about him."

Beatrice leaned forward and whispered urgently, "We've got to get the boys out of the church before the Gestapo find them."

From the doorway a deep voice said, "Josef Gabcik is dead, Bea. And Jan Kubis, too."

Her features sharpened. "Dead? No, Olivia was with them when they parachuted in from England. Josef only hurt his ankle."

"Yes, I know."

Chase recognized Ian's voice before she turned to face him standing in the doorway. She was struck again by his handsome features. He looked even more athletic and muscular than she remembered in his thigh-hugging cycling shorts and the Assos jersey with the Gainsborough logo. The sun caught the brilliance of his reddish hair—the streaks of light emphasizing the stubborn set of his jaw and his obvious displeasure at seeing her. As he yanked off his dark glasses, his piercing blue eyes bore down on her. "What are you doing here, Chase?" he asked. "Did Beatrice invite you?"

"No, Margot Hampton did."

He scowled. "Does she know what you're up to?"

"She should. She's watching me closely enough."

Ian seemed perfectly at home in the room. He strode up to Beatrice and gave her an affectionate peck on the cheek. "It's all right, Bea. Gabcik and Kubis completed their mission. Remember? And Reinhard Heydrich is dead."

"But why Josef Gabcik? I liked him."

Ian cupped her cheeks in his strong hands. "There were so many reprisals after the assassination. Jan and Josef had to sacrifice themselves."

"Olivia could have hidden them in Jarvoc."

"She couldn't, Bea," he said quietly. "The Germans had taken over the steel factory."

"Did they know Heydrich was dead?"

"Yes, Beatrice. They knew."

Chase heard the catch in his voice, and then, uninvited, he flopped on top of the unmade bed. Across the small room their eyes met again. "Don't keep frightening Bea with the past."

Startled Chase said, "Ian, I didn't. She asked me to help Kubis and whatever his name was."

"Gabcik. They were part of the Czech Brigade fifty years ago." He stared at the ceiling. "They were friends of my grandmother, but I suppose you already know that."

"I guessed as much. I've uncovered some other interesting things about your grandmother, Ian. I saw a lovely portrait of her in Oxford and found several articles on her in the library."

He glared back. "Things you intend to incorporate in your dissertation? I told you on the hills of Gascony that I'd stop you."

Her patience exploded. "If I ever find your grandmother's missing manuscript, I'll finish that novel for her."

"If I can't stop you, my grandfather or the publisher will. Besides there is no manuscript and certainly no need for a sequel to her last book."

Beatrice pointed a knitting needle at him. "Then why was Olivia writing it?" she asked.

He gave her a quizzical grin. "Was she?"

"If she wasn't," Chase asked, "then why are so many people trying to stop me from finding it?"

He pillowed his head on his locked fingers, an amused smirk tugging at his mouth. "I bet you chased after leaves when you were a kid or tried to pluck the rainbow from the sky. I did."

"Actually, I tried to catch the wind—especially on a cold day on Long Island or when we were out on a family drive." Before she realized it, she was confiding, "As a little girl, I used to think if I could catch the wind, I'd somehow find

God. But since I've grown up, I don't go for that God stuff any more."

He cocked his head toward Thorpe. "Don't let the old sage hear you saying that. She counts God as one of her best friends." He seemed to be counting the squares in the ceiling. "Your quest for my grandmother's story is like chasing the wind."

Chase laughed. "You're a fine one to be talking. A whole lifetime bicycling and for what? A yellow jersey."

"My grandmother would be proud of me."

At the look on his face, she grew serious. "I would like to have known her. That's what brought me to England."

"I thought the missing manuscript brought you here. And I'm telling you, let it go."

"I'm too close to the truth, right? Her books read like the story of her life."

He swung himself back to his feet, took three steps toward her, and gripped her shoulders. "Please, Chase—let it go."

"No fighting in my room," Beatrice said, waving her knitting needles at them. "Now be good children and kiss and make up."

The pressure of Ian's fingers eased. He winked at Beatrice, and then looking deeply into Chase's eyes, he kissed her soundly.

"What—you," she sputtered. "How dare you."

"Bravo," Bea applauded. "I like to see young people happy."

As her cagey eyes fixed on them, Chase had the uncanny feeling that Beatrice Thorpe was far more aware of reality than the staff at the Eagle's Nest gave her credit for. Beatrice was still grinning when Ian planted a kiss on her own cheek.

"Behave, love," he warned her. "And stop pretending. Chase is on to you."

Bea waited until he stalked off. "I think it would be nice if you could finish Olivia's book."

"I'll have to find it first."

She chuckled. "You're closer to finding it than you think.

But it would be too painful for the Kendalls—and dangerous. Olivia was a spy, you know."

A chill shot up Chase's spine. Bea knit on as she babbled,
her thoughts wandering back to the war years. "The
Renways took Olivia in," she said. "They had their reasons."

She grew tired as her sentences flitted from bombings to
resistance fighters, from war to air raids, from the detention
camp at Jarvoc to Eduard Benes—the exiled Czech
president.

"Benes could have gotten my husband safely out of
Prague, but he didn't." She pointed one crooked finger at
the row of war photos on the wall. "That's all I have left.
Roland died as a war correspondent," she said flatly.

She met Chase's eyes as she spoke again of the assassination of Reinhard Heydrich, a look of vengeance satisfied.
"The Nazis called themselves steel manufacturers and architects," she scoffed, her eyes wary. "Murderers—all of them."

She missed a stitch and trembled, saying, "Ian doesn't
like me to talk about the *designers of death*—but that's what
the historians called them. They're still busy."

They're still busy. Chase had to stop Ian and ask him
whether Beatrice was referring to the wretched war years
or remembering only the books that Olivia had written.

Bea's voice softened to a whisper as Chase stood to leave.
"Henri seemed like such a nice young man," she said sadly.
"Olivia protected him. She shouldn't have, you know—and
then the baby. Henri never knew about the baby." For a
flicker, the faded eyes brightened. "But she got even with
him. She left the baby at St. Michael's Cove."

"In Cornwall?" Chase asked.

"Where else?"

The baby son left behind in Cornwall at St. Michael's Cove.

Like Sayers, Renway had held her own dark secret—a
child born out of wedlock, a truth that would have no place
in Chase's dissertation.

"She was a spy," Beatrice repeated. "That's why she went
back to Cornwall." As suddenly as her head bobbed, her
eyes closed and she slept.

☼☼☼

Chase found Ian outside sitting on the lawn, his narrow-wheeled Hybrid bicycle resting against a white bench. "I've been waiting for you," he said.

"I'm glad. I was hoping to catch you. Ian, is there a steel factory in the town where your grandmother was born?"

"Yes, her brother Dorian still works there."

"Was it always a steel factory?"

"How would I know?" he asked. "I think you've been taken in by Beatrice, the keeper of the Kendall secrets."

"I think she understands far more than she lets on."

"She's old, Chase."

"I like her, Ian. I don't want you to make fun of her."

"Don't get me wrong. I'm fond of the old girl. She keeps my grandmother alive for me."

"What if she's making up all those stories, Ian?"

"It doesn't matter. It adds to what I really remember. When she dies, my grandmother will die all over again."

"You'll still have your family."

"Gramps and my dad rarely talk about her."

"What about her other children?"

He looked surprised. "What children? Forget that Cornwall legend. My grandparents only had one son—my dad, Aubrey."

He stood and swung his leg over his high-speed bike. "I was hoping to have dinner with you. We could dine out here in the woods with the saints at Eagle's Nest."

His strong face was deadly serious. It reminded her of the lovely portrait of Olivia hanging in the alcove at Somerville Manor. He had Renway's coloring and eyes and that pensive gaze, even when he smiled. She felt suddenly kindly toward him. He was, after all, fiercely protective of his grandmother's reputation and memory. "I'll pass on that dinner," she said. "We'd spend the whole time fighting over your grandmother's missing manuscript. Let's part friends instead."

"We could call a truce while we stuff down their starches."

She thought of Luke Breckenridge—as she often did these days. Particularly of his brief phone call inviting her to the Von Tonner Art Museum. "You're too young for me, Ian," she said.

"Twenty-three and I like older women."

She grinned at that. "Ask me out some other time."

"Sure. Twelve years from now when I'm old enough."

She wrapped her fingers around the handlebar. "Ian, on the back cover of one of your grandmother's books, she was wearing a beautiful blue bracelet. Was that a family heirloom?"

"I wouldn't know," he said.

He reached out and tucked a strand of hair behind her ear. "I wish I were old enough for you now, Chase," he said.

"I was talking about your grandmother's bracelet."

"I wasn't. Well, I'll be off then. I'm biking back to Kendallshire tonight."

"It'll be dark before you get there."

"I'm used to seven or eight hours of cycling a day."

"That's self-torture."

"Suffering is part of the job. I'm a professional cyclist."

"Ian, I'd like to ask you—may I come to Kendallshire and meet your grandfather?"

"He won't go for that."

"Could you at least ask him?"

"I could do that, but it will cost you."

She thought of the costly venture with Andrew Forrestal. Uneasily, she asked, "How much?"

"I'll have a few hours free on Sunday. You can have dinner with me there in Kendallshire before our team flies over to France." He pointed to the logo on his shirt. "Without Jon Gainsborough's steel company backing us, we wouldn't be riding."

He cuffed her chin playfully. "I'll talk to my grandfather and let you know whether you can come out on Sunday."

Ian rode off without looking back. He liked this girl, but
he felt as if a windstorm had hit the meadow flowers. Chase
was too curious, too close to a day long ago when his grandmother had trusted him with a bracelet filled with priceless
Kashmir sapphires. "Take care of it for me, Ian," his grandmother had said, "until I ask for it." Three hours later she
was dead.

He sped around the building and pulled up beside
Margot Hampton's parked car. "Well," Margot asked, "what
do you think?"

"She's determined to see my grandfather."

"Stop her."

"Should I run her down like they did my grandmother?
It's up to Uriah whether Chase sees him."

"We don't want her going anywhere alone."

"Mrs. Hampton, she's harmless."

"Harmless? Not if there's a CIA connection."

He put his head back and roared, one foot still on the
pedal. "Now you're sounding as nutty as Beatrice."

"I didn't start the CIA rumor."

"I'll run that one by my grandfather."

"If she goes to the Cotswolds, Peter Quincy goes with
her."

"Fine, but Quincy can have dinner with my grandfather.
Chase and I will be busy." He adjusted his helmet. "It's getting late. I have a long ride ahead."

"Ian, with all this renewed interest in your grandmother's death, stay away from the Eagle's Nest for a while.
Even Scotland Yard is getting involved again."

He turned his eyes toward the meadow flowers, their
stems dark in the twilight. "Then it's up to you to take care of
Beatrice for me. I'll be at the Tour de France for three weeks
in July. Will that be long enough for things to die down?"

"Chase should be gone by then."

"I hope not. But when the Tour de France is over, Mrs.
Hampton, I'm coming back to discard Beatrice's papers. If
a copy of my grandmother's missing manuscript is there in
that pile of junk, we've got to find it before Chase Evans
does."

"Do you want me to start sorting through her things?"

"She wouldn't let you."

"I don't think the sapphire bracelet is there, Ian."

Good. You don't know about the trap door in the bottom of the china closet. He winked, a triumphant twitch of his eye. "I can assure you, the bracelet is not there."

But as he pedaled away, he wondered how he could find time to slip back into Beatrice's room unnoticed and claim the sapphires. If he could just wait until the end of the race. No, he would have to get back there sooner—before the Hamptons gave Scotland Yard or Dudley Perkins an excuse to tear the room apart.

Chapter 19

Eagle's Nest, 9 A.M. Twice during the night Chase heard Beatrice whack her cane against the side rails. Twice she heard the heavy steps of the attendant going to her aid and a constrained voice arguing, reasoning, persuading, cajoling. The attendant's frustrated hissing was countered with Bea's shrill and determined protest: "I want to sit in my chair now."

There was no connecting bath between their rooms—no way for Chase to rush to Mrs. Thorpe's side. She longed to reassure Bea that they were still in the predawn hours, that morning would come. Finally the flushing of the toilet vibrated the walls between them, and quiet settled once more.

Now as she listened for some sound of wakefulness next door, she heard nothing, not even Beatrice's cane against the rail. But something had awakened Chase. She swung to a sitting position and cupped her ear. Yes, there were muffled voices coming from Thorpe's room. She had a sickening feeling that something had happened and that Beatrice was about to make her last exodus from the Nest. While Chase feared the worst, Beatrice came to life, shouting, "Get out. Get out of here."

Chase bolted across the room and cracked her door in time to see Margot Hampton and a broad-shouldered man in a tweed jacket backing hurriedly from Beatrice's room. Chase knew before he even turned that it was Edwin Wallis.

As she listened with pounding heart, they stopped just steps from her door.

"I'll get an order to tear that room apart," he said.

Margot's voice came low and strained. "Don't do that. The shock would kill her. She's just a harmless old woman."

"In this country legally or illegally, Mrs. Hampton?"

There was a marginal pause—time enough for Chase to sense a dark cloud lowering. She kept her hand on the knob, her ear pressed to the door as Hampton said, "I told you, Inspector. Beatrice was born in this country."

"Don't force me to use excessive means."

Chase curled her bare toes as the cloud darkened. Margot was fighting for more than the protection of Beatrice and her ancient possessions. Margot and Nigel felt threatened as well; they were personally involved somehow.

"She's English, Inspector," Margot said. "But she was trapped in Czechoslovakia during the war."

Chase cracked the door slightly, gambling on their anger to hide the squeak as she tried to see their faces.

Wallis rubbed his jaw, his chin cupped in his wide hand. "Thorpe. Thorpe. Roland Thorpe," he said. "A Czech war correspondent. Seems to me he was a friend of the American columnist Ernie Pyle. Maybe they worked together."

"Perhaps. But Thorpe was an excellent photographer. Beatrice took some award-winning shots herself."

"I noticed some of the black-and-whites on the wall."

"They were taken by Thorpe's husband. Ones on the downfall of Prague and the destruction of Lidice. They cost him his life."

They took a few steps away from Chase and paused again. "You still haven't answered my question, Mrs. Hampton. Is Thorpe in this country legally or illegally?"

"I told you. She was born here."

"Yes, but there was some question about her husband's loyalties. His political views."

"No one ever questioned hers. But you're wrong, Constable, about Roland Thorpe. He sacrificed his reputation feigning friendship with the German side. His camera

took him into the heart of the Reichland, into Berlin itself."
She shot Edwin a mocking smile. "You question his loyalty?
Roland filtered back information to the resistance move-
ment. In the end—when the Gestapo caught up with him—
he was imprisoned. He died in a labor camp, but as long as
Beatrice thought he was alive, she refused to leave Prague."

"Then she came back after the war? Mrs. Hampton, I have
only to phone Scotland Yard, and I can have my answers."

"Olivia Renway brought her back to London ten years
ago."

"Around the time Renway was killed? Why did she bother
with the old woman after all those years?"

The whispered answer was barely audible. "They were
friends."

"Spies?"

"I said friends. Really, Inspector, I must get back to my
office. Please leave."

"But first tell me—when did she come here?"

"She's been at our facility for ten years."

"And before that?"

"Maybe with Olivia's family in Czechoslovakia. I don't
know."

"I think you do."

If he had twisted her arm, Margot could not have
sounded more pained. "A year after Heydrich's assassination, Beatrice exchanged her papers with a friend." Huskily,
she said, "The Red Cross was securing releases for some of
the foreigners in prison camps. Beatrice was on the list, but
she wanted to remain in Jarvoc for her husband's sake; she
thought he was still alive. The friend was pregnant—her
husband also with the resistance movement; actually he
was dead, but the woman didn't know it."

"I see," Wallis said. "So officially Thorpe's records are
Czechoslovakian now? Her papers. I'd like to see her
papers."

"There are no records."

"Perhaps in her room. Mrs. Thorpe's room is oddly fur-
nished. Cluttered mostly."

"She chose to keep her own furnishings."

"I see," he said again.

But he didn't see, Chase was certain. And the question in her own mind must surely be in his. If Bea had returned to England—smuggled back into her own country—then how had she brought so many personal items with her?

"I'll be back. Tomorrow morning. I suggest that you don't touch anything in that room, Mrs. Hampton."

"Is it all right if we dust, Inspector? Or pick up the items you tossed around?"

"Leave everything just as it is."

"So you can exile her? She's too old to be tossed about."

His laugh came dry and brittle. "Mrs. Hampton, it is her past that interests me, not her age. I could make it quite difficult for you, harboring that woman here."

"But you won't because of Nigel."

"I'd sell my mother down the Thames if I had to. And I will find the real connection between Olivia Renway and Mrs. Thorpe."

"You'd hang them both for another promotion?"

"I'm due for one," he said calmly. "The Renway question has never been settled. It would be a gold star on my shoulder."

"But why all your interest now?"

"You have Chase Evans to thank for that. She muddied the waters. Since she reached London, MI5 has been on it. Fresh terrorist threats."

"Oh, Inspector, the next thing you'll tell me is that Chase is involved in them."

"Perhaps she is in some way. She's clever enough." To Chase it seemed that Wallis had only enough time to smack his lips before saying, "Thorpe wouldn't even budge out of that chair of hers."

"She rarely does. She'd sleep there if we'd let her."

"Why?" he insisted.

"Because she breathes better sitting up. Good day, Edwin. I'll trust you to see your own way out."

"And Miss Evans?"

"I told you in Beatrice's room—Evans is gone. To the Cotswolds, I think."

"Odd. None of my men saw her leave the Eagle's Nest."

Through the cracked door, Chase watched Margot and the inspector until they reached the end of the corridor and disappeared from view. She stole from her room and went immediately next door. Tapping lightly—so as not to startle Beatrice—she opened the door and slipped inside.

Beatrice was still in her night clothes with the derby hat on her head. "Get out. Out," she cried, waving her knitting needles frantically in the air.

"It's me, Beatrice. Chase."

Bea's eyes squinted as Chase approached. Fleetingly Chase wondered, *Do all blue eyes fade and glaze over? Do all the windows to memory cloud as Beatrice's have done? As Marie's did?* The warmth that she felt for Marie back at Willowglen spread quickly to Beatrice. Without invitation, Chase slid a straight-back chair up beside Beatrice and sat down facing her.

"You had early morning company," she said.

Beatrice was obviously agitated as she pointed toward the closet. The piles of junk seemed even more cluttered.

"That's the way the Gestapo come. In their plain clothes with all their questions. Tearing my things apart. Searching through my books."

Olivia's books. "That was Constable Wallis from Scotland Yard."

"That's what Margot told me. But I know. I know he wants Olivia's diaries."

So do I, Chase thought.

She felt like a traitor, as though she too had come in her fancy clothes, shrewdly, deceptively seeking answers—as the Gestapo had done long ago in Prague, as Constable Wallis had done only moments ago. She had come not in friendship for this old woman but for Olivia's lost manuscript. But diaries? Did she have diaries, too? As Beatrice calmed and took the start of another afghan from her knitting bag, Chase said, "Doesn't Uriah Kendall have Olivia's private papers, Beatrice?"

"Her husband?" The wrinkles turned to frowns, the puzzled gaze focused on the knitting needles. "No, Olivia wanted to protect Uriah. She wanted me to give them to the prime minister."

"To John Majors?"

"To Margaret Thatcher. Everything Olivia did was to protect Uriah. To clear his name."

Instinctively, Chase glanced around the room, shuddering at the mess that Wallis had left behind. She had to find Olivia's diary and papers before Wallis came back. *Shape up, Evans,* she told herself. *You're getting caught up in Bea's crazy stories.*

Her more rational self argued back, *What if she's telling the truth?* She managed her Willowglen smile—the happy, cheerful one that Marie loved. "Beatrice, how can you possibly know how Olivia Renway lived or what she thought?"

The knitting needles in the gnarled hands moved with lightning speed. "Who better than I? I knew that child all her life. She was so much a part of my life—still is. I know all about her—still do."

The derby hat tipped cockily on the silver hair. She poked it back in place with one of her needles and went on talking with only the loss of a stitch or two, like a wavering heartbeat kicking in and out.

"Did you really know Miss Renway?" Chase asked.

Thorpe's watery eyes brimmed over, taking on a bright glow that memory had sparked. "From the time she was born."

"Were you her nanny?"

"Her best friend."

"But you're not Czechoslovakian."

"No, I followed my husband there," she said softly. "England didn't want Roland back, so I packed up and moved to Prague to live with the Pascheks. That way I could be near my husband."

"Olivia's family? I thought her name was Renway."

The cagey eyes took refuge under the brim of the hat. "Not in the beginning. I took over for Mrs. Paschek. She had her hands full with three boys. Another baby was just too much for her. Olivia was a sickly little thing, red and ugly in the beginning—all arms and legs and double fists, not pretty like most babies."

The pictures of Olivia Renway were of a striking woman; perhaps Beatrice Thorpe had never known Olivia at all. The watery eyes brimmed over again. "She was scrawny, her face covered with downy peach fuzz. I never thought she'd grow up lovely, but then her cheeks filled in, and she stopped being fretful. She was a good baby after I took over, so easy to care for."

The ramblings of yesterday seemed more focused, the speech halting but clear, as though Beatrice were sorting out just how much to share with Chase. As they talked, Chase's fingers settled on an old-fashioned photo album on the table beside Thorpe. She flipped the cover open and immediately felt the sting of a needle across the back of her hand.

"Sorry," Chase said, her hand and her mood both smarting.

"That's Olivia's. These belonged to Olivia, too," she said, tapping her dangling earrings. "Lots of her things here."

Chase didn't move. She didn't want to damage the fragile bond between them. Why had Thorpe been permitted to keep so many possessions? The other residents were crowded together, two to a room, their possessions limited to a one-page checklist and a favorite stuffed chair. Yet Bea's room was crowded with personal belongings. Her own? Or did they really belong to Olivia Renway?

Bea paused, the knitting needles still in her hands, and leaned back in her velvety blue recliner. "She's here," Beatrice said. "In this room with me. I promised her I'd take care of her things for her."

Chase eyed the album again. "May I?" she asked.

The lips pursed. "Don't have any pictures of her childhood. They were lost in the war." She tapped her temple. "But I remember her growing up into a sweet little thing. Going to boarding school in Switzerland. And taking her for summer vacations in England—stayed with the Renways. Friends of her parents."

She rocked now, the afghan slipping to the floor. "She

should have stayed in boarding school. Been safer. She was smart as a whip, not haughty at all. Then she came back just before Prague fell—she wasn't supposed to come."

"From boarding school."

Bea groped for answers. "Yes, she was safe in Switzerland. But she came home. She was sixteen. For days she sat with her father talking about the clouds hanging over Europe."

"The war?"

She nodded. "Mr. Paschek saw it coming. Everybody did. He fought it in his own way with the underground press. I think that child knew it—she was a smart one. I think that's why she came back to work with him. He wanted to send his family to the Renways in England, but Mrs. Paschek was afraid to go, and Olivia wouldn't go, not without her father."

"But you said she had three brothers."

"She actually had four. Dorian came after Olivia. The brothers were grown up by then, except for thirteen-year-old Dorian. One of the boys was married and living in Lidice. They tried to persuade Mrs. Paschek and Olivia to go there."

"And you? Why didn't you go back to London?"

She rocked and reflected. "My husband couldn't go, and I wouldn't leave that child. I told them I'd stay and travel back to England with the rest of the family. But it was too late!"

Beatrice's past and Olivia's were tied together in this room. Olivia's private papers could be anywhere. In the bookcase. In the cluttered closet. On Beatrice's nightstand. But in spite of her confusion, she was too shrewd to reveal the hiding place. Chase paced the room with a methodical gaze. The china closet was filled with cups and plates, but were the panels hollow or solid? "The man from Scotland Yard will be back in the morning, Bea."

"To take me away?"

"Oh, no. But he plans to tear your room apart." *To destroy the things that you treasure.*

"You won't let him, will you?"

"I won't know how to stop him."

She squirmed in her chair, pathetically small, her short,

swollen legs barely touching the floor, her ankles almost lost in the ruffled trim of the recliner. "What does that man want from me?" she whispered.

"He thinks you're in this country illegally."

"But I was born in England."

"I know. And Constable Wallis wants Olivia's private papers."

"Hide them for me," Beatrice begged.

"I don't know where they are." Again Chase's gaze went slowly around the room, pausing at the clutter in the closet, lingering a second time at the bookshelves crammed with Olivia's books. Each possibility—each thought was interrupted with another glance at Beatrice. "Where are they, Bea? Tell me. I can't help you unless you tell me."

"I don't remember."

She patted the old woman's hand as she had often patted hands at Willowglen. "It's all right. It doesn't matter. I'll stay with you when the inspector comes tomorrow—"

But how can I stay? Margot told the constable that I've gone. Margot! "Beatrice latches onto every excuse to stay in that old chair of hers," she said. Under the cushion? No! Impossible!

Without asking, Chase carefully extended the leg rest. It scraped as it shot Beatrice's body into a cramped position.

Alarmed, Beatrice cried out, "I never use that leg rest. My chair is old and broken."

Chase bent down and lifted the ruffle. Beneath the rusty support rods lay a small trap door, a tiny keyhole visible on inspection. "There's a door here, Beatrice. Where's the key?"

"Olivia's diaries?" Bea asked.

"Maybe."

"You've discovered them?" Beatrice's eyes were shiny with tears. "I'd forgotten where I hid them. Oh, yes. Olivia's diaries are in there. Four of them. I remember now."

"May I read them?"

"Hide them for me. In your room."

"I won't hide something when I don't know what it says."

Her motions were frantic, her bare legs wiggling. "In here. In here," she cried as she rummaged in her knitting bag. "It's here. The key. Promise me you'll hide them after you read them."

"I promise." She took the key from Beatrice's trembling fingers. "You look tired, Beatrice. Would you like me to help you back to bed so you can take a nap?"

"No, I'm afraid of dying when I sleep. I must not die yet."

"You won't. You're just frightened. I'll stay here with you. I'll read the diaries while you rest."

Bea ran her gnarled finger over the back of Chase's hand. "Olivia would have liked you," she said.

She rose slowly to her feet, Chase's hand tight at her elbow. The steps seemed more halting than yesterday. She backed up to her bed, her knitting bag clutched in her free hand.

"Here, I'll take that for you," Chase offered.

"No, leave it by my pillow."

Chase stayed by the bed holding the fragile hand until Bea slipped into a troubled sleep. And then the soft snoring came—like a gentle wheeze. The outside wind against the curtains and Beatrice's snoring blew gently together.

As Beatrice dozed, Chase went back to the chair and fitted the key into the tiny hole. It jammed, but she struggled again, twisting and turning it, fearful that it might break before the door came loose. Finally the latch turned; the door moved. She lifted four diaries from their hiding place, lowered the leg rest, and settled in Bea's chair. She thumbed through the pages of the first diary and read: "The Germans came today. Czechoslovakia is no longer free. All I can hear is the booted step of marching men."

As Chase backed up to the first page and read through the diaries, she felt the pain and outrage of the youthful Olivia, the heartbeat of a young woman who would do anything to protect her family and her country.

> *February 24, 1939: Father has told me to stay in boarding school and not to leave Lausanne. But I am going home in the morning before any of the others know that I have gone.*
>
> *February 25, 1939: The ticket agent said that the south*

border between Austria and Czechoslovakia is closed. He tells me that he must route me the long way through Munich and on into Prague. Still I have not told my father that I am coming.

February 27, 1939: I am hungry. There have been long delays. There are uniforms everywhere. No one on the train is smiling. I see fear in their faces. I am afraid. A German soldier tried to flirt with me. I pretended I could not speak his language. I wanted to cry out, "Leave me alone. I have some Jewish blood flowing in my veins."

Midnight, March 1, 1939: We spent hours at the border crossing. At last the train rumbled into my country.

March 4, 1939: Father is still angry with me. He says that I have put them all in danger, that I should have obeyed him and stayed in school. But Beatrice was glad to see me.

The farm looks different. Some of mother's favorite furniture is gone, including her small, round table and her china closet. Father has shipped them to the Renways in England while there is still time to send them. He wants the family to fly out this weekend—to go to England until Prague and Jarvoc are safe once again. I will not go unless my father goes with us.

March 13, 1939: Some of the government officials and military have fled the country. My brother Antonin went with them. I worry about Papa. I hear him leave the house each night when we are all in bed. He does not come back until dawn.

He says I am too young to help the growing resistance movement. But he is wrong. I want to work beside Papa. This is my country, too.

March 15, 1939: I am sixteen. At dawn this morning my country was invaded. The Germans have taken over Prague. Even now they are searching house by house. I think they are hunting for my father.

Chapter 20

Prague, March 15, 1939. Sixteen-year-old Olivia Paschek awakened to a foreboding silence in the tiny bedroom above her uncle's shop. She lay motionless, feeling a sudden chill sweep across the room, a nameless fear that wrapped its tentacles around her. The eerie predawn stillness was shattered by the roar of a hundred motorcycles screaming through the streets, the sound of angry voices shouting, the frightened cries of the neighbors. There was a lull in the uproar, and then she heard the booted steps against the pavement. She threw back her bedroll and pattered barefooted across the wooden boards into the other room.

On the radio beside her father, a voice droned on: "Offer no resistance . . . keep calm . . . go about your work as usual."

"Papa, what is it?" she cried.

Only his head turned, his broad stubby finger to his lips. She ran to him, and he held out his arm and pulled her close. "You should have been on the plane yesterday," he said. "Back to Switzerland. Back to safety."

"The planes weren't flying yesterday, Papa."

He cursed the weather, cursed the planes and the trains that had crossed him. His gaze went back to the window, his eyes hardened as he peered through the curtain. Now she saw what he saw. They had awakened to find their country occupied by armed forces—a Panzer division thundering down the boulevard, the neighboring streets blocked off, hundreds of billowing parachutes drifting toward the airport. The road in front of the shop was choked with armored cars and tall, broad-shouldered Germans in gray-green uniforms, their faces harsh beneath their helmets. Across the River Vltava a swastika hung from the top of the Hradcany Castle.

Dawn had brought light to their darkness. Down the street foot soldiers were searching house by house, a block at a time. In spite of the warmth of her father's strong arm around her, Olivia shivered. She knew before she asked. "Who are they, Papa?"

"The enemy." His voice filled with loathing. "They've taken us without a shot. Get dressed, Olivia. We must leave."

"They'll stop us. They're searching the houses."

"We'll be gone before they reach our shop."

"Why would they want us, Papa?"

"They are searching for the voices of opposition—political activists, the country's leaders. Teachers. Journalists."

She frowned. "But you are a friendly voice, Papa."

He smiled. "Not my words in the underground paper. These have aroused fury in Berlin."

"Then Dorian is right. You run the underground press."

"Someone had to."

Zdenek Paschek had always been her strength, her idol. She thought him old and wise, yet in truth he was only forty-five—a short, stocky man whose nose was a bit too wide, his mustache too thick and bushy, his mahogany eyes rich with kindness. Papa had been content to run the print shop and work the family farm and to spend his early evenings drinking Staropramen with his friends in the pub. He was a good provider, better off than most of their neighbors in Jarvoc, and more than willing to stretch his earnings to send Olivia to boarding school in Switzerland.

Only in recent months had his patterns changed. Now he spent long hours at his brother's shop in Prague, often taking the older boys with him. He had always been nonpolitical. Yet here he was admitting to partnership in the resistance movement; growing uprising had fanned across

Czechoslovakia ever since the Munich Agreement handed over parts of the Republic to Hitler.

Papa seemed suddenly grief-stricken. "Your mama said I have only brought danger to my family. The older boys can take care of themselves, but you and Dorian should be in Switzerland."

"He's thirteen. He can't go to a private girls' school."

"You're right," he said. "Now dress quickly. I must get you on the train. Once you reach Switzerland, promise me you will go on to England. The Renways will take care of you. I'll make certain your mama and Dorian and Beatrice come later."

"The borders will be closed, Papa."

"We can send you through Poland."

"I won't go without you."

He brushed her hair from her face with his big hands. "My stubborn one," he said. Outside, the angry shouts of the soldiers came closer. "No arguments, Olivia. Your brother Antonin is already in London. He'll take you to the Renways."

She came back from the bedroom in her brother's clothes, her own dresses shoved into a backpack. "At school they said the Nazis hurt women and girls. They raped some of my Austrian friends."

Pain ripped across his face. He nodded, unable to speak. He took her hand and led her through the storage room, past her uncle's printing press and the shelves of ink and newsprint.

🦉🦉🦉

The depot was surrounded by Wehrmacht troops, the train smoking idly on the railroad siding. Two of the third-class cars with their hard wooden benches had been cordoned off. Four bodies lay limp on the platform. "It's too late," Olivia's father cried. "I didn't get you out in time."

"It's all right, Papa. I didn't want to go without you."

They were lying in the thick grass on the knoll, hidden

behind the bushes. As her father wept, locks of raven hair fell across his creased brow.

The Kommandant ignored the lifeless bodies on the platform, his attention riveted on a frightened family trembling in front of him. "Show me your papers," he shouted in German. "Your identity papers," the Kommandant shouted again.

As the man reached into his pocket, shots rang out. He dropped in front of the Kommandant, his blood splattering over the platform. Immediately, Zdenek's hand covered Olivia's mouth. "Keep still," her father warned.

"That man didn't even resist," she cried.

"But we will."

Overhead came the drone of planes bringing the threat of bombs falling if the people of Prague resisted. Zdenek's rough hand encircled Olivia's. "Tonight—when it is dark—we will go to Jarvoc."

"We can't. They'll stop us. You heard the Kommandant. We need identity cards to prove we work in the factory at Jarvoc."

"The priest will get them for us, Olivia."

"He doesn't know we're here."

"Come, we'll hide in the catacombs of the Karel Boromejsky Church until darkness. We'll be safe there."

❧ ❧ ❧

The Greek Orthodox church, Prague, 10 A.M. From behind the curtain, Yeurgous Papanastasious saw them steal through the sanctuary—slipping through the wall paneling to the right of the altar into the stairwell that would take them down into the crypt. The priest made no effort to stop them. They would be found soon enough. Let each man and woman in Prague grab what moments of freedom they could. Let them have these few hours or days of safety. He would not turn them away from the church. Let them find solace here. Let them set their house in order.

Yeurgous had recognized Zdenek Paschek. The Germans would be looking for him, carting him off to stand trial and die for his part in running the underground press, silencing his right to free speech. But the priest's heart went out to the young girl—and she was a girl in spite of the trousers and jacket that she wore. He had seen the red curls slipping beneath the cap, had known intuitively who she was. She was tall for her age and shapeless like her mother, but spry as she followed her father down into the crypt.

Yeurgous knelt by the altar and prayed, crying in agony for Prague, for himself, and for Zdenek Paschek and his daughter who sought refuge in the church. And in utter despair, he cried, "My God, where are You? Have You deserted even this Your sanctuary?"

It seemed to the priest that his words bounced back from the vaulted ceiling, shelling him with futility. Behind him the door burst open. Soldiers ran down the long aisle. He felt himself torn violently from his kneeling position. He cringed, shrinking back as they dragged him to his feet and thrust him against the altar. Hatred showed in their faces and boomeranged in the sharp commanding voice of their officer.

"Let the priest alone," he told them.

Luftwaffe wings shone on the lapel of the handsome blond German. "Go on with your praying, priest. Prague will need it."

Something in the eyes belied the harshness in his voice. "What would you know about prayer?" Yeurgous asked him.

In the sudden hush in the room came the answer: "It was my country—as my mother would say—that gave you 'Silent Night.'"

🦂🦂🦂

March 16, 1939, 3 A.M. Keeping off the main roads, Zdenek and Olivia crawled and stumbled through the rough countryside in the pitch darkness. They reached Jarvoc while it was still dark, but even in the starless night they could see that the farmhouse was under the control of soldiers. They staggered on to the dress shop owned and operated by Olivia's childhood governess. Beatrice Thorpe opened the door without a word and pulled them to safety. She held Olivia and brushed the straggly hair from her face.

"What are the Germans doing here?" Zdenek asked.

"They've taken over the factory." Her laugh was mirthless. "They've promised us food and safety in exchange for work."

"What's happened to my family?"

Beatrice was a shadowed figure in the darkness. "Your wife and Dorian have gone to Lidice to be with your oldest son."

"Good. They will be safe there. Where are the others?"

"They're waiting for you. I will take you to them. But we must go quickly. Dawn is coming." She gripped Olivia's hand. "You must come with us. We cannot leave you here alone."

۝۝۝

In the caves of Jarvoc. Olivia had long suspected that her father had a mistress. Now as she faced the resistance fighters in the cavern, she knew her fears had been unfounded. She recognized most of her father's friends: Leo Padanansky and the parish priest. The farmer with six children. Margot and Ladislav Dvorak. And Beatrice's husband, Roland, the war correspondent.

"Get your daughter out of here," Leo said.

Paschek refused. "She has nowhere to go. We must take her into our confidence."

"She's only a child."

"It no longer matters," her father said. "We are at war."

"She's too young," Roland Thorpe warned.

"I'm sixteen."

Her father smiled through his sadness and held out his hand to her. "A very grown-up sixteen," he said. "We will need her. She speaks French and German fluently."

Beatrice gasped. "You're not suggesting—"

"That she run courier for us? What else can we do, Beatrice? My sons are no longer available."

"I'm quick on my feet, Papa. I know all the back roads."

"Where's your son Antonin?" Leo asked. "He's late."

"He's gone—in England by now. He flew out in the KLM plane with Colonel Moravec. Ten others made it with them."

"Impossible in that blinding spring snowstorm."

"They had to risk the storm to fool the German agents."

Leo drove his fist against the cement wall. "Then we've been deserted again. First by our ex-president, Benes. Now Moravec."

"We don't need them, Leo. We'll fight on without them."

"President Hacha is warning against that."

"Hacha is old and ill." There was a slight rustling in the cave as her father pulled a spotter's map from his pocket. "Antonin got a message through to me before he left."

You're lying, Papa, she thought. *But I see hope on Leo's face now.* "Hacha meant well, but he has sold our country out to the enemy. Moravec in London is our only hope of setting up a government in exile. If Eduard Benes joins him, they'll be dependent on our underground activities. We won't let them down."

Leo smarted. "What can a handful like us do?"

Dvorak sharpened his knife. "The same things we've been doing. Cutting brake hoses on trains and telephone lines. Spying on German agents. Maintaining our wireless listening posts."

Papa's voice was determined. "We'll keep on resisting. They'll force us to work in their factories, but we'll stage slowdowns. The intelligence files went out in the British pouch with the request for more arms and ammunition. We won't wait. We'll steal incendiary bombs from the Germans to blow up their petrol supply and destroy their equipment." Papa kept his arm around Olivia and gave her an encouraging squeeze as he said, "And we'll send couriers across the borders whenever we need to."

"What about your other sons? Can't they work for us?"

Paschek shook his head. "Torma and his family are in Lidice. Dorian and his mother are with them now."

"And your son Karol?" Roland Thorpe asked.

Paschek looked at the jaded faces. "Karol is one of the few

who listened to me. I tried to warn all of you that the Germans planned something like this."

"We didn't think it would happen so soon."

"Leo, it's been coming for months. Karol and two of his friends plan to cross the Polish border tonight—while the customs officers and police are still looking the other way."

Moodily Leo said, "And if they're lucky enough to succeed?"

"They'll make their way to the French Legion and eventually to England if Moravec can gather a Czech army around him. We'll help them. We must keep our transmitters open so we can send reports through to Czech Intelligence in Stockholm and Geneva."

Olivia had slipped from the meeting and back while the men argued. But even in the darkened cave she heard them talking. She stood before them now, still dressed in her brother's clothes, her beautiful red hair shorn to a boy's cut. "My brothers are gone," she said. "That leaves me to carry your messages. I know Geneva, Papa. And I know French and German. I can get through the lines."

🌀🌀🌀

Eagle's Nest, England. Chase closed the last of Olivia's four diaries and leaned back in Beatrice Thorpe's recliner, her thoughts on the lovely Olivia Paschek. She could envision the youthful Olivia listening with her ear pressed against the cracks in the wall or slipping up quietly on German sentries. Chase was guilty of listening uninvited herself—ever since her brother taught her how to tune in on the intercom at their family home on Long Island. The truth was, she never lost the habit of or delight in tuning a curious ear to those around her.

As she glanced across the room, she was startled to see Beatrice's tired eyes fixed on her. "You're awake. You should have said something. I just finished reading Olivia's diaries."

Bea pulled herself up with the side rails. "You must hide

Olivia's book with the diaries—in case something happens to me."

Chase's heartbeat quickened. "The lost manuscript?"

"It was never really lost. If something happens to me," she repeated, "give it to Ian Kendall. He'll know what to do."

"Ian will be in France for three weeks. I'll put it in my father's lockbox in London. But is that what you want?"

Beatrice pointed her cane toward Olivia's end table where an old-fashioned lamp tilted precariously. "Over there," she said.

Chase popped out of the recliner and ran to the table. She felt around the edges. "Where?"

"Underneath—there's a latch."

Chase stooped down and ran her hand around the underside of the thick tabletop. Her fingernail snagged in the back as it hit a rusty latch. Once released, the drawer came free easily. Chase lifted out a thick and musty manila envelope. "Beatrice!"

The wizened face brightened. "The nurses snooped in my bookshelves and dresser. Margot Hampton even looked in the china closet. But no one knew about the drawer in the table. 'Cept me. And Olivia. And I can trust Olivia. She won't tell a soul."

And if we had left it there until morning, Chase thought, *Constable Wallis would have found it.* Chase made some hurried decisions. She would travel to Prague to talk with Dorian Paschek about his sister. And she would leave the Eagle's Nest early in the morning, hopefully before Edwin Wallis came back.

She took the few steps back to Beatrice's bedside. The aged hand felt cold in Chase's clasp, like Marie's had felt at the Willowglen. "Thank you for trusting me, Mrs. Thorpe. May I read Olivia's manuscript before I give it to Ian?"

"Yes, do." Her eyes flickered and closed, her breathing suddenly shallow. Slowly she opened them again. "Yes, Olivia would like you," she said. Her eyes clouded. "Could you call Olivia and ask her to come have tea with us? I want her to know that the boys from Anthropoid are gone."

Her plaintive cry turned to a wail. "If only we could have gotten the assassin team safely back to London."

Chase fought the tightness in her throat. "I'll ask the nurse to get you washed and dressed."

"Oh, how nice. Dressed up for tea. I think I'll wear my derby hat today. Olivia likes that one."

"It's there on your bed—beside your knitting bag."

۞۞۞

The Cotswolds, England. Standing here on the bridge where it had all begun, Uriah knew that he would one day come back and finish life's journey in the very place where he had been born. He had grown up in Kendallshire, one of those tranquil Cotswold villages nestled in the hills and valleys of Gloucestershire. It was sometimes missed by tourists, lying as it did on one of those roads less traveled. Thus it remained unspoiled, serene, a place to be shared by simple villagers and grazing sheep.

Uriah knew every inch of the village—the Elizabethan manor once owned by his great-grandparents, the half-timbered hotel in the middle of town, the old cloth mill where the paddles squeaked as the gentle waters of the river turned them. The village was filled with two-story cottages with steeply pitched tiled roofs, his own still thatched because he liked it that way. On the other side of the foot-bridge lay the parish church with its lancet windows where four generations of Kendalls had married.

His son Aubrey had been born here, too. Aubrey had spent his early years rollicking over the woodland paths. Even now the sun cast its golden hues on the limestone hills where sheep were grazing. Grover and Ian had only come to Kendallshire for short visits and seldom after Olivia died. Since coming back, Uriah had been calmed once again by the Cotswolds. But his peace was fragile with Nedrick attempting to shatter it with his constant warnings about trouble ahead.

For days Nedrick had tried to persuade him not to meet with the American student, but sooner or later he would be forced to face this Chase Evans—a good-looking young woman according to Nedrick—and hear her out. He would discuss Olivia's literary works, and he would answer simple questions and ask some of his own. "Yes," he would say, "Olivia was Czechoslovakian by birth. Yes, she survived the war but lived out most of it in Britain."

Some of the nasty rumors about Olivia were in public record. To deny these would be foolish, nor would he dispute them. But should he answer any questions about Cornwall? No, for Olivia's sake, he would deny these and tell Miss Evans that Olivia's British family had died before he knew her.

"I thought I'd find you here," Nedrick said.

"It's pleasant standing here—on Olivia's bridge."

"We've got to talk. The news commentator is talking about more bomb threats."

"We're safe here in the Cotswolds, Nedrick."

"They would just as soon drop bombs or nerve gas on this village as not."

"*They?*" Uriah challenged. "You seem to have some particular group in mind."

"Don't you understand, Uriah? The terrorists could just as easily target us."

"You sound so certain," Uriah said sadly. "Olivia predicted these things in her books. The use of nerve gas. The bombing of government buildings. The destructive behavior of madmen."

"Uriah, this threat is real. Some extremist group could be patterning after the subway incidents in Tokyo."

"Miserable rumors." Uriah tapped his fingers together. "I've lived with miserable rumors for years. Kaminsky and Neilson at Langley still think Olivia was connected with an extremist group. Dudley Perkins's doings, no doubt. Perkins likes to point out that Olivia's books were accurate as to time and location of bombings and terrorist threats *before they happened.*"

"What are they trying to do—blame your wife for something she wrote years ago? Or was she really involved?"

"Before our marriage we agreed not to question each

other about the past. Otherwise there would have been no marriage. But Perkins is convinced that she spied against England during the war, working directly with a German agent."

Nedrick rubbed his hands on his trouser leg. "Did your wife point her finger back at someone in Germany?"

"No," Uriah said calmly. He was aware of Nedrick's nervous movements. *I've triggered something here,* he thought. He was reminded of his concerns back in Maryland—Nedrick's keen interest in foreign embassies across the Potomac.

"There's nothing they can do now, not with your wife dead."

"But Langley and MI5 still keep close tabs on me."

"Then with Chase Evans delving into Olivia's past, it only stirs up more trouble. It's already cost Andrew Forrestal his life."

"Then out of curiosity, I will talk with Miss Evans."

"I won't stay around and watch her cut you down."

"Are you planning a holiday? Where will you go?"

Nedrick deliberated. "To a small fishing village in Spain. I was always going to do that with my grandfather."

"Spain, eh? A favorite place from your boyhood, Nedrick?"

"One of the only good recollections I have."

"I have something else you could do first. Perhaps you would like to attend the opening of the Von Tonner Art Museum. I have an invitation for myself and a guest, but I'm not going." He turned and smiled at Nedrick, wondering what twisted thoughts were running through the young man's mind. "The invitation is on my desk at the cottage. Take it if you like."

Chapter 21

arvoc. Altman Russelmann rallied the family out of bed for an unscheduled conference at the dining room table. Hanz limped downstairs in his tartan robe, tying the sash as he joined the others as the uninvited guest.

Altman's eyes narrowed. "No need for you to come."

Hanz remained, studying his son. Altman was well-attired as always, the shades of his tie picking up the blues in the Canali suit and linen shirt. But he seemed overdressed for the office. Gustav sat on the other side of Altman, looking disgruntled. Josef sat at the end of the table, his eyes downcast, his sense of inferiority in Altman's presence glaring. He didn't even look up when Mila came into the room carrying a breakfast tray with an assortment of breads, stuffed eggs, and grilled sausage.

Altman rebuked her. "Where's the strudel I ordered?"

Fire lit in her dark eyes. "I'll get it," she said. As she passed Hanz, she mouthed, "I've got a surprise for you. Later."

Her smile gave Hanz boldness. "Well, what's the emergency this time, Altman?" he asked.

"Whether to continue the Nishokura accounts."

"They're our best buyer, our dumplings and roast pork."

"Forget the bread on the table, Father. They could be our downfall. Ever since the Tokyo disasters, there's been an ongoing investigation."

"Nothing in the headlines about that," Gustav argued.

Altman fought back. "Behind the scenes, the finger is on Sasa Nishokura, the vice-president of foreign sales."

"And we're involved?" Hanz asked.

"We could be if we keep using them. But our records are in the clear, aren't they, Josef?"

Josef always looked miserable under pressure. "I don't know, Altman. Gustav insists on handling that lately. But Father is right. It hardly seems the time to drop a long-standing account."

"If Nishokura Steel goes down, we're not going with them."

"Why would we go with them, Altman? How could our company be in trouble for selling steel to them?" Hanz asked.

Altman ignored his father and glanced at his Omega watch. "Gunter called for a meeting at the corporate office this morning. The president from the Dortmund plant will be there. Gustav, you and I are flying in to represent Jarvoc."

Gustav bounced his unlit cigarette from one palm to the other. "Will Poland have a voice?"

"This doesn't concern their operation."

"Will Gainsborough be joining you in Munich?" Hanz asked.

"That old fool? There isn't time. The less he knows, the better for him, the better for us." Altman tugged at the button on his suit coat. "Jon is too edgy. He doesn't mind stockpiling money, but he abhors breaking the rules."

"We should at least notify Coach Skobla," Gustav suggested.

"Let him keep his mind on training the cycling team for the Tour de France."

Gustav rubbed his fat hands together. "I like that irony," he said. "Imagine Olivia Renway's grandson cycling down the Champs-Elysees in the yellow jersey next month."

"I can't imagine that at all," Altman said. "I have no intention of letting Ian Kendall win."

۞۞۞

Shortly after Altman and Gustav took off in the company jet, Hanz left the house with his toolbox and made his way slowly along the tracks to the old Jarvoc plant. It was true that the blast furnace—which smelted the iron products—belched out the ominous black smoke that often rose above the mill. But at times lately when the winds turned toward the farm, Hanz detected a different odor above Jarvoc.

Altman held the only key to the front entry of the waste plant, but Hanz made his way to the back of the ghostly gray building and went cautiously down the seven steps. He rattled the rusty lock. Time was against him. By nine the trucks and forklifts would rumble past the building toward the waiting train. He took his battery torch, shielded his eyes with goggles, and fought the chain and lock that had been bolted for fifty years.

Once inside, he was surprised at the absence of spiders. He worked his way through the numerous rooms, finding what he knew he would find. Stockpiles of weapons, drums of liquids, and a massive conveyor of rusting pipes that ran deep into the tunnels. Several gas containers bore fifty-year-old labels, the faded letters spelling out the German word for poison. *Gift gas.* He ran his hand along the bulkhead, feeling for a fissure or ruptured fault line that would allow toxic leaks to rise like a foggy mist. Poison gases seeping from the pipes could destroy everything and everyone in Jarvoc.

His uneven steps echoed loudly as he followed the pipeline to the massive steel doors that led into the tunnels. If the rusty pipes burst as the Russian pipeline had done along the Arctic Circle, any contents would spill out and destroy the underground water source for Jarvoc. Hanz could hardly imagine how far the spring thaws and flowing river might carry it.

Hanz moved on to the infamous shower rooms and glanced up at the old catwalk where the guards had once stood. His torch caught the reflection of new sensors on the wall and shiny new shower heads. Someone had been measuring the pipe's thickness to detect the cracks and corrosion that called for repairs. The doors to the shower room had been resealed and one whole section of the pipeline burnished and coated with rust-proof material. Altman? Altman never dirtied his hands. Josef? A quality chemist but spineless. Gustav was a yes-man. Jiri, the clever architect? Jiri and Altman! "Dear Lord," Hanz cried out, "what are they planning?"

Coming out of the shower room, he stopped, unwilling to go farther into the cavernous tunnels that stretched beneath the railroad tracks and forested mountains. He had walked these tunnels as a young man, recoiling then as he did now. He would not look at the chute that had sent its innocent victims into the underground morgue.

Again he regretted the day he had found his firstborn son in Cornwall. His hip throbbed as he turned and retraced his steps. The toolbox in his hand felt heavier. He stumbled and fell forward. Exhausted, he braced himself against the cold cement and wept without tears. There was only one honorable thing to do. Hanz took the old chrome-plated Smith and Wesson from his toolbox, feeling as old as the nineteenth-century weapon. He spun it on his forefinger, sensing the weight and power that it held. Better to die here alone in the tunnel than to face the shame and humiliation of what his sons had become. He lifted the revolver and pressed it against his temple.

۞۞۞

Sunday. Chase had promised herself one sunrise at the Eagle's Nest before she left. She rolled out of bed, showered, and dressed in her Koret City Blues and a soft royal blue shell. She tiptoed from her room, stole down the corridor, and was outside when the first streaks of dawn painted their golden rays on the valley.

She was still curled in the corner of one of the white benches when Peter arrived with her car rental and the luggage she had left behind at the Hamptons. She ran to meet him and felt the roughness of his tweed jacket as he hugged her. "Peter, I'm glad you came. I hated going away without seeing you again."

His lopsided grin spread from one well-shaped ear to the other. "Jolly good. We're friends now that you're leaving. I dare say, what you hate doing is going away without your luggage."

She touched his right cheek. "Your bruises are better."

"Yes, I can even see again." He hesitated as though his thoughts were stuttering. "Chase, I kept hoping you'd fall passionately in love with England and stay forever."

"You and me?"

"That's what I had in mind."

"It would never work. You plan to take up residence at number 10 Downing someday. I'd be an embarrassment to you."

"I might only make it to the House of Commons."

"And you'd be in the Labor Party, and I'd no doubt be on the other side waving a picket sign on Whitehall. We'd argue politics all through dinner."

He caught her hand playfully and kissed it. "I really will miss you. Come back someday and maybe—"

"We'll see." But she doubted their paths would cross again.

They had run out of words, out of time. She wanted to slip the rest of her things into the car before Margot Hampton caught onto her plans, especially the suitcase with Olivia's diaries and manuscript packed in the bottom. "Peter, would you mind getting the luggage from my room?"

He held out his hand for the key. "The room beside Beatrice Thorpe's? I'm to slip in and out unnoticed. Right?"

"That gives me time to say goodbye to Beatrice."

When they reached the end of the hall, Chase broke into a run. She opened Beatrice's door without knocking. "Beatrice, I—"

She screamed. The room was in shambles. Beatrice was gone.

🐚🐚🐚

Chase was breathless when she burst into Margot Hampton's office. "Margot, where's Beatrice Thorpe?" she cried.

Margot's face went livid at the intrusion. Nigel Hampton stood behind her, his hands firmly on her shoulders. Only Constable Wallis seemed unflustered. "Miss Evans," he said with forced politeness, "they told me you had gone to the Cotswolds."

"Where is she?"

"In the infirmary," Nigel said. "But she'll be all right."

"Mrs. Thorpe was beaten rather brutally," Wallis said matter-of-factly. "At approximately one this morning."

"I was in the room next door. I never heard a thing."

"You weren't intended to hear," Wallis said. "But there were two assailants. That's all Thorpe has been able to tell us."

Nigel disagreed. "She told us they spoke to her in Czech."

Chase looked to Margot for confirmation. "I must see her."

Wallis seemed unflappable. "She's resting, and then I will see her first. You do understand the need for that." His smile was wicked. "Her room was torn apart. Apparently they didn't find what they were looking for, but we will."

Chase had the irresistible urge to stick the constable with a pin, but there wasn't one big enough to deflate his ego. The only comfort she had was that the intruders hadn't found what they were looking for. How could they? She had Olivia's diaries and manuscript in her room. "I have to talk to her, Margot."

Wallis stood and beckoned Nigel to follow him. "I'm sure your wife will want you present when I interview Mrs. Thorpe."

As they left, Margot turned angrily on Chase. "Wherever you go, trouble follows you. First it was Andrew Forrestal. Then bomb threats in Kendallshire—and now this. Poor Beatrice."

"Bomb threats, Mrs. Hampton?"

"Another Czech terrorist group, according to Edwin. They're afraid Olivia left something behind that will lead back to them. Chase, I warned Nigel if you came here, it meant trouble."

Chase glanced out the window toward the eastern horizon where the sun had come up with such brilliant colors. An hour ago? Three? Had hope been shattered that quickly with problems for the Hamptons and Bea? *Wherever you go, trouble follows you.*

Her thoughts raced to the notes from the unfinished novel—a steel factory, nerve gas, the annihilation of another generation. Which steel factory? *Who were you trying to identify? Talk to me, Olivia Renway, the way you seem to talk to Beatrice all the time. What warning were you trying to leave behind? None of it makes sense.* She groped for a link between the youthful Olivia and the genteel woman who had died on Downing Street. Czechoslovakia. It was back to the diaries. How many times had Olivia written that she would die for her country? Something had happened on her last trip to Prague and Jarvoc, a threat against her beloved country.

Chase turned back from the window and faced Margot again. "You know that I'm leaving for the Cotswolds, don't you?"

"I guessed as much. I saw Peter arrive with your car."

"Margot, I'm going to visit Ian's grandfather."

"Then Uriah will probably tell you that Edwin Wallis attended Olivia's funeral. He was a young officer back then assigned to protect the Kendall family at the graveside ceremony. The truth is, Edwin and MI5 have always linked Olivia's death to Uriah's old ties with British Intelligence. Edwin and MI5 never gave up that idea." Margot wiped her eyes with her long fingers, as though with the effort she could take away the weariness. "Ten years ago, when she came back from Prague, there were those who believed she was carrying intelligence reports—or possibly even messages to a Czech terrorist group in London. Important papers that have never been found. After her death, Uriah arranged for Beatrice to stay here in the safety of the Eagle's Nest."

Papers that Beatrice had given to Chase. She jammed her hands in her pockets. "I guess he just wanted to protect Bea."

"Because he couldn't protect his wife. He couldn't bear

the thought of his wife's friend being exiled from England again."

"Margot, do you believe the stories Beatrice tells?"

"Do you?"

"I wouldn't dare put them in my dissertation."

Margot sighed, seemingly relieved. "No, I suppose not."

"Did you know that Beatrice had a friend named Margot?"

"Did she?"

"She said she did. They ran an underground escape route in Prague during the war—rescuing the crews from downed planes."

Margot laughed, but the merriment seemed lost. "She does go on about the war days, doesn't she? But then that's what old people do. They go back to the good old days."

"They weren't good days, Mrs. Hampton. They were dreadful."

A faint smile began at the corners of Hampton's thin lips. "You are so transparent when you want answers, Chase—so obvious when you are on to something. I was named for my mother, Margot Dvorak, but I suppose Beatrice has already told you that."

"No, but I guessed." *Olivia's diaries again.*

"Beatrice, mother, and Olivia called themselves the Bronze Network. Right under the noses of the Nazis, they risked their lives leading twenty or more Allied airmen out of the country when their planes strayed over Czechoslovakia and crashed."

"Then it's true—Beatrice Thorpe and your mother were arrested."

"Yes, but, thank goodness, Olivia eluded capture. Beatrice's family here in England went through the International Red Cross trying to get her freed. She was a British citizen—British passport and birth certificate." She looked on the verge of tears. "But Beatrice and mother had already exchanged their identity papers. It was one of those humanitarian gestures in the war. Mother was pregnant, my father dead. Beatrice thought I'd have a better chance born in England."

"But their passports—they couldn't have looked alike."

"They were near in age, dark hair, haggard, war-worn faces. They had been through some rough months, sharing their limited food rationing with the men they rescued. The hoax wasn't discovered until Mother reached London. Beatrice's family was devastated, but they knew their daughter and her love for others." Margot fought to keep her voice even, unemotional. "After that there was no way out of Prague for Beatrice until Olivia found her ten years ago."

"Margot, I don't understand why Beatrice couldn't come back to England after the war. She was born here."

"Many refugees tried to leave Czechoslovakia as the Russians took control, but Beatrice had no proof of her birthright."

Margot stood up from her desk, walked across the room, and hugged Chase. "I told you once I thought we could be friends—under different circumstances. I still think that. Perhaps you can come back someday when all of this is over." Her fingers barely touched Chase's cheek. "Now go on before Edwin and Nigel get back here. But don't go without saying goodbye to Beatrice."

🌑🌑🌑

The infirmary was down the hall from Margot Hampton's office, across from the nurses' station. Beatrice lay quietly on the bed, her hand restrained so IV fluids could flow unhindered, but her fingers grasped the cane lying in the bed beside her.

She looked feeble, even smaller and shorter than her five feet. One hand was swathed in bandages; her mouth and eyes were bruised from the beating. A row of black stitches ran beneath her chin. Chase pulled up a chair and sat down. She reached through the side rails and cupped one veined hand and squeezed it.

Bea's eyelids fluttered open. Behind the large, wire-rimmed glasses, the Mediterranean blue of her eyes seemed paled by pain. Recognition came instantly. "Oh, Chase.

Chase. I was just talking to Olivia about you. She's over there in the corner."

Bea's words sounded so convincing that Chase glanced toward the corner and saw nothing.

"You don't see her?" Beatrice scolded.

"No."

"She's all in white."

Chase swallowed and swallowed again. She remembered her grandmother saying strange things like that in the closing hours of her life. *Beatrice Thorpe, don't die on me,* she thought. She tightened her grip on the wrinkled hand.

"Bea, I'm going to Prague to see Dorian."

"Oh, Olivia will like that. She can't go herself. Dorian knows the truth about Olivia and the steel mill. He'll tell you."

Her energy waned as she struggled to talk. Chase squeezed her hand again. "Don't say anymore. I'll just sit here with you."

There was a slight tap at the door, and then a nurse whisked into the room. When Chase looked down at Beatrice, the old woman's eyes had closed, the mouth lay gaping.

"Mrs. Thorpe." The sing-song voice rose an octave. "Come, dearie. Time for your medicine."

Thorpe's eyelids flicked open. "Not that again."

"Keeps you strong, dearie."

"Keeps me flustered."

The nurse put the plastic cup to her mouth, tapped the pill inside, and forced some water behind it. Beatrice pushed the glass away and swooped the pill around, her false teeth bobbing as she did so. Chase saw the tiny bulge in her cheek and smiled.

"Now come on, dearie, it's time for your morning nap."

"I want to sleep in my chair."

Again the nurse's voice rose for a deaf ear. "You're in the infirmary, Mrs. Thorpe. House rules say the side rails go up."

"You stay with me," Beatrice whispered to Chase.

The nurse tugged Thorpe's spectacles off, brushing

roughly over the bruised cheeks. "We mustn't tire you out. Mind you, Miss Evans can stay two minutes. No more. You need your rest."

"I want to go back to my own room."

"When you're better, dearie."

Thorpe tried to grip her cane and point it in the direction of the attendant as she made her way out of the room. With an angry sputter that erupted from those swollen lips, she spewed the medicine out. "That woman," Thorpe said, "is pill enough."

Chase leaned down and kissed Bea on the forehead. "I love you," she said. "I'll come back after my trip to Czechoslovakia." Even as she made the promise, she doubted that she would be back in time. "You'll be all right. Olivia will be with you."

Wearily, Thorpe turned her gaze toward the corner and smiled. "Yes, Olivia will be here."

۞۞۞

The Cotswolds. When Ian came out of the house to meet her, the softly rolling hills of Kendallshire were bathed in radiant summer hues. The Kendalls' thatched cottage lay hidden at the end of the village road. Roses climbed up the old stone wall and peeked down on a charming English garden filled with wild minty thyme and brilliant geraniums. Trout frolicked in the clear running streams that rippled under an ancient stone bridge, but Chase's attention was drawn to the elderly gentleman standing there.

"Come," Ian said, "I want you to meet my grandfather."

She grabbed Ian's arm. "That's Uriah Kendall? We can't disturb him. He's too deep in thought."

"He's remembering."

She laughed. "Remembering what, Ian Kendall?"

"The day when he met my grandmother."

At the sound of their laughter, Uriah turned to face them, leaning on his cane. He was casually dressed, tufts of his sandy-gray hair dipping over his forehead. "He's handsome," she said.

"I never thought about it, but, yes, they were both good looking. They met here in the middle of this bridge."

"Then it's not right for me—"

"Now don't back out on me. Gramps agreed to see you. Said if you want to know about Olivia, this is where it all began."

No, she thought. *It began long ago in Prague and Jarvoc. In the risks that she took as a resistance fighter. On the coast in Cornwall. In the trust that she placed in a German officer.* "Your grandfather must miss her dreadfully," she said.

"She was his life."

"It's a shame the way she died. If only someone from your family had been with her." She felt Ian's arm stiffen. "Ian—Ian, you were there that day, weren't you? You saw it happen."

The muscles in his face twitched. "I was there. I couldn't do a thing to help her. We were waiting for her in the limousine on Whitehall. And then she was hit, and Charles just drove off."

"The chauffeur?"

"I was only thirteen, Chase, but I'll never forget it. If I ever see Charles again, I'll kill him with my bare hands for leaving my grandmother like that."

"Does your grandfather know about Charles?" she asked.

"We never talk about that day."

She wanted to comfort him, but she might never have another opportunity like this. "Ian, was it really an accident?"

"Does it matter?"

"To you and your family."

"You're not my family." He towered above her, his handsome face twisted with unhappiness. "I begged you to let it go."

"Ian, you weren't driving the car when Charles hit her. Don't blame yourself. You didn't kill your grandmother."

Her words stunned him. "Charles didn't hit her. We ran— but Charles didn't hit her. It was the Renault idling just in front of us. I can remember that car, but I can't remember the driver."

He spoke with his hands as though he could bring back the moment. "Someone spoke to my grandmother just before she stepped off the curb, but his face has always been a blur, too."

He gripped her elbow firmly and steered her toward Uriah. "I think we've kept my grandfather waiting long enough. But, Chase, just keep in mind that he loved Olivia Renway. Don't destroy that. It's all he has left."

She had no time to answer Ian. Uriah Kendall was holding out his hand, smiling kindly. "So this is the young woman who wants to know all about my beloved Olivia."

Chapter 22

Prague, 8:40 A.M. "A Mighty Fortress Is Our God . . ." As Hanz held the Smith and Wesson to his temple, the words from the hymn of his boyhood echoed back over the years. He lowered the revolver. He saw no hope for his sons, but his grandson had been the pride of his life. Hanz wanted to see Nedrick once more, and he wanted the Mighty Fortress to calm the turmoil raging inside him. But had God ever entered this building, this architectural death trap? He dropped the gun into his toolbox and pushed himself up, letting his back and buttocks glide over the rough wall until he had his balance.

With the fading light of his torch, he could make out the time. Ten minutes to get out of this building and back to the railroad before the forklifts rumbled his way. He dragged himself to the exit and gulped in the morning air as he hit the sunlight. The seven steps back to level ground seemed like impossible mountains. He dragged on, stumbling along the railroad tracks, his eyes riveted on the gleaming rails.

"Popshot."

Hanz shaded his eyes and stared ahead along the tracks. He recognized Mila first, and then his heart raced. The tall young man beside her was waving. Hanz dropped his toolbox and began to run, stumbling on his game leg. He staggered along the uneven ground and fell to one knee as he crossed over the tracks. Pushing himself up, he lurched forward—careening toward the only Russelmann worth knowing. The boy—the grown man—was coming lickety-split toward him. Still waving. Still running.

"Nedrick!" Unexpected tears trickled over his stubble of beard. With no strength left, he pitched forward and toppled into those strong young arms. "Nedrick. Nedrick."

"Popshot, you never greeted me like that before."

"I never missed you like I have these last ten years. I never thought I'd see you again."

Mila peered around Nedrick's shoulder. "I told you I had a surprise for you, Uncle Hanz. Oh—your leg. You're bleeding."

"It's nothing. Just a scrape."

"On a rusty rail. Sit down, Popshot. Let me have a look."

He allowed Nedrick to ease him to the ground. Strong fingers tore the trousers to the knee. "It's a nasty cut, Gramps."

"It'll heal. We'll tend it at the house. Mila here is a good nurse. Aren't you, child?"

She smiled, but Ned went on wiping the dirt from the wound.

"Nedrick has come home to us, Uncle Hanz," Mila said.

"But he can't stay."

"What kind of a welcome is that, Gramps?"

"We have serious problems at the plant."

"Nothing has changed, has it?" Nedrick asked sadly.

He watched Nedrick stare across the railroad tracks and deep into the forest. *He knows,* Hanz thought. *He remembers the tunnels. Remembers our fears as we walked along the tracks.* How many times the boy had asked him for the truth. How many times he had hidden it from him. He couldn't let him get involved now.

Hanz had wanted to protect Nedrick, a thin, frail lad, lonely as a goldfish in a pond by itself. Smart as a whip, but friendless. Over and over Nedrick had cried, "The boys in Jarvoc don't like me, Popshot. What have I done wrong?"

"Nothing," Hanz had told him. *Except to be a Russelmann. To have the blood-streaked history of Nazism on your family tree. To be related, without knowing it, to the designers of death who left a stain on Jarvoc.*

Oblivious, Mila kept smiling, content at having Nedrick by her side. "Altman doesn't know that Nedrick is here yet."

The old man's gaze went back to his grandson. "Your father is in Munich on business. But he knows. He's known every move you've made since you reached England. You should never have come back."

"I almost didn't. I planned to go somewhere else."

To the Pyrenees. To Madrid. To the fishing village where I took you as a boy. They had talked about going back there to live one day. An old man and a boy by the sea. They would fish and read Hemingway and take care of each other. It was too late for Hanz, but not for Nedrick. "You can still leave, Nedrick."

"In a few days. But I had to come back and see you. Jiri said you were well."

"Except for this lame leg of mine."

"You ran a fair race a minute ago."

He allowed Nedrick to help him stand, and then with that old independent pride taking over, he limped unassisted on the painful journey back to the farm. When they reached the house, they urged him into an easy chair. Mila ran off for some warm water and towels as Nedrick pulled the boots from his feet.

They think I've grown old, Hanz thought. *And I have.* He ruffled Ned's hair. "I'm glad you're here. But you can't stay."

"Then you and Mila must go away with me."

"Where?" Mila asked, putting the basin on the floor.

Nedrick kept his eyes on his grandfather. "To a fishing village in Spain. What about it, Popshot?"

"You and Mila go on ahead. I'll meet you there."

Nedrick shook his head. "You stay—I stay."

"These have been empty years, Nedrick. Why did you go away?"

"Popshot, you were all that ever mattered to me in this family. You and Mila." Ned cuffed her ear playfully, and then he went back to washing Hanz's wound. "After I knew about Olivia Renway, I wanted to know her, but you'd never talk about her."

Hanz gripped Nedrick's chin and tilted it up until their eyes met. "Why did you go away, Nedrick?"

"When Jiri told me that you gave the order for my grandmother's death, I made up my mind to forget all of you."

Hanz shook his head, stunned. "Someone else gave that order." He felt reluctant to betray Altman. He groped for words and said, "Maybe it was Jiri. Believe me, Nedrick, I would never have harmed Olivia. I loved her."

"Even when you discovered she was Jewish?"

Mila sat on the floor, frowning. "Is that true, Uncle Hanz?"

"It was Warren Renway who told me Olivia was part Jewish."

"You didn't know until then, Popshot?"

"No. I didn't believe everything that Hitler taught, but I believed in the perfect Aryan race. When Warren and Millicent realized that I had fallen in love with Olivia, they tried to warn me. They knew I was going back to Berlin— that I hated saying goodbye to Olivia. I think the Renways wanted to spare us both."

"Did it bother them that she was Jewish?"

"No. She filled the void their daughter had left behind. Their families had been friends for years. I remember staring at Warren—calling him a liar. 'Ask Olivia yourself,' he told me."

"There's Jewish blood running in my veins, too, Popshot, but you've always loved me."

"Because you were all I had left of Olivia."

"You had my dad."

"Altman hated his mother. My fault, I think. I could never convince Altman that I didn't know Olivia was pregnant. If I had known, Nedrick, I would have married her."

"But you had been ordered back to Germany."

"Yes, but I would have delayed a day or two to make arrangements for her. It was cold that night, Nedrick. Bitterly cold the last time I saw her."

London, February 1941. Hanz had felt miserable as he waited on the bridge for Olivia. He was dressed like an immigrant in his high-buttoned, brown-striped suit and woolen shirt. His dark visored cap was tight against his skull, his metal suitcase lying packed at his feet, a borrowed coat on top of it. But the heaviness was inside, the bitter knowledge that Olivia was Jewish. The Renways had taken the risk of telling him. Had they not considered that he would be obligated to report that they were harboring a Jew? Or had they been confident that to betray them was to betray himself?

Dusk was settling in. The entire city would be blacked out if she didn't hurry. And if she didn't come—if he didn't get to say goodbye—and then he heard her. "Henri. Henri."

He turned, but this time he did not open his arms to receive her. He watched her running toward him, her long russet hair blowing against her cheeks. Innocent. Beautiful. And Jewish. She was barely dressed warm enough in an oversized dark jacket, her thin, threadbare skirt almost to her ankles. Beneath the jacket she was layered in sweaters, Millicent's thick wool one on top.

"You're late," he scolded.

She stifled a coughing spasm before she said, "I'm sorry. I went to the doctor today."

"Are you all right?"

She pressed her head against his chest. He felt the warmth of her against him and yearned to hold her, and still he did not put his arms around her. "I have a surprise for you, Henri!"

"I have something to ask you first." He agonized for a moment. "I have to know the truth. Two days ago Millicent told me you are Jewish. Olivia, why didn't you tell me yourself?"

She pushed away from him. "I didn't think it mattered."

The wail of the sirens shattered the stillness around them. He grabbed her hand and his suitcase and began to run. "The bombers are coming early tonight," he said.

"I pray they don't hit St. Paul's Cathedral."

"They won't," he said confidently. "They use it as a beacon light when they fly in."

"I hate them. I hate the Germans."

His grip on her hand tightened. *Like I hate the Jews,* he thought. *But I don't hate this Jewess. I love her.*

As they ran, Olivia's breath came in short little gasps. He heard the drone of the lead planes flying in formation. In seconds now they would drop their firebombs, lighting the way for wave after wave of heavy bombers that would set London on fire again tonight. Tomorrow the Brits would count their casualties, bury their dead, and record the list of firemen killed in action in a ledger.

As the antiaircraft guns fought back, he prayed that nothing would happen to Olivia. And he prayed for courage to tell her he was going away. He could not tell her that he was German, and it struck him that this was no different than Olivia guarding her own nationality. They heard the hissing sounds as the bombs fell. Olivia trembled beside him. He pulled her past the crumbled walls and safely around yesterday's bomb crater, trying desperately to keep her from noticing the flames that were already ravaging the buildings east of the cathedral.

As they reached the air raid shelter, they heard the deep voice of radio announcer Edward R. Murrow saying, "This is London . . . tonight's raid is widespread . . . the city is aflame . . . buildings gutted . . ."

Hanz knew that across the city, 60,000 Londoners crowded together in underground shelters, calm and united in spite of the vibrations from bombs falling outside. In the shelter he and Olivia entered, a few people had bedded down, stretched out on their blankets, trying to sleep as a sailor led those around him in a lusty rendition of "Roll Out the Barrel." Down past a row of cots, a group of women countered with "Kiss Me Good Night, Sergeant Major."

As Hanz and Olivia went deeper into the tunnel, others made room for them. He put his suitcase down, and for the first time she seemed aware that it was his. "Henri, why the suitcase?"

He urged her to sit down and crouched down beside her.

He took her hands, Jewish hands, hands that he had caressed for five months now. "I'm going away. My country—my family needs me."

He couldn't bear the pain as she cried, "No. No, you can't."

"You slip in and out of Czechoslovakia, Olivia."

"That's different. I have to take messages back to the resistance movement for Antonin and Lieutenant-Colonel Moravec."

"Your brother Antonin should take his own messages. Your country is controlled by Germans, Olivia. If they find out that you're Jewish, it won't go well for you."

She put her hand against his cheek. "We promised not to fight about this. You know I will do anything for my country."

"I don't want anything to happen to you."

He realized now that she had not asked him where he was going or what part of England his family lived in. She had not even suggested going with him. *She knew. His little British spy knew.* He reached up and brushed a tear from her cheek.

"Try to understand," he said. "I have my orders. I have to leave you here in the shelter. I want you to go back to the Renways. Cornwall is safer."

As she leaned against the cement wall, she shivered uncontrollably. "Will you ever come back?"

"After the war—we'll be together then."

The Londoner across from them smiled, a plain-faced woman with pincher glasses and a cot blanket tossed around her shoulders. She had been reading a book by flashlight. "I come to the shelter for encouragement," she said. "Down here, watching these people, I know that the Germans cannot defeat us."

Hanz stiffened, wanting more than anything to argue with her. He recognized her now as the plain-faced vicar's daughter, the writer of detective novels. Back in college—a thousand years ago—she had come to Cambridge to lecture on medieval literature. She crawled across the floor. "I'm

Dorothy," she said as she put her blanket around Olivia's shoulders. "Are you all right?"

"I'm nauseated. I think it's the fumes down here."

"Or the smell of human bodies crowded together."

"That too," Olivia agreed.

Hanz wanted the woman to leave them alone, but Olivia found comfort in her presence. "Do you have children, Dorothy?"

"Yes," she said softly. "One son."

"Was he fun to raise, Dorothy?"

"As a baby? I'm afraid he was fostered out to my cousin Ivy." She offered a faint smile and left them.

As Olivia looked up at Hanz, he saw the distress on her face. "I could never give my child away," she whispered.

With the blanket around her and her head pillowed in Hanz's lap, Olivia finally slept. Next week he would once again be flying planes—perhaps dropping bombs on London. His fear for Olivia's safety knotted his stomach. He needed a reason to send her away, perhaps back to the Renways in Cornwall.

As the shelter shuddered violently again, he held Olivia against him. She stirred and then slept again. He ran his hand through her hair, tucking a lock behind her ear. Still she slept. He wanted more than anything to spend his life with this girl, but his orders had come through on the last wireless transmission. His safety was at risk. He must leave her. It was crucial that the message he carried reach Berlin. But would he live to get back there?

He had taken the family heirloom from the bank vault— before the bank itself became rubble in the bombings. Seven hundred thousand deutsche marks or more lay in his trouser pocket, money desperately needed by his family, desperately needed by the Third Reich. The coded messages on British troop movements and military buildup lay in two of the sapphire links, along with a report on the damage estimates against London and the Czech Intelligence movement near Warwick. He wanted to deliver the message in person, but if something happened to him, one way or the other he must get the message through to Berlin. As he looked down at Olivia, he knew what he had to do.

An hour later he awakened her. She sat up groggily, leaned against his shoulder, and put her cold hand in his. "Oh, Henri, the lady who loaned me her blanket is gone."

"Her name is Dorothy Sayers."

"You know her?"

"I know about her. She lectured at Cambridge once. She said she was going off to help the first aid team stitch and splinter the wounded. She'll be back—but I have to go now."

"Not before the all clear. It's still dark out there."

No, a city in flames would be light enough. "I'll be all right." He hesitated. "Olivia, on the bridge you told me you had something to tell me."

"It isn't important anymore, not with you going away."

"I love you, Olivia." From his trouser pocket he withdrew the Kashmir bracelet. "This belongs to my family. Could you take it back to the Renways for me? They'll know what to do with it." He smiled at her in the darkness. "When I come back again—after the war—I'll give it to you for a wedding present."

She stood, and he brushed a kiss across her lips, his bristly chin lingering against hers. "I have no choice, Olivia," he whispered. "My family—my country—need me."

"Go," she said. "Go quickly while I still have the strength to let you escape. Before I change my mind and turn you in."

He hunched forward, his shoulders squeezed into Renway's wool topcoat, and left the shelter against the advice of the warden standing there. With one hand thrust into his pocket, his suitcase in the other, he walked out into the smoke-filled city without looking back at Olivia. Piccadilly Circus was jammed with vehicles that had been deserted when the air raid siren sounded. Some had taken a direct hit, but one motorbike lay against the wall of a blackened building, the keys still in it. With a twist of Hanz's wrist, the engine sputtered and caught.

Above him brave RAF pilots—and he did consider them courageous young men—streaked through the sky, determined to repel the next wave of Messerschmitts roaring toward London. Incendiary bombs and heavy explosives spilled from the air, exploding on contact and forming a firestorm east of the city.

He mounted the bike and sped away over the gutted streets toward the waterfront. The River Thames that Olivia loved was strewn with debris, a tanker ablaze and sinking on its oil-coated waters. Balancing the suitcase between his knees, he accelerated and disappeared into the night as London burned behind him.

۞۞۞

Nedrick and Hanz sat quietly for several minutes. Finally Nedrick put out his hand and gave Hanz a comforting squeeze. "It sounds like my grandmother knew where you were going."

"I think she did, Nedrick."

"She could have stopped you."

"Even as I left the shelter, I thought she would."

Chapter 23

.

Von *Tonner Art Museum, Germany.* Drew Gregory
grinned at Miriam. "Take a look at that sign, *Liebling.*
That's Robyn and Pierre's dream coming true."

"Mostly Robyn's," she said stoutly. "And all on her own."

"Hmm," he agreed, grinning even more. "Except for
Pierre's support, the baron's money, the Breckenridges'
hard work, and the Klees overseeing the project."

"You know what I mean, Drew." Her voice caught. "Robyn
didn't need me this time."

"Oh, she could have used your wisdom."

"My interference, you mean. Is that why you married
me—to keep me out of Robyn's hair?"

"I thought I could keep you occupied."

She leaned over and kissed his rough cheek. "Thank you
for making this possible. I never dreamed we'd be back in
time."

"Pierre and I planned it that way."

"Does Robyn know we're coming?"

"Not if Pierre could keep it from her."

Drew took another look at the shiny new museum sign as
a car whizzed past them on the narrow incline. "That's
some lady driver. We'd better hightail it up the hill after
her."

He hit the accelerator. Their car shot around the steep
curve and sped up the winding road. The electronic gates

swung back allowing them an impressive view of the gray-
ish white mansion high on the hill.

Albert Klee, the caretaker, came rushing forward to greet
them. His keen, dark eyes shone beneath the bushy eyebrows—a warm welcome, unlike Drew's first encounter
with Albert's Mauser rifle. The old man could best be
described as agile and ugly with a mouth too wide, lips too
thin, teeth too yellow; but Albert was more faithful than an
old hound dog. Robyn and Pierre loved him, Miriam was
still in awe of him, and Drew respected him.

"I told your daughter your car was coming," Klee said.

"It's a rental," Drew laughed. "How did you know it was
us?"

Albert gripped his hand. "Got spotters all the way up the
hill. Like I told you, here she comes now."

Drew watched with fatherly pride—his arms outstretched
as Robyn came darting across the well-kept lawns. She was
so much like one of the Gregorys with her shiny auburn
hair, sea-blue eyes, and that cute upturned nose that she
hated. Robyn came straight into her father's arms and then
slipped from his bear hug with tears in her eyes as she
embraced Miriam.

"Mother, I never dreamed you'd come." She shot a scold-
ing glance at Drew. "Daddy just wouldn't promise a thing.
Told me no man would leave his honeymoon for an art
gallery. What happened?"

"Your father is full of wonderful surprises."

Robyn's smile was one of her best assets. It made her face
and eyes sparkle, making Drew doubly glad that he had
come. He touched her cheek. "We couldn't miss your big
bash, Princess."

"Mother, your friend from the Metropolitan Museum of
Art is coming and the curator from Tate Gallery. But if you
two had not come, it would have been a big disappointment." Her eyes were like brilliant blue saucers. "Wait until
I tell Pierre you're here."

Drew winked again. "He knows."

"And he didn't tell me?"

"Robyn, who was that guest just ahead of us?" Miriam asked.

"The one running toward the stables? That's Chase Evans." Robyn didn't notice their surprise. "She's a friend of Luke Breckenridge. She could hardly wait to see him."

"Isn't Sauni here?" Miriam asked.

"Yes." Robyn arched her brows as she linked arms with her parents. "I hope Miss Evans won't cause trouble. I don't want anything spoiling this weekend."

🌀🌀🌀

As Chase pulled through the gates and parked, she dropped the keys into the caretaker's gnarled hands and said, "Captain Breckenridge is expecting me. Where is he?"

The old man's thin lips tightened. "Humph."

He was not a pleasant-looking man with his thick-hooded brows and puffy cheeks. His body was so thin that it made him look weightless, but he was quick on his feet as he moved to the driver's side and slipped behind the wheel of her car.

"I'm Chase Evans. Luke Breckenridge really is expecting me."

"Humph. He's out in the stables with Monarch and Mrs.—"

She didn't let him finish but broke into a run. She was breathless when she burst through the stable door. The chestnut stallion reared and neighed, its nostrils flaring.

Chase drew back as a head appeared above the stall. "You trying to get us killed?" Luke asked, patting the horse's well-muscled neck, trying to calm him. "Monarch doesn't take to strangers—oh, Chase, it's you. Wondered when you'd get here."

"I just did."

"All settled in?"

"No," she said, blushing. "I came right down to see you."

He looked uneasy as another head appeared above the stall—a woman close to Luke's age, with long flaxen hair, a gentle face, and a heart-shaped locket around her slender neck.

"Er—hello," Chase said.

Luke looked embarrassed. "This is Sauni," he said as if that were explanation enough.

"Luke's ex-wife," the woman said softly. She smiled, but she avoided Luke's searching gaze. "Luke, I'll let you finish cleaning Monarch's stall. I promised to help Hedwig with supper."

She walked away, slowly at first, but when she reached the door, she began to run.

"Did I break up something?" Chase asked.

"Regretfully, the breakup occurred a long time ago."

"I didn't know you still saw your ex-wife."

"The subject never came up, did it?" He stroked Monarch's neck again. "Well, Chase," he said, leaving the stall and giving her a brotherly hug, "let me show you around."

When they reached the magnificent ballroom, he pointed to the frames around several of the paintings. "I made them," he said proudly. "It's been a new outlet for me."

"They're nicely carved—and this room is simply elegant."

"It's my favorite. Pierre and Robyn have commissioned me to turn it into a display room—after the big ball on Saturday."

"Will you save me a dance?" she asked.

"Of course. Several."

※ ※ ※

Drew noted that the entry halls had been freshly painted and the marble floors polished to a shine. The art collection that had lain hidden in the tunnels for years now brightened the walls in every room. Even Drew, who could not distinguish one artist from another, had taken a liking to the Rembrandt painting that still hung above the stairs. Robyn—bless her heart—had placed one of Miriam's favorites in the guest room where they were staying. It was one of Monet's lesser-known works of the Thames at sunrise, emphasizing Monet's skill with broken colors.

Miriam turned from the painting and faced Drew, gorgeous in the coral evening gown that he had purchased for her in a boutique in Paris. "Drew, you look absolutely smashing," she said.

"And you're more lovely than ever, *Liebling*. We'd better go down to dinner before we change our minds."

Baron von Tonner sat at the head of the table in his wheelchair, Pierre and Robyn on either side of him. Drew marveled that Felix was still alive, frail and aged as he was, but the baron seemed to sense the excitement, his dull eyes attentive. He managed to get his fork to his mouth twice before his strength failed and Robyn began to feed him.

By the third course, Miriam was engaged in a conversation with Lady Gilmore. Drew turned to Chase. "What are your plans, Miss Evans?" he asked. "Besides your research project."

"Oh, did Luke tell you about that?"

"No, Uriah Kendall."

As she raised her goblet to her lips, she asked, "Did Mr. Kendall also tell you I was going to Prague?"

Drew sputtered and almost choked. Miriam turned at once and dabbed the water with her napkin. He adjusted his cummerbund. "And what is so interesting in Prague?" he mumbled.

"It's Jarvoc that interests me. Mr. Kendall's wife was born there, you know, but something about that town frightened her. I want to find out what it was. And I hope to meet her brother there."

"Did Uriah encourage you to make this trip?"

"Not really."

"You're going all alone then?" Miriam interjected.

"So far."

But you have other plans, Drew thought. *Dangerous ones if they involve the Russelmanns and Dorian Paschek.* How much did this young woman know about Olivia's past? How much was still guesswork? "Jarvoc is a dismal town—just a few homes and a steel factory. It is not a place for tourists," he warned.

Chase's fine brows arched. "I'm not exactly a tourist. I'm researching for my doctoral program, but I keep running into obstacles. I want to know why, Mr. Gregory. And there was a man in her life. A Henri, I believe. Surely there are some people there who still remember Olivia Renway."

They remember all right, Drew thought as he lapsed into silence. He feared for this girl. He managed a couple of smiles for Robyn, but he was making mental notes for a phone call to Troy Carwell in Paris. He wanted permission to contact Czech Intelligence. But what excuse could he possibly give Troy? One way or the other, once he had Miriam safely on the plane at Heathrow, he was flying back to Prague.

At midnight as they crawled into bed, Miriam said quietly, "You're going back to Prague, aren't you?"

"I don't like Chase Evans going alone. Uriah should have stopped her, but he's too busy guarding the Kendall name. I'm afraid the Kendall secrets may disappoint us, Miriam."

"No matter what the Kendalls did, they're still my friends."

Miriam—generous to a fault. Loyal. She was not prepared for the truth. What was happening in the lives of Uriah and Ian Kendall had taken on new dimensions, new risks.

At breakfast Drew glanced across the table at Chase and Luke. "I have a project I want you to do for me if you would, Breckenridge."

"Name it."

"I'd like you to go to Jarvoc with Miss Evans."

Two mouths gaped open. Drew lifted his juice goblet and saluted them. "You'll love Prague. Miriam and I did." But his confidence wavered when he saw the look of dismay on Sauni's face.

🌀🌀🌀

Molly Perkins paused by the hall mirror. She had chosen a bright lavender frock that made her look more cheerful than she felt inside. She missed Dudley intensely, yet she was determined to put distance between them for a while. Still it depressed her that Dudley—engrossed in his work at MI5—might not miss her.

She adjusted her wide-brimmed spring hat with her gloved hands and practiced the smile she would use when she met Miriam Gregory for tea in the mansion dining room. Satisfied, she turned from self-inspection and made her way to the phone in the sitting room. Molly had hoped to find the room empty, but Felix von Tonner was there, decked out in a fine suit that failed to hide his frail body. He hunched forward in his wheelchair, surrounded by the ornate charm of seventeenth- and eighteenth-century furnishings. Logs were laid out in the stone fireplace—but Molly was certain they would never be burned for fear of blackening the two striking eight-foot portraits that dominated the room.

The oil paintings looked regal, frighteningly lifelike. She couldn't take her eyes from the baron's playful smile. Now his strong features were barely recognizable in the shriveled face of the old man. Felix sat in his wheelchair staring up at the portrait of his wife, Ingrid—elegant, charming, and dead now. The artist had caught her enticing dark eyes and engaging smile, but the devious heart lay hidden in this spectacular portrayal of the woman who had planned to steal the entire von Tonner collection.

Molly glanced around and spotted the phone by the bookcase. The von Tonners had posed behind the same brocade chair, the one that she eased into now. As she dialed her number in Chelsea and waited for Dudley to answer, she wondered with all of the artistic display throughout the mansion, why the young Courtlands had left this sitting room essentially unchanged. Was it fair to subject Felix to this daily reminder of life as it once was—and might have been? Ingrid and the past were best forgotten. Or was it for the past that the room remained unchanged—off limits to those who would come to the museum in the days ahead?

Dudley picked up the phone at last, his voice low as he said, "Good evening. Dudley Perkins speaking."

"Darling, I didn't expect to catch you at home."

"Then why did you call here?"

She winced, hurt by his abruptness. "How are you?"

"Lonely. I miss you, Molly. When are you coming home?"

"I don't know."

"Have you worn that lovely gown yet?"

"Tomorrow at the ball. . . . I've met Miriam Gregory."

He punished her with his silence, his disapproval.

"We've talked Rubens and Van Dyke. Raphael and Rembrandt. It's been marvelous. Refreshing actually to have someone know Constable's work. We even talked about the *Dance of the Nymphs*."

"Constable's work?"

He sounded close, as though he were no farther away than the baron. "No, darling," she laughed. "The French painter Camille Corot did that one a hundred years ago."

"I see," he said. But he didn't.

"It sounds as if you and Mrs. Gregory have talked for hours. Does she know who you are, Molly?"

She stared at the unlit fireplace wishing that the logs would burst into flames and wipe away the chill she felt. She forced herself to tell Dudley the truth. "I've been introduced as Lady Gilmore—and Miriam is politely allowing me my anonymity."

"That title belongs to your mother."

Did he realize how painful his verbal jabs were when he was angry? "Dudley, I didn't call to tell you about Miriam Gregory."

"Then why did you call?"

She considered hanging up. But she knew that his coldness was evidence of his anger and humiliation at her going away. "Dudley, Drew Gregory is sending one of his agents to Prague."

He sounded amused. "My dear Molly, did Drew tell you that?"

"I was in the library, staying out of the way of last-minute preparations. The French doors to the terrace were ajar—"

"And you listened in on someone's conversation?"

"I learned that little trick from you, Dudley."

"The library book must have been boring."

She jabbed back. "No, it was about the Greek islands. I can hardly wait to get there." She twisted the phone cord and said, "Gregory asked the American traitor to go to Prague and Jarvoc for him. You know, the marine captain who caused such a stir a few weeks ago. He's here at the mansion, too."

"Luke Breckenridge? He was cleared of all charges, Molly."

"Then why is Gregory sending him to Prague?"

She heard the tightness in her husband's voice as he said, "That's of no concern to me."

She fingered the phone with her gloved hands, running the cord through her fingers, vicariously strangling Dudley in the process. *You are my husband,* she thought. *I may be leaving you—at least for a time—but I do love you. I will help you.*

When she found her voice again, she said, "Captain Breckenridge will be going to Prague with that American student."

"Be more specific, Molly."

"Chase Evans. The girl you told me about."

"Oh yes."

"Like you told me, she seems to know everything about Olivia Renway. She came to the von Tonner celebration as a guest of Captain Breckenridge."

"Then maybe it is just some romantic entanglement."

"No. I heard Drew ask Breckenridge to accompany the girl. They're leaving the day after tomorrow. I think he's working with the CIA now, Dudley, don't you?"

"Hardly. The last time he went on a mission for the CIA, he lost twenty years of his life."

Why was Dudley belittling her like this? She was only trying to help him. "I really must go. Miriam and I are having tea together."

"Wait. Molly, would you go to Prague for me?"

"And follow Breckenridge and Miss Evans? No, my darling. I'm leaving for the Greek islands at the end of the week. Send your golden boy," she said bitterly. "Maybe Lyle

Spincrest will get lost in the Czech Republic. If he never came back, it would be too soon."

"Molly, can you get me the address in Prague where they're staying?"

How? she wondered. "The Gregorys stayed at the Adria when they were there. Perhaps Miss Evans will register there, too."

"And in Jarvoc?"

"I'm certain that you are well acquainted with Jarvoc. Olivia Renway was born there, and you seem to know everything about Miss Renway. Your files on her must be thick enough."

"Molly, will you call me again before you leave?"

"If I overhear something? Of course." Her eyes drifted across the room to the baron. She understood Felix von Tonner. They were both very lonely. Confused. "Goodbye, Dudley."

"Molly, come home. Please come home. I love you."

"Do you?" she whispered softly as the line went dead.

❦❦❦

Chase browsed in the library with several guests, admiring the paintings of Rembrandt and Rubens. Luke was on the other side of the room, deep in thought beneath a large somber Rembrandt.

She heard the door open and felt the intruder's presence before he stood at her side. "I enjoy the swirling action of Rubens, don't you, Miss Evans?" His voice was accented, mocking.

She felt immediate fear. It was the man who had last seen Andrew Forrestal alive, the man who had followed her to Oxford, the man who had surely beaten Peter Quincy. Chase saw violence in Rubens's painting, cruelty in the stranger beside her.

"You're following me," she cried.

His tone was scornful. "Don't flatter yourself. I frequent art galleries. Don't you?"

He gave her a curt nod and cut across the room to Luke.

She watched in surprise as the two men embraced. Luke glanced over his shoulder, laughing. He came to her—a question in his arched brow. "I hear you think one of our guests is following you."

"Who is that man, Luke?" she demanded as the stranger left the room.

"Jiri Benak. He called me yesterday. Told me he had a ticket to the opening of the museum. I was surprised, but what can I say? He had to know the Courtlands to get an invitation here."

"You know him?"

The scar along Luke's neck pulsated. "I'm not proud of it. Jiri and I met at a mercenary camp in the foothills of the Pyrenees."

"Part of your past?" she asked.

"Part of what I want to forget. I had no problems with Benak at the camp. But I admit, I never could decide whether he was a soldier of fortune or had come to recruit a mercenary army of his own."

"I don't trust him, Luke. And he is following me. I must call the police or talk to Mr. Gregory or—"

He grabbed her hand. "Don't do that. It would only involve me again. Please." He looked down at her and smiled. "Benak is a funny guy. I'll tell him to bug off." His smile widened. "But coming to an art show! That's a new angle for Jiri. I hope you don't mind, but I promised to look him up when we get to Prague tomorrow."

She stared at Luke, sensing his betrayal. Benak. Gregory. Even Luke? Were they working together, recording her every step?

۞۞۞

Miriam was proud of her daughter. Robyn had just chalked up a glorious success at the mansion—from being the charming hostess for a hundred guests to the cutting of the ribbons that officially opened the Von Tonner Art Museum. Only three things shadowed the gala occasion: having to leave Robyn moments from now; Sauni

Breckenridge's unhappiness; and the absence of Uriah Kendall. The guest count had been accurate, but where was Uriah? Someone had come to the museum on Uriah's invitation. But who?

She put it from her mind as Sauni ran out to the car. Sauni looked vulnerable this morning, as though she had not slept at all. Miriam said, "You're so unhappy, Sauni. Is it Luke?"

Sauni tugged at a strand of corn silk hair that had caught in the chain of her heart-shaped locket. "I waited so long to find him, Miriam—and for a little while I thought—" Her smile collapsed. "But I want what will bring him happiness."

"Do you think that will be found apart from you?"

"I'll be at Busingen another school term. I'm not sure he'd be content working at the gallery that long."

"Sauni, he could join you in Busingen."

"He talked about studying there—before Chase arrived."

Miriam's voice went up a surprised octave. "Theology?"

"No, economics. He'd like to get into investments."

"You've met Sherm Prescott. Sherm is high up in Kippen Investments. Drew could put in a good word for Luke."

"Do you think Drew would mind?"

"At least he'd mind Robyn. Talk with her. But what about Luke's work at the gallery?"

Her face clouded even more. "Once they get the rest of the collection framed, they won't need Luke anymore."

"Wrong. Robyn plans to rotate the paintings. The Flemish artists one quarter. The Impressionists the next. They'll always need new frames made and the old ones repaired."

"Luke is good at that, isn't he?"

"Yes, and he's too good to let him slip away." She cupped Sauni's cheeks gently. "Now you get back in there and tell him you'll be waiting for him in Busingen. If he doesn't come back, Sauni, then you'll know it was never meant to be. But don't give up without fighting for him. He's a good man. He needs you."

"I thought so—but he's going away with Chase Evans."

"Oh, dear! Didn't he tell you why?"

"I was afraid to ask him, Miriam. After all, Drew asked him to go."

Drew was coming with the last suitcase, Robyn at his side. With hugs all around, Drew helped Miriam into the car and drove away. As they reached the bottom of the hill, she said, "Drew, if ever I saw a woman still in love, it's Sauni Breckenridge."

"Did she tell you that?"

"Some things, darling, just don't have to be spoken."

"Then I've blown it, *Liebling*—insisting that Luke accompany Chase to Prague."

"You can't go yourself?"

"Not and be at the embassy first thing Monday morning."

"But you're going back to Prague, aren't you, Drew?"

"If they need me."

"They'll need you."

"I won't go until you're safely on the plane at Heathrow."

"Are you that anxious to send me away?"

"No, but I'm anxious for the day when you come back again. The sooner you go, the sooner you are mine again."

🏵🏵🏵

Jiri Benak seethed with anger as he drove through the gates of the mansion behind Drew Gregory. He wanted to push Gregory's car right off the cliff, straight down into the Rhine. It was Gregory's fault that Breckenridge and Chase Evans were going to Prague. None of them would rest until they discovered the truth at the Russelmann factory. Jiri had to advance his time schedule.

He would fly back to Prague and set the wheels in motion for an early takeover of the Jarvoc steel mill. He would take the Russelmanns and Van Rindins out with a handful of gas pellets—with one quick twist of the "on" lever. The repairs in the waste terminal would hold—he was certain the showers would work again.

When the authorities came, he would feign regret, shock. His despair would seem real enough as he told the policie that he had found the family all dead on his return from

London. He would express horror at the use of Sarin gas in
the tunnels and utter disbelief at the suicidal pact that had
destroyed two families.

Altman's living trust—forged by Jiri himself—would allow
Jiri to run the plant. He would admit that Altman and
Gustav had boasted about high-level transactions, and he
would acknowledge that Nishokura Steel was one of Altman
Russelmann's private accounts. But to accept that
Nishokura Steel had been selling nerve gas components to
third world countries—impossible! He had known about the
weapons—had tried to discourage their sale. But nerve gas!
Sadly, Jiri would tell them, "In recent months Altman
seemed quite mad, his father Hanz, senile."

Yes, he could pull it off. He knew he could pull it off.

Chapter 24

Kendallshire, *The Cotswolds.* When Uriah opened the door and saw Drew, he gripped his hand warmly. "Where's Miriam?"

"En route to Los Angeles. If everything is going well at the gallery, she'll be back in a few days."

"You'll be lost without her, Drew."

"I'll keep busy. Chase Evans flew to Prague to meet Dorian Paschek. I can't let her walk into trouble without helping her. I've wired Troy Carwell for an extra five days of holiday time."

He saw disapproval in Uriah's scowl and heard it more in his question. "Is the problem in Jarvoc?"

"Yes, at the steel mill where Dorian works. It could be as serious as the illegal sale of weapons to third world countries. That would link them with terrorists. A Russelmann family runs the mill."

Uriah's sky-blue eyes seemed sunken this morning, grief lines framing them. "That's Nedrick's last name," he said.

"I know. You look worried, Uriah."

"I haven't slept well these last few nights. Last week it was Dudley Perkins warning me about bomb threats against the Cotswolds. Had us all looking at every stranger in town who might fit the description of a terrorist. One lodge owner worried about one of her guests. When he left unexpectedly, they found enough explosives in his room to take out our whole village."

Uriah swung one lean leg over the other, looking suddenly weary and lost. "Now there's this thing about Nedrick leaving—if you find him in Jarvoc, be merciful to that young man, Drew."

Drew thought twice and then said, "Olivia's name is not welcomed in that town. Miriam and I thought we knew her, but these rumors about her being a spy just don't line up with her crusade against terrorism. Even her own brother Dorian condemns her with his silence. Why, Uriah?"

"He's frightened—the way Olivia was frightened the last time we spoke by phone. She had just discovered that a family she once knew ran the steel mill there in Jarvoc. I didn't have the courage to ask her if a Luftwaffe pilot was among them."

"The Russelmanns then? They were part of her past?"

"At first—when we married—we agreed that the past was our own. We'd start our lives from the moment we met here in Kendallshire. No looking back. No regrets. No questions asked." He twisted in his chair. "But Dudley Perkins kept digging into Olivia's background—and making certain that his memos crossed my desk."

He grimaced. "It was madness. But Perkins's actions drove me to it. I was desperate to prove him wrong. I looked through some of Olivia's personal effects. I'll never forget the hurt in Olivia's eyes. She crossed the room and picked out two pictures of an infant—with the cliffs of Cornwall in the background—and tossed them at my feet. 'Is this what you're searching for?'"

"Then you didn't know about the child before you married?"

He moaned. "I loved Olivia. Her past didn't matter to me."

Drew patted Uriah's arm. "I never questioned your love for Olivia. That's why I came here before going to Prague. Whatever we unravel there, we may not be able to quell those rumors about her being a spy and running messages for a German agent."

"Don't do this. We're old friends. I know where you're heading, Drew—a connection between the Russelmanns and Olivia; but let the past rest. Nedrick is too young to have been Olivia's son."

"But not too young to be her grandson."

Sadly Uriah admitted, "Nedrick always reminded me of her. Olivia never really came to terms with the war or the losses that she suffered. She never forgave herself for giving up that baby. Apparently the Renways insisted on it—reminding her of the child's German heritage."

He rubbed the back of his neck. "After our grandson Ian was born and she became so attached to him, she finally spoke of her firstborn child again—the child that she never intended to give up. The war cost her so much unhappiness, but the Nuremberg trials nearly destroyed her. She saw little justice in Nazi leaders escaping full judgment. But when she discovered that family in Jarvoc ten years ago, she was determined to expose them."

"Risky."

"She was used to taking risks—she married me."

"She took risks living with the Renways in Cornwall, especially when Warren Renway's loyalty was in question." Drew leaned forward. "Renway was a personal friend of the Duke of Windsor, wasn't he?"

"So was I, Drew. We all served in the Guards briefly."

"The woman in the glass shop there in Jarvoc told us that the duke visited Jarvoc in the forties. An odd place to visit. There are those who still ask whether the duke was an envoy for the British government or a supporter of the German side."

"Rubbish. You're a British history buff, Drew. You know those nasty rumors were not true."

"Even if they were, I would understand, Uriah. The duke had German ties—no doubt a blood line that traced back to Germany. And no one wanted war again."

"We both tried to persuade the duke not to sail for the Bahamas, but to spend the war years in Europe. Poor Warren was certain the duke would be king again."

"Under German control?" Drew asked. "A puppet government?"

"There are other rumors about the duke serving as a loyal British agent, so don't judge him too harshly, Drew."

"All right, I understand the connection between Olivia and the Renways, but I have to know the link between Olivia and the Jarvoc steel mill. She knew Hanz Russelmann, didn't she?"

"How did you find out, Drew?"

"My visit to Jarvoc set the wheels rolling. So a friend with Czech Intelligence did a rundown on the Russelmanns. Origin—Munich. Well-to-do. Art collectors. Their most prized possession—the Kashmir sapphires—was lost during the war. Half a million bucks never accounted for. Apparently the oldest son took it to England for safekeeping. It was Miriam who remembered that Olivia had a sapphire bracelet once."

"She was wearing that bracelet the day I met her, but shortly after we married, she took it off. Said it needed repairs. She called it a family heirloom. I thought she meant the Paschek family. I wanted to give Olivia something special for our twenty-fifth anniversary, so I took the sapphires from her jewelry box."

He sighed, remembering. "I took it to a gemologist to have it appraised and reset so she'd wear it. It was Lionel Shapman who told me it was one of the great pieces of art reported missing after the war. I knew it was expensive, but nine hundred thousand pounds! *And my wife had it in her possession.*"

"You didn't think Olivia had stolen it?"

"Never. But I knew then that the bracelet tied her in with the Russelmanns, and I knew which side of the war they had been on. I had to accept that someone Olivia cared about, perhaps even loved, had given it to her. She never spoke of him. I thought perhaps he was dead."

🌀🌀🌀

Lionel Shapman Jewelers, Maryland, 1974. When Uriah Kendall walked smartly into the jewelry store, he had less than an hour to pick Olivia up for their twenty-fifth anniversary celebration. He had planned a special evening—doing what they liked doing best—a candlelight dinner for two.

He waved at Shapman. "Is the bracelet ready?"

Lionel looked up, his countenance grim. He beckoned Uriah to follow him into the back room. The sapphires lay on a velvet pad—nine princely gems set in a solid gold bangle wristband.

"Magnificent job, Lionel. Olivia will be thrilled." He picked it up and spread it in the palm of his hand. He counted them for the sheer joy of counting. Nine blinding blue gems like the Sapphire of India. Beautiful. Rich and velvety, but as he turned them, a faint hint of violet crept into the end stones.

"What's wrong? The two end gems don't match the others."

"They're replacements. Tanzanites. They're as close a match as I could make. It's going to cost you more than we expected."

Shapman placed the originals under the gem scope and adjusted the lens. "Those are the two end stones that you brought in," he said. "Have a look for yourself."

Uriah's hands went clammy. "There are flaws in them."

"Fakes," Lionel said.

"But the specks—"

"Microfilm. Microdots, if you prefer. Those two fake sapphires had been lasered out by someone. Cleared of their imperfections. Impurities or inclusions as we call them in our business. Once the impurities were removed, the microdots were inserted."

"And the other seven stones?"

"Genuine Kashmir sapphires. You couldn't buy them if you tried today. The mines went dry in the twenties. I believe these are the Russelmann Kashmir sapphires missing since the war. It would be worth a mint at a Sotheby auction." Lionel scratched his head. "Once you pay me my fee, I'm going to forget that you ever brought that bracelet into my shop. What you do with those gems is your business, Kendall. I don't want to be involved."

"Destroy them for me, Lionel."

"Fake gems with wartime codes? Possibly even some of the final Allied invasion plans. German agents tried to steal those. No." He dropped them on the velvet pad. "I'll leave it with your conscience, Uriah."

"But those messages are no longer of value to any country."

An hour later he faced Olivia across the dining table and held out the bracelet to her.

"What are you doing with that, Uriah?"

"You said it was a family heirloom. I had it repaired for you."

Olivia was furious as he put the bracelet around her wrist. She counted the gems and then recounted them. "The two end stones are different. What have you done with them?" she demanded.

"Lionel Shapman replaced them. They were fakes, but the seven middle stones are the genuine Kashmir sapphires."

"Fakes?" She sat there stunned. "Uriah, why?"

"I thought it would make you happy to wear them again." Even in her anger, the gems caught the violet-blue of her eyes. "They look lovely on your wrist, Olivia."

"They belonged to a German family," she said.

"You don't have to tell me."

"I was to take it to the Renways. That's when I realized the sapphires were valuable and would be smuggled out of England."

"They're still worth nine hundred thousand pounds."

"Uriah, please believe me. I meant to give it to the Renways, but something inside me kept saying wait. Even then the end stones didn't look like the others. I'd crossed the border enough to know that coded messages were sent in many ways. By then I knew that Henri—"

"You don't have to tell me."

"I must. I love you, Uriah Kendall. I must tell you." The candlelight made the tears in her eyes glisten. "One night during a blackout I heard Warren slip out of the house. I followed him to the Cornwall cliffs. I watched him light a lantern and wave it out over the Atlantic. That's when I realized that the Renways—my father's friends—were pro-Nazi. I knew Warren was signaling a German sub. It made me sick inside, but where could I go, Uriah? I was pregnant. I needed the Renways."

"Did this Henri fellow know about the baby?"

"No."

He saw the agony on her face and whispered, "It's all right, Olivia. I love you. If you want to find your child, we will."

She nodded. "But he'd be a grown man by now."

"It doesn't matter. We'll try and find him." He reached across the table and took her hands. "You haven't asked about those two gems I replaced, Olivia."

"Did you turn them over to British Intelligence?"

"No, I destroyed them."

۞۞۞

Uriah met Drew's gaze again. "That's the whole story, Drew. She knew then that I knew, that I had forgiven her, that I loved her." Old age crept into his voice. "We went back to Cornwall once, but there was no trace of her son. I thought by then that perhaps he, too, had died. But there was no way of knowing."

"What did you do with Olivia's bracelet after her death?"

"I don't have it. When Scotland Yard showed me Olivia's possessions, her briefcase and the sapphires were both gone. An ordinary thief on Downing would not have known the value of those sapphires, so for a time I thought one of the underlings at the Yard might have stolen them." He smiled, an exhausted the-world-on-my-shoulder smile. "Back then I never admitted to Scotland Yard they were missing. I knew the bracelet would condemn Olivia. I couldn't let that happen. Whatever she had done—or been— it was over. No lives were lost. Only her own."

"How can you be so certain?"

"Drew, the codes in the bracelet were never delivered to the Germans. The Russelmanns in Jarvoc are the only ones who would have benefited by taking both her briefcase and her bracelet."

"So you think the sapphires were taken to Prague?"

"Where else?"

"What do you plan to do about Nedrick, Uriah?"

"Nothing. Nedrick is gone. Perhaps it is best. Ian doesn't know about his grandmother's illegitimate child. It would be more humiliation than he could handle."

"Perhaps Ian has more strength than you realize."

"I'm fond of Nedrick, Drew. There's no way that he would have stayed with me all these years just to betray me."

Drew thought differently. He knew the mindlessness of intelligence agents. A sleeper would remain hidden five or ten years in blind obedience, waiting to be useful, waiting for instructions. "We've got to locate him. He may be in trouble."

"That's what I used to think when he drove the streets of Washington. I never told you—never told anyone—but Ned had an uncanny interest in the embassies and consulates in Washington. Particularly the ones on Spring of Freedom and Reservoir Road."

Germany and Czech Republic, Drew thought. Had Nedrick been receiving messages from Jarvoc right on embassy row?

"Drew, didn't you see him at the opening of the Von Tonner Art Museum? I gave him my guest tickets."

"He wasn't there. The count was right. A hundred guests—all accounted for, but Nedrick was not among them."

"Then someone else used my tickets."

◉◉◉

Jarvoc, Czech Republic. Altman Russelmann looked out on his massive complex and the acres of land that were his. True, they were still in his father's name, but not for long, and Josef would be dealt with quickly once their father was gone. Nor would he allow the company to fall into the hands of Nedrick, that weak, disloyal, despised son of his.

From the time Nedrick could walk, he had always run to

his grandfather, never to Altman. From the time he could speak, his words to his father were, "No! Go away. I do it myself!" It was always Hanz he adored. Only moments ago Altman had dismissed Nedrick from the room after a heated argument about the Kashmir sapphires. If there had ever been a moment in time when he loved Nedrick, he could not remember it.

Yet he had no question about his feelings for the man beside him. He despised him, but he needed Jiri Benak more than his own family. There was a cleverness about Jiri, an architectural genius, that Altman still found useful; but he did not trust him for a minute. Someday, before Jiri tried to take control of Russelmann Steel, Altman would send him away. Or put him away.

"You've been in the waste plant again, haven't you, Jiri?"

"You have the only key."

And you know where I keep it, he thought. "Your shoes are muddied on the side."

Jiri glanced down. "I was out by the tracks checking out the Nishokura shipment."

"And was it to your specifications?"

"To yours, Altman." There was mockery in Jiri's voice as he said, "Twenty- to forty-foot steel rails and angles and 3 x 2 rectangle steel tubing. All descaled and coated with oil."

"And bound with black steel strapping?"

"Crated. Nishokura must be shipping it somewhere important."

"The destination is not our concern."

"The contents hidden in those steel cylinders is. What does he put on shipping labels—supplies for highway construction?"

"It's for a pharmaceutical plant in Libya."

Jiri laughed. "More likely a chemical weapons facility. Nishokura Steel does take risks."

"As long as we don't."

"Paschek was there loading the train. Why do you trust him?"

"I don't trust any of my underlings. Particularly Paschek.

There is too much hatred building in him. The men look up to him."

"Don't tell me you fear an uprising among the men?" Jiri scoffed.

"Best to be prepared. And Paschek, for all of his apparent weaknesses, has the potential for leadership. Why else do you think I keep him out in the yards stuck on that forklift? He's too clever to allow him to work inside one of the plants."

"You won't trust Chase Evans either, once you meet her. She's another clever one, and she's already in Jarvoc."

"Josef told me that your Miss Evans and a male companion have taken lodging at the Rosners' place. Are they married?"

"No, he's just another American. They've already tried to get in touch with Dorian Paschek."

"CIA?"

"He was once. I met him at a mercenary camp in Spain."

"A mercenary, eh? Then he's useful to us."

"Doubtful. He's the ex-marine with a hero's welcome in America."

"Any man can be bought."

"Not him."

"Will he recognize you?"

Jiri squirmed, hesitating. "Breckenridge and I spoke briefly at the Von Tonner Art Museum opening."

"You're a fool, Jiri. How much does he know?"

"He promised to get in touch with me when he got to Prague. He knows by now that I gave him a wrong number."

"Brilliant."

"I had them followed from the airport." He glanced at Altman. "While they're prowling around in Jarvoc, I'd better stay out of sight. I could have Pavel keep an eye on them."

"Pavel? We can't depend on him. He'd be taken in by a pretty face. Besides, he couldn't even manage to set off a bomb in Kendallshire."

"He did run," Jiri admitted, "but at least he got out of the Cotswolds with his life. But someone—you perhaps,

Altman—warned the British that Czech terrorists were there."

"You're a fool, Jiri."

"And you, a liar, perhaps. Never mind. What should we do about the Americans, Altman?"

"They are expendable. Do it any way you please."

ⓦⓦⓦ

Hanz was working the compost pile when the girl approached, her steps confident and graceful as she came toward him. He couldn't decide what appealed to him most—her healthy complexion or her youthful good looks. Hanz couldn't even remember back to being that young and energetic. She had to be in her mid-twenties, a fair cut between wholesome and attractive, her smile a hair between shy and sly. But there was nothing cunning in her expression as she said, "Hello. You must be Mr. Russelmann."

"One of them."

"I'm Chase Evans."

She offered her slender hand, but he shrugged, showing her the dirt on his palms. He leaned against his pitchfork, easing the pain in his hip. *Chase Evans.* This was the student Nedrick had talked about. Petite and stylish. Her hair as silken as a rose, her large hazel-brown eyes compelling. But a CIA agent? If so, he would beat her at her own game.

"You're the American student who knows so much about Olivia Renway. My grandson told me about you." Before she recovered from her surprise, he said, "Renway was born in Jarvoc, one of the Paschek children. Did you know that?"

"Yes, but I didn't know you had a grandson."

"Until last week Nedrick worked for Uriah Kendall."

His hands took a tighter grasp on the pitchfork. This woman, this American, could bring them all to their knees. As much as he hated what his sons had become, he did not want them destroyed. "Why have you come to Jarvoc?" he asked coolly.

"To meet you and Dorian Paschek and to visit the

Russelmann Steel Mill as Olivia Renway did on her last visit here."

His eyes narrowed. "She was not well received in this town," he said. "Questions about her will only anger the people."

"Because she fell in love with a German pilot?"

"Did she?"

"Some of your neighbors say she was a German spy."

He put his head back and laughed. "Because she loved a German pilot? No, that little resistance fighter did not work for the Germans. Dorian knows that. He was merely tricking you." Sickened by the charade, he said, "I think you know who I am."

"You're Henri. She wrote about you in her diaries. I thought you were in love with her."

There was contempt in her voice. She despised him as Olivia had despised him that last night in the air raid shelter. "I was in love with her, but we were on opposite sides in the war."

He gripped the pitchfork, blinded by a sudden rage. Olivia had betrayed him—left written notes behind that would ruin all of them. *If this young woman is CIA, then she knows about the Nishokura accounts. She knows about the waste plant full of weapons.* Olivia had known. Olivia had died for it.

Before he could put vengeance into action, he saw Mila ambling down the path toward him. "Uncle Hanz, where are you?"

"Go, Miss Evans. I don't want anyone to see you here."

"Your niece Mila told me where you were. And, oh—I forgot. I was to tell you that Nedrick had gone to the waste plant. I didn't know he was your grandson."

Hanz recoiled. Nedrick must not discover what was hidden there. He had to get back to the plant—tomorrow, this afternoon, soon—and set explosives enough to destroy the arsenal stored there. If it took the entire steel plant, all the better; he would set a spectacular farewell fireworks and he would die with it. Anything to salvage Nedrick. Nothing mattered as long as his grandson went free.

"Mr. Russelmann, you weren't listening to me," Chase said.

"I told you to go."

"I will, but I keep wondering, why did you desert Olivia when she was expecting your child?"

He thought of explaining that he had been called back to Germany, that war necessitated obedience, that Olivia was not pure Aryan. Instead he said what he had wanted to say for years. "If I had known about the baby, I would never have left her."

❦❦❦

Jiri waited in the shadows outside the local pub—waited for darkness, waited for Dorian Paschek to stop downing his lagers and go home. Paschek came out thirty minutes later with two friends—Ludvi Rosner, the town's artist, with shocks of gray hair showing beneath his skull cap, and Ivan Koch, with his curved pipe dangling from his mouth. Koch, who was barrel-bellied and barrel-chested, could out-chuckle and out-drink anyone in Jarvoc.

Jiri kept in the shadows as he followed the three of them to the corner. He knew from their slurred speech and raised voices that they had lingered too long over their Budvars. Paschek had the longest distance to go, two blocks beyond the others.

As Dorian turned down the lane to his three-room cottage, Jiri called out, "Paschek."

Dorian turned. "Mr. Benak, is something wrong at the plant?"

"No, but Altman sent me. Mr. Russelmann is unhappy about that friend of your sister's visiting you."

Perplexed, Dorian said, "I have no guests."

She's been in town twenty-four hours and hasn't contacted him? "You haven't seen Olivia Renway's friend?"

"My sister is dead."

How well I know, Jiri thought. And he knew by the coldness in Dorian's voice that he had sobered quickly. He shoved Dorian roughly against the stone wall that separated the Paschek dwelling from the neighbors. "I don't have time to waste. I'm talking about Chase Evans. The American CIA agent."

That suggestion hit its mark. In the light of the half-crested moon, he could see Paschek's bleary eyes narrowing with hatred and fear. Dorian was a big man, muscular, known to win in a pub brawl, but the pistol in Jiri's pocket was ample protection. He would actually delight in shooting Paschek at close range.

"Mr. Benak, I don't know any of Olivia's friends."

He pinned Dorian against the wall, his doubled fist tight beneath Paschek's jaw. "Don't lie, Paschek. It could cost you your job. We know about the Gregorys visiting you at the plant."

"I swear. I never met them before. They told me they were friends of Jon Gainsborough."

"Jon barely knows them."

"Go ahead. Check out my house, Benak. I'm hiding no one."

Jiri heard fear in Paschek's voice and smiled. "Mr. Russelmann does not want an American agent roaming around Jarvoc."

"I—"

Jiri's knuckles came down hard on Paschek's mouth, cutting off Dorian's protest.

From the window above the glass shop, a head appeared. "Quiet down there," the woman yelled. "Or I'll call the *policie.*"

Jiri lowered his voice. "If the American shows up, you are to let me know. Arrange for her to meet me at the waste plant."

"No one ever goes there."

"Safe then."

"I can't—"

He silenced Dorian with another crashing blow to his face. Dorian doubled over, but Jiri knew he would make no attempt to fight back. He treasured living—treasured being employed. Surely Dorian was aware that he might himself end up at the waste plant where other employees had disappeared over the years.

"Don't make it necessary to meet with you again, Paschek! The Russelmanns do not tolerate opposition."

"No." Dorian turned away and spit—blood, Jiri was certain.

"As soon as she contacts you, we must know. Come to Altman's office in the morning and let us know what she said."

Dorian held his mouth and nodded.

"Good. And good night, Paschek."

Jiri watched him slouch off at an uneven gait and disappear down the alley toward the house. No lights went on. *What are you doing? Watching me now? No matter. You will do as I have asked.*

He took a Havana cigar from his pocket and lit it, puffing contentedly for a few minutes. He was confident that the longer he lingered out front, the more fear he could instill in Dorian.

🝙🝙🝙

As Dorian reached his door, he heard a rustling sound by the bougainvillea bush. Before he could turn to investigate, a strong hand clasped his mouth, intensifying the pain of his split lip; an arm circled his chest in a Herculean grip. Jiri? No, not Jiri. The man behind him was too tall, six feet or more.

"We're friends," the stranger whispered. "Friends of your sister. You've got to help us."

Dorian nodded. He was not in a position to bargain.

"I'm going to release you, Mr. Paschek." The stranger's voice was deep, hypnotic. "But the man who beat you is still out front. Cry out and he'll come running back, and if he's armed—"

Dorian stopped struggling. The blood in his mouth and nostrils blocked off his air, gagging him, choking him, but the prospect of death at the hands of Jiri was even more terrifying.

"We've been followed to Jarvoc, Mr. Paschek, and we want to know why. Only friends knew we were coming here."

As the iron grip loosened, air stung the raw wounds on Dorian's face. He swallowed the blood in his mouth, fear souring his stomach as he turned to face his assailant.

"I'm Luke Breckenridge," said the towering man, his coal-black eyes glinting in the shadows. "And this is Chase Evans."

The American CIA agent! As she stepped from the shadows to Luke's side, Dorian could tell that she was young and beautiful, as Olivia had been. "Go away," he said. "My sister is dead."

"But the things that frightened Olivia are very much alive. And Beatrice Thorpe is still alive, too," she said.

"Still alive! How is she?"

"Someone tried to kill Mrs. Thorpe the other day, Paschek," Breckenridge said. "Czech terrorists, according to Scotland Yard. I'm voting on someone from the steel plant here in Jarvoc."

The girl was more gentle. "I saw Beatrice in the infirmary and talked with her. She told me everything about Olivia and Jarvoc—even about the night you were forced to betray Bea."

He felt the gnawing fear he had felt as a boy—the terrible pounding in his head as the secret police threw him against the wall. "Your sister. Where is your sister?" they had demanded.

He had lied and led them instead to the cave where Beatrice Thorpe and Margot Dvorak were hiding. Beatrice had wheeled around and glanced back at Dorian as the Gestapo led her away.

He didn't want to hear any more. She knew about Olivia's unfinished manuscript. Knew too much about the ruins of Jarvoc. Knew enough about the steel plant to lose her life as Olivia had lost hers.

Jiri's voice! Jiri's words. *If the American shows up, arrange for her to meet me in the waste plant.*

Dorian's hands shook as he turned and unlocked the door.

They followed him inside, the man moving stealthily around the room to draw the curtains; the girl stood motionless by the closed door, so close that Dorian could feel the warmth of her body and hear the sound of her breathing. As the lamp went on, he could see them clearly. The girl looked sympathetic as she watched him—the man alert and mistrustful, the jagged scar down his neck making him look even more fierce.

"What do you want from me, Breckenridge?"

"The Nishokura file from the steel plant."

"I work out on the grounds driving a forklift."

"Then get us a key so we can find the file ourselves," Breckenridge demanded.

"Leave," Dorian said, "while you still have a chance to leave Jarvoc alive."

Chapter 25

The next morning Dorian rode his bike to the steel compound and flashed his I.D. badge as he passed through the gate. His mind was numb, unable to make clear decisions, as he pedaled toward the six-story glass complex that housed Altman's office.

The waste terminal and six product plants lay behind the executive building. Ivan Koch worked by the blast furnace, Ludvi Rosner at the coke ovens, other old friends in the plant that made galvanized pipes. They rarely mentioned the war years; Altman had infiltrated the town and pubs with spotters who constantly threatened their jobs. Except for this privately owned steel mill, Jarvoc would still lie in ruins. After last night, Dorian felt backed against a human wall, even as the waste plant was backed against the forest of spruce and firs.

Chaining his bike, he went up the steps and into the lobby. Convinced that his legs would buckle if he took the stairs, he stepped into the elevator and pushed the button for the second floor. He owed nothing to Luke Breckenridge, nothing to Chase Evans. Yet sweat poured down his back as the door slammed shut leaving him trapped alone in a moving cell. His mind filled with old horrors. "Out. Out," the soldiers had shouted. And his father, a prisoner, had stumbled out of the crowded truck.

On these very grounds, Dorian thought. *Out by the rusty railroad track.* His sister Olivia had fought back as a resistance fighter, striking out against the enemy with a violence that frightened young Dorian: spying on troop movements, setting the radio beacon to guide the British bombers toward their targets, stealing past sentries to set explosives in the barracks. Olivia had always stepped to a different drummer. *And I've never fought back. I have gone on blindly here in Jarvoc, living out my life in fear. I have,* he thought bitterly, *been less than a man.*

As the elevator door opened soundlessly, Dorian wiped his swollen lip with the back of his hand and thought back to that time years ago when the Gestapo had swung a stick across his jaw. Staggering, he had tried to run toward his papa. As they yanked Zdenek Paschek from the truck, he had glanced over his shoulder and smiled—actually smiled—and whispered, "Be brave, son."

Dorian had fallen to the frozen ground, whimpering as his father was herded down the seven steps. In all those years since, Dorian had never felt like anything but a coward. Even now his boots felt like rocks as he stepped from the elevator into the carpeted hall across from the Russelmann suite. What right had Olivia had to make him look so small in the eyes of the people of Jarvoc—coming back in all her finery for Lisa Anne's funeral? Even his friends at the pub had insisted that she leave as hurriedly as she had come. She had brought back the bitter remembrance of reprisals in Jarvoc because of the Bronze Network. How dared Olivia come back and stir up so much trouble at the steel factory. His job had been in jeopardy ever since.

But he had been wrong to hate her. For the first time in ten years, he grieved for Olivia, mourned for the childhood that had been taken from them when the Nazis marched in. He grieved for Olivia as he still grieved for his wife, Lisa Anne!

"Someday, my beloved Dorian," Lisa Anne had said, "you will find the courage to break away from the Russelmanns' control."

Tears stung the back of his eyes; a miserable tightness rose in his throat. During her illness, she had forced him to watch a documentary film on the disposal of nuclear wastes. These had been transported by convoy truck to a freighter and over the ocean to an incinerator on an isolated island in the Pacific.

Dorian had been outraged as he snapped off their tiny television. "Fool politicians," he had said. "Endangering the lives of people all along the route."

"It had to be done," she told him. "And we must clean up the tunnels in Jarvoc. Otherwise our town risks total disaster." She had patted his rough cheek. "You will think of a way someday, Dorian. After I'm gone. You were meant for leadership."

Had the time come for resistance—for the revival of his sister's Bronze Network? Tonight. Or perhaps tomorrow. He would speak to the boys in the pub, and they would drink to freedom from the Russelmann reign.

But at this moment, Dorian had only the heart of a coward.

He stepped into the reception room without realizing he had moved. As the receptionist glanced up, he removed his hard hat and turned it in his bare, work-worn hands. "I'm here to see Mr. Russelmann and Mr. Benak," he said.

Altman stood in the door of his office, looking stern like a Gestapo agent. "Come in, Paschek. Jiri and I have been expecting you. We have something we want you to do for us."

"Did you see the girl?" Jiri asked.

"Yes, Mr. Benak." Dorian kept his eyes downcast, his heart racing. "I told Miss Evans that you would meet her at the waste plant this morning."

"Good," Jiri said. "I will be there waiting for her."

🏵🏵🏵

Chase set out on her own at dawn that morning, determined to catch Dorian at his shacklike dwelling. During the war, the Gestapo had turned the Pascheks' sprawling farm into the secret police headquarters. At war's end, Dorian sought to claim the land again, but Communist communal living took over; the vast acreage was parceled out in cubbyhole-size segments. Fields once planted by the Pascheks lay uncultivated. Look-alike houses in drab yellow were brightened only by lovely lace curtains and window boxes where summer flowers struggled to bloom. Chase found it difficult to imagine the lovely town that Olivia had described in her diaries. Had Olivia forgotten that Jarvoc was dominated by a factory with dark smoke pouring from its smokestacks?

Chase shuddered as she went down the alley, past the spot where the man had hand-whipped Dorian. The bougainvillea bush wound itself over the narrow porch rail, almost as determined to survive as Dorian was. Chase tapped lightly; the urgency of her knock increased when there was no response from inside.

From Dorian's yard, she could see the Russelmann farm and the factory with its eerie ring of smoke curling up and losing itself in the treetops. *What were you trying to tell us, Olivia? What is there about that steel mill that frightened you so?*

The Russelmann farm was an easy walking distance from where she stood. She set out, pacing herself to the heat of the summer day and was tired when she reached the house. Again her knocks went unanswered. She circled around to the garden and the compost pile where she had first found Hanz. His pitchfork was still plunged into the ground where he had left it.

Shading her eyes, she glanced up at the back bedroom window. The curtain moved—not windblown, but a man's hand letting it fall into place. Fear tingled her spine. She ran back to the road. Glancing frantically to her left and right, she knew that the factory was closer than the Rosners' lodging place. *Oh, Luke, I should have waited for you.* Behind her, she heard the sound of a car's engine turning over. She hid in the bushes and waited, too well hidden to even see the driver's face.

Five minutes later she brushed the weeds from her skirt and walked rapidly toward the freight train. The back gate to the compound was open, a forklift rumbling toward the tracks. Again she sought refuge—creeping around the ghostly building and down the seven steps. The rusty lock was broken, the door cracked. As she made a move to open it, a strong hand clamped around her mouth. She caught the whiff of chloroform and went limp against a man's muscular chest as he dragged her inside.

🏺🏺🏺

At 2 P.M. Drew Gregory dumped his overnight duffel on the chair in Luke's room. He was still gripping his laptop computer when he asked, "Where's Chase, Luke?"

"Missing."

"Missing?"

"I haven't heard from her for five hours. That's when she insisted on going back to Dorian Paschek's alone. From there—if I can believe the woman at the glass shop—Chase disappeared." With a distraught hand sweep through his disheveled hair, he said, "If I didn't leave, she threatened to call the *policie*."

"Luke, I told you not to let Chase out of your sight."

"Don't look at me like that, Drew. Chase had different plans. She was out of her room at the crack of dawn. She likes me—that's obvious, but she doesn't trust me anymore. We've got to find her."

"If she's really missing."

Drew set his computer on the table, loosened his tie, and tossed a map at Luke. "Troy Carwell alerted Czech Intelligence from Paris. Now they're taking us seriously and sending Leos Cepek and the *policie* from Kladno." As he changed his shirt, he said, "Fortunately, Dudley Perkins is staying in London. He'll check out Gainsborough's steel mill. We'll handle this end."

Luke shoved the map away. "I don't need a map to tell me there are plenty of places for Chase to disappear. The steel mill. The caves. Russelmann's farm. Dorian's place—I've been there. And a lot of tight-lipped people who won't help us."

He was on his feet, starting for the door. "We can't wait for your friend Cepek to arrive, Drew. We've got to take this town apart and find Chase. We've got to get to her before Jiri Benak does."

"That friend of yours who was at the gallery opening?"

"He works at the steel plant. Chase was afraid of Jiri. Said he was following her since London. I really didn't believe her."

"Then Chase is in serious trouble."

❂❂❂

2:45 P.M. Drew was in no mood for politeness. He walked into the farmhouse through the open door and met an astonished Hanz coming down the stairs with a large tool-box in his hands. "Hanz Russelmann, we meet again," he said.

"Most unfortunate. This time it seems as though you have invaded both my home and my town."

"Chase Evans is missing."

"The CIA agent? But she was here earlier."

Gregory stepped toward Hanz. "She'd be flattered to hear you call her a CIA officer. Where is she, Russelmann?"

He had regained his composure. "I have no idea."

"British Intelligence is shutting down your operation in England—at least temporarily."

"Poor Jon! I assume it's my old connection with the war?"

"That will come out. That and so much more."

Hanz flashed a tired smile. "Poor Jon," he repeated as he reached the porch. "It was never Gainsborough's choice to work with us, but after the war we needed a foot back into the United Kingdom. A German family heading up a steel company there was out of the question."

"So you used Gainsborough?"

"We used what we knew about him. The Gainsborough money was gone, the family possessions dispersed." Russelmann eyed Drew impatiently. "My family didn't just sit back and wait to lose the war. We saw surrender coming. We kept our lists of collaborators. The Renways in Britain. Two of Gainsborough's family in Germany."

"So you came out of the war with your reputation and

your wealth intact—all except for the Kashmir sapphire bracelet?"

Hanz groped for the porch railing. "You'd better leave, Gregory."

"I don't intend to leave Jarvoc without Chase Evans."

"She is not here." He pointed to the woman coming toward them. She was young and smartly dressed in a belted jumpsuit, a black-and-white dog at her side. "There's my niece. Ask her."

"Uncle Hanz is right. I haven't seen Miss Evans since early this morning."

Mila stepped aside as Gregory stormed around the corner of the house, but he heard her say, "What did Mr. Gregory want?"

"The truth, Mila. The bitter, miserable truth."

"Wait—where are you going, Uncle Hanz?"

"To the waste plant to find the girl—if she's still alive."

⚙⚙⚙

Drew stepped back onto the path as Hanz limped away with the collie dog at his heels. Mila's expression was as black as her hair and eyes. "Mr. Gregory, we were going to leave for Spain today," she said. "Nedrick promised to take me away if his grandfather would go with us. But you have angered my uncle. Now he may never go away with us."

"Go later. The American is in danger if we don't find her."

Mila's eyes filled with mistrust. "Hanz thinks she's in the waste plant, but Altman has the only key." She plucked a flower from the bush beside her and pulled off the petals one by one. "There's another way into the tunnels. Nedrick and I played there as children. Mr. Gregory, if you help me get tickets for Spain—"

"I'll help you," he promised. "Tomorrow."

She latched onto his words. "We'll have to go through the old drainage ditch beneath the railroad tracks. We'll need a weeding hoe or sickle in case it's grown over."

As he chose a hand sickle and hedge shears from the shed beside the compost pile, she said shyly, "If you're not afraid to ride with me, we'll use Pavel's motorbike. We can beat Uncle Hanz that way; he walks slowly on that bad leg of his."

Drew clung to her narrow waist with one arm and to the tools with the other. As they bounced over the rutted ground along the railroad track, she swerved to the right. They leaped over the rails, coming to a jolting stop by a cement sewer pipe.

He could see as he swung his leg off the bike that weeds and twisted vines had formed an impassable web at the entry of the ditch. He attacked them with a vengeance, fighting time and nature with a sickle. Then he tossed the tools aside. "Let's go."

Mila scrambled ahead of him through dirt and debris and rat droppings. All he could see were the heels of her multicolored running shoes and the wild lavender shoelaces as he belly-crawled behind her. Halfway through he smelled a foul garlic-like odor in the ditch—as irritating as nerve gas! Colorless, tasteless, and deadly!

🜚🜚🜚

When Luke Breckenridge reached the shimmering glass complex at the Russelmann compound, he was surprised to see Nedrick Russelmann coming out of the building.

"Nedrick," he said seriously, "Chase Evans is missing. Could she possibly be with your grandfather?"

Nedrick's gaze strayed out toward the railroad tracks and slid back again. "He might be out there. He's been trying to persuade my father to close down that waste plant. That's why Popshot keeps putting off our trip to Spain."

"Take me out there, Nedrick."

"I'll ask the receptionist for the key, but she's all upset this morning about some unexpected guests from Prague—potential customers, I think. Josef is showing them around the grounds."

Good, Luke thought. *Leos Cepek has arrived.*

Nedrick came back with the key, but he looked distressed as he said, "Pavel is out looking for my grandfather. We'd better cut through plant six—just in case anyone is watching us."

Inside plant six, Luke's attention was drawn to the man on the elevated catwalk near the blast furnace. He stood there, his cold eyes on them.

"My father," Nedrick explained.

"What's he doing in here?" Luke asked.

"Overseeing production probably. He's the boss."

Luke felt the heat of the blast furnace even from where he stood. The furnace was mounted on rockers; the molten metal was hot and glowing, ready to be shaped into beams and rods and tubing. The sealed room directly behind Altman held the computer-controlled instrument panel lined with dials and gauges.

"My father modernized the plant twelve years ago. Jiri's idea and design. It stepped up production when they installed the automated high-speed equipment and the computer system." The glaring overhead lights made Nedrick's skin look a sickly yellow. "We've got the whole works now—instrument specialists, computer programmers, engineers, metallurgists—"

"Nedrick, we can't stand here admiring your father's assembly line. We've got to find Chase Evans and your grandfather."

Ned's jaw clamped down. He gave a casual wave to his father, led the way to the exit, and headed out toward the plant by the railroad track. Above the smokestacks, streams of black smoke polluted the air. The waste plant looked like a military barracks, its gun-metal gray forming a ghostly apparition. A wheel loader, tractor, and dump truck were parked by the building with empty freight cars visible in the rear.

Behind him, Luke heard a vehicle rolling toward them. He jerked Ned to safety as the forklift bore down on them. It veered to the left—Dorian Paschek at the wheel—riding so close that Luke felt the frame brush his skin as the forklift passed them.

Paschek drove straight for the front entry of the waste plant, the carriage and forks ramming into the bolted door.

He reversed and rammed again. His face filled with rage as he slid from the forklift and mounted the cab of the wheel loader. Within seconds, he charged toward the door again, the bucket teeth and cutting edge of the blade tearing into the two-foot-thick door. Forward-reverse—he went back and forth on the heavy-duty wheels. Forward-reverse. He seemed void of expression as the truck scooped up the splintered wood into the yellow bucket.

When they reached Dorian, sweat was streaming from his face. "Dorian," Ned shouted, "Chase may be in there."

Dorian's lip curled in contempt. "I was here when she went in."

Ned held up the key. "You didn't have to wreck the door."

There was no indication that Paschek heard him. He switched vehicles again, driving off in the forklift as though nothing had happened. A few feet away, he barked out orders to Rosner and Koch. Rosner buggered off on the run, Ivan Koch taking to Ludvi's heels with his potbelly bobbing—both of them beating a retreat toward the office complex.

Dorian glanced back at Ned, loathing on his face.

"Paschek, what are you doing?"

"Resisting for the first time in my life. Nedrick, we've got to stop your family from destroying the Nishokura accounts before Jarvoc lies in ruins again. I've sent Rosner and Koch to the fifth floor to salvage the files."

"My father's office is on the second."

"Nishokura's bogus office is on the fifth. Go on," he said, pointing to the battered door. "Do what you must."

As Dorian drove away, Nedrick and Luke tore down the remaining boards with their bare hands and crawled through the opening. Inside, it was empty, the rows of windows barred and painted an opaque white. "Chase isn't here," Luke said.

ⓦⓦⓦ

When Drew and Mila entered the tunnels, Mila ran off in search of Hanz. Drew prowled more cautiously, his search for Chase turning futile, but his discoveries unnerving. When Nedrick and Luke caught up with him, Drew was in the storage room pulling down two cardboard cartons, rotted and mildewed by the years.

Nedrick choked from the dust as Drew opened the containers. The remains of shoes filled one, eyeglasses the other. Nedrick watched stony-faced as Luke helped Drew lift down a third carton—more shoes and moth-eaten clothes. Drew picked up a pair of baby shoes and slapped them into Ned's hand. "Someone—someone from your family—overlooked these at the end of the war." He pointed toward the shower room. "A room down there was the end of the line for these people."

Color drained from Luke's face. "I didn't think they had extermination camps in Czechoslovakia."

"Only on a smaller scale—never fully developed, Luke."

"No," Ned protested. "Jarvoc was a labor camp. That's all."

Drew snatched up an old blueprint from the floor; it tore as he unfolded it. "Obviously they had bigger plans for Jarvoc. I've already found the morgue chutes and the dressing rooms. And now these boxes of clothing," he said with utter contempt. "My guess would be that Jarvoc had large deposits of coal and a good supply of water—and the railroad depot at their disposal for this godforsaken factory."

Luke grabbed Drew's wrist. "Chase is in this mess somewhere."

"I haven't found any sign of her yet. Maybe she's safely back at the Rosner lodging. But come. We'll go the length of the tunnels if we have to—but prepare yourselves. There are more horrors in the tunnels."

He led them into a storage area surrounded by stockpiles of weapons, a subterranean arsenal. Rifles. Handguns. Missile heads. In the next cave were fifty-five-gallon drums on dollies, silver canisters of fertilizer, tanks filled with chemicals, and shelves with containers marked "liquid gases." The yellowed inventory list hanging on the wall was chilling: "Zyklon-B. Nitromethane. Stoff-146."

From behind them, a deep voice cautioned, "Don't pry

that lid open, Mr. Gregory. Not when we don't know what it contains or what would happen when it hits the air."

Drew looked up. Hanz Russelmann stood yards from them, an old man listing on his game leg, one hand braced against a wall carved with the names and dates of prisoners who never left the tunnels. The black-and-white collie whimpered at his side.

"What is this place?" Luke asked Hanz.

"It's what it once was that sickens me." He met Nedrick's despairing glance. "I won't be able to go to Spain with you, my boy, but you and Mila go. Go for me."

Ned started toward his grandfather. Hanz held up his hand.

"Jiri is in the tunnels somewhere. I have to find him. You go back to the house for me. Olivia's missing attaché case is in my room. Find it before Altman discovers I've taken it. It'll clear your grandmother's name." When Ned hesitated, his voice grew firm. "Go on. Miss Evans is safe. Go through the dressing room. You remember—I took you there once as a boy. It's the only way out. And take Patek with you."

The dog refused to move.

As Nedrick stumbled back through the tunnel, Drew said, "Hanz, your niece came in here with me. Where is she now?"

"She's with her brother Pavel, but Jiri found him first. He's in the shower room—dead. Miss Evans is with her— she'll be all right. Now all of you get out. I'm the one Jiri wants."

Drew thumped one of the gas containers. "Hanz, are your sons planning to blow up the steel factory or the whole world?"

"We don't discuss things like that."

"Stockpiling chemical weapons is a direct violation of the Geneva Protocol." His voice was iced, colder than the tunnels. "We should have listened when Olivia labeled the Russelmanns and Nishokura as terrorists. Is that why your family silenced her—so you could go on making your billions in profit?"

"I had no part in Olivia's death."

Drew underlined the words on one container. <u>Zyklon-B</u>. "This was used by the Nazis back in the 1940s, Hanz. And this one—innocent enough. Hydrochloric acid—alone, no problem. But by mixing it with other chemicals, your sons could make a nerve gas."

Drew caught the look of surprise on Hanz's face. The man was vacillating between loyalty to his family and utter revulsion at what his sons had become. "Pure speculation," Hanz said.

"Tell me, Russelmann, are Libya and Iraq constructing roads with your products or building underground chemical plants?"

"Very clever, Mr. Gregory." Jiri Benak's voice filled the room. "But be assured, if the Russelmanns had not come along, there would have been other terrorists." Jiri chuckled dryly. "And good afternoon, Breckenridge. I see you've discovered my place of employment."

They looked around and saw no one. All they could hear was Jiri's mocking laughter over the loudspeaker.

Luke doubled his fist. "I'm going to take you down, Jiri."

"Not likely."

Faintly and then in increasing volume the music of Wagner and Mozart echoed through the tunnel. The wall sensors began to blink red, the dials moving slowly to the right.

"He's turned something on," Drew warned.

Hanz's face went ashen as he glanced at the pipes above their heads. "Then we don't have much time."

Looking around again, Drew spotted Jiri standing on the catwalk by the control panel. He was wearing a trench coat with an unlit cigar jammed in his mouth and his snow-blond hair combed neatly in place. "My grandfather was one of the architects here," he boasted. "Tell them, Hanz. Tell them how our families helped design this facility for ethnic cleansing."

Drew retched. *The designers of death.*

Over the loudspeaker the music had changed to the triumphant notes of a hymn, "A Mighty Fortress Is Our God."

"Go," Hanz pled. "Chase needs your help to escape. She's out cold, but she's still alive. Go while there's still time."

Luke shook his head. "Jiri knows me. I'll keep him occupied. You go, Drew, and see if you can get Chase and Mila out of here."

"No," Hanz said firmly. "I'm the one to stay behind. I know these tunnels. I can keep Jiri at bay for a little while."

Jiri's mocking voice came over the loudspeaker again. "Hanz, I'll kill every one of them," he said, "unless you go into the shower room. Your life for theirs."

Hanz's smile was vague as he turned to Luke. "This has always been an evil place. I begged my son Altman to destroy this plant and these tunnels. I should have done so myself years ago."

Drew wasn't sure whether to despise Hanz or pity him. "Czech Intelligence will take care of that for you. Come on, Luke."

Hanz detained Luke, saying, "I'm not apt to come out of here alive. That hymn—'A Mighty Fortress'—I knew it as a lad. I know I don't deserve mercy—but can you tell me how to get to God?"

The muscles in Luke's face contorted. "I don't know— Hanz, I'm—I'm not a confessional. I—"

"Come with us, Russelmann," Drew called back.

"No, Jiri is armed. He would take us out one by one."

The music still played as Hanz obeyed Jiri's command, the collie staying faithfully by his side. Hanz dragged along, his limp more pronounced as though he were giving Drew and the others time to crawl to safety.

As they all entered the shower room, Chase opened her eyes, looking dazed and confused. Her face was streaked with dirt and tears, her eyes frantic as she saw Pavel's body and Mila moaning beside him. Drew and Luke knelt beside Chase.

"Someone grabbed me," she cried. "Dorian, I think, or Hanz."

"No," Luke told her. "It must have been Jiri Benak who brought you in here. And I'm getting you out."

"I thought you were working with him."

"No, Chase. No." Cutting the ropes that tied her wrists, Luke lifted her into his strong arms and held her tight against him as he ran out the door.

Drew tried to force Mila to her feet. "Come with us, Mila," he begged. "You can't help Pavel now."

She shook her head. "I won't go."

"Then I'll send Nedrick back for you."

"No, Mr. Gregory. I know he will never go to Spain without his grandfather. Let me stay with Uncle Hanz. He needs me."

Drew stepped into the dressing room, ready to charge off to find Nedrick. Behind him, he heard a metallic clanging. He whirled around and ran back. The gas-tight door to the shower room had been slammed tight and secured from the other side. He peered through the peek hole. It was fogged, steaming hot water pouring from the shower heads down on Mila and Hanz. Hanz had knelt down and pulled Mila to him as she bent over the inert body of Pavel. The collie whimpered beside them.

Drew caught the sickening sensation of an unknown odor and knew that Jiri had thrown gas crystals in through the ducts. He turned and sprinted back through the tunnel. His long legs cramped as he burst from the darkness into the glorious fresh air outside and collided with Nedrick.

"My grandfather lied to me," Ned said. "The attaché case wasn't in his room."

"He wanted to save your life, Ned."

"I'm going back in and save his."

Drew grabbed Ned and wrestled him to the ground, pinning him there. "You can't go back in there, Nedrick. It's too late. Nerve gas is pouring into the room where Hanz is."

Chapter 26

Drew waited beside Nedrick, but his attention was on Leos Cepek—standing aloof, grim-faced, his gray eyes alert as more agents poured onto the compound. Work at the steel mill had come to a standstill. Many of the employees were already herded together in holding areas for interrogation, their frightened wives and families on the other side of the locked gate begging for answers.

At a signal from Cepek, the Kladno *policie* took the Russelmanns into custody. Altman sneered. Josef kept his head downcast. Gustav's fat jowls sagged. In a strange way, Franz Van Rindin seemed relieved to have his hands cuffed behind him.

"Wait," he told the officer. "I have a confession to make."

"Shut up," Altman told him.

Franz lifted his dark, brooding eyes as they manhandled him into the car, his expression one of regret as he glanced back toward the ghostly plant with ominous smoke rings curling from its smokestacks. "I drove the car that killed Miss Renway," he said.

Drew felt no surprise. He was convinced that even if Franz were executed for the murder of Olivia Renway, he would welcome it as relief from his darkness.

Only Altman resisted. Even with his wrists restrained behind him, he scorned the others. He twisted his shoulders adjusting the fit of his Canali suit coat and then with his stern, well-shaped chin, he flicked some dust from his shoulder. He thrust the officer's hands from his arm and glared at his son.

"Father," Ned choked, "I'll find the best lawyers I can."

Altman's frigid gaze fixed on Nedrick. "Don't bother. I have never needed you. I don't need you now."

He nodded toward the officers. "Shall we go, gentlemen?" he asked. "But I must warn you, you've made a grave mistake in allowing Mr. Benak time to escape. When this is over and I'm free, I will make certain that you wallow in the gravel for a false arrest."

He gave a curt bow to the guards and slipped into the car, like a gentleman off for an evening concert at the National Theater. *Altman was probably right,* Drew thought. He had run his vast steel empire with cunning, and in spite of the billions in profit from the sale of firearms and nerve gas, the records would be in his favor. Gustav and Josef might hang, but Altman would have planned ahead for his own future.

Drew felt the convulsing of Ned's shoulders as he spun the younger man around and forced him toward the farmhouse. Ned's skin looked ash-white, like dirty soap suds left in a wash basin.

"It should have been my dad in there instead of Popshot."

"Ned, Hanz could have left the tunnels alive, but he chose to give the rest of us a chance to escape."

"But Mila didn't make it," Nedrick said, grief-stricken.

"She wouldn't leave Pavel nor your grandfather."

"Pavel is dead, too?"

"He was already dead when Jiri turned on those shower heads and fed in the gas pellets. They went quickly, Ned."

As they caught up with Luke and Chase, Ned said, "Popshot was a good man. He was the best friend a boy could have. We used to walk along the tracks and make plans to catch a train out of here to Spain. He wasn't like the others, Drew. He wanted nothing to do with the Nishokura accounts. You've got to believe me."

"The records will prove that."

Behind them a violent explosion erupted. Drew dropped to the ground, pulling Ned and Chase down beside him. He risked looking back. The explosion had come from deep within the forest, beyond the railroad tracks. Another major rumble shook the ground, spewing giant spruce and fir trees into the air; they disintegrated into dust and ash chips, thick as smoke, as they drifted back toward Jarvoc.

"What happened?" Ned asked.

"I'd say Jiri Benak just secured his escape route by blocking the tunnel with debris and doubling his chances of getting away. He most likely set the blast off by the steel shoring in the mine shaft. No one can follow him now."

Luke crawled over to them. "You okay, Drew?"

"We'll make it, but if that explosion put fissures in any of the containers in the plant, we're dead meat."

"Jiri's not that stupid, Drew. Once he turned on those shower heads, he secured the entry to the tunnels with those iron doors before he took off. He's a genius," Luke said glumly. "And that includes firearms and explosives."

Ned stumbled to his feet. "We've got to stop him."

"Ned, what we have to do," Drew said, "is get out of here. Jiri must know the exit to the caverns. He's long gone by now."

Nedrick stood his ground. "Won't Czech Intelligence want to talk to me? I'm a Russelmann. I have to face up to—"

"Leos Cepek told me to get you out of here. As far as he understands, the youngest Russelmann left Jarvoc ten years ago. Let's keep it that way."

"Cepek?"

"Czech Intelligence. He's an old friend of mine. I vouched for you, Ned. And I'd say you're more like a Kendall. Wouldn't you agree, Luke?" *Dear God,* Drew prayed. *I can only hope that Uriah agrees.*

Dorian Paschek came lumbering over the fields in the forklift. He veered toward them, pelting them with gravel and creating a dust screen as he pulled to a stop and saluted.

Paschek leaned down, his weather-beaten face streaked with soot. He pointed back toward Cepek. "He sent a message, Gregory. Said for you to leave quickly. Thought it best not to have American Intelligence involved."

Drew nodded. "Good man."

"His colleagues might not agree," Dorian cautioned. "Some of them are more touchy about American interference."

Again Drew nodded.

"I've got an old truck behind my house. Take it," Dorian offered. "Get out of here—before the town folk turn against you." He dropped the keys into Drew's hands and glanced at Chase, silent beside Drew. "We don't want any of you involved. Just leave the truck at the airport."

Ned protested, "Dorian, I can't leave. I've got to make certain my father didn't destroy the Nishokura files."

Dorian's anger flared. "They're safe. The boys and I made certain of that. And you, Nedrick—you've always had trouble taking orders—even when you were little. Like Mr. Gregory said, they don't know about you being back in town—that's the way Hanz wanted it. Now get out of here—all of you."

Drew saw new strength in the craggy face. He gripped Paschek's callused hand. "Jarvoc is at risk with all those hazardous components inside the plant."

"My wife told me what to do about that a long time ago. The boys and I used to talk about it at the pub—after a few drinks to give us courage. But we couldn't see a way to sabotage the plant or to destroy what's hidden there."

"And now?" Drew asked.

"As soon as they stop interrogating the employees, I'll have the men load those containers on the train as quickly as they can. We'll put distance between the danger of explosion and the village."

"You'd be destroying evidence."

"We're trying to save our town. Czech Intelligence agrees with me." His grin turned sly. "Mr. Cepek will help us. He has ties to this old town—married one of the girls from here. Even if he doesn't, as long as he turns a blind eye for a day or two, we can send some of those tanks and shells on a truck convoy over the back roads out of Jarvoc."

"You'd risk lives along the way," Drew warned.

"It's been done before, Mr. Gregory. We'll do what those people did to rid their towns of nuclear wastes. And we'll ask Prague for enough firefighters and riot *policie* and planes overhead to ward off any terrorist groups who might try to steal our shipment."

"You can't just leave it on the back roads."

"We won't." He brushed a tear from his eye. "I saw myself this morning for the miserable, weak man I was. But all morning at the plant we've been passing word man to man, 'Remember the Bronze Network. Remember the Bronze Network.'"

Olivia's old resistance movement, Drew thought.

"I only wish my wife and my sister could be here to see us clean up this town. We'll make it. We'll ship those chemicals and weapons to an isolated island in the Pacific. The island is nothing but a toxic wasteland, but they've got an incinerator there equipped to handle massive disposal efforts."

"You're risking international opposition."

"Better that than the whole world eventually becoming a wasteland."

"What about Jiri Benak?"

"We'll seal off the shower room, Mr. Gregory." His face was anguished, a man who had been acquainted with more than his share of grief. "Benak only had time to feed a few pellets into the room. I'm certain he didn't plan on running, Gregory. He planned on taking over the plant."

"It's too bad he didn't get locked in the shower room."

"No, Mr. Gregory, I wouldn't wish that on any man, not even the man who planned my sister's death." He cleared his throat. "Olivia was fond of your wife, Gregory."

"The friendship was mutual. Miriam was proud to have been a friend of Olivia's."

"A better friend to her than I was. Go. Please. All of you."

Still Drew hesitated. "Will you be all right, Dorian?"

"For the first time in fifty years, I'll be all right."

Drew watched him mop his sweaty brow, thinking, *Paschek, you've got the makings of a leader. If anyone here in Jarvoc could pull off salvaging the steel plant, you could.*

"Dorian, work with Czech Intelligence. You can trust Leos Cepek. He's a good man. I know him."

He nodded. "He's promised us more investigators and firefighters from Prague and Kladno. Chemical weapons experts from Munich and London. Paris, too, Cepek said. We'll get through this one. I better go back now. Cepek will have some questions for me, too."

Paschek saluted once again, then turned the forklift back toward the factory, and rumbled away. "There goes a man," Drew said, "who could use half a million dollars."

He gave Nedrick and Chase a gentle nudge. "You heard the man. Let's get out of here."

◉◉◉

Ruzyne International, fifteen kilometers northwest of Prague. As the four of them sat in the airport coffee shop waiting for their flights to London and Zurich, Luke checked his watch and cracked his knuckles in disappointment. They had forty minutes more to keep a low profile, but he half expected other members of Czech Intelligence to burst into the room and detain them. Drew—typing furiously on his laptop computer—could take care of himself, but there'd be no fight left in Nedrick or Chase. She sat beside Luke, hunched forward, lost in thought. Ned was at a table alone, his eyes glazed; dust from the explosion still speckled his hair and shirt. Luke went back to looking at Chase and tried to coax a smile from her.

"You looked at me that way the first time we met," she said.

"I remember. You asked me if I had missed the Bartholomew nose. There's a streak of dirt on the tip of it right now."

She brushed it away, a tear with it.

"Don't go weepy on me. We're going to make it. Right, Drew?"

Drew grinned wryly. "Count on it. We'll be in London in a couple of hours, Chase."

"But I hate saying goodbye to Luke."

"Then don't," Luke said with more cheer than he felt.

"Just stand up when the time comes and say, 'So long, Luke. See ya.'"

"It's not that easy. You—you saved my life." She flipped the hair from the back of her neck. "I'm a mess, but poor Nedrick looks worse. I wish he would sit with us."

Drew said, "He needs space to sort out his losses."

"Will he lose Uriah Kendall, too?" she asked.

"I don't know, Chase." He pointed to his computer. "I've started my Jarvoc Report. I'll make sure Uriah gets a copy. If he understands everything that happened—"

"Ned is Olivia's grandson," Chase defended.

"Uriah will take that into account."

"I feel so badly about Hanz Russelmann," she said softly. "Imagine how Nedrick feels."

"I can't imagine," Luke told her.

Time was running out, takeoff for London getting close. He hated seeing the others fly out ahead of him. "Maybe I should tell Nedrick what happened back in the tunnel," he said.

Drew scowled. "Spare him a repeat of that. He already knows that his grandfather was gassed to death."

"That's not what I meant. Back in the tunnel, Hanz grabbed my arm and said, 'I'm not apt to come out of here alive—you've got to tell me how to get to God.'"

"What did you tell Hanz?" Chase asked.

"I called after him, 'Russelmann, my mother always says that God's Son is the way to peace.'"

"Jesus? Is that what you believe, Luke?"

"At that moment, Chase, I was never more certain of anything in my life."

"Then perhaps Hanz died with that name on his lips."

"It's for certain that I will." Luke cleared his throat as he turned to Drew. "Well, it's all over now. All behind us."

"No." Drew nodded toward Nedrick. "The half-million-dollar Kashmir sapphires are still unaccounted for."

Luke rubbed his jaw to ward off a grin. "You're looking at the wrong man, Drew. Nedrick didn't play chauffeur to Uriah Kendall for ten years with that kind of money in his back pocket. Maybe the Russelmanns invested it in the steel business."

"No. Dorian Paschek said his sister was wearing that bracelet when she attended his wife's funeral."

Luke whistled. "Imagine flying all over Europe with half a million dollars on your wrist."

"At least that much," Gregory said. "But it's not worth a thing now because no one knows where it is."

Chase rallied. "Wrong, Drew," Chase said. "I don't think it's really lost. In fact, I'm quite sure I know who has it."

Before they could argue with her, she snatched up her carry-on bag. "I'm going to go change clothes and freshen up a bit before our flight."

Luke watched her saunter away toward the lady's room. "Now what was that all about? She's all uptight about some bracelet that doesn't even belong to her."

"I'll see what I can find out on the flight to London, but, Luke, have you told her about you and Sauni yet?"

"I haven't figured out how."

"She's fond of you."

"My fault, I guess. I thought she knew we were just friends. But you're wrong about Sauni and me. That's a closed door, too."

"Not according to Miriam's predictions. She already has the wedding bells ringing."

"Hope she's right." Luke cracked his knuckles again. "Do you think Dudley Perkins will ever apologize to Uriah?"

"Unlikely. Dudley's point was well taken. Gut feeling tells me that Olivia knew Hanz was German. Does love cover that, or did she cross the line when she took that bracelet and allowed him to walk out of that air raid shelter?"

At the mention of his grandparents' names, Nedrick came out of his stupor. "Maybe that day she was praying Hanz would blow with the next bomb. There was no reason to believe that my grandfather would ever get back to Germany."

"Ned, I have to settle something before we reach London."

Nedrick looked uncertain, but he stood and moved to their table and faced Drew. "About Uriah?" he asked.

"It affects him. You spent a lot of time in Washington, riding near the foreign embassies."

Solemn eyes sought Drew's. "That always bugged Uriah."

"Was it a drop point for you, Ned?"

"What? You mean Uriah thought I left messages there—the old chalk-on-the-mailbox routine?"

"Did you? Did your family send you messages?"

A frown wedged between Ned's thick black brows. Miserably, he said, "My father was well known in Prague. Wealthy. Powerful. I hoped that if I went by the embassy, I'd have a chance to see him and settle our differences."

Chase stood beside them now looking stunning in a designer suit with tiny violet stars in its pattern, her dress pumps easily giving her another two inches.

Luke handed her a cup of coffee. "You look great."

"Too fancy for me," Drew said. "I'd better shave so you won't be embarrassed traveling with me." He set his laptop on the floor beside Luke. "Come on, Ned. Join me."

After they got up and walked away, Chase asked, "Was that planned?"

"Drew's idea—so we could talk."

"About us?"

"Chase, I'm really sorry. I never dreamed—"

"It's my fault, Luke. When you told me to look you up in Europe and you'd introduce me to some of your friends, I just thought . . . and then when you carried me out of the tunnels—"

"You thought I meant more by it?" He put his broad hand over hers, a warm brotherly gesture. "I'm twice your age."

"Not quite. Besides, I like older men."

"What about Ian Kendall?"

Her chin stuck out stubbornly. "He's too young. Besides, my dad would never approve of a cyclist."

Luke laughed. "Would I have met your dad's standards?"

"I think so. But I'm embarrassed I read you wrong—about us. My dad always asks me how come I'm so dumb when I'm so smart."

Luke watched her wide eyes swim with tears. He ran his long fingers over her hand as he did with Sauni when she was hurt. "It matters what your father thinks, doesn't it? It was that way with the admiral and me—always trying to please him."

"But no matter what I do, it never pleases my father."

Luke thought back to the Columbia campus and Chase's exuberance for life and solving problems. "You have helped wipe out a lifetime of pain for the Kendall family and given Olivia back her good name."

"And unraveled her old love affair. Uriah won't thank me for that. Seems I've messed up a lot of things this trip."

For a while Luke watched the planes landing and taking off, willing Drew to come back to his rescue again. The scar on Luke's neck throbbed as he thought about the emptiness of facing life on his own. "I understand you, Chase. We're a lot alike."

Above the brim of the coffee cups her dark eyes met his. "There'll be someone for you someday, Chase. Much better than I would have been. You'll see."

Luke pushed back his chair. "There's Drew and Nedrick. They'll be calling your flight any minute."

"Luke?"

"Yes."

"Thank you for being honest with me. Are you—are you going back to Sauni as soon as we leave Prague?"

If I'm not detained by the Czech policie *after the rest of you leave,* he reflected. "Straight to Busingen from the Zurich airport."

"Does she know you're coming?"

"She asked me to come. She's my one real chance for happiness."

As he helped Chase stand, she gripped the handle of her carry-on. "In Jarvoc I never expected to live long enough to get back to London."

"It's been hairy," he said. "But it's over now."

He slipped his arm around her shoulder as he walked her toward the boarding gate. "Chase, you're a special lady."

"As special as Sauni?" she quipped dryly.

"Almost." He leaned down and kissed the top of her head, turned, and walked away—praying that he'd still get out of Prague before Czech Intelligence stormed into the airport.

EPILOGUE

L ondon, 3 A.M. The phone in Chase's hotel suite rang on her bedside table. She lifted her head from the pillows and groped blindly in the darkness, finally knocking the receiver from its hook. Fumbling again, she muttered, "Yes . . . hello. What? Oh, Drew, what do you want at three in the morning?"

"Sorry. Just checking on you. Have you called home yet?"

"Drew, you're crazy, but, yes, I called home. That time change is a killer. This is Mother's day for golfing and committee meetings." Chase was still grumbling but awake. "I tried Dad at the office. His secretary—the glamorous Iron Lady herself—would only take a message. She protects Dad like he's Fort Knox."

"He'll explode when he finds out it was you."

She put her head back on the pillow and stretched. "He'll have fits and fire Melba on the spot; then—she's quite a looker—he'll rehire her three hours later. But don't worry, Drew, Dad has eyes only for Mother. Now what did you really call me for at three in the morning?"

"I've been up talking with Uriah. Can you be a sweet thing and be at the Hungerford Foot Bridge at eight in the morning?"

Irritably she asked, "Are we taking a walking tour?"

He remained annoyingly good-natured. "Maybe we'll go for a swim in the Thames. Now be a sweetheart and be on time, and jot yourself a note to bring Olivia's unfinished novel with you."

Suddenly she was fully awake. *How,* she wondered, *did he know about that?*

"What manuscript?" she hedged.

"The one you came to England for—the one you've been hiding."

"How—how did you know about that?"

"Ian pried the truth out of Beatrice Thorpe."

She chuckled. "Beatrice is the one who asked me to keep it safe for Ian."

"Well—Uriah wants it back."

At 6:25 A.M., still dripping from the shower, Chase toweled down and, with nothing unpacked, shook out a soft shell blouse and put back on her Escada suit. Wiggling her narrow feet into the lavender high-heeled pumps, she remembered the novel and groaned. Except for one folder with Olivia's notes and first chapter, she had placed the manuscript in the bank vault where her father held his British account. Drew would never believe her. She picked up her oversized shoulder bag and shoved the folder inside.

Outside the Ritz Hotel, London's weather was as unpredictable as ever—what was expected to be a sunny summer day was muggy with mist, the distant clouds threatening rain. She reached the embankment with four minutes to spare and leaned against the railing watching the swirling mist drift across the River Thames.

"Good morning, Chase."

She recognized the deep voice at once and turned to face Ian Kendall. The morning mist had dampened his hair, teasing it into waves. He was more attractive than ever in dark slacks and a blue tennis shirt that turned his eyes a cerulean blue. "I was expecting Drew," she mumbled. "Or Uriah."

"I was afraid you wouldn't come if I called."

"Thought you were in France with the Gainsborough team training in the Alps."

"I was, but my grandfather and I had an appointment at Scotland Yard; Constable Wallis had been in touch with Czech Intelligence. Gainsborough expects me back in

France by midnight, or I'm off the team. It doesn't matter—
I just had to see you."

"But why here at the river?"

"Drew's idea. He said it was going full circle."

"Because it's Olivia's river?"

"I think that's what he meant."

"Did Drew tell you all about Prague?"

"He said you almost got killed in Jarvoc. I'm sorry. I
should have stopped you from going. But you were so
determined."

"You couldn't have known about the Russelmanns."

"Beatrice Thorpe tried to warn me, but I didn't want to
hear bad things about my grandmother. When I was a kid,
she was the most perfect person I knew. I couldn't destroy
those memories."

"Did you really believe she was a spy?"

He nodded. "Dudley Perkins convinced me that she spied
against Britain—that she was a spy right on up to her death.
I felt it was my duty to protect the Kendall name at all costs."

"Ian, I know who has the Kashmir sapphires."

"How would you know that?"

"There was only one family member with Olivia on the
day she died. You have your grandmother's sapphire
bracelet, don't you? You've had it all along."

As surprise whipped across his lean face, the muscles in
his jaw flexed involuntarily. In that split second, he withdrew, shutting her out. *Come back,* she thought. *Don't run
away this time.* For his sake, for Olivia's, she refused to back
down. "You do have it, don't you?"

He looked down at her, the feverish intensity in his eyes
reproachful. "She gave it to me the day she died."

"It's worth half a million."

"So Beatrice told me. We often looked at it together. She
let me hide it in her room at the Eagle's Nest."

"But someone tore her room apart."

"I know—I was there to get the bracelet and move it for
safekeeping. If I hadn't scared those men off, she would be
dead, but she sent me away. Told me not to admit that I'd
been there."

"She was hurt, you know."

"I know, but in Beatrice's eyes I'm still Olivia's little grandson—someone to protect. She doesn't realize how responsible I feel toward her." His eyes seemed riveted on the Thames as though he could no longer meet Chase's gaze. "I'm the one who lifted Beatrice back into bed—and put the call light on. Then I went out the window and waited until the nurse came. Beatrice was hurt—badly I could tell—but, ironically, the sapphires were safe in the trap door beneath the china closet."

Chase watched a patrol boat cut the aquamarine waters of the Thames as it forged a billowy path under the Waterloo Bridge before admitting, "She asked me to hide Olivia's manuscript."

He stiffened. "Yes, Bea told me you had the unfinished novel."

"Yes, it's in my father's bank vault." She tapped her shoulder bag. "Except for a few pages that I brought with me."

She took them from her bag and held them up. "It's all here, Ian. Your grandmother's story—her life in espionage," she said lightly.

His reaction was swift. He knocked the papers from her hand. "Don't speak of her that way."

"Oh, no Ian," she cried. "Why did you do that? Those papers, the trip to Jarvoc—they proved her innocence."

He had no answer. The breeze caught the pages and swept them down the embankment. They drifted into the veiled white mist on the River Thames. Whirlpools formed by the patrol boat sucked them under and drenched them. They floated defiantly back to the top—white blotches against the gray-blue river. An early morning sightseeing boat cruised by, shredding the paper with its motor, leaving in its wake a surge of waves that sucked up the pages. At last Olivia's notes sank beneath the waters.

As they slipped from view, Chase squeezed Ian's freckled hand and leaned her head against his shoulder. "It's over, Ian," she said softly. "There's no need to protect your grandmother's name anymore. Now it's more important than ever that you win the Tour de France for her."

"That's what I promised the last time I saw her." He seemed suddenly shy, less tense, his smile creeping back. "I want you to be there, Chase. For me. Will you stay over for the race? I want you there cheering me on."

He seemed older somehow, mature, frightfully good looking. She blushed, remembering that stolen kiss at the Eagle's Nest.

"Well," he urged. "Will you come?"

"I'll think about it. Let me check my calendar for July," she said.

They stood quietly for a moment watching the patrol boat on its return run, cutting its engine as it moved slowly toward the dock. Then Chase asked, "Did Drew tell you about Nedrick?"

"Yes, we talked half the night through. But like I asked Drew, why didn't you leave Nedrick in Jarvoc?"

"He doesn't belong there anymore. He broke his ties with his family. Those who mattered to him are gone. Both of them dead."

"The girl?"

"Mila Van Rindin, his second cousin. They really cared about each other. . . . She died trying to help Nedrick's grandfather. Nedrick doesn't have anyone left unless your family helps him."

"Why should we?"

She ran her fingers over his freckled hand once more. "You're related actually. He's Olivia's first grandson."

"Yes, the legend of Cornwall is true. My grandmother did have another son. That's tough to swallow. My father won't like that."

"That won't change anything."

"Nedrick is nothing to my grandfather," he persisted.

She smiled as the swirls of mist rose from the river, spraying their faces with droplets. "Somehow I think Uriah won't agree with you. Nedrick is part of Olivia. That's what will matter to your grandfather."

🏺🏺🏺

Kendallshire, the Cotswolds, 9:00 A.M. Drew circled Kendall-shire, walking the willow-lined streets of the village and fin-ishing out a sleepless night at the church courtyard where Olivia was buried. He snatched up the lone weed that poked its ugly head at one corner of the grave and polished the marker with the palm of his hand. *Be at rest, old friend,* he thought. *Be at rest.*

Ambling on over the woodland trails, he breathed in the sweet fragrance of the meadows as the golden brilliance of the morning sun caressed the limestone cottages. He saw the young man standing alone on the old stone bridge and felt a knotting in his stomach as he turned into the narrow lane that led to Uriah's cottage.

He let himself in, joining Uriah in the parlor. Uriah sat in his club chair, deep in thought with his palms together as though he were praying, his fingers to his lips. A copy of the Jarvoc Report lay on the round table beside him, his wire-rimmed reading glasses on top of it. With nostalgia Drew remembered that Olivia and Uriah always had matching chairs wherever they lived; he knew with a sense of sadness that Olivia had once occupied the one he had just taken.

"Uriah," he said, "Kendallshire is most beautiful at this time of day."

"Yes. Olivia loved the early mornings."

In the quiet that followed, Maddie rolled in the teaploy with a pot of steaming tea and a plate full of scones and jam on it.

Drew and Uriah sipped companionably, not even stirring when Dudley Perkins rang the doorbell. Maddie ushered Perkins into the room and set out another cup and a fresh plate of scones for him.

"I'll be going now," she said, "and do the marketing."

Uriah barely nodded, his attention fixed on Perkins, his eyes showing neither warmth nor surprise at the new arrival.

"Uriah," Dudley said, "I didn't expect to get back to Kendallshire so soon."

"Drew's idea."

Perkins sat down facing them and placed his hat and

briefcase on the floor beside his walking stick. "I assume it's about this Jarvoc affair. I've read the report completely."

"More likely it's about Olivia," Uriah said.

Dudley focused on Maddie's freshly baked scones. "May I?"

"That is what they're there for."

This is not going well, Drew thought. He took a quick bite of another scone and said, "Dudley, everything I wrote in the Jarvoc Report is true." He glanced apologetically at Uriah. "Fifty years ago Olivia Renway fell in love—*for the first time.* Hanz Russelmann was a Luftwaffe pilot whose crash landing during the Blitz forced him into the role of a German agent."

Talking to Dudley was like trying to stir cement that had already set. Perkins kept his lank hands wrapped around his cup, his stony expression making his gaunt face even more homely. But Drew kept explaining. "Olivia knew the agent as Henri, as an Oxford graduate. As far as she knew, he was British to the core. Handsome. Adventuresome. But he was as committed to his cause as Olivia was to hers. She didn't know he was a German agent until that last day in the air raid shelter."

"You seem to be well informed, Gregory," Perkins snapped.

"Olivia's brother, and Uriah here, filled in some of the small print."

Perkins thumped the Jarvoc Report. "You're asking me to believe all of this—that I wrongfully accused Olivia Renway of spying against Britain?"

"You did. It's all there in the report. In detail."

"She should have stopped Russelmann right there in the shelter. All she had to do was cry out, 'A Nazi. He's a Nazi.'"

"And watch the fury of other people turn against him?" Drew asked. "Perhaps lynch him in front of her? She was only a kid herself—seventeen or eighteen at most."

"She was pregnant, Dudley," Uriah said calmly. "Perhaps that more than anything else affected her decision. No doubt in Olivia's mind, she was not helping a German spy escape. She was protecting the father of her child."

Dudley forked a scone and stared back, disbelieving, his mouth full. "That wasn't in Gregory's report. A baby? Not—not Altman Russelmann?"

"Yes," Drew confirmed.

Perkins wiped his fingers on his gangly knees. "That poor woman." His sympathy was short-lived. "But she did spy against Britain. The records at MI5 are against her. Some of the messages that Olivia carried reached Berlin. I have files to prove it."

Drew's tone hardened. "Olivia took intelligence reports across the channel between Britain and Czechoslovakia for the Czech Brigade in London. She made mistakes. Serious ones. We all do, but if some of those reports showed up in Berlin, Olivia was unaware of it. Up until that last day in the air raid shelter, she trusted Russelmann, loved him."

Drew was hit by silent opposition. He shot another apologetic glance at Uriah. "Russelmann and Olivia obviously spent time together. It would have been easy enough for him to make copies or memorize the codes while Olivia slept, even photograph them with a mini-camera. I'm not here to defend what Olivia did or didn't do. The facts are all in the Jarvoc Report."

Uriah said, "If your files at MI5 are accurate, Dudley, you already know she was active with the Czech resistance right up to the end of the war. Two months after the birth of her son, she flew into Czechoslovakia to help prepare the way for the Anthropoid team. That spring only a violent case of flu kept her from being part of the team that took Reinhard Heydrich down."

Uriah's quietly modulated tone was frightening, yet filled with pride. "Even toward the close of the war, she carried pre-invasion plans through to the resistance fighters. It was as though she constantly tried to make up for falling in love with a German agent." He shook his head. "But what good did it do? There has always been little recognition for resistance fighters. Even the Anthropoid team have only a small memorial in Leamington Park—nowhere near the country they fought and died for."

Perkins wouldn't quit. "I suppose you have excuses for her work with Beatrice Thorpe and Margot Dvorak, too?"

"Dudley, are you blind to everything that concerns my wife? The Bronze Network personally assisted twenty or more airmen safely back to the Allies. That's how Thorpe and Margot Dvorak were arrested and marched off to the labor camp in Jarvoc."

"But Olivia remained free," Perkins mocked. "Did the Germans protect her for working with them?"

This is not going well, Drew thought again. *My fault and it all boils down to Olivia—to the man who won her hand and the man who didn't.* He said, "She hid in the rafters in the barn covering a dying RAF pilot with her own body. You had a pilot-son, Dudley. Killed in the Falklands, right? Wouldn't you have liked someone like Olivia willing to sacrifice herself to protect him?"

Drew had touched a raw nerve. "The reprisals in Jarvoc were blamed on Olivia, Dudley. There's the possibility that if she had turned herself in—revealed the hiding place for that young pilot—perhaps there would not have been so many deaths in Jarvoc that week."

Uriah moaned and said, "But to hate my wife for that and seek vengeance all these years."

"Unfair," Drew agreed. "But emotions ran high." He turned back to Dudley. "You went to great effort to destroy the Kendalls because of Olivia."

Dudley snapped to his own defense. "When Olivia held on to those Kashmir sapphires, she kept nine hundred thousand pounds for herself."

Over the years Drew had carried a lot of things in his pockets from firearms to forged passports, from Miriam's diamond ring to surprise presents for his daughter Robyn. But this was the first time he carried something worth half a million, and it wasn't even insured. He reached deep into his pocket, wrapped his hand around the Kashmir sapphires, and placed them on the teaploy beside the empty teacups. Brilliant sparkling gems.

Shocked, Uriah asked, "Drew, how in the world did you

get that bracelet out of Prague without a hassle from customs?"

"It's been in England all along. Olivia gave it to Ian in London the day she died."

"Why would Ian hide it from me? Didn't he know its worth?"

"Money was never the issue with Ian. The bracelet was a trust from his grandmother. A few hours ago he asked me to give it back to you. He couldn't face you with it."

The light from the windows caught Uriah's strong, well-cut features. He was still a handsome man, his thick hair a distinguished gray, but the permanent grief lines around his eyes had increased in the last few weeks. "Nedrick should have this," he said. "It's a Russelmann heirloom."

Perkins stared at it as though it were venomous. He pushed himself to a standing position, his shoulders still slouched forward. He jerked his hat on and picked up his walking stick and briefcase. Gathering up as much self-respect as he could salvage, Dudley said, "I owe you an apology, Uriah, but it's too late to retrieve an old friendship."

Balancing the stick and case awkwardly under his arm, Perkins took a snapshot from his wallet and dropped it beside the sapphires. "This is rightfully yours, Uriah," he said.

The cottage door slammed closed behind him. Then came the tapping of Dudley's stick on the cobbled walkway. They watched from the window as Dudley's car rattled over the village road, stirring up dust until it disappeared in the distance.

Turning the frayed snapshot over, Uriah stared wistfully down at the face of his wife—a solemn, yet alluring look in those wide, pensive eyes. She was glancing back over her shoulder, young and beautiful in her sleek charcoal gray trench coat, the sapphire bracelet visible on her wrist as she waited on the old stone bridge in Kendallshire.

"This is the way Olivia looked the day I met her. Mystical and melancholy even then. I loved her, Drew, but I've wasted so many years trying to protect her name when she was never a German spy."

"Olivia of all people would have understood. But, Uriah, I wonder if she realized what a special person you are."

A whimsical smile touched Uriah's face, putting the old spark back in his eyes. "She told me often enough." As he stood, the weariness fell from him. "I'm going for a stroll," he said.

"To the bridge where you and Olivia met?"

"Yes, would you care to go with me?"

"No, someone is waiting out there for you."

Uriah glanced out the window. "Nedrick!" was all he said.

"I encouraged him to come back to the Cotswolds to see you. I asked you once before, Uriah, what are you going to do about Nedrick?"

The blue eyes turned misty. "We've had ten good years together—Nedrick and I. Do you expect me to throw them away?" He squared his shoulders. "That's Olivia's grandson—*my* grandson now." His voice remained husky. "Are you coming with me, Drew?"

"No, I won't intrude. I have a heavy date back in London. If I work it out right, I'll have just enough time to get home, air out the apartment, get my dirty clothes off the floor, and be at Heathrow when Miriam's plane hits the runway."

🕸🕸🕸

Drew stood by the open window reluctant to leave the peaceful scene. No wonder Uriah loved this place. The river with its moss-covered banks ran through the middle of the village, the gentle sounds of water turning the paddles of the old weaving mill. Drew would take the sights and sounds of Kendallshire away with him—the weather vane spinning on top of the whitewashed cathedral, the limestone hills filled with honey-colored villages, the Cotswold sheep nibbling contentedly in the golden meadows. And the sight of his good friend Uriah standing on the arched bridge embracing Olivia's grandson.

Drew wondered how much he would tell Miriam about Prague and the Russelmanns. He would answer her questions—be honest as much as he dared, but he would skip the details when he told her that Hanz Russelmann had died sacrificing himself for his grandson and the rest of them. But this moment between Uriah and Nedrick he would gladly share.

He was just tempting himself with the last scone on the plate when Uriah's phone rang. He picked it up. "Kendall's cottage," he said with his mouth still full.

"Drew, is that you?"

Miriam! "*Liebling*, where are you?"

"Cruising at 37,000 feet. Or higher maybe."

"You sound like you're in the next room."

"And you sound a thousand miles away."

"I was just leaving—heading back to London."

"Don't worry about dusting or airing the condo," she teased. "Just pick up your dirty clothes."

"You're coming in on time?"

"I gave the pilot strict orders when I boarded."

"*Liebling*, I'll be there. I love you." He cradled the phone, sensing her nearness. "How's everything at the gallery?"

"Everything's just fine. I'm so pleased."

"And I'm pleased you're coming home."

"You're all right, Drew?"

"Yes. Everything's fine here, too. Olivia's name is in the clear, her reputation intact."

"I'm glad. I always believed in Olivia."

He heard the catch in her voice and knew she would flood the jet with tears if he didn't give her something to smile about. "Miriam, I've got more good news. In the next few weeks—six months max—I'm expecting a wedding invitation."

"Sauni and Luke's?"

He swallowed his disappointment. "How did you know?"

"I just talked to Sauni."

"At 37,000 miles in the air?"

"I was worried about you, Drew. When I didn't reach you at the condo, I called Robyn and Pierre. No answer there either. So I called Sauni. I—"

Static. He shook the phone. He'd sue the airline if the call disconnected. "Repeat that," he shouted.

"I said Luke is already there. *Very much there.* They'll be married in the college chapel in Busingen as soon as Luke's parents can fly over." Her voice was joyful. "And, Drew darling, I'm not supposed to tell you—but I'm going to anyway. Luke wants you to be his best man."

Drew grinned as he hung up the phone. He grabbed his car keys off the round table and strode out of the house whistling. Easing into his Renault, he drove out of Kendallshire. He was a man at peace with himself, going with the flow, following the Thames from its source back toward London. *Back to Miriam.*